"In *The Rules of Falling* into a delightful Regency-lovers' romp filled with clever banter, heartfelt faith, and a romance that dances to the tune of decorum and desire. A heartwarming gem for fans of sweet romance with a divine hand. A delightful read for anyone who believes in laughter, love, and God's unconditional love and perfect timing."

Melissa Ferguson, bestselling author of *The Perfect Rom-Com*

"A charming contemporary romance set at a Regency-themed singles' retreat, with a swoony, reluctant hero and a spunky yet vulnerable heroine. The writing is smart and sassy with humor and touching moments sure to please lovers of rom-coms, Regency romance, or Jane Austen period dramas."

Julie Klassen, bestselling author

"Fans of Becca Kinzer and Rebekah Millet are sure to enjoy this new addition to the Christian romantic comedy genre. Filled with whimsy and Regency delights, *The Rules of Falling for You* is sure to entice readers in search of a lighthearted romantic romp through the pages."

Sarah Monzon, author of *An Overdue Match*

"*The Rules of Falling for You* is a warm, winning charmer with heart. Fans of Angela Ruth Strong's *Husband Auditions* and Shannon Hale's *Austenland* will feel right at home in the cozy, witty world Mollie Rushmeyer has created."

Bethany Turner, award-winning author of *Brynn and Sebastian Hate Each Other: A Love Story*

"*Bridgerton* meets Pepper Basham in the charming, offbeat, and wholly unique *The Rules of Falling for You*. Mollie Rushmeyer has captured the zeitgeist of current romance tropes with a whiff of Regency goodness. An utter delight with characters I couldn't help but root for, this sweet love story is full of whip-smart lines and heart-pounding chemistry. A total win from an author at the top of her game!"

    Rachel McMillan, bestselling author of *The Mozart Code* and *Love in Three Quarter Time*

The Rules of Falling for You

Mollie Rushmeyer

a division of Baker Publishing Group
Minneapolis, Minnesota

© 2025 by Mollie Joy Rushmeyer

Published by Bethany House Publishers
Minneapolis, Minnesota
BethanyHouse.com

Bethany House Publishers is a division of
Baker Publishing Group, Grand Rapids, Michigan

Printed in the United States of America

All rights reserved. No part of this publication may be reproduced, stored in a retrieval system, or transmitted in any form or by any means—for example, electronic, photocopy, recording—without the prior written permission of the publisher. The only exception is brief quotations in printed reviews.

Library of Congress Cataloging-in-Publication Data
Names: Rushmeyer, Mollie, author.
Title: The rules of falling for you / Mollie Rushmeyer.
Description: Minneapolis, Minnesota : Bethany House, a division of Baker Publishing Group, 2025.
Identifiers: LCCN 2025000962 | ISBN 9780764244421 (paperback) | ISBN 9780764245749 (casebound) | ISBN 9781493451333 (ebook)
Subjects: LCGFT: Christian fiction. | Romance fiction. | Novels.
Classification: LCC PS3618.U74325 R85 2025 | DDC 813/.6--dc23/eng/20250224
LC record available at https://lccn.loc.gov/2025000962

The Scripture quote in chapter 36 is from Isaiah 43:2.

The Scripture quote in chapter 37 is from Matthew 11:28.

Scriptures taken from the Holy Bible, New International Version®, NIV®. Copyright © 1973, 1978, 1984, 2011 by Biblica, Inc.® Used by permission of Zondervan. All rights reserved worldwide. www.zondervan.com. The "NIV" and "New International Version" are trademarks registered in the United States Patent and Trademark Office by Biblica, Inc.®

This book is a work of fiction. Names, characters, places, and incidents are the product of the author's imagination or are used fictitiously. Any resemblance to actual events, locales, or persons, living or dead, is coincidental.

Cover illustration by Nate Eidenberger
Cover design by Laura Klynstra

Published in association with Books & Such Literary Management, www.booksandsuch.com.

Emojis are from the open-source library OpenMoji (https://openmoji.org/) under the Creative Commons license CC BY-SA 4.0 (https://creativecommons.org/licenses/by-sa/4.0/legalcode)

Baker Publishing Group publications use paper produced from sustainable forestry practices and postconsumer waste whenever possible.

For my girls, Rya and Nova,
who "put up with" my Jane Austen obsession
but love to brainstorm stories with me.
You fill my life and heart with immeasurable joy.
I love you both so much.
Remember, no dream is ever too big for God. ~Mark 11:23

1

Zoe

I refuse to have a *Pride and Prejudice* pity party... again. The 1995 BBC version, of course. The only correct version, in my opinion.

Okay, maybe that's exactly what I need right now.

Goodness knows I'd much rather be on my couch in my favorite "I love Darcy" pajamas, eating my own recipe of banana/chocolate no-added-sugar ice cream, than here in this trendy downtown Minneapolis restaurant, scanning the exits for my date, who excused himself to the restroom fifteen minutes ago.

Another dine-and-dasher? Seriously?

Despite all of this, I'm still here, trying to give the guy the benefit of the doubt, even if he did live stream ordering a platter for us of the one food on the planet I loathe—salapao. It is a first date after all. He couldn't possibly have known I can no longer stomach the little pork-filled steamed buns, or that my mouth waters upon sight or savory scent, but in the I'm-about-to-dash-to-the-bathroom kind of way.

While I wait to see if my date shows his face again, I fish my phone from my reticule-inspired purse. At this point, either this Thai food is exacting swift revenge on my behalf if he's a would-be ghoster or he's jumped out of the nearest window and made a run for it.

Either way, it's not the first time.

Opening my phone, I check my blood glucose levels on the app synced to my continuous glucose monitor attached to the back of my upper arm. Normal range. Perfect, because I accidentally left my extra insulin in the car inside my insulated travel case to keep it cool.

Then I hit "new note" in my notes app under the folder labeled: "Dear Modern Lord Pembroke," the dashing hero from my favorite Regency-era novel by A. Nathaniel Gladwin. I can hear Lord Pembroke now in his baritone British accent: "Miss Zoe Dufour, would you do me the honor of permitting me to call on you? I can no longer remain silent about my deep affection for you."

Sigh.

My dearest M. L. P. I type the words into the app. Later, I'll write this out by hand in a letter, my preferred method of communication, and add it to my collection of letters I'll give to my future husband. No one writes letters anymore, and it's a shame. Handwriting expresses so much about the human soul. Not to mention the bravery it takes to turn thoughts into ink, staining the pages for generations to come. I like to imagine that my husband will enjoy reading through these letters someday, and maybe my future children will, too.

Where are you? I've poured my heart out to you for years. Saved these words to share them with you when I finally find you. I don't think this bathroom sabbatical guy is you, by the way. As a reminder, my thirtieth birthday is soon. So if you could hurry up, I'd appreciate it.

I swirl the remnants of my khao soi—sweet and spicy Thai coconut curry noodle soup—with a broad, shallow-basin spoon. The ceramic makes an obnoxious screech against the bowl and earns me a glare from the couple at the next table. *Sorry.* My mouth forms the silent apology. They look happy. What's their secret?

Grateful for the din of surrounding conversations and clatter of dishes, I groan to myself. I'm practically an old maid by Regency standards. Even by modern measures, I'm only a handful of years and a few felines away from becoming a lonely old cat lady.

I guess I'm already a plant mom, with more plants in my house than people in my cell phone contacts. Maybe that's the next phase in my transformation into forever spinster. While everyone else pulls out their phones to show pictures of their families, I'll be there sporting my "It's Not Hoarding If It's Plants" T-shirt while sharing glamor shots of my fur babies and memes of Mr. Collins.

The phone vibrates in my hand.

My thumb slides over the phone screen to answer. "Hey, Eden."

"Hey, yourself."

My tense shoulder muscles relax at the sound of Eden Lundquist's voice—my best friend since grade school, talented broadcast technician, and sometimes co-host on my trending Regency-themed advice column podcast, *Love According to Miss Gladwin.*

"You still on that date downtown? The new Thai place? Cough if you need a rescue from a snooze-inducing troll. Give me a birdcall if he seems like a sociopath who'll follow you home. Blink twice if—wait, no."

A chuckle bubbles up at her quick jumble of words. She's what I would call a fast talker. "That took a dark turn. Relax, I'm fine. I'm just feeling a little nauseous with this half-eaten platter of salapao staring me down."

There's a sharp intake of breath like air sucked between teeth on the other end. "Sawyer's favorite food? Yikes. Even I don't like the sight of those things since . . ." I can almost see the wince on Eden's face as she trails off.

"I threw my own engagement party before I was actually engaged and was left with a ring in my hand, not on my finger? Not to mention a freezer full of steamed pork buns?" With a shrug, I sigh. "It's okay. You can say it."

But the heat of humiliation prickles up my neck for the millionth time.

"I'm sorry for the ex vibes, Zoe."

I blow a long, cleansing breath before answering, "It's all right. This guy isn't Sawyer. Not sure he'll end up as more than another dead-end date. But, hey, barring the salapao, I had a great meal—man, I've missed Thai food—and he seems harmless enough."

"Way to look at the bright side, my friend." Eden's tone is warm, light. "Something's up though, right? Who has a dinner date at 4:30 in the afternoon? Is he an octogenarian?" She loses the rabbit trail and meanders, "Not that there's anything *wrong* with being elderly, of course."

"Right. And, no, he's not my grandpa's peer." I rub my chin. "I don't know. He insisted we come here at this time. A two-for-one special."

"Romantic." Her tone is dry.

"I know. I'm not sure why I'm still here. I guess I was hoping for a frog prince situation. That maybe there was some other level to him I haven't seen yet. Thankfully, he hasn't jabbered on about his mom." *And at least I have no close, personal witnesses to another potential romantic catastrophe this time*, I silently add.

"Not that there's anything *wrong* with loving your mom," she says, drawing out the words.

"Of course. But there's a fine line between sweet and—"

"Creepy." She finishes my thought. As usual.

I squeeze my linen napkin into a ball. "But he went to the restroom fifteen minutes ago and hasn't come back yet."

She huffs in my ear. "Nobody skips out on the check and a perfectly lovely time with my friend."

I throw a hand up, knocking water out of my glass with the gesture, and sop it up with my napkin. "I have to hold out hope for my perfect match, Eden. He's out there. I have to believe my happily-ever-after wasn't ruined before it ever began with the engagement that never was. And honestly, if I have to go out with every ninety-year-old catfish—"

Eden sucks in a sharp breath like mentioning that particular real-life disaster in my dating history pains her.

"—and unemployed basement dweller with an unhealthy attachment to his mom in the Twin Cities, nay, all of Minnesota, then so be it." I slap my hand onto the table, winning me more stares.

"Hear, hear."

There's applause through the phone. I must be on speaker while she concocts her usual afternoon green smoothie. "But beware, all you ungentlemanly rogues," Eden declares. "In the words of Gandalf, 'You shall not pass!'" There's a *thwack* like a spatula slamming the counter.

How someone could allege she's an equal fan of Regency stories and J. R. R. Tolkien as Eden claims, I have no idea. Different universes. But then, Eden herself is a walking juxtaposition. Spunky, but kind and caring. Dressed in flowy feminine skirts and dresses—probably channeling her inner Tolkien elf—offset by her nose ring and lavender hair.

"Thank you, by the way, for enduring all manner of terrible

dates so the rest of us don't have to. Your quest for love is like skimming the dating pool for all of us."

My head bows in acknowledgment as though she can see me.

But she's not done. "And you know nobody's out there skimming the pool finding something good. No, you see somebody take out that long-handled net, you know what's floating—"

"Okay!" I say brightly, hoping to force this conversation elsewhere. "Yes, you know me. I'm like that person royalty used to have. The one who tried all of their food and drinks, checking for poison—"

"Cupbearer!" she supplies.

"Yup, that's me. The dating cupbearer. I do it for the good of humanity, myself, and our dear podcast listeners."

She gasps. "Oh! I almost forgot, speaking of the podcast, I found us a new audiovisual engineer and show producer."

"What? Awesome, who is—"

There's movement out of the corner of my eye, someone headed this way. My long-lost date.

"My date's re-emerged from the restroom," I whisper to Eden. "I'd better go. Fill me in later."

"You got it, and you better call me after with the play-by-play. By-ee."

My date, Trevor, slips back into his seat with a clueless smile, as if he hasn't been AWOL for almost twenty minutes now.

I smile back, determined to end the date on a positive note. After all, he hadn't made a run for it. Sadly, that has become a unit of measurement for a date's success these days.

"You all right? You were gone a long time."

His brows furrow for a moment, then shoot up. "The restroom? Yeah, I'll be fine. Thai food does that to me."

I resist the urge to ask why he picked this place, then.

He rubs his stomach. "Wreaks havoc on the ol' system, ya know? My mom—"

Okay, one mention of his mom isn't weird.

"—always says, 'Don't go to restaurants with spicy food. You know what it does to you.' But I couldn't pass up the early bird special. Mom always says to look for the best deal. You know what they say about early birds, right?"

"Mm-hmm." I clamp my mouth because *my* mom always said if you don't have anything nice to say, don't say anything at all.

He proceeds to take another pork bun and indicates the three left on the platter, saying, "Want one? I'll never finish these." The words are thick around his mouthful.

I exhale instead of repeating my "no, thank you" from earlier. Nor do I warn him he'll likely earn himself another visit to the restroom. I'm not his mom, after all. With a click of my tongue, my shoulders roll back and straighten.

"You know what? Yeah, I will have one." Silently adding, *This is silly. I'm a big girl, and a year and a half is plenty of time to get over a phobia of my ex's favorite food.*

Despite it being a little cold, the soft, pillowy bun and the slightly sweet and salty filling melt on my tongue.

Trevor's eyes brighten as I take my second bite. "Hey, I brought something to show you." He retrieves the cross-shoulder bag strapped to the back of his chair and pulls out a thick book.

Scooting closer to my side of the table, he leans in. "Speaking of my mom..."

So *many* mentions of his mom now. Help.

"She always says to put your best foot forward. So I made this photo album. It's all about me and the things I've done in my life."

This is an infinitesimal step down from "I prepared a slide show presentation documenting my birth through present day. Want to see it?" I know my polite smile is sliding into a grimace.

He pats the floral cover of the photo album that, if I had to guess, his mom picked out. "This is me in a nutshell." Flipping to a page in the front, he points to a picture of him with a woman in large, wire-framed glasses and tall hair. "This is Mom and me in our prize-winning hand-knit Christmas sweaters last year." He turns the page. "Oh, and here's one of our most recent trip to North Dakota—"

"No!" I didn't intend to shout it.

Mr. and Miss Happy Couple are standing to leave and give me one last cocked-brow stare.

"Sorry. I mean, no, I should probably go. I'll have to get more insulin." I hold up what's left of the bun. It's not a lie. I do need more insulin.

Shoving the rest of the salapao in my mouth to demonstrate, I try to grin, but my cheeks are full like a chipmunk's prepping for winter. That's when I feel another set of eyes on me. At the other end of the restaurant, a twinkle dances in the dark blue gaze I'd know anywhere.

Harrison Lundquist. Eden's brother. He quirks an eyebrow at me, the corner of his mouth tipping to the side.

The one and only witness to my epic rejection a year and a half ago, whom I haven't seen since that fateful night. And he's with a gorgeous blond woman. Figures. I can tell she's tall and slender even though she's seated.

The food in my mouth seems to congeal. Harrison shoots me a two-fingered salute as I try to swallow. But the bun sticks halfway down my throat, immovable. Clutching my neck, I jump to my feet and wave frantically at Trevor with the other hand. He stands but backs away. Everything is a blur, but there's a hush as nearby patrons realize what's happening. The room starts to spin.

A large shadow passes over me. Someone's strong arms wrap around my middle from behind, under my ribs, and there's a squeezing sensation. Forceful and sure. The food dislodges like a shot out of a cannon and flies straight at Trevor and his photo album. It lands with a *splat* on the ugly Christmas sweaters page. I gasp and cough, sweet air filling my lungs again.

Ignoring for now the indignant noises from Trevor as he sputters, "M-my photo album. You've ruined it!" I tip my head back to find Harrison's upside-down face peering at me. Incredulity and concern are etched in tandem on his angled, lightly bearded face.

"Harrison? What are you doing here?" I croak, my throat raw.

"Same as you, having an early dinner." Harrison's thumb indicates the woman at his table, and I crane my neck to see she's now staring wide-eyed in our direction.

He turns me around so we're facing each other.

"No, I meant here in Minnesota. Are you visiting?" *Please be visiting.* I've managed to avoid him for almost a year and a half, why now?

The entire restaurant has gone silent, nary a knife or fork stirring, as he grins and says, "Nope. I'm moving back to Minnesota, and not a moment too soon, it seems."

His hands gently grip my shoulders as his eyes scan me. "Are you all right?"

Like a bobblehead doll, Trevor glances between us with his mouth agape.

Harrison takes the liberty of reaching over for Trevor's hand, giving it a shake. "Hey, I'm Harrison."

"My best friend's brother," I supply. Gesturing across the table, I add, "This is Trevor."

But Trevor's not paying attention, fussing over his photo album and scrubbing at the page with a napkin.

There's a flash of something in Harrison's deep indigo eyes in the awkward silence that follows, but it's gone just as quick, and he quirks a grin down at me. "Ouch. Save your life and all I get is 'best friend's brother'?"

I shuffle from foot to foot, cheeks burning. "You hardly—I was working it out—"

"You were turning purple." His arms cross over his plaid-covered chest. He never was one to dress up, even in a nice restaurant. But then, no one has ever worn plaid as well as Harrison does. "I'll take that as a thank-you, so you're welcome."

He winks, and my glucose monitor emits a series of earsplitting beeps—as if people don't have enough reason to gawk—and my mortification is signed, sealed, and delivered.

2

Zoe

Standing at my open car door, body bent inside over the front passenger seat after giving myself an injection of insulin, I spend an extra few seconds sending a furious text to Eden:

> Thanks a lot! Didn't know your brother was back in town. Why is it that every time he's around, I'm in the middle of making the biggest fool of myself?

I add the face-palm emoji, growl as I hit send—not worrying the text will make no sense to her right now—and throw my phone back into my purse.

Harrison leans his tall body against my short-by-comparison MINI Cooper. "Well, you sure know how to show a guy an exciting time."

When I squint up at him, he jabs a thumb in the direction

of the restaurant across the street from the parking garage. "Trevor. That's a date he'll never forget."

"Me either." Slapping a hand to my forehead, I roll my eyes. "Nor his mother. I'm sure she'll be getting an earful about the evil girl who ruined their photo album. I said I was sorry—"

"You know, I don't think I've ever seen someone run so fast out of a nonburning building."

His lips twitch, and he scrubs at his chin as though to steady it, but a low chuckle escapes anyway, the sound warm and familiar. For a moment, it's as if the last year and a half melts away. And I have my surrogate big brother back.

I swat his arm. "Stop. It was a horrific date, don't make it worse."

The golden rays of the fall afternoon sun mix with his sandy blond hair, setting it aglow. "Thank you, by the way." Heat fills my cheeks despite the crisp for the first week of September breeze ruffling my long, wavy hair around my face.

He shrugs off my thanks as he shoves his hands into his jeans pockets.

And . . . it's uncomfortable again. What came after my failed proposal, what Harrison said, how he looked at me, the suffocating tension that followed rushes back.

A pang slices through my chest. Things used to be so easy between us. The boy I grew up with, like family to me. He and Eden both.

My fingers cover my mouth with another realization. "I'm so sorry you had to leave your date, and you did *not* have to pay for mine. I'm paying you back."

After Trevor fled, Harrison insisted on paying for our check. I only let him because I didn't want to cause more of a scene than I already had. Plus, I needed my insulin.

"That wasn't a date. For me, I mean." Palming the back of his head, he shakes it twice. "It was for my new job."

"So, you're like *back* back, then? For good?"

"Yup, I'll be working at a news station. Security." He lifts a broad shoulder. "But I'm hoping to work my way up to a producing job again at some point."

I nod. "Good for you. I know Eden will love having you back." I keep my own mixed feelings to myself.

He studies me for a moment, then adds, "And you're not paying me back. Besides, I'm about to be ridiculously overpaid for a new side gig."

There's that grown-up boyish grin again, though maybe not as open and unguarded as it once had been. I narrow my gaze, but he doesn't elaborate.

Instead, he says, "I better run. Never know when someone will need a spotter for chewing or a witness to the longest restroom break in dating history."

"Haha. Very funny." My hand lands on my hip. "Wait, bathroom break? You saw that and didn't come over earlier?"

"I was enjoying the view." His grin widens as he starts backing away.

"There's something wrong with you. You know that, right?" *Tsk*ing, I point at him. "You should get that checked out."

He touches his forehead and gives a little bow as though doffing a cap, then starts toward his big red truck that belongs in a country song. Over his shoulder, he tosses, "See you around."

Back in my car, heading toward home in the suburb of Shoreview, I reply for myself alone, "But maybe not too soon."

How often will I run into him, though, even if he *is* living in the Twin Cities again? It'll be fine.

My heart lightens as I near my little neighborhood-within-a-neighborhood of four townhome complexes. It's quiet here. Surrounded by old-growth trees, wide sidewalks, and well-kept mid-century homes and yards, this feels like small-town USA rather than a quick jaunt back to the freeway and the hustle and bustle of Minneapolis/St. Paul.

Home. When my podcast numbers climbed higher than I

dreamed they would, and with the income from my part-time work as a host on a faith-based radio station, I could finally afford a real home.

I started the podcast because of a passion for the topic, but I honestly assumed I'd be rambling to myself and Eden. Who knew people would take a shine to a little podcast about finding love in a modern world using wisdom from my favorite Regency authors?

Ironic. The listeners are relying on me for advice and help in their dating lives. But so far I've failed to find a modern-day gentleman of my own.

I cringe, reviewing the Date of Doom this afternoon even before the whole choking incident. Aren't there any true gentlemen left in the world?

My answer comes with a flash of my soft-spoken father and the way he cares for my mom, who has primary progressive multiple sclerosis. My dad is the epitome of a gentleman and has never complained or begrudged his role as husband and caretaker. Their love is like something from my favorite Regency romance stories. Better, actually.

I need to step it up. Not only for me. For my listeners, too.

The question is, How?

Eden is dancing in her living room with her dog when I pull into the shared driveway. Through the window of the townhouse across from mine, I can see Eowyn Elizabeth's paws on Eden's chest. Eden always says her golden retriever–mix rescue dog's names represent the best female characters of both worlds.

Inside, something is waiting for me on my kitchen counter. There's a small wrapped package, and next to it is a plate with a single brownie. Eden and I have keys to each other's places, so no doubt this is the famous (to me) low-sugar zucchini brownie she learned to make when type 1 diabetes found me in the sixth grade. Vegetable brownies might sound disgusting to most, but they're moist and delicious and an easy way to adjust my life to my condition.

My mouth waters at the sight. But there's a note taped to the front of the small rectangular gift.

> Hey, that date sounded rough. Sorry for not telling you about Harrison. I just found out myself. Speaking of which, there's something I need to talk to you about tomorrow morning. But, hey, I'm glad you're okay! Brought you a couple of things to cheer you up.

A growl rumbles in my still-sore throat. He must've told her about me choking. Heap on the mortification. There's a lot to digest there, but not right now. The whole situation has exhausted me.

I rip off the gift's paper. It's a book. She knows me so well. The worn cloth cover, yellowed pages, and earthy scent tell me it's old. I flip it open. Elegant writing, faded in spots, but clearly a high-quality reproduction of the original handwritten pages. Inside the front cover is printed: *Yours Truly, A Diary by A. Nathaniel Gladwin*. Underneath, it states the volume contains the author's own words.

This is a rare find. Gladwin's personal writings are the reason historians determined Gladwin was female, but they've never uncovered her true identity. Her published journals have been out of print for years. I clutch the little book to my chest. This one is now mine.

Eden's parents are rich, with all of the connections to go with it, including in the art and literature world. They attend a ton of charity auctions. Eden knows I've always wanted something like this.

A page toward the back has been bookmarked. Along the top is scrawled in Gladwin's own hand, "Thirty Ways to Meet and Secure a Suitor." A grin pulls at my lips. After tonight, I'm game for anything. *Is this what'll finally help me fulfill my dream of finding my person, of starting a family before it's too late, God?*

But I don't wait for an answer. I don't have that kind of time. None of us knows what tomorrow holds, and I need to stick to my plan if anything is going to get done and get done right.

Look out, hunky but humble lords and esteemed gentlemen. Here I come.

"Isn't it supposed to be 'Thirty, Flirty, and Thriving'?" Eden eyes me over her open laptop at my kitchen table as she preps for our podcast recording this morning.

"Yes, and it is. But I'd rather be flirting with my husband, and first, I have to find him." That inner clock starts to tick and with it, prickles of sweat form on the back of my neck.

I cast her a cheerful grin as I shuffle through my notes for the podcast episode at my kitchen counter. "That's why I'm going to use Miss Gladwin's list, 'Thirty Ways to Meet and Secure a Suitor,' from the diary you gave me. My own ideas have failed, *obviously*, so maybe this will be the key to finally finding my modern-day gentleman."

"But, Zoe, why thirty, why—"

"Did you know in 1805 Jane Austen basically lost everything? Her father died, and she, her mother, and her sister were left poor and dependent on her brothers for support."

Eden's lavender brows scrunch together. "And?"

"She was thirty." I tug my bottom lip between my teeth. "And then there's Miss Gladwin. We don't know who she was, but in her journal"—I hold up the book Eden gifted me for emphasis—"she wrote about how approaching her thirtieth birthday, she was considered an old maid. Unmarried. A social pariah after a broken almost-engagement with a prominent bachelor, kind of like me."

"I still don't understand. I only gave you the diary reproduction because I thought you'd enjoy it." A crease forms on her otherwise smooth forehead.

Gritting my teeth, I square my shoulders and reply instead, "And did you know when my mom was thirty, in one fell swoop she found out she could never have another child and was diagnosed with multiple sclerosis? Her entire life changed in an instant. When she was this age, *my* age."

Eden's mouth drops open. She stands and moves toward me until she can wrap an arm around my shoulders. "Just because that's your mom's story doesn't mean it's yours. You can't live in fear of what could be."

Squeezing her back once, I step out of her embrace and give her a small smile and raise my chin. "I'm not. But that's the point. I can't take a day for granted. I want a family. I want to have a partner in life. What's so wrong with wanting to move along the process?"

I lift a hand. "And what could it hurt, using Gladwin's suggestions? We know she did eventually find her very own real-life Lord Pembroke, who she based her character on. She must've known what she was talking about."

Eden is quiet, studying me for a moment, but then a slow grin spreads, her eyes rounding. But as she starts to respond, "You know what? That's actually a brilliant idea," my BBC *Pride and Prejudice* theme music doorbell plays.

Eden's gaze darts toward the stairs. "Oh, I meant to tell you—"

"Just a sec." I hold up a finger as I dash to the front door.

Yanking it open, I gasp at the sight of Harrison standing on my front step. His tall, broad frame fills the doorway.

"Harrison, what are you doing here?" I don't mean to sound so accusatory.

"Hello to you, too." His sandy brows shoot up. "This is the second time in twenty-four hours I seem to have shocked you with my presence. No unchewed food in your mouth this time, I hope?"

I huff and roll my eyes.

Eden appears at my side. "Harrison! Come on in."

I find myself backing up to let him by but aim an incredulous look at Eden.

In answer, she returns my scowl with a too-bright smile. "So, Zoe, remember how I said I found us a producer and audiovisual engineer replacement?"

We had started our podcast with just the two of us about six months before the proposal-incident-that-shall-not-be-named, but quickly realized we needed help. A coworker from the radio station had filled in here and there, but we were on our own again a couple of weeks ago when he moved.

Harrison, already at the top of the split-level stairs, turns and points to himself. "You're looking at him."

I catch up to find him making himself at home in my kitchen like he always used to, like I haven't just spent the last year and a half avoiding him. Although it wasn't too hard since Harrison had moved to Cincinnati for a lead-producing job right after the whole thing with Sawyer.

Tipping my head to the side, I cross my arms over my chest. "Lucrative new side gig, huh?"

He shrugs, his eyes full of mischief. "Well, I may have exaggerated that part. Unless you're looking to give me an immediate raise. In which case, I'll say that's completely proactively justified. But otherwise, I will work for coffee, especially if you're going to insist on the early morning recordings." He's already rummaging through my cupboards.

Eden joins us and chimes in, "I convinced Harrison to help us, and he agreed because it'll be good for his résumé while he's applying for news-producing positions."

He places a hand on his chest as if struck there. "I'm offended. What I think you meant to say is that out of the goodness of my heart, I'm here to offer my much-needed charm and expertise to this operation."

But with a gesture to me, he adds, "If that's okay with you, too, Zo."

His tone is soft, uncertain, putting away his usual jovial-with-a-hint-of-sarcasm attitude for now. The sweet, vulnerable side he doesn't show everyone. The side that always plucked at something in my chest. And then there's his use of his nickname for me since we were kids. . . .

Finally, I pinch the bridge of my nose even as I feel myself give in. We do need the help, after all. "Fine. But keep your opinions to a minimum."

Before the words even fully leave my mouth, I know that'll never happen. He hadn't been shy about letting us know how ridiculous he found the concept back when we started the podcast.

"You know me. Always on my best behavior." He chuckles as he adds my freshly ground dark roast coffee to the coffeemaker.

After starting a big pot to brew—the curls of steam already filling my kitchen and combined dining room with the rich aroma—he turns and rests his hip against the counter. Retrieving the diary reproduction sprawled on top of my show notebook, he thumbs to the marked page in the back with the thirty tips. The notepaper I've already filled with ideas on how to use the list for the podcast and myself falls free.

"What's this?" One brow slants low while a corner of his lip hitches up as his finger traces the list.

I grab it out of his hands, my shoulders arching back. "It's a list of ways to meet and—"

"Secure a suitor," he finishes. "Yes, I can see that. Don't tell me you're going to try doing these things."

"Yeah, isn't that a great idea, Harrison?" Eden's chipper voice carries from the corner of the kitchen where she's prepping our coffee mugs. Even without Harrison here, it's always been our number one rule. Coffee first. Podcast second. I bring my notes to the table, and he asks if I still keep our audio equipment in the hall closet. After I nod, he retrieves the mic, cords, and small soundboard.

"It'll be fun," I insist. "Plus, we'll document everything for the podcast. We'll call it, 'Thirty by Thirty: Regency Courting Tips.' Get it? My thirtieth birthday is in November."

I don't add that, though our podcast has an overall positive audience reaction, there has been some kickback in the comment section demanding what I could possibly know about love when I'm not in a relationship. So this list has both a personal and professional objective.

He breezes past me and sets the equipment on the table to sort through and eyes me. "So you're going to blindly follow these old dating suggestions from the 1800s?"

His considerable shadow falls over me and my papers. With his height and wide shoulders, he always made my five-foot-two-inches look diminutive. Not that we ran in the same circles back in school. Our two-year age difference meant something when we were teens. And the fact that he was the popular football star, while Eden and I were the drama club/artsy/start-a-Regency-book-club outcast type.

"Look at this stuff." He scoffs, pointing. "'Attend a ball or assembly,' 'Go for a horseback or carriage ride with your potential suitor,' 'Take a promenade in the park'? 'Enjoy a friendly competitive parlor game such as conundrums or whist'? 'Write and receive letters—'"

"Oh, that's a good one. I wish someone would write me a love letter." I tap my chin and flutter my eyelashes.

Eden snickers. "I can hardly get people to text full sentences. A love letter might be out of the question." She hands us our coffee, made just the way we like it—his black, mine pale beige with unsweetened almond milk and my homemade sugar-free creamer. A preference that always makes my dad tease, "Want a little coffee with your creamer?"

Eden's lavender hair is twisted back in a complicated braid today, and her round blue eyes, a shade lighter than her brother's deep indigo ones, are set off by the long-sleeve boho dress she's wearing. Her hair used to be the same color as Harrison's, golden blond with natural caramel undertones. I was always jealous since mine only came in one color—brown. Not something romantic like chestnut or auburn. Just medium brown with eyes to match.

Harrison takes a sip and grimaces, probably from the scalding contents, but he doesn't make a sound. He's not big on emoting unless it's to express his displeasure at the Vikings. Which happens a lot. But when Harrison has something *more* to say, he doesn't hold back. Whether we like it or not.

Except the night I proposed to Sawyer. The way Harrison looked at me. Unsure, nervous, so very unlike Harrison. Had he held in something more he wanted to say? What he did manage to say still sets off a gnarled jumble of feelings in my chest.

I brush the thoughts away. If there had been anything unspoken, he'd probably been about to say how sorry he felt for me as I made such a fool of myself with Sawyer. I certainly didn't need his pity or to hear those words out loud. And the thing is, that wasn't the first time he saw me in such a pathetic situation with my heart broken. Back in high school, he'd witnessed my jock boyfriend humiliate me in front of the whole school—and Harrison had looked at me in much the same way then. Whatever words were behind it, if there were any, are a mystery, and frankly, it's fine if they stay that way.

"Are you really doing this one?" He bends over my shoulder to tap number four on the list, now open on the table. "'Attend chaperoned activities with your potential suitor'? Do you need a babysitter to tag along on your dates? That's ridiculous. Who's gonna go for that?"

Not that *he* would ever have a problem acquiring a date, chaperoned or otherwise. A certain hammer-wielding superhero comes to mind when I think of Harrison—golden and buff but in plaid flannels—although that's as far as I've ever let the thought go. Okay, *maybe* for a hot minute in junior high I let myself crush on Harrison, but that's it. Otherwise, he's always been the snarky, sports-fanatic older brother of my best friend. A jock, but a nice one. I've had run-ins with the not-so-nice kind. I guess we all have our battle scars.

I prop a hand on my hip. "Yes, I will be doing that one. A chaperone isn't a babysitter. In Regency days, they helped preserve a woman's reputation, confirmed intentions were honorable, and offered advice and support to ensure both were making a good choice. Why wouldn't that be worth a try?"

Eden's head bobs, matter of fact.

Harrison, on the other hand, eyes me again with one eyebrow quirked. Eventually, he shifts gears. "We'd better get ready for the show. I have to be to work in an hour and a half."

With a check to her cell phone, Eden says, "Yup, and I set up a caller question for you." She sits behind her laptop at the kitchen table, where she typically monitors our recording program to ensure it's running smoothly and fine-tunes as we go. "I told her you'd call at 8:30 a.m."

"Right." Fifteen more minutes. I gather my notes while Harrison carries the microphone to the plant-filled four-season sun porch that doubles as my studio and sets it up with my laptop at the desk in the corner. I adjust my ring light and boop the small rounded leaves of my Jade Austen plant. "Looking handsome enough to tempt Darcy, Miss Austen." She's shoulder to shoulder with her proud hero, Darcy the Dracaena, who's doing his best not to be overshadowed by Lord Ficus.

I smile to myself and adjust each one, including my fussy, high-maintenance but beautiful fuchsia moth orchid I've nicknamed Caroline Bingley. "There's sun enough for each of you."

Harrison chuckles at my one-sided plant conversation and grabs the soundboard, which I bought from the radio station Eden and I work at when they upgraded. He runs the extension cord from the soundboard to my laptop through the sliding glass doors. We keep the sliding door mostly closed while I'm recording, and Eden and, I guess now, Harrison work at the kitchen table listening and modifying along the way.

Slipping on the headset Eden offers him, Harrison shrugs his shoulders. "I still don't see who we'll find to go along with this."

I smile at the use of "we," as if he's already a part of this little show of ours.

Eden stops the pre-podcast checklist I made for her. "We'll think on it, won't we? But, Harrison, maybe not—"

"What?" He scowls. "You don't want me setting her up with someone?"

I share a smirk with Eden.

Propping an elbow on my desk, I raise a palm. "You're not exactly a romantic, Harrison. I mean, when's the last time *you've* been on a date? And no, that dinner meeting yesterday doesn't count." I shrug. "Look, most of your friends think all a date requires of them is holding in their burps at the dinner table and using a toothpick flosser before going in for the good-night kiss—"

Eden snorts and leans back in her chair at the table, crossing her arms. "Right. The height of romance. And the rest of your friends who *are* mature and well-mannered are already married."

He doesn't refute our claims, but instead points to the invisible watch on his wrist.

"All right, people. Places."

Squaring my shoulders, I slip into my ergonomic chair, put on my headset, and check my microphone.

I let my plants' sharp, earthy scent and super-oxygenating powers seep into my lungs, calming my before-show jitters. "Here we go. Showtime."

Now if only the advice I give others would work on me.

3

Harrison

"Do a quick sound check for me, Zo." I stand right inside the kitchen at the sliding glass door to the porch, headset in place.

This is strange and familiar all at once. Back here, seeing Zoe, talking to her like nothing happened eighteen months ago. It's taking everything I have to keep this up. Fake it until you make it, I guess. But I'll do it. I'll tolerate it all. Anything to sweep away the months of not talking, knowing she was avoiding me anytime I came home for a visit. Anything to fill the void left in my life without her in it.

If only she knew she's the biggest reason I'm back . . . and the reason I left in the first place.

She draws a breath, which is a light brush against my eardrums, then gives me a thumbs-up. "'In vain have I struggled. It will not do. My feelings will not be repressed.'" She recites Mr. Darcy's words with passion.

Not what I was expecting, and it catches me off guard. My coffee slides down my windpipe, and I start hacking.

Zoe leans in her chair to peek through the sliding doors at me. "Should I return the favor with the Heimlich?"

Eden stands and starts slapping me on the back until I shoo her away.

"I'm fine." Another cough says otherwise. "It's the coffee."

Her brow tilts. "Or perhaps too early for Jane Austen?"

"Much. I haven't even had my breakfast yet. You should really give a guy some warning before spouting love declarations."

It's her turn to sputter—which I much prefer. Her full lips open and close several times before she spits out, "I didn't—that wasn't—"

Eden claps for our attention like a mom between fighting toddlers. "All right, you two. Do I have to separate you? You're worse than siblings, and I would know."

"It's time, ladies." I jump in to refocus us but mostly to turn my own mind back to the task at hand.

Rolling her eyes, Zoe rotates back to her computer and uses a recording program to call the podcast listener. The caller won't be on camera, only audio, while Zoe will be on both so that we can release the audio-only version on Spotify and then the video version will be posted to their YouTube channel.

Eden plays the Regency-esque with a modern twist music intro and Zoe's recorded "Welcome to *Love According to Miss Gladwin* with me, your host, Miss Zoe Dufour. Here's where we examine love conundrums and dating strategies through the lens of our favorite Regency-era fiction."

Zoe introduces Lisa, the caller, then she hops right into her question.

"So, Miss Dufour . . ."

Lisa sounds like she's in her late twenties to early thirties. Their audience sweet spot. Eden and Zoe might think that as a guy I wouldn't keep up with their show, but I listened while I was away. Even though I thought some of the Regency stuff was absurd, I was impressed with what they'd achieved. Plus, listening in, hearing Zoe's warm, caring voice, had felt like a little piece of home in the middle of a city where I knew no one.

"What if you're keeping a secret for the sake of someone else?" Lisa says. "Someone you care about. I don't want to hurt this person. What should I do?"

Taking a moment that I will certainly need to edit out, Zoe sits as tall as a person of her petite height can before answering, "In her book *The Season of Secrets*, Miss Gladwin wrote, 'Secrets are lies we tell ourselves.'"

The secret part makes me swallow hard. It's loud in my own ears, but at least my headset is muted for Zoe at the moment. I pull at my collar.

"I remember that story." Lisa's words are quick. "I read it as a teenager for English class, but then went home and immediately read it again. One of Gladwin's best."

Seeming to warm to her topic, Zoe grins into her laptop camera. "Indeed. I think I've found a kindred spirit in you, Lisa."

Zoe's pen spins and drops from her hand. Another edit. She straightens again, poised in her seat. "For those who don't know, *The Season of Secrets* involves love and intrigue during the London Season, sometimes referred to as the Marriage Mart by Gladwin's contemporaries."

She turns the briefest smile to me, still at the doorway. "The Season ran from April to July and then from October to Christmas, and consisted of balls, receptions, and social events. It was *the* place for eligible bachelors and young ladies to make a marriage match." She sighs. "But back to your question, Lisa. Can you fill in a little context?"

"Sure." Lisa's voice trembles a bit. "The secret is about my relationship with this guy. There's nothing terribly wrong with him. He's faithful, as far as I know. He doesn't treat me badly. But he's not *the one*."

Oof. Poor dude. I expect Zoe'll need to call in every ounce of her psychology and broadcasting/communications degrees for this one. Propping her elbows on the desk, Zoe bows her head. Sending up a quick prayer maybe. Two seconds. Three. I'm about to send her a signal. I need some signs or something to communicate while she's recording. We can't reach the dreaded four seconds of dead air. Not that I can't edit that too, but old habits from the newsroom die hard.

Then her head pops back up and she says, "How do you know?"

"He doesn't open doors for me. I know that's small, but it's the little things, right? He doesn't leave me notes or hold my hand when we take a walk or shop together. He doesn't plan dates. He doesn't do romance. And when I asked him if he felt that special spark when we kissed for the first time, he looked at me like I'd suddenly pronounced myself Duchess of Minneapolis. Don't you always tell us to wait for a gentleman, never to settle?"

Lisa's words spill over each other, breathless. "But how can I tell him how I'm feeling? I'll hurt him. Besides, what if this is my only shot at marriage?"

"I get it, Lisa. Sometimes it feels like there's a shortage of modern gentlemen out there and we must settle for what's in front of us instead of the very best for us. But I think Miss Gladwin was trying to say that when we keep secrets from others, we're telling ourselves it's for their good. To protect them. To protect our own hearts. But it's a lie we tell ourselves to avoid doing what's right."

My booted feet shift beneath me, my jaw clamping tight.

There's a pause then a long exhale on Lisa's end. "So you think I should tell him the truth?"

"I won't tell you what to do, but it's my firm belief that honesty is the most important component of a healthy relationship." In Zoe's reflection on-screen, she blinks at herself. "Maybe he's willing to work on the romance side of your relationship once he sees how important it is to you. Or . . . maybe not. But at least you'll know, and the truth may set you free."

Lisa's quiet but heartfelt "Thank you, Miss Dufour" brings a swelling sense of awe into my chest. The Regency bit is still silly, but Zoe's . . . amazing.

Zoe thanks Lisa for being on the show and listening to the podcast before connecting her with Eden for the business side of things—when it will air, her agreement to broadcast it, and so on.

With a deep breath, Zoe turns off her mic and hangs up her headphones. When she stands, she licks her lips as though she's thirsty, and there's a wobble to her steps.

No food plus caffeine?

I open the sliding door for her while Eden finishes up on the phone. Crossing her arms, Zoe stands before me as if daring me to snark about the episode. "What, no sarcastic comment about my advice?"

I throw a hand up in defense and slide my headset off one ear. "No, it was . . ." My glance skids from her wide, chocolate brown eyes and back to my clipboard, where I'm already jotting ideas on how I can give direction during recording and where else we could expand the show's reach. "It was good."

She seems stunned into silence for a moment, and then her lips slope into a frown. "Really? When it comes to my brand of love advice, we don't tend to agree on much of anything. When Eden and I spent our teen years watching the BBC miniseries of *Pride and Prejudice* on repeat and reading all the Regency romance we could get our hands on before starting this podcast, you said, and I quote"—her fingers curl into air quotes, and her face pinches, a caricature of me as some grouchy old guy—"'I can't believe you guys believe in this fluffy, ridiculous, Regency fairy-tale stuff.'"

My mouth opens, and to my annoyance, I'm fighting the urge to laugh, but Eden hangs up with Lisa and her hand shoots into the air. "I know the perfect guy! I don't know why I didn't think of him before."

"Who?" both Zoe and I ask in unison.

I slide into one of Zoe's mismatched painted kitchen chairs. Zoe grabs a glass from her kitchen cupboard and pours a full cup of orange juice.

She guzzles it down in three swallows.

Blood sugar. It was her blood sugar. The sheen of sweat on her forehead and upper lip, the unsteadiness, the dry mouth. Sure enough, there's the beep from her monitor. She swipes her phone to stop the alarm.

I should've known. I used to know every sign. We used to be so in sync. At least as far as our friendship went, but I broke everything in one night. It'll take time to rebuild. *Help me have patience, God. She's worth it.*

Eden slaps the table, a self-satisfied grin on her face, and I blink, trying to remember what we were talking about. "Ben Rowley," she says. "He's the guy who can go on that chaperoned date with you. Great show, by the way."

My sister's foot taps a rapid beat. She's always needed to keep a part of her body moving even while sitting.

I groan at the name, the topic finally registering. "Seriously? What would Ben and Zoe even have in common?"

"Hello? Who's Ben Rowley?" Zoe glances between us.

Eden is already scrolling her phone for what I'm sure is Ben's contact info. "Family friend. His parents know our parents." Sending a pointed glare at me, she continues, "And they'll have plenty in common." Then to Zoe, "He's an Ivy League graduate."

"Pfft." I cross my arms. "Yeah, and his parents never let us forget it."

"They're proud of him. You would be, too."

A parent's pride? I wouldn't know a thing about that.

The tips of Zoe's fingers make a circle on her chin. "Okay . . . that guy? I think I remember you mentioning some Ivy League guy. But didn't he ask you out?"

Eden swats that out of the air like a pesky mosquito. "A million years ago. We were still kids, before college. Then he went away to Yale, and that was that. I saw him in passing at one of Mom and Dad's"—she directs this at me, and my fingers immediately clench into fists—"fundraiser events a couple of months ago. He moved back to Minnesota. And, trust me, that's *so* ancient history."

Numbering his qualities on her fingers, Eden continues, "He's super smart, into classic English literature and old movies—"

"AKA boring." Rolling my eyes, I snort as I remove my headset and throw my navy Twins baseball hat on backward. I don't mean for that edge to sharpen my tone, so I add a chuckle.

"Romantic." Eden corrects me with a scowl. "You'd have tons in common. What do you say?"

Zoe angles her head. "Where have you been hiding this modern Lord Pembroke? But, seriously, why haven't you brought him up before?"

"Like I said, he just moved back to Minnesota, too. Like Harrison." Eden gestures to me.

Great. And he seems to have swooped right in ahead of me. Not that I could've gone on a date with Zoe. Not that we'll ever be more than friends. She's made that very clear.

Eden chews the nail on her pinkie—a sure sign there's more.

Zoe plants her palms on the table and stares Eden down. "And? Do I have to give you the talk I had with Lisa about honesty?"

My hand covers my grin by rubbing my jaw.

"Fine." Eden squeezes the phone in both hands. "But you have to promise not to freak out."

"This is so hard to watch, but I can't seem to look away," I mumble to myself as I start the process of returning the audio equipment to the hall closet. Clearly, we'll have to talk podcast logistics another time with all of this ultra-important dating stuff going on.

Zoe's eyes narrow. "Okay . . ."

Eden sucks a breath through her teeth. "He thinks the 2005 adaptation of *Pride and Prejudice* is the best version." The words are so fast I almost don't catch them, and they end with a grimace.

"What?" Zoe's back snaps straight. "There's no way . . ." But after a laugh from me, she amends through gritted teeth, "I'm sure everyone is entitled to their opinion."

"Since when?" Eden's mouth pulls down to one side. "Never mind that. So, you're willing to give him a chance? Despite his unenlightened views on Jane Austen adaptations?"

I shove a hand in my pocket and shake my head. "I think a better question is, Do you think he's the kind of dude who'll go along with this whole chaperone thing? And if he is, doesn't that worry you a little?"

They turn twin withering glances my way and continue without a pause.

Eden scrolls her phone's contacts again. "Only one way to find out."

She greets Ben on the other end after only a few seconds and explains the podcast experiment.

This is giving middle school memory vibes of the time Zoe asked Eden to call her crush. Hopefully, this is a less traumatic experience for all involved.

Ben's answer must be positive because Eden gives us a thumbs-up. "Great idea." Eden smiles and nods at Zoe. "We'll meet you there. Friday at seven. You're going to love her, Ben. Thanks."

A flush of red crawls up Zoe's neck as Eden hangs up.

Eden fills us in, and my stomach is a roiling mix of everything I've been keeping in, growing by the second at the thought of some other guy—especially Ben—free to go on a date with Zoe.

Zoe's the first to ask, "Ben wants to go roller-skating? As in the 1980s pastime of choice?" Her jaw is rigid and her eyes are wide as she plays with the hem of her top. She isn't exactly known for being coordinated, nor have her limbs ever cooperated in any physical activity or sport in her life. Well, except for her rowing.

"Why on earth did you agree to that?" Zoe pulls at her long, wavy hair, made fuller by the plant-humidified porch.

Eden's brows knit together, but she reaches over and pats Zoe's shoulder. "You'll be fine."

"She most certainly will not." I lean back against the kitchen counter, running a hand over my mouth, trying to hide a smirk. I don't think Ben's ready for roller-skating as a contact sport.

Zoe ignores me. "Eden, will you be my chaperone?"

Raising my arm, I insert, "We'll both be your chaperones."

Eden and Zoe share a look.

"Why?" Zoe blurts.

My shoulders rise. "Because this I've got to see."

Maybe helping her will give her a reason to trust me again. And maybe I need to see her on a date with someone else to help myself—psych myself up for this friend mode again. It's what I've always been to her, and it took eighteen long months to realize I'd rather have Zoe as a friend than not in my life at all.

So I grin and give her shoulder a light squeeze. "I'll be there."

4

Harrison

This might be the most inane thing I've ever been a part of. That may be harsh, but come on.

Here I am, gripping the steering wheel of my truck, headed for the roller-skating rink, about to become a chaperone for this disaster-in-the-making date. Being back in my home state is great. This is what I told myself I wanted, but maybe I should be pointing my truck to my uncle's cabin up north for the weekend. The woods have always been a refuge for me. I tell myself it's to get a little practice with my bow. It's almost hunting season after all, which coincides with football season, making fall the best of Minnesota's four seasons.

Even so, I agreed to this. Volunteered for it, even. It's what a friend and now a colleague would do. But it'll be painful to watch for so *many* reasons. Maybe a little funny, too. Zoe is not what I would call graceful. I remember trying to teach her and my sister how to play soccer when they were little. Let's just say I never knew bruises came in those colors.

I will give Zoe this: When she's determined to do something, she doesn't quit. Kind of like graduating top of her college class and starting her own podcast.

This, though? Using the stuffy old advice of someone who's been dead for two hundred years? How is turning back the clock on dating going to be helpful?

I blow out a loud lungful of air, my hands tightening on the wheel as I ease onto my exit. I'm working for Zoe on the side because the job I really want, a producer at a serious news TV station—I'd even take my old role as an audiovisual engineer—was stolen from me a few months ago. By someone I thought I could trust.

If I keep biding my time as a security guard at a news station here and keep my skills sharp by helping my sister and Zoe with their little podcast, maybe I can advance to a better position and get my career back on track. And if not, I can always look for a job out of state again.

But I have to admit, the podcast isn't so little. No one's more surprised than me that Zoe might be looking at syndication soon. Eden filled me in with the numbers, and people are eating this stuff up. The twenty- and thirty-somethings love it. Basically, anyone secretly holding out for their own personal Mr. Darcy or that Lord Pembroke Zoe's always going on about.

Sometimes I forget Zoe's a grown-up, and even if it's not my thing, she does do some good for other people.

I pull into the skating rink parking lot, the neon lights near blinding.

"Means to an end," I remind myself as I grab my audio equipment and video camera bag. I've been assigned as the videographer as well as producer while Zoe continues building her YouTube channel presence. She'll have me capture behind-the-scenes content of her podcast and footage like this for special episodes away from her house.

Everyone's favorite part of the episodes is when Zoe reads one of her sappy letters gushing to the invisible Mr. Perfect Gentleman she thinks she's going to marry.

I don't want to hurt her feelings, but . . .

Reality in the romantic department is as much her forte as, let's say, horseback riding or . . . roller-skating.

Through the swinging doors, I'm hit with raucous '80s music, dizzying disco lights, and the scent of stale rented skates and cheap nachos at the concession stand.

There's another job to do here, apart from filming. As her almost big brother and designated chaperone, I'll ensure she doesn't hurt herself too badly and watch out for her where Ben Rowley is concerned. Never cared much for him, to be honest. There was always something about him. But "judge not lest ye be judged" and all that. Thanks, Grandma and Grandpa. They'd made sure Eden and I attended church every week even though our parents refused.

Ben and Zoe are already at the skate rental. She laughs. It's not her real laugh. If you've known her as long as I have, you know this is the way she laughs when she's uncomfortable or nervous. Or both. When she's *really* laughing, it's full but somehow still feminine, and the bridge of her nose crinkles the same way it always has since she was a kid. She used to laugh that way for me. Maybe she will again.

Zoe waves as Ben passes her a pair of rented skates. I give the two-finger salute, then hold up one finger to say, "Just a minute." I step away and send a quick text to Eden.

> Harrison
> Where are you?

Three little moving dots, then:

Eden
A complete sentence, good for you. I'll have to tell Zoe there ARE guys who can text full sentences. It's a short one, but it's a start!

I clamp my jaw. Sisters. They grow up, but how are they still so annoying?

Harrison
Ha. Seriously, where are you?

Eden
Sorry. Can't make it.

Harrison
That's a fragment

Eden
Very funny. I was called to the station. A tech is sick for the evening show. I texted Zoe, but maybe she didn't see it. Please tell her I'm sorry.

Harrison
You should apologize to ME. Nothing like being a videotaping third-wheel weirdo on someone else's 1st date.

I add the eye roll emoji and hit send.

Eden
Sorry, bro. Get some good footage and try to be encouraging. I know this mushy stuff is difficult for you, but she deserves someone nice. A true gentleman. So. Don't. Poo-poo. It.

Harrison
I would never.

Even as I hit send, I know that's not true. I find it hard to keep my opinions in check, especially with all this gentleman/

Regency/romance nonsense. Emotions are sometimes harder to express. But I'm a tell-it-like-it-is kind of guy when it counts. Maybe a little too truthful at times.

Before Eden's bubbles start again, I text:

> **Harrison**
> You sure this is a good idea? Ben, I mean. I don't trust that guy.

> **Eden**
> Why? 🤤

> **Harrison**
> He cheated every year at the country club medallion hunt. I caught him once, and he didn't even deny it.

Her response is almost immediate:

> **Eden**
> What? He did? I didn't know that!

> **Harrison**
> Yes.

> **Eden**
> Younger me would've been furious. I always wanted to win that prize pack. But . . . we were kids. I think we've all grown up since then.

I don't want to argue, but to me, that showed something of his character I'm not so sure he could grow out of.

Eden's three little bubbles turn into,

> **Eden**
> Gotta go. I'll text you when I'm done at the station in case you guys are still there and I'll head over.

> **Harrison**
> K. C. U. L8TR.

> **Eden**
> Great. Degraded to single letters and numbers. Good thing we don't depend on you to do the closed captioning.

> **Harrison**
> LOL

I chuckle as I stash my phone in my flannel jacket pocket and make my way through the crowd of families with kids and giggling adolescents meeting up sans parents. Who knew? Skating is still a thing.

Zoe and Ben are near a wall of built-in benches with cubbies above for people to stash their shoes. Ben is bent in front of Zoe, helping her into her skates. Okay, bro, good start. He's already wearing his own official-looking pair of skates, their monogrammed carrying case beside Zoe on the bench.

Her face brightens when she spots me. "Hey, Harrison."

"Hey." Uneasiness settles in. But it's good to see her actually look happy to see me, so I paste on a grin. "You guys ready? Ben, you know what you're getting yourself into?"

"Good to see you, man. Yeah, should be fun." Though a bead of sweat drips down his forehead as he continues to force the skate onto Zoe's foot.

She winces and sucks a breath through her teeth. "I think I might need a bigger size."

The words "Watch it, dude" are on the tip of my tongue, but I keep them locked behind a clenched jaw.

"No, no. It's better too tight than too loose. You could twist an ankle."

I feel like I'm witnessing some strange, updated version of *Cinderella*. Yes, I know about *Cinderella*. Eden watched every

Disney movie on repeat until she outgrew them and moved on to her Regency romances.

Finally, the skate pops into place and Zoe jumps. "Ow!"

My teeth grit as Ben apologizes. "You okay?"

She nods, but there's tightness in her eyes. She blinks it away.

The other skate slips on more smoothly. "There, nice and secure." Ben stands and thrusts a hand out to shake mine.

I grasp his hand in return. Maybe more firmly than is strictly necessary, but hey. "How's your family? Your parents?" I'm not great at small talk. I feel like Darcy when he awkwardly asks about Elizabeth's family on repeat and she's too polite to tell him to get a grip.

Ben shoves a hand in his pocket and avoids eye contact. I get it. I don't like talking about my parents, either. A distant mom and a never-satisfied father. "Great, I'm sure you'll receive the invite through your parents to the annual harvest party."

"Sure, sure." *Annd* . . . that's about my chitchat limit. I reach for the portable clip-on microphone packs inside my bag. "Well, let's get you guys mic-ed up. And hey, thanks for doing this, man."

Zoe clicks her tongue. "Don't say it like that." She tries to stand and slides right back down onto the bench with a thud. This will not end well.

"What?" I frown at her.

Ben does the equivalent of shuffling his feet in skates, peering between Zoe and me.

She pins me with her signature look. "As if Eden only set us up so he could be on the podcast. This is a real date . . ."

Ben's mouth widens into a goofy grin.

"And we happen to be filming it." She turns to Ben. "Thank you for agreeing to that, by the way."

I throw a hand in the air. "That's all I meant."

She tries to stand again. It's like a newborn fawn on ice.

I need a life. Is this really what I'm doing on my Friday night? Watching someone else have a first date?

Ben coaches her to stand with her knees slightly bent and legs farther apart for stability—made more difficult by the long, flowing dress she chose to wear. Only she would wear a fluffy thing like that roller-skating. She looks like she belongs in one of her Regency books.

I give her a tentative thumbs-up, then hand Ben his microphone. "Put these on so the audio picks up your voices without so much interference." Ben clips the small mic to his Oxford button-up near his tie. Odd choice for this activity, too. Maybe Eden's right, and they're meant for each other.

When Ben's mic is in place, he takes the other microphone pack from me and places Zoe's hand on his arm to keep her upright. He starts clipping the mini-mic to the neckline of her dress where it touches the curve of her collarbone. Something in me bristles.

I stifle the urge to growl, *Watch it!* As her chaperone, I have a responsibility here.

Her neck to her hairline flushes pink. "Why, thank you. What a gentleman."

After fiddling with their mic volumes, I start my camera. The owner of the rink is cool with us filming as long as we blur out other people's faces and give the business credit in the caption of the video. Zoe has already enticed her listeners/watchers with a description of this series of episodes devoted to the list of courting tips.

And what's my role again? Protector? Both virtue and limb. I resist the impulse to ask if she's checked her blood sugar.

"All right, kids, have fun." I count down silently with my fingers and point as I hit Record.

This is going to be a long night.

It's a rough start, and my shoulders ache from holding my arms in one position with the camera. Man, those cheap nachos are starting to smell pretty good. I forgot dinner.

For long minutes that feel like hours, Ben skates backward in front of Zoe, holding her hands. She's stumbling and slipping every inch of the way.

The conversation is polite but boring. Where they live, what they do for fun, and if they have any pets, to which Zoe claims proudly she's a plant mom and dog aunt to Eden's dog, Eowyn. Somehow she's laughing even though the guy is as dry as the toast I had this morning because I forgot to restock my favorite sour cherry jam.

Her nervous/uncomfortable chuckle makes a gradual shift to her loud and free laugh. The lilt of it vibrates in my headset, a sound that always pulls my mouth into a grin, no matter the day I'm having—chaperone duty or not.

But he seems to eat up the fact that he's a better skater than her. Weird flex, bro.

"The Final Countdown" by Europe blares from the sound system. A local oldies station is hosting the music tonight, so we have to listen to their commercials for area restaurants and upcoming events between songs.

Other skaters, even kids, zoom past Zoe and Ben. His longing glance reveals that he's not thrilled with being saddled with the skating equivalent of a toddler. At this rate, the blooper reel will be longer than the footage I'll have to hunt through of her staying upright.

Ben guides Zoe to the half wall encircling most of the rink. "Do you mind if I skate on my own for a while? I want to stretch my legs."

"Oh, sure. No problem." She crawls along the wall, hand over hand, and tumbles hard onto her backside, dress caught in the wheels.

"You all right?" He helps her up.

"I'm fine. Come on, let me see those skills."

"You don't have to ask me twice." He winks, then he's off, weaving around her in a series of complicated zigzags. Okay, he's pretty good.

He makes a loop around the rink and nears Zoe again, who's still inching along. "Eden said you went to an Ivy League school. Yale?" I can see his shoulders roll back from here.

"Is it as pretentious as it sounds?" Her tone is wry but teasing. My mouth twitches at the corner.

Ben throws his head back and laughs without so much as a stagger. "Even more so."

"Hey, what'd I miss?"

This is not in my headset but at my side. Eden's here. Finally.

"Thought I'd show up to see how it's going. Oh, they look cute together!" She makes a high-pitched noise only dogs and brothers can hear.

"Shh." I turn my head without moving the camera. "Grab some headphones."

"I'm sure it is," Zoe is saying. "What was it like? What's your degree in?"

"Oh, stuffy, beautiful, you know." His voice is casually bored. "I studied economics."

"What brought you home?"

"Family. I wanted to be closer to my family."

She gazes up at him with a soft expression. "Family is important to me, too. I'm really close with my parents."

After a long exhale, she asks, "So what do you do, Ben? I've never met someone with an economics degree."

He seems to hesitate, pulling at his collar, which makes the mic scratch and hiss in my ears. "I'm teaching at the University of Minnesota. Nothing glamorous."

She touches his shoulder and makes a sound of delight in her throat. "That's amazing! I so admire teachers. Are you back for good, then?"

He glances down at her with a grin. "Yes, definitely. I'm a Minnesotan through and through. I've always known I'd settle here after college."

"Me too. I never want to be far from the Cities."

"So, all the questions at once, huh?" He does a 360-degree turn and then drops into a squat position.

He's not much better than the tight flock of teens zooming at breakneck speeds around the rink trying to impress each other.

Showing mercy, Ben pulls over at the half wall not far from Eden and me.

Zoe stops beside him. "Isn't that what we do on first dates? Ask all the questions and do our best to charm the other person?" Her tone is warm. I've never heard Zoe flirt before. It's weird, like catching your grandparents kissing. It's okay behind closed doors. I just don't want to witness it. Not any more than I had wanted to watch her propose to someone else, but I'd agreed to be the videographer anyway to be a good friend.

"'There is no charm equal to tenderness of heart.'" Ben's voice is low.

Yup, this is weird. Eden and I both heave a sigh—for very different reasons—I'll need to edit out later.

"Ben's not so boring after all, hmm?" Eden whispers. I've told her before I'll have to edit the audio if she talks. It doesn't matter at what volume.

Zoe sucks in a sharp breath, and I have to zoom in to make sure she's not hurt. "Jane Austen! That's from *Emma*. You know it?"

Eden smacks my arm. "See? Told you."

"I love English literature, especially from the nineteenth century. Isn't it divine?"

How does Ben—or Zoe, for that matter—keep a straight face when he says *divine*?

"Yes. Me too. But I don't know who I love more, Jane Austen or—"

"A. Nathaniel Gladwin?"

"Exactly!" Zoe's voice is breathless. "You know historians have determined Gladwin—"

"—was a pen name." Ben taps the top of the half wall like he's buzzing in on Jeopardy. "Gladwin was a woman."

Zoe angles her head back, gazing up at him. A playful smile curves her lips as she taps his shoulder. "But, hey, I have a bone to pick with you about your *Pride and Prejudice* adaptation preference...."

They start a jovial debate about the merits as well as the faults of each that my brain blocks out.

My eyes roll. I might be a little like the poor sap the podcast caller described. It's not that I don't like romance, but I don't get this Regency stuff. From what I can see, it's a lot of broody stares that border on creepy, polite yet clever tête-à-tête without anyone actually saying what they're thinking, and rain-soaked declarations of love that come only after the gentleman's yearly income is established. What am I missing?

Ben pulls Zoe away from the wall and skates much too fast around the circle, her hand in his.

The radio announcer starts another advertisement as "I Love Rock 'n' Roll" ends. I turn my focus back to the task at hand.

"Ladies, are you looking for a gentleman? Maybe you're a gentleman ready to find the right lady to sweep off her feet." The announcer's silky smooth tenor booms over the sound system.

"Well, I have just the thing for you. You're cordially invited to a Regency era–themed singles' retreat, the Minnesota Marriage Mart, from October nineteenth through the twenty-fifth."

Eden gasps next to me at the same time Zoe does in my headset. This is not good.

"Enjoy a variety of Regency activities, nightly formal dinners, a ball, of course, and a chance to meet and spend time with as many suitors as you'd like, all while living out your *Pride and Prejudice* fantasies in historical attire. Visit Wyndmere Hall's website or call to reserve your spot today. Located thirty-seven minutes from Minneapolis, outside of Stillwater. Step back in time to find love that lasts today, tomorrow, and forever."

I cringe at the commercial copy.

Zoe and Ben skate toward where Eden and I stand at the rink's entrance/exit in the half wall. Ben flashes a smile for the camera and lets go of Zoe's hand. Her arms flap. They're coming in fast, but for once, Zoe stays upright.

"Hey!" Zoe calls. "Eden, did you hear that? A Regency retreat!"

Eden steps closer to the opening in the wall. "I know. We have to go. No way we can miss—"

Eden shrieks.

It's like in the movies where everything turns to mayhem in slow motion, but there's no way to stop it.

I reach for Eden, trying not to drop the expensive new camera, only managing to pull her into the direct line of fire.

Zoe flails her arms as Ben shouts, "Toe down!" and arcs away from the impending doom.

"Comin' in hot!" Zoe's tone is both panicked and resigned. I push Eden out of the way, though she falls anyway, as Zoe barrels full force into my chest.

Oof! The air leaves my lungs in a painful gush, and we both go down.

We're heaped on the floor, everyone staring. This is the human equivalent of a three-car pileup.

Thankfully, the camera's still in my hand above my head. I'm nose-to-nose with Zoe. Her eyes widen and consume my field of vision. What is that scent? Something floral, like my mother's rose garden in summer, and something homey, like freshly laundered sheets. I gently push her into a sitting position. Her cheeks redden, and she lets out a shaking laugh.

"You guys all right?" Eden sits up and rubs her shoulder where I shoved her.

"Sorry about that." I gesture to her arm. "I was trying to move you out of the way."

Eden stands. "No worries."

"Thanks for breaking my fall." Zoe starts unlacing the skates, face still red.

I lift a shoulder. "What are chaperones for? I mean that seriously."

She bats at me as if to say, "You're hopeless." Blood oozes from her knee, exposed as she bends it to remove the skate.

I point. "You're hurt."

She groans. "Good thing I always carry Band-Aids in my purse. Kind of tools of the trade as an accident-prone person."

Ben swerves over but stays back as though we're about to grab him and throw him to the ground with us. "Are you—oh, oh"—he covers his mouth, shoulders convulsing like he's gagging as he eyes her knee—"Yeah, you know what? I think I'll head out. Long day." The words are muffled behind his hand.

Zoe's fingers freeze on her laces, her head whipping up. "Oh, o-okay. Sure."

The waver in her voice wrenches something in my gut.

"It was nice to meet you, Zoe. See you, Eden, Harrison." He nods at us in turn and hands me his mic.

He takes off as if those fancy skates have turbo boosters.

Zoe frees herself from her death traps on wheels. "Well, as date escapes go, a quick exit by roller skates is new."

I stand and pull Zoe up.

We return to the bench. I tuck the camera and mics away in my bag. With my thumbs now hooked on my belt loops, I quip, Regency-style, accent and all, "As your chaperone, I must say I don't believe that suitor *suits* you."

Zoe places a Band-Aid over her knee. A small quirk of a smile peeks out from behind her curtain of warm-chocolate-brown hair. "Oh yeah?"

"Yeah." I cross my arms. "He's not your MVP or whatever."

"M. L. P. Modern Lord Pembroke." Zoe slips into her shoes and settles her skirt over her bandaged knee. "The hero from Gladwin's famous last novel, *Twice the Gentleman*."

My face is blank. I can tell by the way she's looking at me like a deer caught in my crosshairs.

Eden raises a hand. "That means we keep looking. And I think I might know where to start."

They put their hands palm to palm, something they've done since grade school whenever they're mutually excited over something.

"The Minnesota Marriage Mart," they say together.

"I can save some of the 'Thirty by Thirty' list for then because where else am I going to attend a ball or assembly anyway?" Zoe gushes.

"Right." Eden already has her phone out, looking up the retreat. "It says registration includes a pre-retreat boot camp with dress fittings, Regency dance instruction, and etiquette lessons."

Zoe covers her mouth. "That sounds like a dream come true."

I blink. "No, that sounds like a waking nightmare."

Eden points at my chest. "And you're coming with us. We'll document everything for *Love According to Miss Gladwin*."

This sounds like more Regency ridiculousness I'll have to endure before I can land that "real" job.

All I know is, chaperoning these people is about to become a real, full-time job.

5

Zoe

A quick burst of air flaps my lips in an embarrassing noise I hope no one misinterprets. The makeshift dressing room curtain set up in one of the Regency Society of Minnesota's meeting rooms flutters as I struggle with this confounded corset. I'm glad we arrived early to meet with the retreat coordinator, Victoria, so we're the only participants here at the moment. And Victoria is busy with the seamstresses on the other end of the long, rectangular room.

"You all right in there?" Eden's voice lofts from the fitting room beside mine.

"If by 'all right' you mean feeling like an over-stuffed sausage, then sure." I swat a lock of frizzy hair out of my eye while sweat trickles down my neck. "I'm supposed to feel like an elegant lady. Instead, I feel like a fool playing dress-up."

She laughs. "If you are, then so am I. But I guess I'm used

to playing dress-up, with Comic-Con and all those *Lord of the Rings* conventions."

I finally finish lacing the front of my full-length corset. Okay, it's all right once it's in place. Thank goodness, nothing like the super-tight, stiff Victorian-era corsets. "I don't know about this, Eden." I peek out of my curtain and tap hers until she pops her head through.

"What's the matter?"

"Maybe this is as ridiculous as Harrison said." I duck back inside and start pulling on the high-waisted petticoat. "Where is he anyway? He's supposed to be here to film a little promo for our first day of retreat prep."

I hear rustling, so I know she's back to dressing, too. "He had something to finish up at his new job. He'll be here later."

Eden and I signed up for the Regency-themed singles' getaway immediately after hearing the commercial at the roller-skating rink. The mandatory pre-retreat boot camp sounded fun, a chance to build on my extensive Regency knowledge built from years of poring over every book, movie, and website devoted to this time period.

This is it. My chance to prove myself right on everything I've been preaching on my podcast, everything I've told myself and my modern-day gentleman in years' worth of letters. I can put Gladwin's advice as well as my own list of nonnegotiables into practice. And the timing couldn't be better. Turning thirty has always meant something to me it probably doesn't to others—a transition from young adulthood to a true "grown-up." But it's also much more than that.

I sigh and swallow, a bittersweetness coating the back of my mouth and mind. Thirty isn't a deadline exactly, but knowing what can happen, what *did* happen to my mom and dad, makes me all the more anxious to finally find my perfect match. It means security. It means having someone there for you and with you through the thick and the thin of life, just like my mom and dad are for each other. They are truly best friends, and I want that so much it aches deep down to the bottom of my soul.

The pressure builds in my chest, and I blurt to Eden still in the next dressing room, "What if I can't find someone who checks the boxes on my list? Or worse yet, what if I think I do and he—he's not who I think he is?"

Another flap of the curtain. "Hey, Zoe?"

I stick my head out again. "Yeah?"

Her lavender brows stitch together in the middle. "You know this isn't another Sawyer situation, right? We're setting our phony baloney radars to high alert, remember?"

I try to swallow, but my throat constricts and I splutter. "Yes, I know. But I'm not so sure about my judgment at the moment. He was supposed to be my 'perfect on paper' guy. I thought we wanted the same things—you know, have 2.5 children, advance in our careers, all of that. But that loosey-goosey plan wasn't enough."

Her features tighten, eyes filled with grief for me. I don't need to tell her the ending of this story—how a year and a half ago I found out Sawyer was cheating on me with someone who was his and my exact opposite, a total unplanner who flitted into his life at an art gallery, and he was swept away from our lovely, well-thought-out life before it ever truly began. This is the news Sawyer chose to share with me the night I proposed ... in front of Harrison and his rolling camera. Talk about adding insult, with a squeeze of lemon and a dash of salt, to injury.

Eden reaches over and finds my shoulder to squeeze it. "I know it's hard to try again. Like *really* try again."

"What do you mean?"

She pauses as though considering her next words carefully. "That if you choose to go out with guys you don't really know—like a match on a dating app where all you had to do was swipe right—or who don't seem very promising to begin with, there's less at stake for you if it doesn't work out. You were only dipping your foot into that dating pool, so who cares if he's a dud, right? That way your heart can't get broken again."

Were my many blind date fails halfhearted attempts to find love? That can't be right.

I start to say so, but she holds a hand up. "I don't want this retreat to end up the same way. Don't be afraid to really jump in, get invested, okay? How will you find love if your heart isn't actually open to it?"

Pinning her with a look, I jut my chin at her. "But, hey, you can't sit back, watching me crash and burn at love, either. At some point, you have to get out there too. Meet people. Date. There may be bad dates, but it only takes one good one with the right person."

"I don't know." Her tone's already closing off.

It's the one thing Eden has a tough time discussing.

"Not every guy is like Colton Hayes, Eden. Some of them go out into the world to seek their fortune and truly do come home. Instead of . . ."

"Finding the woman of his dreams elsewhere, marrying her, never to return? Yeah, I'm a real Anne Elliot. Only my Captain Wentworth never came back for me." Her tone is droll, but she can't hide the ache underneath.

My gut writhes. She has her own Ghosts of Relationships Past to deal with.

"I'm sorry. But he wasn't the man you deserve." I tug at my chemise's neckline. "You gotta get back out there. Besides, even a failed date is more fodder for the podcast, right? It'd be nice to feature someone else's checkered dating life for a change."

She grumbles a noncommittal reply, and I press my lips together. "Anyway, that's why working from a nonnegotiable list and this structured retreat are exactly what I need to get on track. Maybe you, too."

I step back into the dressing room, slipping into the blush

satin empire-waist gown I'm supposed to try as a sample so they can take my measurements. "You know, I thought I could randomly meet and fall in love with my forever person like my parents did. I tried, not only with Sawyer but with all of these haphazard dates, too. It didn't work. But now I have my list and a plan, and I'm not deviating from it. This is how I'll find my perfect gentleman"—*who won't break my heart with his duplicity and blow up my plans for the future*—"if he's even out there."

And with honesty on the list, something so lacking with Sawyer and many of my failed dates, I'm making it my top priority now.

My shoulders roll back. "Besides, this is what I've wanted since we were teens. You know me, I've always wanted to step into the pages of our favorite books. Into the BBC adaptations, into the literal shoes of Elizabeth Bennet." Eden inserts an *mm-hmm*. "As if I could turn back the clock to a simpler time with clear rules of conduct. Of courting. Etiquette. A time when proper, gentlemanly manners were an expectation and a given instead of the rare exception they seem to be today."

"Yes!" Eden adds in a muffled voice as if wrestling on an article of clothing. "Maybe this will make finding our modern Lord Pembrokes as easy as counting the times Mrs. Bennet complains of her nerves."

We laugh.

For now, I squelch the worry about what I'll do if this doesn't work, if living a Regency dating life isn't all it's cracked up to be, and I never manage to find my M. L. P. Keeping up a Regency-themed romantic advice podcast might be tough, for one.

There's the commotion of more women arriving now, a cacophony of excited chatter and giggles.

I emerge from my dressing room at the same time Eden does hers. We help each other fasten the backs of our gowns.

"But what if there's something wrong with me? I mean, I'm such a disaster. I managed to scare Ben so badly, I think I saw smoke billowing from his roller skate wheels as he made his escape."

"You are *not* a disaster. And Ben felt terrible about leaving like that, he texted me. He has a blood phobia." She taps her chin, right over a thin white line of a scar. "I guess that explains why he ran screaming the time I split my chin falling off a swing as a kid."

"Anyway . . ." Eden bends closer to ensure our words are for us alone. "Listen, we have no control over what happens during this retreat, okay? Who will be there, any of it—"

"That's the only thing I don't like about it."

Squeezing my elbow with gentle pressure, she goes on, "We have to trust that Someone who knows us better than we know ourselves has a plan. And His plan is what's best for us."

Being a witness to Mom's ongoing health struggles—her condition worsening over time since I was eight with her more progressive form of MS, and in the last few years having to use a wheelchair full-time—I sometimes wonder about that. Are we really supposed to leave things like this up to some master plan we aren't allowed to consent to? With so much at stake, why wouldn't I know what—or who—is best for me?

But this isn't the time for a spiritual existential crisis, so I shoot her a tight-lipped grin.

My satin gown swooshes around my ankles as we move to the three-sided mirror at one end of the room.

The morning sun cuts through the Regency Society of Minnesota's high arched windows, lighting the pale blue silk of Eden's empire-waist dress to a shimmer. The color is a complement to her eyes and, oddly enough, her lavender hair.

The society, tucked into a second-floor corner of the historic Landmark Center in downtown St. Paul, could almost make me believe we truly stepped back in time. The building features a four-story columned and glass-ceilinged atrium, dark ornate woodwork, and an exterior of conical turrets, cylindrical towers, and pink granite.

"*Okay...*" Eden draws out the word as she turns a coy smile to her reflection. "I could get used to these flowy Regency gowns."

Eden fluffs the loose fabric around her middle.

Stepping to her side, I adjust my own dress and admire the split-skirt style—about a foot too long, but otherwise, fits well.

"Right, no need for polite salads whilst in this thing." I lift my chin at mirror-me.

"Whilst? Love it. Already diving headfirst into the Regency era." Eden laughs as she spins again, the silk making a *whoosh*. "Same, by the way. My dates might as well know I eat like a hobbit right from the start."

"Right. What's the line from *Lord of the Rings*? We've had one breakfast, yes. But what about 'girl lunch'?" I wiggle my brows at her.

Eden giggles.

"Second breakfast," a cheerful voice corrects, wafting from the nearest dressing room. A woman with a thick fringe of bangs, large burgundy cat-eye glasses, and a wide grin pokes her head out. "Hi, I'm Sophia. Sophia Tuffin. Would you mind helping me, please?"

"Sure. No problem." Sophia steps out of the dressing room, turns so her back is toward me, and I tug the two sides of her sunflower yellow dress together to continue the buttons up the back. She'll need the bust let out a bit, but otherwise, it's a lovely color for her complexion. "I'm Zoe Dufour, and this is my friend, Eden Lundquist."

When I finish, Sophia whirls around. Mid- to late-thirties? There's the tiniest crinkle around her brilliant green eyes—widened as she studies me.

"Zoe Dufour? As in *the* Zoe Dufour from the *Love According to Miss Gladwin* podcast and YouTube channel?"

I exchange a smile with Eden. "Yup, that's me. And Eden is my broadcast technician and sometimes cohost." Is this one of those fan situations, or will we get a laundry list of things we should change? Please let it be the former. . . .

Braces gleam from Sophia's mouth as she squeezes Eden's forearm and shakes my hand for what seems like forever. "Oh, I'm such a huge fan. I'm a total Gladwin Girl." My shoulders relax.

One palm covers her heart. "I love everything about your show. I grew up reading Austen and Gladwin. I especially love when you share one of your letters to your future husband, your modern-day gentleman. That's what I'm looking for, too."

There are a few sideways glances from the other ladies nearby.

"Thank you. I'm so glad you—"

"Don't hate the show." Eden finishes for me with a wink. "Haters are scary, and they feel free to say anything these days."

"Hater? Of course not." Sophia finally lets go of my hand when my teeth rattle. "Sorry. I guess it's a good thing we'll have etiquette lessons, huh?"

Victoria, a tall, imposing brunette with a cool smile sweeps through the room, tipping a brow at Sophia. "Yes, and I can see some of you will need it more than others."

The crowd of about twenty-five women trying on dresses or being measured by seamstresses from the Behind the Times Modiste & Costume Shop stops to stare at Victoria. It's a sea of bright and pastel hues as well as silks, satins, cottons, and muslins. But the sea stills as Victoria commands the room with one loud clap, reminding me of my militant eighth-grade gym teacher.

"All right, ladies. If everyone could please make their way out of the dressing rooms." She waves us forward to crowd around a dais at the other end of the room. "I'm Victoria Snelling, your Regency Society of Minnesota hostess and activities planner for our Regency Singles' Retreat, which we're calling 'The Minnesota Marriage Mart'—"

Eden nudges me and whispers, "Do you think finding a guy will be as easy as strolling down Aisle 12?"

I cover my snicker with a cough.

Victoria clears her throat and shoots invisible daggers at us. I straighten and clamp my mouth shut. "As I was saying, we're working with the historic Wyndmere Hall outside of Stillwater as our pristine venue. And we're calling it 'The Marriage Mart' as we're modeling it after the London Season during Regency times, which was filled with social activities and balls with the main purpose being—"

"To spouse shop." Eden's whisper is low enough Victoria doesn't catch her this time.

Victoria explains the historic use of the term *marriage mart*, then clasps her hands together. "Now, I'd like to lay out some rules and expectations for you."

Here we go. I rub my palms together.

"I hope Harrison gets here soon." Eden glances toward the door.

Victoria sends us a sharp glare and continues with the last half of something I missed. " . . . also, don't forget, no modern clothing—with one exception, the trivia night—and no devices during the retreat. We are focusing on a fully immersive experience."

"*Psst*." It's Eden. Again. We're right back in school. "We should probably take some footage with our phones if Harrison doesn't make it."

I nod, then place a finger over my mouth, smiling so she knows I'm not annoyed. Always the one to say exactly what pops into her head, anytime, anywhere. It's just Eden. The rolling dialogue with plenty of pit stops and rabbit trails along the way is part of who she is. And I wouldn't change her for the world.

Victoria's voice ratchets up a few decibels. "The one exception to the technology rule is standing right there." She gestures to Eden and me by way of introduction. Every eye turns to us.

I raise a hand in greeting.

"Hi, I'm Zoe Dufour, and this is Eden Lundquist. We work for KNZW Elevate Radio, and I'm the host of the podcast and YouTube Channel *Love According to Miss Gladwin*."

There are murmurs, some excited. Sophia grins ear to ear. Another younger woman, maybe mid-twenties, with vibrant copper curls whispers something to a taller and older woman with a softer, graying version of the same hair. They smile at Eden and me. Meanwhile, a handful of women who arrived together and kept to themselves in a loud, giggling group eye us. The one at the center, a blonde, seems to be the leader.

Great. Can we please have a snooty clique like we're back in high school? That's *not* the kind of "step back in time" I meant.

I clear my throat. This is so different than talking to people through a microphone or even a camera. "We will be collaborating with the Regency Society of Minnesota as well as the staff at Wyndmere Hall to help promote both wonderful organizations"—maybe if I compliment them, Victoria will stop looking at me like I've already ruined Christmas, New Year's, and her birthday, as well as her precious retreat—"and we'll take footage for my YouTube channel during the retreat. We will try to be as unobtrusive as possible. Both Eden and I as well as our producer, Harrison—"

As if on cue, Harrison bursts through the door, looking completely out of place not only because he's the only guy but also because he's the only one in twenty-first-century clothing. But it doesn't faze him. He's always had an innate sense of confidence. It's not arrogance, but a comfort in his skin I admire.

Eden waves him over. "This is Harrison. He's late."

She gives his shoulder a playful tap, but he ignores it. A

strange expression drifts across his face. His gaze stays with me. My face heats. Yes, I'm sure I look ridiculous to him in this dress. Eventually, he greets Eden and waves to the ladies, who nearly swoon as if Darcy himself just walked in. Victoria herself seems to warm and soften as a small smile breaks through her icy facade.

Even I must admit he casts a striking figure, standing at least a foot above everyone else, with windblown golden hair, a leather jacket over a red plaid button-up, rugged short beard, and those eyes. . . .

He turns them to me, catching me staring. A glint appears as does a side smirk that makes my mouth dry. He may be off-limits—like he'd ever be an option for me anyway—but I'm not *dead*.

There was a time, a moment in high school actually, when I thought maybe he thought of me as more than Eden's friend. That he'd been doing more than comforting me after a breakup. But nope. If he'd ever had those types of feelings for me, he'd had plenty of opportunities to say or do something about it over the years. Of course, there was the thing he said after Sawyer dumped me. . . .

Eden clears her throat, snapping me out of it.

"Where was I? Oh, right." I point to the three of us. "We will be dressed like you"—there's a groan from Harrison—"and Eden and I will participate in the activities like everyone else. We have release forms to sign if you're okay with us showing you on camera. This is a blanket release and does allow us to use any and all footage from the retreat on any platform. But no worries if you're not comfortable, we will blur your face during the editing process. Any questions?"

The dress fitting and introduction to the retreat ends with only a few questions, and most of the women let us know they'd love to be a part of the filming, especially the enthusiastic Sophia. Even the clique members sign the waivers, but

I sense it's for what they hope will be their fifteen minutes of fame.

Harrison snaps a few shots of us in our gowns and again I feel exposed, but it has nothing to do with the bare neckline I'm not used to. His gaze, usually light and jovial, is somehow more intense since he returned home but especially today.

Before I have a chance to ask him what's up, he pulls his buzzing phone from his pocket.

He holds up a pointer finger. "Just a sec. It's work. Maybe they're calling to say I can't go with you on this little adventure. Sorry." But his tone and one-shoulder shrug are anything but.

For some reason, the wink he shoots me on his way to the door sends heat rushing through my cheeks and no doubt red splotches, which always accompany blushing for me.

Eden doesn't seem to notice as she sidles up beside me, hands on her hips. "I bet he's trying to get out of his menswear fitting."

I cross my arms. "And the retreat . . ."

6

Harrison

Bracing myself, I answer, "Hello?" even as I run a hand through my hair, trying to escape whatever happened inside me when I saw Zoe in that dress. Which is weird when those Regency dresses look like nightgowns.

At the thought of Zoe in a nightgown, I smack my palm against my forehead. *Snap out of it!*

The brash, commanding voice of Bill Kellsner, owner of the news station where I work, barks out, "Harrison Lundquist?"

My eyes squeeze shut. I need to focus. It's not like I haven't seen Zoe in a dress before or even noticed she's a beautiful girl. No, woman. Those deep, soulful brown eyes and the light shining through her rich brown hair. The pink flush of her cheeks when she caught me staring like an oaf . . .

It's thoughts like these that led me to act in a way that scared Zoe off all those months ago and put a wall between us.

"Lundquist? Are you there?" His voice is growing impatient.

Get a grip, man. It's Zoe. She's off-limits. I know this. But I'm also not dead. I'd have to be not to notice her.

I clear my throat. "Yes, sorry, sir. This is Harrison."

"Harrison, this is Bill Kellsner."

"Yes, Mr. Kellsner. I know who you are." What I can't say is, "I tried to see you about a possible producing job at the station, and you wouldn't take an appointment with me."

I forge ahead so I don't have to hear the words that, a few months ago, sent the career I'd worked so hard for into a spiral—*"You're fired."* Never again.

"Sir, Mr. Kellsner. I apologize for requesting a week's leave. I know I haven't been there long." I wince. It's only been a few weeks on this job. "The news station is really important to me. But I've made a commitment to help my sister." Though it's Zoe's hopeful expression when she asked if I could help them that flashes through my mind. "See, I've been—"

"Running that dating something or other podcast. Yes, I know."

"I don't actually run it, sir. It's my sister and her best friend who—"

"Right, right. My wife, Delilah, doesn't miss an episode. Always going on and on about it." He snorts. "Between you and me, I don't really get it. But that's not the point."

"I know it's a lot to ask, sir. If you'd rather I have my sister and her friend find other arrangements, I'd be happy to." I almost sigh in relief thinking of avoiding the dreaded Regency menswear fitting. Suits—whether the kind my chronically disappointed media-investor father wears or the 1800s variety—and I don't mix.

I walk around the balconied hall overlooking a wide foyer below as the women from the dress fitting start trickling out, in their regular clothes now. They openly watch me as they load into the elevator.

There's a gruff noise on the other end of the phone. "No,

no. That's just it, Lundquist, I want you to go on this Regency dating thingy."

"Sir?"

"My wife has been bugging me to consider investing in this little podcast. I may not understand all the hubbub about this Lord what's-his-face Penbrooke or Mr. Barcy, whatever. I think it's all a bit ridiculous"—I cover a snort with a cough because, honestly, I *still* think it's ridiculous—"but there's a real audience for this kind of thing. I'm seeing the numbers. So, if you can leverage this experience for an even greater reach and really make the most of it on your platforms, I'd like to talk about syndication within our online news sources afterward. Publicity, too, throughout our daytime talk shows and light news hours. Depending on your film edits, we could talk about a segment or a show of its own."

My feet carry me from one side of the marble-floored balcony to the other. An enormous grin steals over my face. This is going to make her, I mean, *their* day.

"I'm so honored. Thank you, Mr. Kellsner. That's great news. I can't wait to tell them and to shake your hand, sir."

"Well, it may be sooner rather than later because my wife's already made me sponsor this retreat, and we'll be making our obligatory appearances. She's dying to meet Chloe."

"Zoe," I correct. "I'm sure we'd all like to meet your wife, sir. Sounds like we owe her a thank-you."

"Oh, and Lundquist?"

"Yes?"

"I know about your background." Here it comes. He knows what happened at my last job. "And I know you have experience in producing as well. I heard you tried to see me when you got back in town, before you started in our security department. Sorry, I was tied up with some things at the time. We do have some slots in our investigative news hour and a few other places. How about we chat about it after the retreat?"

I stutter. "Yeah, that'd be great." But then I lower my voice to sound more nonchalant. "Let's do that."

"I'd need you to give everything to the producer role, if it comes to that. Besides, our only vacancies are at our national news station in Chicago, so I'm afraid you'd have to leave this little project."

I knew I was doing the security gig and the podcast until I found a "real job" back in my field. And I'd always said I'd be willing to move for the right job like I did for the one in Cincinnati. In fact, when I was a teen enduring my family's oppressive expectations, I'd said when I became an adult I'd move away and never look back, except to check on Eden. But I just moved home, and suddenly the idea of quitting the podcast trips me up.

"You understand, Lundquist?"

This is what I've been working for since my life was derailed by doing the right thing but trusting the wrong person. This should be a no-brainer.

"Mr. Kellsner, thank you, sir." I pause, running a hand through my hair. "Leave the podcast? Well, I—no, of course, sir. I'd give up just about anything to produce again."

"Good to hear."

"Right, I'll show you I can handle it with this retreat series."

"I also had a little birdy tell me your father is Arnold Lundquist, as in Lundquist and Associates, Media Investment Firm? That's certainly a family tree I can trust."

As if someone has thrown an invisible punch to my jaw, I toss my head back. Why is he asking about my father's business? The business I won't step foot into, much to my father's disappointment and ire.

I make myself unclench my teeth. "Yes, he's my father."

"I'd love to talk with him about the possibility of joining up for this little venture. Perhaps he'd come out to the retreat and we can all sit down and talk business, and have his investment firm throw in their support for the show as well. What do you think?"

I've told my father I want nothing from him, which seems to suit us both just fine. I can't be seen crawling back to him for support now, especially not with the podcast he finds even more absurd than I do. "Sir, I would really rather keep this in-house if you don't mind. My father knows of the show and has never seen the value in it."

There's a huff. "Fine, fine. I'll keep it to myself for now. But we will need backers if we're looking at anything more significant for the future."

"Thank you, sir."

Zoe and Eden exit the door with the last few stragglers.

I say goodbye to Mr. Kellsner and lower my phone.

Zoe and Eden cast me twin quizzical looks.

"Hey, bro. What was that all about? You haven't looked this excited since the Vikings beat the Saints in the Minneapolis Miracle." Eden tries to keep up with sports, which I appreciate. Plus, she was dating a die-hard Vikings fan at the time.

Zoe, on the other hand, waves. "Can someone please interpret?"

"I wouldn't know where to begin on the football reference." I smirk at her sassy tilt of the head. "But I *can* tell you what the phone call was about."

I fill them in on my conversation with Mr. Kellsner. But for some reason, I can't bring myself to mention the fact that he'd expect me to quit the podcast if this leads to a producer job offer, as well as move to Chicago.

They both squeal and do their jumping hug thing. Eden pulls me in. I try not to think about having an arm around the small of Zoe's back and how maybe I wish my sister wasn't a part of this embrace.

We pull apart. Zoe studies her feet and tucks a piece of hair behind her ear.

"You know what this means, don't you?" Eden crosses her arms.

"What?" both Zoe and I ask, even though Eden is staring me down.

"You can't get out of your menswear fitting now."

I groan. "Don't remind me."

7

Zoe

"Dear listeners and devoted Gladwin Girls." I lean closer to my mic and use the moniker a group of the podcast's superfans like Sophia have given themselves. Who knew we'd have superfans?

Harrison spins his finger and reaches for one of the handmade signs he decided to create to let me know what he thinks of what I've said or to give direction as the producer during the show. No one, I repeat, *no one* asked him to make these. But I'll give him this, he's always been a skilled artist. He holds up a caricaturized emoji with a talking bubble from his post at the patio door.

"Instead of a letter to my hopefully-not-too-distant-future M. L. P., I'm sharing something different to end our episode." I straighten, clasping my hands on the desk.

"A. Nathaniel Gladwin's character Lord Benedict Pembroke is an unlikely hero. I've always been captivated by the rough-around-the-edges stable hand elevated to swoony gentleman who wins the heart of Lady Aurelia in *Twice the Gentleman*"—Hmm, I never thought about my favorite novel having a Ben in it before. Too bad I scared the real Ben away—"and I realized it's because he has the characteristics I'm looking for in my own M. L. P."

Harrison lifts a sign of a sleeping, drooling emoji, and I keep myself from rolling my eyes and having to edit it out.

"You know I love a good checklist, so about a year ago I scoured the book and created a list of characteristics and qualities I'm looking for. It is a truth universally acknowledged that a single woman in possession of a good list must be in want of a husband, am I right?" I pause for a laugh, then tap my hands on the desk. "Now, drum roll, please . . ."

Eden plays our sound effect, then cuts it at Harrison's direction.

I read from my journal.

"*1. He's chivalrous*

"You're a grown woman, so he doesn't have to do everything for you. But he makes sure you feel special and cared for. This can include opening the door or offering his jacket on a cool evening. He doesn't have to pay for every meal, but he shows up prepared to do so."

I lean closer to the camera, conspiratorially.

"I feel like I shouldn't have to say this, but some of my past dates suggest otherwise . . . can we agree he should keep his mouth closed while chewing and his bodily gases to himself? Maintain a little mystery, guys. Manners matter."

Harrison snorts a laugh into his hand, which vibrates into my headset. I manage to forge ahead.

"*2. Similar interests*

"I want something more than the weather and the health of our families to talk about. Regency fiction should be on their list of interests so we have some common ground to stand on. Just like a sports fanatic and I wouldn't have much to talk about."

There's a scoffing grumble from Harrison. Let him. He's the one who'll have to edit it out later.

"*3. He's honest*

"I will not budge on this one. Honesty isn't the best policy. It's the *only* policy." I press my lips together. The knot in my stomach whenever Sawyer comes to mind twists tighter and tighter like a rubber band about to break. My heart hammers in my ears. Will the microphone pick it up?

I lower my head for a moment then glance toward Harrison and Eden. They're staring, brows gathered. Harrison scribbles on a blank laminated sign, "You okay?"

I swallow and let a slight lift of my chin and rollback of my shoulders answer for me. "The dating scene is full of people wearing a mask, but people who you've known awhile can fool you, too. Be careful out there."

To expel the memories, I blow out a long breath. If only past-me had heeded this advice.

"*4. He's well-groomed*

"Personal preference here, but I feel a gentleman should have enough respect for himself and his lady to take time and pride in his appearance. Clean clothing, clean-shaven—though I do allow for swoony side-whiskers. I mean, imagine Darcy without his side-whiskers.

"*5. Shared beliefs*

"This may not be on everyone's list, but as much as I sometimes struggle with certain aspects of my relationship with God, it's still the most important relationship in my life. And a foundation built on God is something I really want to share with a significant other and, ultimately, with my future spouse.

"*6. He's heroic*

"He doesn't have to save me from a burning building or locked tower. But think, for example, about the ways Mr.

Knightley is heroic in *Emma*. How he aids Emma's friend Harriet Smith by dancing with her when she's snubbed by Mr. Elton. And how he stands up for the ridiculed Miss Bates.

"7. Proximity

"In the modern world, we can meet people from anywhere on the globe without leaving our living room. And there are cases where people fall in love that way and somehow make the distance work. But I, for one, want to be in the same time zone, zip code even, and they'll have to know up front that I never want to live more than a short driving distance from my family. It's really important to me to visit them and be available if anything—"

I almost say "goes wrong" but then swallow the fear and instead add, "Be around if they ever need help."

"8. Strong and steady

"I won't say no to physical strength. Right, ladies? But I'm also looking for internal strength of character, the type who's not going anywhere. Who'll be there with me through the thick and thin of life."

Interlocking my fingers, I rest them under my chin. "Are these qualities too much to ask? As someone with a history of failed suitors with qualities ranging from Mr. Collins's buffoonery to Mr. Wickham's rake vibes, I think not. It's what I know I want and need. So, what's on your list?"

Eden throws me a thumbs-up, but I can't decipher Harrison's expression. It's not his usual brand of good-humored smirk. Maybe he's thinking of the call with his boss before recording. Mr. Kellsner is sending an extra cameraman with us on the retreat to help capture footage. Harrison didn't seem too pleased.

"That's all the time we have for today. Remember, as Jane Austen once said, 'To you I shall say, as I have often said before, do not be in a hurry, the right man will come at last.'"

I fill them in on the details of the retreat and sign out as Eden plays the outro.

"Great show, Zoe." Eden greets me back in the dining room, where she's still clicking away at her laptop.

"Thanks."

Harrison eyes us while clinking around in my kitchen cupboards. Ever since the dress fitting a few days ago, he's been unusually quiet.

His boss's interest in the show is great news for everyone, especially him. I know he doesn't want to work on this podcast forever. Maybe he's feeling the pressure of impressing his boss.

I grip the back of one of my painted antique chairs, a light sheen of sweat forming across my forehead and upper lip. I've always been extra sensitive to the symptoms of high or low blood sugar, often noticing something's off before my blood glucose monitor even goes off. Though annoying sometimes, noticing these symptoms helps me make the minor and sometimes larger adjustments throughout the day that I need and that, ultimately, save my life. There are good days and bad days. Some days my body cooperates with the food and insulin I inject, and some days it doesn't. It's just another thing to manage, to make sure I'm following all the rules the best I can.

As I open my mouth to say I better check my blood sugar, Harrison places a cup of mango-carrot juice and a yogurt in front of me.

"Sit." He indicates the chair. "You looked like you were getting low toward the end there."

I squint up at him, but my mouth waters, and I obey. "Thanks," I say between bites. And there's my glucose monitor as it hits my low threshold alarm. I push the button to stop the beeping.

Harrison crosses his arms, his heather gray T-shirt straining against his biceps. I have the impulsive urge to squeeze his arm. Where that intrusive thought monster came from, I have no idea. But I stuff the little weirdo back in its cage and appease it with more yogurt and a lullaby of reasons I can't look at Harrison that way. Ever. It must be my blood sugar.

My cheeks burn at the memory of his strong arm holding my back after the dress fitting.

His head cocks to the side, a small smile forming at the corner of his lips.

Eden removes her headphones. "So, speaking of making a list and checking it twice, have you heard from Ben since—"

"The calamity on wheels?" I throw out jazz hands.

"I was thinking while you were listing qualities how Ben fits so many of them."

I shrug. "After my display of record-breaking clumsiness, I'm sure he's long gone. He practically left a trail of smoke behind him. I don't think even Mr. Collins left the Bennet sisters after the Lydia/Wickham scandal as fast as Ben left the skating rink that night."

Harrison scoff-grumbles. "If Ben is scared away by that, then he wasn't worth the time it took you to put on those four-wheeled death traps."

Eden lifts a hand. "Wait a minute. He has a blood phobia. Maybe he's embarrassed by his own reaction and doesn't know how to reach out to her."

I sip down the last of the tangy juice and sigh. "Unfortunately, I can't read minds. So unless he calls me, I guess I'll never know."

Eden moves to the fridge, pulling out the ingredients for her smoothie, while Harrison crosses his arms and legs, leaning against the end of the counter.

A crease forms on his tan—for a born and bred Minnesotan—forehead. "If you want to know, why can't you call *him*?"

Breezing by him to bring my bowl and cup to the sink, I say, "Well, call me old-fashioned—"

"That's a glaring understatement."

My eyes narrow. "I like a guy to make the first move and ask me out."

He points with his thumb at Eden behind him. "So many rules. Why wasn't that on your Declaration of Independence-length Lord Bibbity list?"—he uses the lovely nickname he invented for Lord Pembroke— "And by the way, didn't Eden ask him out for you last time? That's basically you asking him out."

Eden apologizes before she starts my bullet blender.

"Yeah, well, you should know better than anyone what happens when I do the asking," I mutter, the blender drowning out the words.

"What?" Harrison leans closer.

Picking at imaginary lint on my sleeve, I shake my head. "Nothing." Then, making eye contact, I continue, "Eden did the asking last time. This time, if Ben wants to apologize for leaving our date without a goodbye and ask me out, the ball is in his end zone or hoop or whatever."

"Court." His hand slides down his bearded cheek and angled jawline.

"What?"

"The expression is court—"

At my blank expression, he pulls his phone from his back pocket. "Never mind. I have to go. I have my suit fitting downtown." This slips between his gritted teeth.

Eden taps his shoulder as she returns to the table with her green smoothie. "Hey, we'll see you at etiquette lessons tomorrow?"

"Yup. I spoke with Victoria"—the way she eyed Harrison with a possessive quality crosses my mind—"and she's cool with me attending the women's etiquette lessons. I'm only going for the show anyway." The men and women won't meet until the retreat.

"Come on, bro. Why not do a little dating while we're there? Zoe and I will be dating along with everyone else." She wiggles her brows at him. "Besides, when's the last time you were on a date?"

"No way, I—" He's already waving his arms in front of his chest.

"I'm sorry to play boss lady, but we do actually need someone there who's more focused on the production and filming side of things while Eden and I participate in the activities." I try to soften it with, "Of course, you're welcome to join in whenever possible."

He sends me a sober salute, but there's mischief in his wink. "Aye, aye, Boss Lady. That's fine. But I don't think I'm about to find the woman I'm supposed to marry at this ridiculous thing anyway."

Grabbing his flannel jacket, he heads for the stairs.

"Famous last words!" Eden calls to him in a singsong voice right before the door closes.

His deep baritone laugh echoes from the driveway.

8

Zoe

"Now, we're not expecting you to know all of the Regency-age etiquette rules, of course." Victoria sweeps a magnanimous hand over the women sitting at two long tables that replaced the dressing rooms from last time at the Regency Society of Minnesota. Harrison sits to my right, and the cameraman Harrison's boss sent, Jake Rydberg, sits across from us next to Eden.

Harrison squirms in his chair. The boredom oozes from him in the form of a glazed, slack-jawed expression. All he's missing is drool. I elbow him in the ribs harder than I mean to.

He yelps and rubs his side, giving me the side-eye.

"Sorry," I whisper.

Victoria lectures on expectations, embracing the etiquette of Regency times, and what she calls, "a fully immersive experience."

Even I, the rule-lover, have to admit I'm feeling antsy.

"... but in twenty-first-century style, ladies are welcome to invite a gentleman to dance or to participate in an activity. And vice versa."

Victoria strides around the room, shoulders back in a way that would have made any society mother proud. "That said, you have all completed a compatibility questionnaire. You will begin the retreat by spending time with your top-tier matches. But afterward, you're free to mingle with anyone of your choosing. Understood?"

I liked that quiz. So organized. All of this seems worth a shot to me.

When everyone bobs their heads, she brings her palms together. "We will, however, have chaperones to accompany couples during their one-on-one dates as well as during group activities. And I must tell you we have a strict policy on spending unchaperoned time with the opposite sex. This is not a frat-house party."

One of the young women in the clique group giggles. "If that worked to find a husband, I'd already have one."

Sophia, sitting on my other side, ducks her head. "That's fine with me. I was never invited to those anyway."

Victoria snaps her fingers to gain our attention again. "I see it as adding an incentive for genteel behavior.

"And ladies, remember," Victoria continues, "a curtsy when you're introduced is expected. You may offer a hand to a gentleman, and he may kiss the back of it lightly but should not linger. We'll also continue to practice fan etiquette, which is, as you know, a language all its own."

Harrison is studying me. When I catch him and raise a brow in question, his lips quirk to the side. I mouth, "What?"

Before he can answer, Victoria swoops in, spearing herself into my space, sending a waft of her expensive perfume. Her cascade of shiny raven hair slaps me in the face, catching me right in the eyeball. "You looked like you had another question, Harrison. Is there anything else, *anything* at all I can help you with?"

I rub the sting out of my eye. Eden and I share an incredulous gaze while Jake covers a grin.

Harrison, however, seems unaffected. "Nope. I can't think of anything."

She waits a moment before straightening and tossing him a wink. "Well, you know where I am. . . ."

We stand to practice polite greetings and curtsies for the women and bows for Jake and Harrison.

Eden curtsies to Jake, and he bends in a theatrical bow, sweeping an arm low to the ground. Eden giggles, then points at Harrison. "You better watch out. Someone's got it bad for you."

Harrison's eyes dart to mine for some reason, then back to Eden. "What? Who?"

She slaps a hand over her forehead. "Seriously?"

I can't help the *pfft* that tickles my lips on its way out.

Even Jake smirks and scratches the back of his head beneath his shaggy dark curls. "Dude" is all he says.

"Victoria, Harrison. *Victoria*." I try to whisper, but the words come out as a harsh grumble. "She was all over you. What does she have to do? Skywrite it?"

He swipes a hand through the air.

Bending myself into a wobbling curtsy, facing Harrison, I pretend to hold my nonexistent dress. "I guess you must be so used to women who look like supermodels throwing themselves at you, it doesn't even register anymore." I try for a cheeky grin and elegant rise from my curtsy, but my feet tangle together. I'm falling.

Harrison catches me, and I land in his arms with an *oof!* His face is close like the night I fell on him at the skating rink. Like the night of the nonengagement . . .

He holds me there a foot from the ground. That tattletale heat creeps up my neck, flooding my cheeks.

Victoria saunters by, breaking Harrison's intense eye contact, and stage-whispers behind her slender hand, "You think that's bad, you should see her dance steps."

I scramble out of Harrison's arms with a huff. Yeah, we had the first dance lesson. Mr. Collins wearing Lady Catherine de Bourgh's heeled slippers couldn't have done worse.

Sophia, working with the younger of the copper-haired mother/daughter duo, shares an encouraging smile.

Joan, the mom, gestures to me. "It's okay, dear. I don't know how I'll make it through these dances gracefully. All those steps!"

"You and me both. The BBC miniseries made it look so easy."

When I face Harrison again, one of his hands is shoved in his pocket and his eyes are narrowed like he's trying to decide something. "Why do you always do that to yourself?" His voice is quiet, a deep rumble for me alone.

"Do what?" I straighten. "I can't help that I have the coordination of a wavy inflatable-arm guy."

"Not that."

My hand plants on my hip. "Then what, Mr. Cryptic?"

"You said something about people who look like supermodels flirting with me. What's that supposed to mean?"

I blush again. "I mean, yeah. It's always been like that for you, since junior high. You never notice. But that doesn't have anything to do with me—"

"But it does. It's like you're comparing yourself to that woman. Like she's at some level above you, and in your mind, you've come up short."

I lift my chin. "I, well, that's just . . . a poor excuse for a short joke."

It's a poor excuse for a response, too, but I can't bring myself to dig deeper. I hadn't compared in a negative way, had I?

"It's not a joke, Zoe." His tone is rough but not angry. "You shouldn't do that. You're—you're . . ." He hesitates as if he wants to say more but thinks better of it. "I hate to see you sell yourself short."

His somber expression lightens, and he lifts a hand. "And no, that's not another short joke. Okay, maybe a little that time."

I shuffle my feet. At least we're joking around again like we always used to since we were kids. "Thank you. Really." I'm not sure what else to say.

Is he right? I guess I never looked at saying things like that as a reflection of how I feel about myself. But then I flash back to the epic rejections of a certain jock, Chad Summers, whom I had an enormous crush on in high school that led to a school-wide humiliation. And fast forward to Sawyer. Then there's the string of dates gone wrong in between. . . .

It's no wonder my self-esteem has taken a hit over the years.

But I know better now. I need to lean into what I want and deserve. Stick to the list. No straying = no broken heart.

Thirty is approaching fast, and being engaged or married by then is looking less and less likely, but I can't give up. I smile as my mom comes to mind. Her warm laugh, the way she and Dad still have goo-goo eyes for each other. How he cares for her without reproach or complaint—as he says, he didn't take the vow "in sickness and in health" lightly—like a true gentleman. Who knows what the future holds for my mom and her illness? It would make her so happy to see me settled down with my own modern-day gentleman, and it would be the realization of a dream I've had since I was a girl. To have a family of my own, to love and be loved like that—it's the next chapter of my life I can't wait to start writing. I don't want to wait anymore.

I have to swallow the sudden lump in my throat.

Eden and Jake curtsy and bow too close to each other and bump heads, which sends them into a fit of laughter. Victoria descends like a curmudgeonly crow to squawk at them to take this seriously.

Harrison steps forward, does the half bow, and waits for me to curtsy with a solemn gaze. For someone who doesn't want to be here, who's never pretended to like anything Regency, he looks the part. He doesn't need to practice that smoldering Mr. Darcy stare. He's got that nailed down and superglued.

He bends over my offered hand, completely enveloping it in his own. A warm, calloused cocoon.

I tip my head forward in acknowledgment like I'm supposed to. It's his move, and he draws my hand toward his mouth. I'm about to tease him that he shouldn't linger—it would be improper and bring down Victoria's wrath upon us. But before I can, his lips touch the sensitive skin on the back of my hand in a featherlight kiss, his eyes never leaving mine, piercing through his thick fringe of dark golden lashes. Even though it's only for a moment, the warmth of his lips seeps into my skin, sending a jolt through my arm straight to my chest.

The room silences and stills around us, and I can't break his intense gaze.

But then everything grows loud again. The room's abuzz and seems to spin, or is it my head?

I don't mean to gasp or to wrench my hand away like he's scalded me, but I do. A shadow passes over his expression, but it's gone as fast as it forms. He scratches the back of his neck, turning away, while Eden watches from across the room.

What on the good green earth was that? I can't believe I reacted that way.

It's Harrison. It's just Harrison, for crying out loud. A few weeks ago, I could hardly stand to be in the same room as him.

This plays on repeat as I try to calm myself. But that's the problem. It's Harrison. The guy I grew up with, my best friend's brother. Not to mention, he's so far outside of anything I'm looking for in a perfect gentleman. Nothing can ever happen between us.

He's chatting with Jake now as the class wraps up. Looking totally unaffected. So, I imagined the little zing when he kissed my hand, right? He certainly didn't feel it. And I need to pretend that split second of electric eternity didn't happen for me, either.

We're good. We're *all* good.

9

Harrison

*L*ast night was weird.

My thumbs drum an unknown rhythm on my truck's steering wheel as I drive toward Zoe's house to drop off equipment. I need to shrug off whatever that was at the etiquette lesson.

It was a kiss on the hand. It's not like the earth shattered. But why had it felt like it?

Even though the skin on the back of Zoe's hand was softer than rose petals and smelled even better, there's no reason to get all worked up. The fact that it made me—for a fraction of a fraction of a second—wonder not for the first time if her lips were just as soft is nothing. It's fine. I'm fine. Everything is *fine*.

But the way she yanked her hand away like I'd hurt her stings.

I turn down her street and wave to our old principal, Mr.

Bolstadt, raking up the scattered red and gold maple leaves. His grandkids run and jump into the piles, slowing his progress. But the twinkle in his eyes as they meet his wife's says he doesn't mind. It's a picture of family, all the things I want for myself. At least, once my career's solid.

That's why I can't waste my time reading more into Zoe's and my relationship. Our friendship. She started out as my sister's best friend, but somewhere along the way, we became friends, too. I don't want to ruin that.

The truth is, adorable or not, Zoe and I are most certainly *not* compatible in a romantic way.

I pull into the parking spot in front of her garage and draw in a long breath before grabbing my bag and heading for the door. After a quick knock, she calls, "Come in!"

As I climb the stairs and step into the living room, Zoe waves in greeting. There's a moment's hesitation that quickly dissolves into a smile.

She's on a video call with her mom, Rena, who looks frail in her motorized wheelchair. But her cheeks are flushed like Zoe's, and her brown eyes alight. Her mom must have a phone stand, too, because her hands are limp in her lap.

"Mom, no. I'm not doing the Macarena at your funeral."

Zoe rolls her eyes and curls a finger at me to come in.

Only her family could make me chuckle at a topic like funerals.

I wave to Mrs. Dufour. "Hi, Rena. How's David?" After the respect and titles thing my parents hammered into me with their upper-crust acquaintances, it's still hard to call Zoe's parents by their first names. But they insisted. Repeatedly.

Her smile widens. "Oh, hi, Harrison! He's in the kitchen whipping us up some lunch." Their four-season porch behind her, not unlike Zoe's, is filled with plants, making Rena look like she's sitting in the middle of a tropical rainforest. "So good to see you, dear. Please tell my daughter that there will be dancing at my funeral, so she better brush up on her chicken dance, electric slide, and yes, the Macarena."

I nod. "Sure, but not too soon, right?"

Zoe makes a disgusted sound in the back of her throat, but if I'm not mistaken, there's more than a little fear behind her eyes, too.

Rena's hand waves that away with her typical shaking movements. "Only God knows, but I don't think so. David and I are updating our wills and wishes for what we like to call life celebrations, that's all. Because as I always say, live to the fullest today because tomorrow is never promised. We never know what's going to happen, do we?" Her tone is matter of fact.

Is that another dose of terror in Zoe's eyes? She seems to be doing her best to school her features, but there's strain in the lines of her face.

Zoe crosses her arms and blows out a breath that flaps her lips together. "Fine, Mom. You win. I'll do the Macarena. I'll dazzle everyone with my version of 'Can't Touch This.' I'll even throw in one of these Regency reels if I can ever stop each of my limbs from dancing to its own tune."

Suddenly I'm sure I'm out of place. I should go.

But Zoe cracks first, then Rena. They're laughing, and I can't stop my own grin. They may disagree, but at least they speak their minds and never stay upset for long.

Unlike my parents, who say everything but what they mean. Kind of like the tortured, repressed couples of Zoe's Regency stories. Never truly saying how they feel.

David comes into view and leans too close. His right eye and balding head fill the screen. "Hey, kiddo! How are you? Hi, Harrison. You kids working on the podcast?"

We exchange pleasantries, then Zoe says we have to go, and it's kind of a disappointment.

They've always felt like an extended family to me. They actually ask how I'm doing and care about the answer. And the way those two lovebirds still look at each other after over thirty years together . . .

It pulls at the ache in my chest, the one that longs for the same kind of companionship, trust, and love.

David steps back from the phone, and they both wave. Rena holds out one shaking finger, her arm never still. "Hey, Harrison. Teach this girl how to dance, will you?"

"I'm not a miracle worker."

Zoe swats my stomach. "Hey!"

I smirk and wink at her. "*But* I'll do my best."

As we're saying a good ol' thorough Minnesota goodbye, David stops us. "I'm not sure that Jane Austen singles' mingle thing is the best way to find *the one*."

He adjusts his glasses and leans in again. "In our day—"

Zoe groans. "Please. Don't tell me in 'your day' you had to walk uphill both ways in the cold and rain to get to your first date."

When David grins, it's the one of adoration I've seen a million times when he stares down at his bride. "No, but things were a lot simpler then. There were no dating apps or themed singles' retreats. Which certainly sounds fun, but you need to be sure the connections you make are real. The real you. The real them."

Rena nods, glancing up at David. "Find someone who cares—you know, the gentleman who'll give you his jacket on the first date."

It's a story I've heard before. Both Zoe's grandma and mom knew they'd found "the one" when the guy gave her his jacket. Both had/have long and happy marriages. So it's a thing, I guess.

"All right. I will." Zoe's tone is sincere.

David's forefinger aims at me again. "Can you watch out for her, Harrison? She's kind of got a streak of bozos in her wake. So far they've been harmless bozos, but you've always been like a big brother. I'd sure appreciate it."

"We both would," Rena adds.

A rush of fierce protectiveness but also something akin to agitation courses through my veins. Yes, I've used the phrase *surrogate big brother* in relation to Zoe, but it rankles something inside me now. Regardless, I cross my arms and answer, "Of course. Always."

Zoe's hand slides to her hip. "Excuse me. I don't need a nosy bodyguard. I can take care of myself, thank you very much."

"I know." Palms lifted in surrender, I send David and Rena a secret nod before we sign off. I will always protect her. I can't help it.

Once she returns her phone to the kitchen counter to charge, I notice her laptop on the TV stand, open, and a video is paused of men and women in Regency clothing, facing each other in two lines.

"What's this?" I gesture to the video.

She grumbles. "I'm so bad Victoria emailed me a bunch of videos to practice as homework."

"Let's see those dancing skills." I lean onto the arm of the couch.

"Fine, but you're not allowed to laugh." She taps the laptop and then moves to the middle of the living room. "And I'll have you know I was never so bad at the Macarena and I could dance a pretty epic YMCA back in the day, too."

A memory of Eden and Zoe laughing on the sidelines blinks to life in my mind. They always looked like they were having way more fun than me and my high school friends. At her sophomore prom, my senior prom, I'd had a sudden urge to ask Zoe to dance. But I didn't. I wish I had.

I move toward her, bow low, and reach for her hand now. "Well then, may I have this dance, Lady McDanceton of Macarenashire?"

She giggles and places her small hand in mine. I twirl her, and my feet immediately remember my lessons years ago.

The music from the laptop plays, and the dancers begin, stepping toward their partners, spinning and weaving through each other.

Her lips pucker to the side. "Hmm, what's your Regency name, then?"

I tilt my head in an imperious nod. "You may call me Lord Bibbity of Fancypantston."

This time she throws her head back with a full belly laugh. It's a beautiful sound.

Zoe starts circling me but turns the wrong way, and I gently guide her in the other direction. "How are you so good at this, Lord Bibbity? Have you been secretly attending the Regency Society annual ball all these years while making Eden and me believe you hated this stuff?"

Adjusting our arms as we touch palms, we circle again. Is my hand hot or hers? "I do have a secret, but it's not that." I waggle a brow at her.

Her full lips pucker into a heart shape. I've tried to forget about the curve of her top lip and the full, pouty shape of the lower. I'm not sure when I started to notice her lips and how very kissable they look.

I give myself a mental shake and focus back on her eyes. Okay, that's giving me trouble, too. Those big, round, deep pools . . .

Clearing my throat, I straighten and keep her from tripping over my foot. "My mother made me take dance lessons growing up to ready me for all of her society functions. Plus, my football coach liked it. It kept my footwork nimble on the field."

Her eyes widen. "Really? How did I not know that?"

"Because I made sure no one did. Do you think I wanted people to know I could waltz or tango or even dance these ridiculously elaborate Regency quadrilles and cotillions?" I grimace.

Another stomp to my foot and her winced apology make me laugh. "You could always stand on your partner's feet on purpose. That's what my grandma always did with my grandpa."

Her smile warms.

With a chuckle, I add, "At least then he'd *know* his feet will be stepped on. No surprises."

I twirl her under my arm at a measured pace, the back of my other hand stays on the flat of my back. "Actually, the dance lessons weren't so bad. And it was something that was just mine, you know?"

Her palm lands on my shoulder for this part. An accidental graze of my neck sends an electrical pulse down my vertebrae. She stops watching the video and her feet. Instead, her gaze meets mine. "I get it. The thing that's yours alone. For me, it's rowing."

"So I've always heard. You know, I shared my secret talent with you. . . ."

On impulse, I lower her into a dip, my arm bracing her back. This is too close for me to keep my head. Too much like the two times I biffed it with Zoe—in high school and then again after her almost-engagement party. I seem to have impeccably bad timing, and now she'll probably never see me as anything more than Eden's brother.

"I'm going rowing tomorrow. You should come." The words tumble out one faster than another like she can't stop them.

After pulling us up, I step back. My hand grasps the back of my neck. I've pushed her into a corner. That wasn't a real invitation. I've upset her like last night. "No. It's your thing. I don't want to crash your quiet time."

Her bottom lip catches between her teeth. "Really. You should come. We can ask Eden if she wants to come, too. It'll be fun."

An internal sigh of relief and a prick of annoyance war together when she mentions my sister.

"Sure, okay. Tomorrow, then?" I stash the equipment in the closet, the original reason for my visit, and gather my jacket.

"Yup, it's a date. I mean . . ." She ducks her head and tucks a piece of hair behind her ear. "You know what I mean."

Right, a three-person outing where one of those people is my little sister is *not* what I would call a date, either.

10

Harrison

Dawn is still a greenish glow on the horizon but is slowly illuminating all that night hides. Maybe in the light of day, my agreeing to go rowing with Zoe is a bad idea. This feels different, more intimate than hanging out at Eden's place or Zoe's or working on the podcast together. And, honestly, the last year and a half is still weighing on me—the invisible wall between us. If there's any opportunity today, I need to knock down that wall.

Zoe asked me to meet her on the Nazareth Hall side of Lake Johanna. This is on the campus of her and Eden's alma mater, St. Paul's University of Northwestern.

I park in the Nazareth Hall parking lot, pull on my knit Vikings hat, and button my flannel jacket. Zoe's beside her MINI Cooper, which is dwarfed by the long, thin boat strapped to the top.

There's a bite to the air this morning, but thankfully, no wind. My breath becomes puffs of white as I approach.

"Hey, where's Eden?" I reach for the strap she's struggling with. "And how in the world did you maneuver this clown car with this telephone pole down the freeway?"

Her startled expression melts into an exasperated grin. "First off, I couldn't get Eden's lazy behind out of bed. Sorry. She said she never wants to see the pre-dawn side of the day. Ever. I should've known better." She gestures to me. "I'm kind of surprised you're up, actually."

Zoe's always been the morning person out of the three of us, as long as she has her coffee. As she likes to say, she can't "people" without caffeine, no matter what time it is.

"Also, that *clown car*, as you call it, is directly proportionate to its driver." She waves a hand over her petite frame. "As is yours." Then she points up at me and over to my four-by-four truck.

"You got me there." I jut my chin toward the boat. "I guess there's no turning back now, huh? Unless you want me to go . . ."

Why does my voice sound like I'm back in middle school asking my first crush if she likes me or *like* likes me?

"No. Don't go. I mean, not if you don't want to." Her gaze turns shy. We're both acting weird.

I don't know if I want to row or not, but I *do* know I want to be here with Zoe.

"Nope, I'm not going anywhere. You're stuck with me."

Her timid expression lingers for a moment, then brightens. I move toward the boat. "Here, let me get that for you."

"You sure? It's—"

I grunt as I heft the unwieldy thing over my head.

We make our way to the path leading down to the lake.

She takes the long oars two to each shoulder. Okay, tough girl.

"So, you ready for our dance lesson tonight? Did our practice help?" My mouth dries out, and I swallow. Making conversation with someone I've known all my life suddenly seems incredibly difficult.

She adjusts the oars on her shoulders. "No and no, but thank you for trying. I'm dreading Victoria's scowl of doom at my lack of improvement. That woman is legitimately scary."

We approach the bridge between the shore and Chapel Island, where a lone 1920s chapel sits amidst the trees. A quiet refuge in the middle of a bustling city. "This thing is heavy. How do you carry it down here on your own?"

Setting the oars on the sand, she turns and helps me ease the boat onto the small strip of beach. "I have a one-seater when it's just me. This is the triple scull my parents taught me on. Mom and Dad used to take me out before she wasn't able to hold herself up in the boat anymore and it became dangerous for her."

"I've never really asked you about your mysterious solo pastime. So, your parents taught you?"

Her grin softens as she hands me a life jacket that was strapped to the inside of the narrow boat. "Yeah, they loved to row. In fact, that's how they met. They both rowed for the University of Minnesota. That was way before . . . you know. I haven't been out with anyone since they stopped rowing. I always go by myself now."

"Right. I'm sure it was hard to give up rowing, but knowing your dad, he'd willingly give up anything for your mom."

"He would," she agrees. "Of course, she told him he could still go, but he hated the idea of doing something alone they once enjoyed together." She tilts her head. "They found other hobbies to do together, though, so it's okay. They love to garden, indoors and outdoors."

"And they play a mean adaptive floor hockey."

Her smile warms.

She starts to thread her arms through her life jacket armholes, but I stop her with a touch to the shoulder. "Hey, can I talk to you about something first?"

Blood rushes in my ears as she goes still, her face paling. "About what?"

Hands digging into my jacket pockets, I blow out a long, fogged breath. "I think we should clear the air about, you know, *that* night."

The scene of Sawyer rejecting her proposal, telling her he'd started seeing someone else, the devastation contorting her beautiful face, wallops me in the chest every time I think of it. But there's something else I need to address, the thing that still keeps me up at night.

Her gaze darts from me to the shoreline to the trail behind me like a cornered animal looking for its escape routes. "I, well, it's nothing." She can't seem to make eye contact.

"So much nothing that you managed to avoid seeing me the entire time I was away?"

She picks at her life jacket buckles. "I wasn't avoiding you. It's not like I could run into you, could I? Not when you lived in Cincinnati."

I tilt my head and wait for her to look at me. "I came home every month." I don't mention I'd hoped to run into her, but I'd been too much of a coward to call her.

Plowing a booted toe through the soft sand, I lift a shoulder and continue, "Anyway, I don't blame you. If you were avoiding me, I mean. I know it was a horrible thing that happened with Sawyer, and I was trying to comfort you afterward"—I drag my hand across the back of my neck, this is so much harder than I thought—"I didn't mean to weird you out or anything."

Her expression, vulnerable and caught off guard, is so similar to that night. It's like I'm watching back my idiocy all over again on a replay camera. Zoe and I standing outside of her engagement party, the moon's light turning her tears silver on her cheeks. Eden, friends, and family unaware inside Zoe's townhouse. This was the second time I stood before her in the aftermath of a broken heart, the first in high school, and I couldn't stand by and do nothing.

I'd taken Zoe's hand in mine and brushed the tears from her cheeks with the backs of my knuckles. Then the thoughts and feelings I'd pushed down for years surfaced again as I said, "If it were me, you wouldn't have had to ask."

Her eyes had widened then shuttered in the same breath, a pain behind them as if she was trying to find the words to let me down gently or maybe, worse, tell me how dense I was to say something like that at a time like this.

But I'd saved her the trouble of trying to find the words. I'd backed away, saying I had to go. When I'd offered to help break the news inside before I left, she'd told me it wasn't necessary. Her voice had been soft when she'd said I should go, but the words cut deep. And . . . that was that.

I want to smack my forehead all over again but instead scrub at my beard. "I'd wanted to tell you how special you are and it was his loss, but it came out wrong." I swallow hard. "And I regret leaving you there and what I said . . . I didn't mean"—I scuff my boot against a rock—"What I meant was that with the right person, there'll be no question on either side. No matter who asks, it'll be an easy answer."

And that is the truth. It just doesn't come close to covering everything. Nor does it explain how I allowed my own feelings to speak instead of being sensitive and supportive like she needed me to be. She needed a friend, and instead, I'd blurted something that confused her when she already felt vulnerable. "I didn't mean to upset you, Zo. And I would never want to hurt you," I finish.

For a long moment, she's quiet and still, studying me. Then a hint of a smile tugs at her lips. "It's okay, Harrison. And I'm sorry I've been avoiding you."

My own mouth hitches up, and I let out a breath that feels like it has been in my lungs for eighteen months. "Really? So you forgive me for making an awkward situation a hundred times worse with my big mouth?"

Laughing now, she gives my arm a playful shove. "Yeah, that's nothing new. You usually mean well."

"All right, you. Thanks a lot." A weight seems to lift from my shoulders, and I rub my hands together. "Now, let's get this sliver of a boat in the water and see if we can defy the laws of physics by staying upright."

Wrestling myself into this one-size-fits-no-one life jacket (except for maybe a certain petite brunette) proves more difficult than I thought and requires her help. Finally, she loosens the chest straps to their longest length and clicks the buckles closed.

Despite the cool autumn air, a sheen forms on her forehead. She wipes it away before buckling her own vest. "Whew! Admittedly, I didn't buy these life jackets with a giant in mind. You can swim, though, right?"

I try to cross my arms, but the pressure of the jacket straining against my chest stops me. "Of course. I grew up visiting my Uncle Sebastian's cabin every summer, remember?"

"Right-o." She directs me to the seat at the back of the boat. "Here, you sit in the bow seat. I'll take the stroke seat. When we get out there, you can watch me and match my rowing speed."

Plunking down onto my micro seat almost capsizes the scull into the foot of water. "I don't know if this thing is built for someone my height."

"Don't worry, you can do it. I'll take it easy on you with the pace." She flashes a mischievous grin and claps me on the shoulder before pushing us off, then slips seamlessly onto her seat in front of me. I'm digging this confident, competitive Zoe. And the lighthearted conversation flowing between us again feels good. So natural, like it always has been.

Her oars slice through the water as she thrusts her seat backward. "Here's to our nondate, right? May we stay upright and our life jackets hold true."

"Amen to that." It takes me a bit to stop shaking the boat and almost tipping us.

With a glance over her shoulder, she says, "Find your balance. Take a deep breath. You can join in with your oars when you're ready. Watch how I do it."

Her body glides forward in the moving seat, her arms cross each other as she pulls the oars through the water and then out and up. Her back remains straight but at an angle.

Who could not admire her? I've never seen her quite so in her element, other than when she's recording the podcast. "That's more like it."

"Hmm?" She slows us to a stop. The sun has fully risen now, but the steam from the water cocoons us in. The drifting fog almost blocks out the multicolored shoreline of reds, oranges, and golds of the maples, birches, and oaks.

"This seems like you. Although I've never known you to—"

"Have a coordinated bone in my body?" She turns a raised brow and smirk to me.

"You said it, not me." My chuckle echoes across the quiet, still water. "But I have always thought of you as confident in your own way, even in all of your modern gentleman nonsense—"

This earns me a *hmph*, but I continue. "The other day, with Victoria"—her shoulders tip back, rigid—"I wanted to say don't put yourself below anyone, okay? Be as confident in yourself and what you have to offer as you are about most everything else."

"Thank you." Her tone is grudging but sincere. "And you, sir, have things to say, so don't hold back. And Eden's right, you never know if you might meet someone at this retreat, too. So you should be ready."

"Mmm" is all I acknowledge. "Are you ready for a whole slew of potential suitors?" I grin to myself at remembering to use her Regency term, but it quickly dissolves. Zoe is attending this retreat to find a guy. Somehow, I have to make my peace with that.

She starts rowing again, and I try to join in, but my timing stinks and it actually slows us down. Indignation makes me grip my oars tighter, trying harder to match her speed.

"You sound doubtful. Do you have so little faith in this process?" Her words huff between breaths.

Could she hear my grunt? "What about you? Do *you* really believe in all this stuff? Like some guy is gonna step out of your favorite Regency story and stride across a misty field to say"—I put on my best impression of Mr. Darcy—"'Miss Dufour, you must allow me to tell you how ardently I admire and love you.'"

"You have Mr. Darcy's love declaration memorized?"

I try again to keep my oars in time with Zoe's. Is it just me or did she speed up?

"How could I not with you and Eden watching that BBC miniseries every other day? It played so often, I repeated it in my sleep. And then you started playing *Pride and Prejudice* bingo to spice things up—"

"Yes! That was so fun. Spaces for every time Mrs. Bennet mentions her nerves, for anyone discussing a gentleman's yearly income, and of course, for every brooding glance from Mr. Darcy . . ." Her words are hushed, wistful.

"It was incessant. I accidentally answered a question in my Language Arts class in high school in an English accent. Badly, might I add. Everyone thought I was trying to be funny."

Her laughs shake her shoulders and the boat. "I know I should apologize, but it's too amusing. With that much apparent brainwashing, shouldn't you be buying into Regency courtship by now?"

"I'm not saying modern dating doesn't leave much to be

desired, but at least it's real. It's not sticking your head in the sand or creating unrealistic expectations."

"Unrealistic expectations?" She slows as a pair of mallard ducks float by.

"What about this wish list you went on and *on* about the other day?"

"I thought you appreciated my confidence. Well, I'm *confident* in what I know I want and need in a partner. And I won't compromise on what's most important to me. The last time I did—"

She doesn't finish the thought, but her volume rises and I don't press it.

"But don't you see that you're setting yourself and anyone else up for failure?" My frustration leaks into my tone.

Her oars hover over the water, her back is set in a stubborn line, and her long dark waves swish when she shakes her head. "You know what your problem is?"

"No, but I have a feeling I'm about to find out."

So much for knocking down the wall between us.

Zoe

His words grit under my skin like a layer of sand. Why does his disapproval of my dating methods matter? But for some reason, it digs sharp talons into my flesh.

My oars carve into the water's surface with surgical precision as if they can sever this unsettled feeling. We've barely made it around Chapel Island. Why in the world did I invite him into this sacred space?

I gather my thoughts and then let them loose. "The thing is, if a woman has expectations or, heaven forbid, standards, suddenly she's picky, cynical, and high-maintenance. Right?"

"Oh no, no, no. I'm not touching that with a ten-foot oar."

"They're nine feet, six inches." I can't keep the words lassoed behind my lips.

His movements are erratic as he tries to keep my speed. I should slow down.

"I'm not saying you're any of those things, Zo, but you do seem to have a pretty poor view of men. It's like you assume they're all villains and rakes from one of your stories if they aren't perfect. If they don't measure up to this impossible list you've created and this faultless vision of what you think they're supposed to be."

His voice is gruff, upset. I can probably count on one hand how many times I've heard Harrison upset. Sharp wit? Sure, that's his go-to. A little annoyed, especially at Eden when we were younger? Absolutely. If anyone hurts Eden, or even me? You better believe his inner protective bear shows his claws. Right now, however, he's upset. With me. It hurts, but I'm not conceding, either.

Before I can reply, he says, "It wouldn't be so bad if you were only filling your own head with this nonsense—"

"So you think what we're doing is nonsense?"

"—but now you're telling all of these impressionable young women they have to wait for this perfect guy, too. I hate to break it to you, Zoe. But he doesn't exist. He's not out there waiting to ask you to the ball or to ride off into the sunset or whatever. That's a fantasy."

The statement is like a punch to the chest. No, *through* the ribs, straight to my heart. My breath and any words are stolen for a moment. I grapple for an intelligent reply, a counterpoint. "What about Ben Rowley? Sure, I haven't met the other men attending this retreat"—the information had passed from

Harrison and Jake to Eden then to me that the guys had run into Ben at the suit fitting and he's coming to the retreat—"But I already know he and I have lots in common. He might be the *perfect* modern-day gentleman I've been waiting for."

"Ben? Really? You can't be serious. He ran at the first sign of trouble." His laugh is caustic. Not like his usual chest-deep rumble of warm mirth.

"You said yourself he told you to tell me he's looking forward to seeing me there and he's sorry about our first date."

The boat sways as if he let go of the oars and they now dangle from the oarlocks, sending out a ripple around us. "I don't trust the guy. All right? And you know what? Perfect *isn't* real. Don't you think you're leading yourself and all of these women into false hope for something or *someone* that'll never appear?"

I stop rowing. There's no point if he's not moving and I have to drag his oars along. But then he begins to row again and so do I.

"Hope? That's exactly what I'm trying to give them. And myself." I steer hard to starboard, and he's trying to follow me. We're not attempting to circle the small lake like I normally would. "I'm trying to let them know they're worth the wait for someone who cherishes them, respects them, *loves* them enough to treat them the way they deserve—like ladies. That's what I mean by a gentleman, Harrison. It's not for the faint of heart or someone not ready or willing to commit. It's not supposed to be easy."

There's a prick of worry at the statements I spout. What if no one can ever love *me* that much?

"And you think Ben is all of those things?" He spits the words like an accusation.

I shrug, and the boat lists to the right. "I don't know, but I'm not too scared to find out. To put myself out there unlike *some* people I know. One bad experience shouldn't—"

The hint at the ex-girlfriend he left behind in Cincinnati hits its mark, and our trajectory swerves as one of his oars stops. I dig in with my oar on the opposite side to steady us, and we even out. "Hey, you have to get in sync with me!"

That water looks mighty cold on this chilly morning.

"Yeah, well, that's the problem. I don't think I can."

We're not talking about the boat anymore, which is headed back toward the sand beach at an alarming rate.

"What you're looking for is a puppy! An obedient puppy. Or a robot. Not a man who thinks and feels for himself. But someone who is there to fulfill some laundry list of requirements and lift you onto a pedestal while he's at it."

"It's actually none of your business what I'm looking for. And I'm doing a world of good for women. I'm encouraging them to think for *themselves* by not settling for the scraps of attention the selfish Willoughbys of the world are willing to toss them. To look for something, someone . . . *more*."

"Right, well, I hope you find the guy who'll buy into all this stuff. You're right, maybe you and Ben are perfect for each other." The words would seem supportive if they didn't sound forced between clenched teeth.

"Maybe we are." I can spit words through my teeth too.

"Fine."

"Great."

He's rowing faster than me now. I try to slow us.

He lets an oar drop. At this speed, we slide to the side like we're skidding on ice. This is my dad's boat. We can't wreck it. This emblem of my parents' love story, what he was willing to lose for love.

As soon as we grate to a sudden stop on the sand, I jump out the front to assess the damage. The boat seems fine, and I let out a gust of air. I barely register the yelp from behind me until I hear a *splash!*

I turn to find that my sudden exit made Harrison topple

out of the back. He sits waist-deep in water, fire burning in his eyes.

My own submerged feet and ankles ache with the cold burn of the frigid water.

"Worst nondate *ever*," I mutter.

The angles of his face seem chiseled from stone as he answers, "Finally, we're in sync about something."

11

Harrison

How did Zoe go from sweet but benign friend of Eden's to this infuriating woman who invades my thoughts every waking moment? My dreams too. It's unwise for so many reasons.

One, what would Eden say? Eden's my family. Sometimes she seems like my only family. With a mother who doesn't seem to care to talk to me and a father who, whenever he does, only criticizes and finds fault with my choices, I can't chance a rift between Eden and me. Second, knowing everything I do about Zoe's stubborn ideals, as explosively demonstrated earlier, I'm probably the last man on earth she'd be looking for.

Zoe, across the room at the Regency Society, catches sight of me. Her arms cross, eyes narrowing. I wait for steam to start blowing out of her ears like it does in cartoons. Any hope that she may have forgotten this morning vanishes.

Shame at my raised voice and angry words gnaws at the

lining of my stomach. I stand by what I said, but I could've had a gentler way of saying it. What frustrates me more—that she might be setting herself and her listeners up for disaster or that I don't know if *I* could ever measure up to her list?

In my experience, the nice guy usually finishes last, and you can try to do everything right and still lose. Just another reason this whole idea of the perfect gentleman is absolute garbage.

Jake steps beside me dressed to the nines in his long-tailed jacket and cravat monkey suit. He tilts his head my way. "Hey, I heard what happened this morning. You good?"

"I'm fine. How'd you know?" How humiliating.

"Eden." He scratches the back of his neck. "I went over to her place to help edit some footage for the podcast, to get a feel for how you guys do things"—he's talking fast as if this will ensure I don't feel weird about him being alone with my sister—"and Eden told me. Don't worry, Zoe will come around. But, man, I hope you don't mind me saying I wish I'd been there with my camera."

He shakes his head and laughs.

I try for a smile but know I'm baring my teeth when his laugh dies away. My hand reaches for my flannel buttons. "Anyway, Zoe come around? It's not like we're . . ."

Why are my fingers so big and clumsy? I fumble with the buttons of my shirt like that'll somehow make me appear more formal and presentable for dance lessons. I must've missed the memo about wearing the suit. We'd all been sent one set of our period clothing. The rest will be waiting for us at the retreat.

"Right. Of course." Jake claps me on the back as we approach Zoe and Eden at the end of the line. He veers off to the side to start filming.

Zoe is standing at the end of the row, looking everywhere but at me. She doesn't have a partner. I have no choice but to stop next to the friend they've made, Sophia, across from Zoe.

My boss has made it clear that he'd like me to be on camera as much as behind it—part of the reason Jake is here to help with filming.

Victoria starts the music. I step toward Zoe, who won't meet my eye, chin angled to the ceiling, as we begin the reel.

Despite her steely silence and still stepping on my toes every few minutes, it seems natural to be this close. With her in my arms. Towering over her, her hand warm in mine as her deep brown eyes gaze up at me, finally making eye contact. But she's not wearing an adoring or even friendly expression.

The next stomp on my foot seems to come with an impish gleam in her eye.

I answer it by spinning her faster than is necessary and tilt my mouth into my own wicked grin. She yelps and flaps her arms, but she's in no danger. I've got her. I twirl her in toward my chest, which she thumps against with an *oof!*

Her nose lifts with the dignity of a queen as she steps down hard, aiming for my foot again. I snatch it out of her way, sweeping it behind her knee instead, which tips her off-balance. But my arms are there to catch her and set her upright again. This earns us a scowl from Victoria and her reminder, "Stick to the choreography!"

Zoe's nostrils flare and a blaze ignites in her eyes.

With clamped jaws and glares at one another, we prance our way to the end of two long lines. We spin and part through two other dancers and rejoin our lifted hands. I try to give the impression I wouldn't rather have my head glued to the floor and have all these women dance on it as we near Jake filming us. Finally, I clear my throat. "Zoe, listen. About earlier—"

"I know we're never going to agree on this, Harrison, but I don't want to fight with you about it, either." Her forehead creases. "We're friends, aren't we? Or at least I thought so after all these years. I started as Eden's best friend, but I'd like to think you and I are friends, too. And now you're finally back, and we're speaking again. I'd like to keep it that way." She keeps her chin up. "God's approval is the only one I need, but for whatever reason, I'd like your approval, too."

"Of course we're friends." I straighten. Yes, *friends*. "And it's not that I disapprove."

"But I wish you'd understand this isn't coming from a shallow or picky place."

"You're not shallow, Zoe. You're one of the kindest people I know. You genuinely care about every caller, not just pretend to listen because you have to. You truly want to help each person. I admire that." Picky, on the other hand? I'm not touching that one. I clasp her forearm behind our backs, and we walk to the other end of the room again. She still stumbles, but she's doing better.

She snags her full bottom lip between her teeth and hesitates. I should definitely *not* look at her lips. Not if I want to be truthful about being her friend and friend only.

Her dress catches on her feet, and she trips but rights herself this time. "With my mom's primary progressive type of MS, I don't know how much time she has left." The words hang heavy in the air despite the light music playing in the background and excited chatter and laughing around us. "And who would care if something happens to her, to me, to my dad? I know I have friends, you guys, who care, but I don't have a partner in life. Someone I can lean on and who can lean on me, you know?"

Her shoulder rises and her chin wobbles for a moment before she clamps it in place. My finger itches to run along her jaw, the one she's holding so steady. "It would bring Mom and Dad peace to see me settled, but I don't want to *settle*—if you know what I mean. I want to find a true gentleman because I want to find true love. Someone who'll love me the way Dad loves Mom. Then they won't have to worry about me."

My neck heats as I watch her face, so real and raw. It's like no one else is in the room. But isn't this really one more way she's worried about her parents?

I give her hand a gentle squeeze. "What can I say? When you put it like that, the root of all this nonsense somehow makes... *sense*."

Her lips spread in a wide grin. It's like a beam of morning sunshine suddenly lighting across her face even though the sun is now setting outside the line of windows. A playful twinkle glints in her eyes. "And come on, you can't tell me you want to stay an indefinite bachelor like some of your forever-frat-boy friends—"

"Hey, some of my friends are married." I flash a wry smile.

"Precisely. And I bet that looks pretty good, doesn't it?"

This line of questioning makes my throat close. Why is it so dry in here? Blips of my screaming parents, slamming doors, and protecting Eden pop into my brain like '90s sitcom freeze-frames.

"I mean, yeah, but..."

Then there are stills of my grandparents. And Rena and David. They make marriage look enjoyable, fun even. I can see why they want that for their daughter. The responsibility of their request to help and protect Zoe swells in my chest.

One of her brows drops. "You want that for yourself, don't you?"

Yes, but it's more important that I help you find it.

I swallow the dry rock of a lump in my throat. "Well, yes, at *some point*"—Victoria sweeps by, grazing a hand along the back of my upper arm, and I stiffen—"if I ever find someone where there's mutual respect, who's ready for commitment, who I can have intelligent conversations with. Who's driven, smart, kind, who I can share a laugh and my faith with... then yes, of course that's what I want."

Her mouth is slightly parted, then snaps shut. "Right. See? You have a list of qualities you're looking for, too. You just say it differently and don't broadcast them on a podcast or write letters about them to your future spouse. Or wait, do you?"

I know that giddy, excited, I-got-an-idea look. "*Pfft.* No. I assure you, I do *not.*"

"Hey, maybe that would make a good twist on the podcast. Dear Lady Aurelia—"

"Absolutely not."

"If you say so." She winks, her lips curling up to one side. It does something inside my chest. My pulse quickens. Is it hot *and* dry in here? The separation is needed for a moment as she twirls around someone else and then steps back to my side. I told myself not to look at her lips.

"I've already done a lot of silly and embarrassing things for the podcast. Case in point"—I gesture to the room at large—"but I'm not doing that."

I lift a hand. "Besides, I won't need letters when I choose to share my feelings with a woman. I'll look her in the eye . . ." We're close again for this part. We've begun a waltz, which was sort of scandalous back then, and now I can see why. You have no choice but to look into your dance partner's eyes, to stand close enough to feel the heat of their body merge with your own.

We've stilled. The room seems to have halted, too, but hasn't. It whirls past us like we're standing motionless at the center and everyone else is on a spinning carousel around us. ". . . and tell her," I finish in a rough whisper.

Zoe's pupils dilate, and for a moment, it's like I'm about to be swallowed whole by her searching gaze.

Throat sufficiently cleared, I say, "Anyway, I might have some general ideas about the type of person I'd be compatible with, but I'm willing to leave a little room for surprise. For something I *didn't* have planned. Let God do what He does best."

Her back goes rigid beneath my hand.

Zoe

Everyone is already not-so-subtly pretending they aren't listening in, might as well give them an earful. Stepping back from Harrison's touch, I slip my hand to my hip, a move that's not as dignified as I'd like in this dress.

"Are you really giving me the 'let go and let God' lecture? My mom *invented* that lecture."

Victoria is calling attention back to her at the head of the room, and I drag Harrison off to the side. My flustered fingers need an occupation, so I reach up and start unbuttoning Harrison's misbuttoned plaid shirt that's been driving me nuts all evening. His eyes flare wide.

I mutter, "Sure, you can ask Jesus to take the wheel. But sometimes you're on a bus full of cranky toddlers demanding to see Disney World and a hundred flapping chickens. Someone needs to get this thing under control."

He snorts a laugh, but it dies away when I pin him with a pressed-lip glare.

"You can live by a 'it'll happen if it's meant to happen' and go in without a plan or a list all you want. But the last time I did that, I got burned." I'm a little rougher on the button at his throat than I meant, and his Adam's apple bobs, warm against my fingers.

I take in a measured breath. "You know what's great about the Regency era? You knew what was expected of you and everyone around you. You knew what would happen, how to act, what, and who to say yes to. Who to politely decline. There was etiquette for every situation. There was such a thing as perfect manners, and they kept you from embarrassing yourself and protected you from getting hurt."

I brush a hand down the front of his shirt to smooth it, suppressing the awareness of the muscled chest beneath the fabric. Done.

A smirk plays at the corner of his lips. It's that boyish grin he's always had, but all grown up. "I thought we weren't fighting about this anymore."

I cross my arms. "We're not."

"You don't need my approval."

"I know I don't—"

He raises a hand like a white flag. "But you have it all the same."

My shoulder muscles held tight now relax. "And about this morning—"

"Thought we were done hashing that out, too. Sorry I lost my temper."

The teasing tilt of his head makes me laugh. "Me too. After our fight, I thought you'd quit the podcast for sure." My fingers reach out, clasping his hands in mine. "Even though I know we don't exactly see eye to eye on this—"

"That's pretty hard to do when you only reach my chest." His innocent expression doesn't crack.

Letting go of his hands, I give his arm a playful shove. "Really? Another short joke?" A groan earns me a "shh!" from the cliquey ladies.

"You walked right into that one. Which is also tough to do since you're so short, but then, the bar *is* pretty low. . . ."

"Okay, you." I mock glower up at him. "Anyway, you've been great for the show. You've got such an eye for storytelling through your editing and audio production, plus you do all of the things I hate—"

His eyes gleam. "Ditto."

"So I won't tell you you have to come to the retreat. I know

Eden said you have to, but you really don't. But will you? And stay on the podcast?"

A shadow seems to pass over his eyes, but then it's gone. "Of course. I already said I'd come, and I never back out of my commitments."

"Don't be so excited. You make it sound like an appointment for a root canal. I'm not twisting your arm here."

He scuffs the floor with his boot.

"But can you try to come to the retreat without preconceived notions and cynicism? If for no other reason than you know better than anyone that nonbiased stories make the best stories."

This makes him stop, frozen, but then he thaws. His hand extends, taking mine. I must have all things Regency on the brain because for a second I think he's about to kiss it. But he shakes my hand twice and releases it.

"Deal." He shoves his hand into his pocket. "You can't expect me to not make *any* jokes or snarky comments while we're there. How would it even be fun, then?"

"Fine."

Pretty soon people head to the changing area and gather their things.

Eden waves me over.

The handful of women still loitering around are staring at Harrison. I lean closer to him, and a waft of spice, mint, and whatever the woodsy scent I associate with him hits me. "If that's how they look at you in your flannel and jeans, imagine how we'll have to pick them off like ticks when you're wearing your tails jacket and cravat."

He grumbles something unintelligible and pulls at his collar. Is that a flush creeping up his neck?

"You're forgetting one thing." He tips a brow at me.

"What's that?"

"We may not be fighting about this anymore, and I will be

there to document the process for the good of the podcast, but that doesn't change my mind about it. This is still a ridiculous way to meet the love of your life."

But all that echoes in my ears as he walks away, a deep rumbling laugh trailing behind him, is "love of your life."

Yup. That's the plan. He's close by. I can feel it.

"We'll see about that!" I call after Harrison.

I'll show him.

12

Zoe

"It's like I went to sleep in twenty-first-century Minnesota, and woke up in Pemberley, Mr. Darcy's grand nineteenth-century home. I feel like Jane Austen herself might knock on the door at any moment." I spin around, taking in my gorgeous shared room at Wyndmere Hall, the rich wood-trimmed room filling with the late-morning sun.

Eden squeals as she flops back on her four-poster bed across from mine.

Turning onto her side, she props her head on her hand. "I know. It's weird we're only a little over half an hour from Minneapolis, but it feels like we're in the English countryside."

We truly stepped back in time when we were made to park in a designated parking lot at the edge of the two-hundred-acre estate, then brought to the sprawling mansion by horse and carriage.

"Do you think Harrison is here yet?" I turn after placing

my unmentionables—yes, I was born in the wrong era—in the drawer of an antique dresser. From our time as college roommates, I know Eden will not unpack. Her suitcase will somehow grow in volume until it takes both of us sitting on it to zip it shut before we leave on Wednesday morning.

"Jake texted me five minutes ago that they're here and settling in over in the gentlemen's wing." Eden moves to the ornate wood-carved fireplace and rubs her hands in front of the flames dancing inside. "What I would've given to see my brother bouncing along in a carriage."

I snort. "Same." Stepping closer, I cross my arms. "But don't think you can slide that juicy little morsel of info in—'Jake texted me'—and assume I won't say anything. Since when are you two on a texting basis?"

"Texting basis?" One of her lavender brows shifts upward.

"Yeah, like the equivalent of being on a given name basis in the Regency era."

She walks her fingers across the mantel, avoiding my gaze. "It's not a big deal. We bonded over J. R. R. Tolkien, and I think his foreign correspondent film footage is brilliant, but it's *nothing*. I promise you."

"Don't make promises you can't keep. And why not?" I prop a hand on my hip. "He seems nice, his gorgeous, dark curly hair and his old soul eyes give him the tragic, romantic air of a nineteenth-century French poet, he's talented—the man won a Pulitzer for crying out loud—and he understands your fascination with elves and small people with big hairy feet. What's not to like?"

"They're hobbits." She plops down on one of the floral upholstered chairs with carved wood detailing and shrugs. "I think he's carrying a lot on his shoulders. I get the feeling something happened on his last assignment. All he said was that he's happy to be back here and covering something light that'll make people smile for a change. But when I said something about meeting someone here, he quickly shot it down and said he isn't looking for romance...."

"Right. But you never know. He says that now, but he hasn't seen all of the charms"—I put on the airs and accent of an upper-crust English aristocrat—"and wiles Miss Eden Lundquist has to offer yet." I bat my lashes like a debutante.

She laughs. "I don't know about that, but I can see us becoming good friends, and that's okay. That's enough for me."

"Pish posh. You have enough friends." I wave that away as I peruse the spines of the two full walls of books in the Lady Aurelia Room. Each room is named and themed after a Regency heroine or hero.

"Hey, since we're on the subject..." Her voice is hesitant with impending doom. "I don't want to be weird, but I've noticed something. It's you and Harrison...."

"What?" I try for light and casual, but my voice cracks. Why? It's not like anything is going on. And there never will be. There's a little gnome of irony cackling my words back to me, "Don't make promises you can't keep!" I shove him in with that intrusive thought monster.

There's a bloated hush. Eden wrings her hands. "I can't tell if you like each other or hate each other sometimes, and there was the thing when he would come home to visit and you always had a reason you couldn't see him"—her hand gestures speed up, as do her words—"I never wanted to bug you about it. Maybe it was a coincidence, but then he moved back and there was this silence-filled weirdness between you. Now, there's something else I don't really know how to describe."

She takes in a deep breath as though she needs it to forge ahead. "Is there anything happening between you and Harrison? Because if there is, you know I love you both. I've always thought of you as a sister, so if you guys were ever to, you know, get married... well, we'd be sisters for real. It might be a little strange at first with you two dating, but—"

"No!" I clear my throat to calm my shrill tone. "I'm sorry, but no, we're not together. It's not like that between us. I mean, why would you even suggest that?"

Her brows furrow. "The way you two have been bickering about this whole singles' retreat among other things. Not to mention the way you danced with each other, you could hack through the t-e-n-s-i-o-n with a rusty chainsaw—"

"Right. See? We can't even see eye to eye about dating methods. Our argument *was* the tension. And the thing about avoiding him was just a misunderstanding before he moved to Cincinnati, but we've sorted that out." I drop my chin in a precise nod, as if this settles it. "Now we've agreed to put away our differences for the sake of the show."

"Okay, but . . . I know him. And there are these times."

"What times?"

"When he thinks no one's watching him and he looks at you. I've never seen him look at anyone like that. And the girl he was with when, you know, he was let go from that news station in Cincinnati? I knew he was never serious about her. He never even brought her home to meet us."

We both knew very little about the situation. Only that Harrison had been seeing someone he was working with, then somehow she was promoted at the same time he was fired. The next thing we knew they weren't together anymore and he'd moved back.

"I can assure you, Eden. He doesn't look at me like *anything*. I mean, we grew up together, like you and me. He's practically a big brother to me, too." Why is it the more I say this the less it feels true?

When her brows slant and her mouth puckers to the side as she studies me, I add, "Look, maybe I do see him as more than my best friend's brother." My stomach twists. "We've become friends in our own right. But, trust me, no one will ever replace you as my best friend."

"No, of course not."

A quick succession of knocks interrupts. Sweet, merciful knocks.

I race toward the door. "I'll get it!"

On the other side of the door is Sophia. She's already in a pale peach gown. "Hi, Zoe." She peeks around me and waves. "Hi, Eden. I think I'm the only one who didn't come here with someone I know. I hope you don't mind me coming over here."

"Not at all. Come in." I step back.

"I'm next door, and I could hear you chatting." Sophia scurries in.

Great. Does everyone know Harrison and I have been giving each other "looks"? Nonsense. Although there was that night, the intense gaze when he kissed my hand . . .

Sophia seems to catch the awkward silence. "Oh, no, I didn't hear anything you said. I-I only wanted to chat, too. I'm nervous about meeting everyone. How about you?"

Before we answer, she indicates her ivory lace fan. "I could just as easily tell someone 'I wish to be rid of you' as 'you have won my heart' with this thing."

We laugh, and I raise a hand. "Well, I'm so accident-prone I'm more likely to poke out a gentleman's eye with that thing than say anything at all."

Eden bobs her head in teasing empathy. "Yes, I think it's in the best interest of all retinas involved that you use your fan *very* sparingly."

Sophia's creased face relaxes slightly. "I couldn't sit still, so I didn't even wait for the lady's maid to dress me." She lifts the side of her dress and spins.

"You look amazing," I gush. She sparkles, not only from her braces and the reflection in her glasses. There has to be the perfect guy who'll see it.

Her cheeks flush. "Oh, thank you. Are you two nervous? It's

hard not knowing who'll be here and hoping they're here for the same reason I am, you know?"

Eden holds up a finger. "I guess we do know one person, other than my brother and our assistant cameraman, Jake. Ben Rowley, a family friend, will be here." She gestures to me. "Zoe's already been on a date with him, so she has a head start."

Sophia props herself at the edge of my bed. "Ooh, what's he like?"

"Well, he's a huge fan of Jane Austen and A. Nathaniel Gladwin." I count his characteristics on my fingers. "He's a Yale graduate, so obviously intelligent and driven, an expert-level roller skater"—this earns me a laugh from both—"and afraid of blood, apparently. Which if I'm honest, doesn't exactly bode well for me as an extremely clumsy person."

"Maybe," Eden says. "But I think for the right person, he can get over that."

I raise a shoulder. "He might not be looking to reconnect with me. He might be looking for a fresh start here."

Eden's mouth gathers to the side. "I don't know, that's not how he made it sound to Harrison."

There's another knock. It's a woman dressed in a light floral print empire gown, an apron tied around her waist and a white cap on her head.

She bobs a curtsy. "Greetings, Miss."

I find myself dipping a little curtsy in return. Staying in character is so easy here. "Hi, I'm Zoe."

Her smile is polite. "I'm Anne. I've been assigned as lady's maid for this side of the hallway for the duration of your stay. I'll be assisting you in dressing, hair, and anything else you need." She strides inside with purpose.

Her lips pinch together when she sees Sophia has already dressed sans help, but then her face returns to its polite expression. Behind a woven antique dressing screen, Anne assists Eden and me into our dresses for the kickoff tea/luncheon.

I choose the blush-pink satin dress to start, while Eden picks a pale blue silk one for herself. When our hair is perfectly coifed and our makeup toned down to a natural finish, we thank Anne and she bids us adieu for now.

I hardly recognize myself in the full-length, wood-framed mirror as we head to the door.

"This is it." I blow out a breath. "Be yourselves, ladies."

It brings back something Harrison said. Am I demanding perfection of guys and none of myself? A sliver of doubt wedges its way into my poised head. But I do my best to pluck it out like the one stubborn recurring hair that sprouts from my chin like I'm related to that poor old Michael Finnegan from the nursery rhyme.

Excitement and trepidation dance a reel in my stomach as we fall in line behind the other ladies descending the wide curved staircase leading to the expansive foyer.

My slippered feet keep catching on the front of my dress. "Klutzy person problems." I mutter the words out the side of my mouth, indicating my feet while clutching the railing with my short kid leather-gloved hands.

Eden glances back with a frown. "Be careful."

When my gaze connects with Harrison's at the bottom of the steps, his lips lift to one side.

Eden reaches him and turns to wait for me.

I have to admit, he looks good in his Regency attire. Strangely, it suits him. He's like a more rugged, bearded Mr. Darcy. I've never seen him this dressed up. Ever. As always, he doesn't seem to notice the appreciative female stares.

Four steps to go. I can do this.

And . . . my foot catches on the front of the dress, and I skid down the last few steps. I grapple for the rail. But it's too much momentum. I'm falling.

In. Front. Of. Everyone.

"Zoe!" Harrison's voice booms. He runs forward, arms open.

But out of my peripheral vision, a blur dashes in front of him. I land with an inelegant grunt but safely inside a strong pair of arms.

I look up and find Ben staring down at me, a bemused smile on his handsome face. His evergreen-flecked hazel eyes sparkle with humor.

My face is hot. I know it's blotchy and red. I try for a sheepish laugh, but it's too jittery. "I can't seem to stay on my feet around you."

Ben's sharp chin softens as his grin broadens. "I'm just glad I caught you this time."

He sets me on my feet and asks if I'm okay. I assure him I am.

The clique leader—Samantha, I've found out—stage-whispers to her group, "I guess she's got the whole damsel in distress thing down already. What a Marianne Dashwood drama queen."

Hmph. I'm clearly an *Elinor* Dashwood, thank you very much. A woman with a plan, not given to silly whims.

Ben places my hand in the crook of his elbow and leads me toward the dining room. We let the silent room gape after us.

Maybe he does deserve a second chance. He might be the gentleman who'll check all of the boxes. And I'm here for it.

13

Harrison

This is what we're here for. To find Zoe her perfect guy. I try to pound it into my thick skull.

She'll interact with the guys, go on dates with them, maybe even fall in love, ride off into the sunset on a white horse toward the picket fence, the whole shebang. She'll marry him—my thoughts spin faster and faster like I'm caught in a whirlpool with no escape—have children, grow old with him. . . .

Get a grip, Lundquist.

As her friend, I should want to help her find someone who loves her like she deserves.

But this faceless dude who sweeps her off her feet is suddenly filled with Ben's face.

My hands clench at my sides as I walk behind *Lord Smarmington* himself while he leads Zoe into the dining room, her small hand tucked into his bent arm. Is he flexing his bicep?

A snarl prowls behind my lips, but I keep it locked behind clenched teeth.

I clear my throat. "Zoe, are you okay?"

Over her shoulder, she tosses back, "Yeah, I'm fine. Good thing Ben happened to be right there."

"Right place, right time." Ben shrugs, and it's anything but casual.

No, *I* was in the right place at the right time until he swooped in. Of course, he had to go all knight-in-shining armor or whatever the Regency equivalent is. Mr. Willoughby rescuing Marianne? That dude turned out to be the villain. Just saying.

"You okay, bro?" Eden is studying me.

"Of course. Why wouldn't I be?" My tone is more brusque than I intended. I straighten my spine along with this constricting frock coat.

She doesn't comment, but her puckered brows say she's not buying it.

Good thing Jake's covering the filming right now, but I try to snap out of my daze. On our way into the dining room, where one long table is set for a feast, we whisper logistics and agree I'll take over partway through the luncheon. A fire in the fireplace and a crystal chandelier add to the glow streaming into the room from the line of windows against one wall.

Zoe's lilting laugh at something Ben says travels back, hitting me square in the chest. The same place that seemed to split apart when Ben's arms had encircled Zoe and she'd stared up at him with those big melted chocolate-brown eyes.

I'm seated across the table from Ben and Zoe. At least I have the relative safety of having my sister beside me. Their new acquaintance, Sophia, beams up at me from the other side, the chandelier light catching on her braces and glasses, and I smile back. It's so like Zoe and Eden to befriend the shy woman.

"Is that the Ben Zoe was talking about?" Sophia inclines her head toward the two now talking closely.

"Yeah, that's him." I try not to snarl. "She was talking about him?"

"Oh, yes!" Sophia's hands spin and dive with her enthusiasm, reminding me of my sister. "She thinks he checks most of the things on her list. Isn't that exciting? They might be the first to pair off."

I mutter a noncommittal "Mmm."

All right, I still like Sophia, but I don't care for her assumptions.

Our hostess stands and spreads her arms wide, which we've come to recognize as her "shush your mouths" stance. The excited chatter dies down.

"Welcome, ladies and gentlemen, to the Minnesota Marriage Mart Retreat." Victoria smiles. "I anticipate this will be a great success, like the London Season of old."

Victoria steeples her hands. "Now for some rules and reminders."

Zoe's face brightens. No surprise there. She retrieves a miniature notepad and pencil from the small, near-useless bag hanging from her wrist.

"The west wing of the house is for the men, and the east wing is for the women. There will be no comingling in those spaces." She turns a stern gaze to each person at the long table.

With more levity, she continues, "The middle common areas of the manor, as well as the grounds, you are welcome to explore individually and as couples—with a chaperone, of course."

There's a low communal grumble. But this doesn't deter Victoria. "They are here to provide a fully immersive Regency experience." I mouth the last four words along with Victoria, as they seem to be her tagline. This makes Zoe cover her mouth to stop a laugh.

Victoria adds, "And as a reminder, you are to stay in your Regency attire while in common areas or on the grounds—"

"So this is like a week-long LARPing." This comes from a guy who appears to be in his late twenties or early thirties, who I think is named Darren. He says it like he's not new to Live Action Role-Playing.

Eden perks up beside me.

With a curt nod, Victoria agrees. "As you know from our registration materials, there will also be a daily schedule. This isn't a spa retreat, so no sleeping until noon. Even at a Marriage Mart, it takes time and work to find the right match." She taps her fingers together. "There will also be a friendly competition throughout our time here where you can earn points toward a prize at the end. We'll talk about the details more later."

Competition? Now she's speaking my language. Maybe this won't be completely drop-dead boring.

"For now, let's go around the table and introduce ourselves and share why we're here." Victoria sits and indicates the person to her left, a quiet guy who looks to be around forty with horn-rimmed glasses and a mop of mousy brown hair.

He bends closer to the table like it'll hide him from the attention focused on him. "I'm Milton." His voice makes me think of a mouse, too. "Milton Birtwhistle. I'm here ... because my mom thought it would be a good idea."

Mentally, I flinch. Shucks. Too bad, my man.

His small eyes dart from side to side. "She and my sisters heard about it on the radio and know how difficult it is to meet anyone out there. So I thought I'd give it a shot. . . ."

Decent save.

There's a string of other introductions, including a widowed mother and adult daughter, Joan and Wilhemina respectively, and a group of women Eden and Zoe referred to as the clique who seem like they never left the high school power-trip-hierarchy thing. Then several guys who appear to be nice, normal, gainfully employed men looking for love—

like Matthew, maybe a little older than me, who keeps casting covert glances at Sophia—and a retired architect, probably in his early sixties, named George.

I'm surprised at all the guys here. This is not a normal way to meet a woman. But then, I suppose, there are plenty of men like me who aren't into the two modern dating staples—dating apps and the bar scene.

When it's my turn, I stand and make it clear I'm here for the podcast and will begrudgingly participate in the activities I'm required to. "Basically, I'm here to do what Zoe makes me do. But I won't be participating in the ball. Filming only."

Yes, I'm here for the podcast and Mr. Kellsner. But deep down it hits me. If Zoe's responsibility is to be the cupbearer of the dating pool, then I'm the guy who makes sure no creeps get close to the queen. My shoulders square, and I draw up my full six-foot-four-inches as much as I can while seated, surveying the table full of mouth breathers—I mean, potential suitors.

I was an offensive lineman in high school and college, and more specifically, a left tackle. It was my job to protect the quarterback on his blindside. No one got to him except through me, and they didn't call me Brick House Lundquist for nothing.

After our introductions and a silly but delicious meal of tiny sandwiches too small for my large hands, fruit, and pastries, Victoria calls our attention back to her. "Everyone, you're free to mingle in the drawing room for an hour. You are welcome to make plans with someone of your choice for this afternoon. We'll start our compatibility speed dates tomorrow. A list of activities available to you for today will be on display, if you'll all follow me."

We men remember our manners and assist the women with their chairs. I pull back Sophia's. Jake strides forward to help my sister, and I send him a grateful smile and let him know I'll take over filming now.

I grab the camera as he stretches out his neck and arm.

People gather around a framed, calligraphed list of activities. I zoom in on Zoe, her delicate silhouette shadowed and highlighted in the firelight and sun streaming in, standing with Ben. I'm sure she'll choose to spend her first date with Mr. Checks-All-Her-Boxes himself. But that shouldn't bother me.

On paper, we make no sense at all. Zero. Zilch.

I'm not into all this Regency stuff, for one, and I'd rather watch Sports Center or play a game of pickup basketball any day over this. We don't really have any interests in common, and our outlooks on life couldn't be more different, save our faith maybe. I don't even have the facial grooming she prefers—no beard. And above all that, she's made it abundantly clear on more than one occasion she has no interest in me that way. I let out a long-held breath, noisy in the mic. More editing.

Now, if someone could convince this gnawing ache that seems to have taken up a permanent stakeout in the center of my chest, I might survive this retreat. I need to snap out of it and help her like I promised her folks. Like a good friend would.

14

Zoe

The afternoon sun tilts its golden head in that posture only present in autumn. Like a playful farewell to summer before the long Minnesota winter settles in. I shield my eyes from the dancing light by pulling down my lace-trimmed bonnet and securing the satin ribbon under my chin. The winding, shrub- and once flower-lined but now waning garden of Wyndmere Hall is behind us, while the lawn bowling green spreads out before us.

The rays reach through the rust-topped oaks, the vibrant yellows and marigolds of the birches, and the brilliant crimsons and oranges of the maples, setting them aglow like fluttering jewels. The rippling waters of the small private Willow Lake belonging to the estate sparkle like a million little diamonds. The sprawling house is a Minnesota version of Pemberley from this vantage point.

Eden, Jake, Harrison, and I wait for Ben and Darren, who

Eden met at the luncheon and invited to lawn bowl with us. He seems like a great match for her since they both love Tolkien and cosplay.

"What do I know about lawn bowling? It's like a sport, right? I had no business agreeing to this." I squint over at Harrison, who chuckles. "What?"

He scrapes a thumb over his chin with a smirk. "I've seen you row, like an Olympian might I add. I don't think you can ever complain of not being coordinated enough for sports again."

The compliment sends a flush to my cheeks.

Harrison and Jake set up equipment and mics. Jake clips the battery pack to the tie in the back of Eden's dress. *Ooh!* The look he gives her would put the broodiest of Regency heroes to shame, and her immediate blush . . . *Okay.* I cast her a look that says, "We're discussing this later."

I smooth my dusky rose long-sleeve day dress I've changed into—a little warmer for our outdoor excursion—and pull my leather gloves more firmly into place beneath the cuffs of my short spencer jacket to ward off the chill in the breeze. "Thank you for comparing me to an Olympian, but that's different. And there were all manner of activities listed. I could be painting right now. Or taking a lovely, *safe* promenade around the grounds. I mean, even I couldn't hurt myself walking."

He wags an eyebrow, pure mischief in his sun-illuminated indigo eyes. "I wouldn't be too sure. If anyone could manage it, I'm absolutely certain it would be you."

I squint at him, resorting to my childhood comeback, and stick out my tongue.

"You two." Good-natured exasperation edges Eden's tone.

"Etiquette, Miss Dufour. What would Victoria say?" He winks, and my heart does a little loop-de-loop. Since when? I clap a hand over my sternum like it'll quell the sensation.

This is how Ben finds me, mouth still ajar from my less-than-ladylike gesture.

"Hello, Zoe." Ben's long strides make quick work of the hill down to the large, flat rectangular bowling green with six lanes, or "rinks." It'll be a two-on-two game—Eden and I against Darren and Ben. That way we can take turns—me, Ben, Eden, then Darren. Plus, the competition between guys and gals sounded fun.

Ben's slim, athletic build is enhanced by his gentlemanly attire. One of his tousled chestnut waves slips onto his forehead as he smiles down at me. He's tall. Not as tall as Harrison or as broad-shouldered. But then, everyone is tall to me, and I'm not sure why Harrison is the measuring stick with which I'm comparing my date.

There's a waft of mint, like an overpowering amount of sharp peppermint—hey, at least he cares about his dental hygiene—and an expensive-smelling cologne with notes of sandalwood, black pepper, and warm vanilla.

Jake calls me over to record an on-location update for our social media.

"I'm sorry. Would you excuse me a minute?"

Ben inclines his head. "Of course. Do what you need to do. I'll be right here waiting."

At the end of the promo, I add, "I've been working on my 'Thirty by Thirty' list for about a month, but now that I'm here at the retreat, I know I'm going to be crossing off items left and right. I've already crossed off 'Attend a private tea or dinner party' and I'm about to check 'Spectate or participate in a lawn game.' I'm off to lawn bowl. Hope to see you on the other side, unscathed!"

I wave to the camera, and Jake calls, "Cut," while Harrison murmurs, "Famous last words."

Ben beams when I step back to his side. "Great job. You're such a natural on camera." His smile is warm as he greets everyone else. Then turning to Eden, "I apologize, your suitor is otherwise engaged. He sends his regrets."

He's taking this Regency etiquette to the next level, and I swoon a little at his gallant manners. But I'm not pleased with this Darren.

"What do you mean? Where is he?" I blurt before Eden has a chance to respond.

Eden taps the air like she's patting my shoulder. "It's fine. We didn't have plans etched in stone. Put your claws away, Zoe."

Ben's straight shoulders lift, and he drops the upper-crust gentleman facade. "He's my roommate, actually. He said he wanted to take some 'time to observe and explore other connections' right now." The tip of his head to the side is apologetic.

Eden rolls her eyes, but soon her easygoing grin is back. "Hope he finds what he's looking for. But that messes up our plan for two-on-two lawn bowling." She layers one arm over the other, fingers tapping her elbows. She points to Ben and me. "You two could play on your own. I can hang back and help with filming."

"Nonsense," both Jake and Ben say together.

Sweet for different reasons—despite what he said, Jake seems taken with my friend, and Ben checked off "he's chivalrous" on my own nonnegotiables list.

Jake raises his arm, still holding a camera in the other. "If it's all right with you, Harrison, I could play on Ben's team. You know, to keep both Eden and Zoe in the show." He's quick to add, "Unless you want to play?"

Harrison arches a brow. "I'd rather eat one of the bowls"—he indicates one of the oblong balls used for the game—"whole like one of my grandma's Swedish meatballs, thanks," he deadpans.

Harrison takes the camera from Jake and adjusts a headset onto his ears.

Ben lightly touches my arm. "All right, that's settled, then."

We briefly run through the rules. The object is to underhand throw a ball or "bowl" as close as possible to the smaller white ball or "jack" without rolling it into the gutter at the ends of the long rectangular bowling lane. The rules sound easy enough, but I make Ben repeat them a second time, which he patiently does without protest.

Harrison points at us and counts down from five with his fingers. "We're losing daylight, people. Let's do this."

I roll my eyes at him right before he says, "Action!"

"Ladies first, I insist." Ben bows to me.

Eden shoos me forward to go first.

The bowl is heavier than I thought, and when I pull back my arm, swing it forward, and let go, it wobbles and limps over onto its side a good six feet from the jack like one of those exhausted hedgehogs acting as croquet balls in *Alice in Wonderland*.

Ben squeezes my elbow. "Great job, Zoe. Don't be afraid to give it some power."

He throws his bowl, and it cracks into mine, which sends it spinning off to the side and his right next to the jack.

He and I will alternate and each bowl four times before it's Jake and Eden's turn. When one team reaches twenty-one points, the game is done.

"Here, let me help you this time." Ben steps next to me.

"Sure. Mixing me and throwing heavy objects is usually cause for villagers to flee."

"I can attest to that." Eden raises her hand. "Softball week in gym class meant helmets."

"And bubble wrap," Harrison adds, amusement in his eyes.

Ben's lips twist with mischief. "A menace not only on roller skates, then? Good thing I like a bit of danger." He winks at me, and I'm faintly aware my heart doesn't do that little flippy thing it did when Harrison did the same. But maybe I'm too focused on not making a fool of myself.

Ben curves his body around mine. Even though my back doesn't quite touch his torso, this feels intimate. Warm. Disconcerting. Ben reaches around me, taking my hands in his as we cradle the bowl between them. His chin brushes the top of my bonnet-covered head. A roaming retreat chaperone clears her throat, and Ben withdraws a fraction.

As he helps me pull back one arm, his hand wrapped around mine and the ball, and we underhand throw it toward the jack, there's unmistakable heat from a set of eyes. It burns through me. I glance up to find Harrison across from us, staring. He's gone so still he could be carved of stone like one of the many lifelike statues guarding the grounds.

Intense and unreadable. I swallow an imaginary dry patch like I'm in the desert, parched. No, maybe it's more like drowning. Like I can't breathe. I don't know what it means or if it means anything at all or if I'm imagining things. But for some reason, I can't look away. He doesn't move or blink in this infinite millisecond. The only thing that moves is a tick in the crook of his jaw.

Only when Ben steps back and lets go of my hands does the minor existential moment break. I blink. So does Harrison, who runs a hand down his face before straightening.

"You'll get there. Don't you worry." Ben indicates what I hadn't noticed—my bowl not only landed in the gutter but pushed his in as well.

I blow out a breath to clear my head. "Maybe I'm better at the 'meet me in the library' sort of activities. And, honestly? That sounds like my dream date."

Ben chuckles. "I've always been a bookworm. Maybe we'll have to do that sometime." His smile is kind and inviting, and I return it.

I need to shake off whatever *that* was with Harrison.

Again, my gaze finds Harrison's. His expression has lightened. He's still watching me, but now with a slight upturn at the corner of his full lips. Wait, did I notice his lips? If I'm truthful with myself, this isn't the first time. I remember stealing glances at my best friend's brother over the years. Never intending to do anything about it, of course. But one can objectively appreciate lips like that. Full but masculine. Soft? I bet they're soft.

My own mouth hangs open. I snap it shut and realize Ben is saying my name like he's said it a couple of times. Harrison's smirk turns into a wide, boyish grin.

It's my turn, my last bowl before we turn it over to Eden and Jake, who are talking and laughing, patiently awaiting their turn.

I pull my arm back on my own this time, but the ball is so big in my petite hand that it slips to the ground.

"Oops." I pick it up and ready my aim, but Ben steps up behind me again.

"I'd be happy to assist you again, Miss Dufour."

Harrison strides forward like he's about to say something as Ben touches my hand holding the ball. But his touch startles me, and I drop the bowl. On his foot.

Ben's yelp echoes into my ears and throughout the bowling green, where every other couple playing stops to stare.

He's quick to say while sucking air through his teeth, "I'm all right. No worries, Zoe. Everything's fine."

But it's not, especially because I allowed my distraction to cause this disaster.

15

Harrison

I'm not *happy* Ben took a heavy bowl to the foot this afternoon. Seriously, I'm *not*. I wince at the memory. Ben played it off, but judging from the slight limp throughout the rest of the miserable game in which somehow Zoe and Eden won by a hair thanks to my sister's mad skills at lawn bowling—another result of our youth spent at stuffy parties with our parents—it hurt. Bad.

But I can't say I was sorry he kept his physical distance from Zoe after that. He didn't offer to help her throw the ball again and stayed clear while she took her turns.

I don't know what came over me, but when he wrapped his arms around her . . . it was like this protective instinct had risen inside me.

It wasn't jealousy exactly. Not a desire to tackle the guy or anything. More of a fierce desire to shield her from potential harm. And if I'm honest, more than a little wishing I could trade places with him. I can almost imagine the warmth of her body as I curl my arms around her, completely enveloping her, and the sweet scent of her hair and skin that close....

"Hey, you okay, buddy?" Jake walks through the door to the room we're sharing for the week.

He flops onto his dark wood-framed bed across from mine.

Why is he calling me buddy? I hardly know the guy. And I'm still not convinced he's not a spy for my boss, who's already called twice to check on me. Besides, I need Mr. Kellsner to know this is a job I can handle on my own.

"Yeah. Why wouldn't I be? And why do you and my sister keep asking me that?" I drag my fingernails across my scalp until it burns.

But my stomach immediately squirms. I finish zipping my equipment bag and toss a glance over my shoulder. "Sorry. Didn't mean to bite your head off, man."

"It's all right. But you didn't seem too happy during lawn bowling." He doesn't meet my eye, picking at nonexistent lint on the dark comforter. "I wondered if it had anything to do with Ben having his arms around Zoe."

Now he pins me with a knowing look. A mini-war rages inside as I try to decide if I can or should talk to Jake. Zoe and Eden were right about my friends—many of them haven't moved on from their carefree twenties, and the few who are married with children or babies on the way are busy with their own lives, which I understand. But here I am, a man of thirty-two whose closest friends are my sister and Zoe. Not that there's anything wrong with that, but I can't exactly tell Zoe about my conflicted feelings for *Zoe*. Nor my sister.

And despite my suspicions, Jake does seem like a stand-up guy and hasn't given me a reason to distrust him.

I lean back on the wooden post at the corner of my bed and cross my arms. "It was that obvious?"

"I thought I was witnessing the transformation of a werewolf at full moon." He laughs and sits up. "Am I missing something? Do you like Zoe, and if you do, why haven't you told her?"

I pinch the bridge of my nose, a sudden headache forming.

"She and I, we're friends. She was like another little sister growing up—"

"Wait, wait." He turns his head, lifting his hands. "The look I saw on your face did not say friends, and it definitely did *not* say sister."

He's right. The same line I've told myself a million times sounds even more ludicrous out loud.

Gripping the back of my neck, I walk across the room, but without a destination, march back. "You caught that, huh?"

"I did, and if I'm not mistaken, so did she."

There was that moment when our eyes locked . . . but nah. I'm seeing what I want to see.

My chest tightens, sweat slicking my palms. "No, she didn't. Trust me."

"How do you know?"

The words tumble out. "I've knocked on that door already. Twice." I run a hand down my face, then hold up two fingers as a flash of a further-back memory bursts through my brain. An electrically charged moment years ago in high school. "My senior year in high school, her sophomore. She'd had her heart broken by this jerk I played football with. He'd humiliated her and rejected her in the most cruel way possible." My fingers still curl into fists thinking about it. "I found her in the empty gym after school, hiding behind the bleachers, waiting to leave until everyone else was gone so she didn't have to face them."

The laughter and cruel words hurled her way that day still ring in my ears, despite my attempts to tell them all to shut up. Eden had been sick that day. Zoe was on her own.

Jake nods for me to continue, his concern drawn in two lines on his forehead. I don't know why this story is leaking out, but now I can't seem to stop it.

"I sat with her. Quiet. You know, in solidarity until she was ready to stand. Without thinking, I pulled her to my chest. I only meant to comfort her, to protect her"—as if my body alone could shield her from everyone and everything ready to hurt her—"but there was this—this—"

I groan. "This second when she tilted her head back to look up at me—like she trusted me, man, more than anyone else in the world in that moment—and I misread the situation. Or maybe let myself believe something that wasn't there. I went in for a kiss and . . ."

Jake sits up from his reclining position. "And what?"

My eyes squeeze shut, head bowing at the image of her heart-shaped lips forming an O as she ducked out of my arms.

"She ran." Palms up, I add, "We were quiet and weird for a while afterward but eventually came out of it. She seemed dead set on never talking about it and pretended it never happened. So I took her lead."

With that same rock in my stomach, I explain what happened a year and a half ago.

I shake my head. "I'm the poster boy for the phrase *wrong place, wrong time.*"

"That was a while ago, man. Things might be different now if you're honest with her."

Honest. Yeah, that's one of the traits on her list. A dealbreaker. But this is one of those truths that isn't helpful, to either of us.

"I know where she stands, and where I've always stood with her. Firmly in the friend/surrogate big brother zone. Besides, you've heard her podcast. I'm not that guy. Maybe I check off a few things. But all this?" I flick the cravat I've tried tying exactly one thousand and one times and am about this close to throwing into the fireplace.

"All this stuff isn't me. I had my chance at living like the 'modern gentleman,' as she likes to say"—Jake has asked me about my father and our family's large media investment firm, so he nods his understanding—"and that's not the life I want. I want a simple life. No courtship rituals or dating games. Just two people who fall in love and stay that way. Real and honest."

There's that word again. So I'm expecting honesty without giving it in return? Is it *honest* to have feelings for someone and then not tell them the truth? To tell her I'd support her search for love when the reality of watching the process makes me want to crawl out of my own skin?

Jake crosses to his wardrobe and pulls out a dinner jacket since we're expected in the dining room soon.

"All I know is life's too short not to tell people what's on our minds." He shrugs his arms into the jacket. "I came back here from my coverage of the Middle East with a whole new perspective and an appreciation for the brevity of life. We have to use every minute and not let any go to waste."

This dude obviously doesn't mind going deep even though we've only known each other a short time. I guess it's the whole life-is-short thing. Somehow it makes me less tight-lipped than I usually would be.

I step in front of the mirror and try to make my fingers cooperate in tying this cravat once and for all. "Speaking of telling people the truth, you seem taken with my sister. . . ."

Taken? Maybe this gentleman stuff is infiltrating my brain.

Jake stills, and his fingers stop knotting his own cravat. "She's great. I already feel like we've known each other forever. But I'm only looking for friendship. I think I might've brought home more than my rolling luggage, if you know what I mean. Romance isn't something I'm interested in right now."

Even though I think I genuinely like this guy and can already sense a friendship forming, I will always put my sister first. I narrow my eyes at him. "I don't want you leading her on."

"I would never do anything to hurt Eden. I want you to know that." He moves a hand to his chest. "We already talked about friendship as the goal *and* endgame. Nothing more. Don't worry, we're on the same page."

I draw a breath, straightening my dark blue jacket. The cravat is as good as it's gonna get. "Come on, let's go be the double chumps *du jour* who help the two best girls in the world find love." I let out a ragged sigh.

Somehow Jake and I make it through watching the charade of a roomful of twenty-first-century adults pretend they've been plunked into the middle of a Jane Austen story come to life.

Jake and I focus on the filming instead of participating this time. We take turns standing off in a corner, scarfing down bits of the beef roast, candied carrots, and freshly baked buttered rolls. It's great, but a craving hits and I whisper at one point, "What I wouldn't give for a cheeseburger with everything on it and a stack of hot, crispy fries."

Zoe catches my eye and agrees with a mouthed "Me too."

All through dinner, Ben makes Zoe laugh. Her full laugh where she tips her head back, exposing the curve of her neck, and her cheeks turn rosy.

Something deep in my chest silently churns. *That's my laugh.*

But it's not, and I don't have exclusive rights to it. It's hers to give away to whomever she chooses. *God, please, give me the strength to support her and do right by her no matter what that means.* It's hard not to wonder, especially in this moment, why doing the right thing results in me losing. Again.

We're excused into the drawing room, which has been transformed into a small ballroom, the furniture now lining the walls. The large ballroom on the other side of the mansion is reserved for the ball on Tuesday.

Ben didn't seem to hold a grudge during dinner over Zoe's accidental foot bludgeoning and whispers into her ear while they line up to dance, her expression warming at whatever he says.

Victoria slides by me, her arm brushing against mine. "Mr. Lundquist, a cravat suits you." She glances back at me, the handle of her fan touching her lips.

Accidental or part of the Regency fan language? If so, I have no idea what it means. Maybe I don't want to know.

I keep my face polite with a tight-lipped smile instead of telling her I'd like to throw this cravat into the nearest fireplace along with the rest of these strangling clothes.

After I endure filming a dance, Zoe in Ben's arms—I'll give him this, his patient directions and compliments keep her on her feet—Victoria stops the music with one snap of her fingers.

Then her hands come together in one loud clap like she's corralling kindergarteners. "Our lady's maids are passing out dance cards to you ladies. In Regency times, women received these to record who asked for a dance, but the cards you're receiving now"—all of the women now hold a small booklet and miniature pencil attached with a ribbon—"will be for your accelerated compatibility dates tomorrow. Use them to take notes about each one so you can reflect later."

Pointing to a table in the corner laden with baskets of parchment paper, quills, ink, and wax, as well as trinkets like chocolates, snacks, and small floral arrangements, Victoria adds, "At any time, please feel free to use the items on our love tokens table to write notes and leave gifts for anyone you wish. Ask a retreat staff member to deliver tokens to their rooms."

Victoria raises a hand, then drops it like she's signaling a drag race. "Now, go! Dance, mingle. See if you can guess your top matches."

After an hour, Zoe strides my way along the wall and breathes a sigh.

"Looks like you're already belle of the ball." I nudge her elbow with mine and lower my camera.

She scrunches her nose, showing off a smattering of freckles along the bridge of her nose and cheekbones. "Who knew being a near thirty-year-old almost-cat-lady obsessed with Lord Pembroke would prove to be such a hot ticket item?"

"You're doing it again."

"What?"

"Selling yourself short." Her eyes narrow, so I add, "And no, that wasn't a short joke this time."

She fidgets with the little notebook and pen. "Actually, I'm kind of nervous. That's an eight-hour workday of dates. And I'm supposed to know who to allow to call on me again after that? Who might be *the* one? What if none of them even like me?"

Even though this is hard for me, the trepidation and pleading in her voice grip my chest and make my mouth open before I can clamp it shut. "I'll help you."

I vowed to help her with this retreat, after all. To be her friend. It's time I start acting like it.

Propping a hand where my belt loops would normally be, I bend closer. "Meet me later. In the library." My words breeze out in a rush, but I'm warming to an idea. "I'm gonna help you NCAA March Madness basketball bracket this thing."

"What does that even mean? And after curfew? You know we can't. Victoria will have a conniption."

"I'll explain." I dip my head toward hers. "Later. In the library."

She glances across the room at our hostess, then adds in a hushed tone, "You, sir, are truly scandalous. If anyone catches us, I'll be utterly ruined and you labeled a rake."

A slow grin pulls at my lips.

"You're always such a rule follower." I don't know what makes me do it, maybe I'm enjoying the flustered blush I've caused her, but I move toward her until my lips almost touch her ear and whisper, "But maybe there's a time for rules to be broken."

The little hairs at the nape of her neck rise, but she straightens, muttering, "Oh, all right."

I can't help the full smile overtaking my face now.

People start to disperse toward their separate wings of the mansion.

She agrees to meet me at 11:30 p.m., an hour after our curfew, when everyone should be asleep or at least in their bedrooms.

I bid her goodnight for now, and I catch a sideways glance from Jake as we head for the stairs.

"What?" I avoid his eye.

"That can't possibly end in disaster. Just friends, huh?" Jake claps me on the back, and his laugh reverberates down the hall.

If he overheard our plan, I can only hope no one else did.

I pull our door open and toss over my shoulder, "I'm helping her *as* a friend. And breaking some rules in the process, but it'll be worth it. She's worried about these speed dates tomorrow."

Do I wish I could be one of her eight compatibility dates tomorrow? Yes. But I keep that to myself. The reality is, a compatibility test would likely show what we already know: We aren't right for each other.

Good thing you don't need lists or a compatibility test to be friends. And that is exactly what I'll be. I will be honest by showing her I care about her . . . as a friend. Even if my heart pummels my ribcage, demanding, begging for more.

16

Zoe

It was kind of embarrassing to explain to Eden that I'm secretly meeting her brother in the library for a late-night speed dating strategy sesh, but after a pause, she waved me off. "Have fun."

Instead of arguing with her wry, knowing smile, I slipped out the door and down the hall on tiptoes.

This feels a little like the only time I sneaked out of the house in high school to hang out with Chad Summers. He was so not worth being caught and immediately grounded over.

Memories of Chad swim through my mind as I pad barefoot through the silent halls—of the day he publicly humiliated me. My genius plan was to ask him to the homecoming dance at lunch. I blamed my lightheadedness on nerves, not realizing my blood sugar had dropped to a dangerous level. I was still learning the symptoms of low and high blood sugar at the time. They can still catch me off guard even now.

I passed out, right there in the cafeteria in front of everyone. Chad's popular friends took pictures and videos and passed them all over school. I awoke to the school nurse hovering over me, squeezing that disgusting glucose gel into my mouth, and everyone laughing and taunting me for "fainting from an epic rejection." I ran, finding solace under the bleachers in the gym.

Harrison found me and sat with me, his mere presence all the support I needed in that moment. A solid rock, unwavering in the storm of my hurt and humiliation. The way he'd taken me in his arms, the look on his face when he'd leaned in . . .

My heart gallops like it did then. All these years later, I can still feel the tingle down to my toes, remember his outdoorsy scent like fresh-cut wood and something earthy and spicy, almost like the dried autumn leaves scattering the grass outside right now.

But that was a long time ago, and the memory of a heartbroken teenager shouldn't be trusted. He probably hadn't been about to kiss me and wouldn't dream of it now. He'd been trying to comfort me, just like the night Sawyer and I broke up. Harrison and I are friends, good friends.

I pull my robe tighter around my nightgown and place one careful step in front of another, holding my chamberstick higher to light the way. I feel like Catherine Morland in Jane Austen's gothic satire, *Northanger Abbey*, sneaking into the forbidden room.

I finally fumble my way into the library deep in the heart of the manor-like house. Far from either sleeping wing. Quiet and dark.

The large room is something out of a dream for bookish, historical romance–loving gals like me—wall-to-wall books, a rolling ladder, even an open-balconied second story with more books and cozy sitting areas beckoning visitors to curl up with a good book and hot beverage. It brings to mind the Beast's library in *Beauty and the Beast*, and suddenly Belle's

"You know what? Maybe being a prisoner isn't so bad. Stockholm syndrome, Schmockholm syndrome" makes so much sense.

A fire still burns inside the tall marble fireplace, sending light dancing with the shadows.

One of the shadows beside the fireplace grows, almost obscuring the flickering orange glow. Tall and imposing. I gasp.

The form nears. Harrison. My shoulders relax, though I clutch my racing heart. He takes the chamberstick about to fall from my hand. "Zo, it's me. Who'd you think it was?"

"Sorry," I whisper. "I was thinking of *Northanger Abbey*."

He chuckles, and the warmth of it fills the dark space, making it seem brighter, chasing away the dark. "You know there weren't any actual specters or boogiemen in that, right?"

"Yes, of course," I hiss.

"You don't have to whisper, by the way." His lips crook to the side in that boyish yet masculine way of his. "No one knows we're in here. We've got the place to ourselves."

Something about that seemingly innocent statement brings heat to my face, making the cover of darkness and flickering amber light a necessary camouflage.

Taking my hand, he helps me maneuver around the furniture to sit in front of the fire on an antique wood-framed sofa. He sits beside me and retrieves a teacup and saucer from the side table.

"Here, I started a fire for us and made you some herbal tea in the kitchen."

I try a sip. Hints of honey and floral, like chamomile and lavender. "Mmm. Thank you." The warmth of the fire and the tea, but maybe the gesture, too, work to thaw my chilled extremities.

"Sure. No problem."

His gaze travels from my bare feet up to my hair, which I'd let fall down my back after taking out the many pins from

Anne's expert coif. He pulls at the already unbuttoned neckline of his own crisp white linen shirt, his Adam's apple bobbing. He's still in his trousers from dinner but no jacket and no cravat.

I'm suddenly very aware I'm in a blush silk nightgown and matching robe, and although I'm covered from ankle to neck with the robe pulled tight, I've never felt so exposed in front of Harrison. It's not like he hasn't seen me in pajamas before. But this feels different—alone in a big empty library.

I try for a dignified sip of tea, pinky out, but it trickles down my chin and windpipe instead. While I sputter and hack, he pats my back.

"Hey, you okay?"

When I finally catch my breath, I rasp, "Yeah, wrong tube. No Heimlich needed this time."

He removes his hand from my back, and my skin cools.

I take a slower sip and clear my throat. "So, how do you think you can help me with my speed dating? And what's this about March Madness? There won't be any actual basketball involved, right?"

"No, absolutely not. Did I say I wanted anyone to die?"

Tilting my head, I glare. "Ha, ha."

His body angles toward me, and he braces his elbows on his knees. "I was thinking we could look at your and Eden's semi-speed dates like a basketball bracket." The way he says "we" is endearing.

"Okay . . ." I draw out the word like a question, set the now-empty teacup on the table, and lean forward, mimicking his posture.

"You each will go on your dates and decide who you're compatible with or not, right?"

"Mm-hmm."

"Then you and Eden take the dates up against—well, not against, but compare them to—each other by spending more time with the ones who you each feel mutually *connected* to . . ." There's a slight strain to his tone. He swallows. This must be weird discussing his sister's and friend's dating life.

He straightens, continuing, "Anyway, you continue the brackets from tomorrow's dates to the others you'll have throughout the retreat, and keep comparing and whittling your list of suitors down until there's one fortunate guy left at the end. We could make a chart if that helps."

"Okay. But you make it sound so easy. This isn't the basketball playoffs. This is my life, potentially the rest of my life. My forever person."

He jumps to his feet and walks to the fireplace, leaning over the mantel, his broad back to me. "If he's here, I know we'll find him for you."

At his use of "we" again, the corners of my lips twitch.

I try to work up enthusiasm, especially since he seems to have put thought into this plan. But for some reason, I can't do more than sigh, and my shoulders sag with the effort.

He turns back to me. "What's wrong?" A shadow of a crease forms on his brow. "I was trying to break down the process so it doesn't feel so overwhelming. I'm sorry, I didn't mean to mansplain or tell you what to do."

Planting a hand near his waist, he rubs his jaw with the other. "You're right, it's your life."

Standing, I step toward him. "No, no. It's not that. Thank you for helping me."

Is it the heat of the fire or being this near Harrison in the darkened room that compels me to move away? This feels dangerous. Ben's sweet, patient attention digs firmly into the forefront of my mind as I stagger back. "The whole retreat"—my hand sweeps out—"is more overwhelming than I thought. I don't think I was fully prepared for this."

A chill seeps through my silk nightgown and robe the farther I roam from the fireplace, but my head's clearer over here.

I run my fingertips along antique leather bindings, passing classics like *Wuthering Heights*, *The Great Gatsby*, *A Tale of Two Cities*, and of course, several Jane Austen and A. Nathaniel Gladwin favorites.

His footsteps near, and I focus back on the lovely novels. I wasn't kidding when I told Ben my dream date would be right here in the library.

"I didn't know what to expect, but I guess even with everything organized and planned for me, it seems so . . . out of my control."

"Do you need everything to be in your control?" His tone isn't accusatory or admonishing, just thoughtful.

Lips pressed together, I overturn a palm. "I've seen what happens when I'm not following a plan or when life just *happens*." I chance a glance up at him, and he's closer than I had realized, studying me.

A flash of my mom's devastating diagnosis when I was young runs through my mind. How it turned our lives upside down. Then my diabetes diagnosis only a few years later. Not to mention not having a list, a firm plan with Sawyer. Boy, did I learn my lesson with that self-important rake in disguise. Someone who in retrospect would've never checked off my list. A total Mr. Willoughby who ran off when a better offer came his way. Now I'm prepared. I know what I'm looking for as I put myself out there to find love.

"If you have everything planned, how is that any fun? Besides, even when we think we're controlling things, we're really not. Surrender is acknowledging the fact that God has it under control, has our backs, and loves us. We don't have to carry the burden of making everything right." His eyes flare like the words jab at something in his own chest.

Normally I'd squirm under such words, but said with the sincerity and matter-of-fact care I've come to expect from Harrison, they make me pause. Consider.

"Do you know me at all?" I touch his shoulder with a playful shove. "Me and surrender aren't exactly acquainted. Who would I even be without my checklists and nonnegotiables?"

"Free." That one word, rumbled from his chest, seems to sweep through the darkened room. To fill the shadows with warmth, to brighten the candle and firelight. But that light exposes a part of me, too. A part I don't want seen. A place that terrifies me. A place where I've learned to hold tight to the reins of my life and its destination. And I'm not about to hand over control.

Yes, I believe in God. Yes, I believe He loves me. But I can't seem to reconcile that truth with the unexpected pains in life. Even if my soul aches with the effort of keeping everything together, the way I think it should go.

He runs a hand through his golden waves, making them stick up at odd angles. The amber light sets the unruly strands aglow. They look so soft, and I wonder what it would feel like to run my fingertips through them.

I'm not usually the night owl like Harrison and Eden. Maybe the late hour is affecting my judgment.

17

Harrison

How is it possible a cast of firelight changes Zoe's eyes from chocolate to warm honey? They're round, vulnerable after my question about her controlling everything. I didn't mean to upset her. But my desire to know what's going on in that list-making, rule-following, and frustratingly stubborn, albeit pretty, head of hers keeps me up at night. Literally.

With the stretching silence, I figure a little levity is in order. "How about a ride on this ladder?"

I stride over to one of the rolling ladders attached to the long wall of bookshelves and waggle my brows at her.

She giggles. "Don't be ridiculous."

"That's my word. And, yes, this entire thing is ridiculous"—I wave a hand, gesturing to the mansion—"but here we are. Let me help you live out your *Beauty and the Beast* fantasy. I know how much you loved that library."

That got her. She takes a bare footstep forward. "I thought the same thing about this place when I walked in." Her silk robe and nightgown billow out as she walks toward me. It constricts my throat. I have to clear it twice to swallow.

"Won't we wake someone?" There's the tiniest twitch at the corner of her mouth.

"Nah, no one's around. Don't whoop too loud and we'll be fine."

She climbs two rungs, her cool, smooth hand in mine. The back of her head is at eye level for once. Her hair, down around her shoulders, wafts its soft floral scent and brushes against my nose. This is dangerous.

"All right, hang on tight."

Keeping my arms on either side of her, gripping the ladder, I run her down to the end of the wall. Her laughter bubbles out, musical and free.

Then I start us back to the other side. There's a little rumble as we go, but they must keep this thing well-oiled.

"This reminds me of when we were kids." Her tone is bright. "When you'd take Eden and me to the park by my house. Do you remember us begging you to keep pushing us on the merry-go-round?"

"Yes, I was your personal pack mule. More, Harrison! Faster! Again!" I mock their childish voices.

"You were such a good big brother. Still are." I slow us on another run to the other side. "And friend." Her voice is wistful now.

So that's how she still sees me. A big brother. A friend. Nothing more. It doesn't surprise me, but it still twists a dull knife into my gut.

"I'm so glad you were part of my childhood," I say.

"Me too. I love that we grew up together. Knew each other as kids."

When we stop, away from the fireplace now, she turns

the top half of her body. We're nearly nose to nose. I can hardly make out her features. Not that I need to, I've had them memorized—every freckle, every lighter fleck in her deep brown eyes, every expression her full lips can make—for years.

There's a gleam in her eyes, dancing in the dim light. "I remember your Zac Efron–hair stage back in his *High School Musical* days."

"And I remember the first and only time you got those blond highlights that turned yellow then somehow green."

She shudders. "Don't remind me." Her mouth puckers to the side, and her nose wrinkles. "I've witnessed you burp the national anthem."

"Hey, it was the fourth of July, I was being patriotic." I flash her a wide grin. "And I've seen you in your rebellious phase"—but I amend when she swats my stomach—"not that you had much of one." When her lips thin, I add, "A week, tops."

Tilting her head, along with her smile, she adds softly, "You didn't really have one either. You were always *you*. Funny. Good and brave. Even when we were kids."

She thinks I'm good and brave. My words to her return to haunt me. This burden to do everything right, to *be* good enough is so heavy sometimes.

"But you're not a kid anymore." My words escape in a gruff almost-whisper. "And neither am I."

Before I can tell it to stop, my left hand travels toward her face. When my calloused fingers make contact with the softness of her cheek, there's a swift intake of breath, and I'm honestly not sure if it's her or me. My thumb rubs a slow circle in the hollow beneath her cheekbone. Her eyes widen, locked with mine, as she gulps air. So do I.

Her lips part. Is she about to tell me to back off? Or the other thing . . . the thing I dream about? Her lips look so inviting. My head dips forward an inch.

But then she stills. Too still, like a deer who's spotted me with my bow in the woods. Too much like the other times I've messed up with her.

I start to lower my hand. "I'm sorry, Zo. I don't know what I was thinking." Unsure what to do with the offending appendage, I shove it down to my side.

But I *do* know what I was thinking. Something I find myself thinking of often, and what I've only admitted to myself and a little bit to Jake, of all people.

She hasn't moved yet, but her mouth opens and closes as if gearing up to speak.

My other hand scrapes at the back of my neck. "I—"

There's a creak behind me. I turn to find Victoria sweeping through the doorway. "Well, well, well. Look who thinks just because they have certain privileges with their *little* show, they can do whatever they want."

Victoria's scowl is as furious with me as it is with Zoe. Good. Maybe she'll stop her pointless flirting.

Zoe clambers off the ladder, pulling her already secured robe closer to her neck. If she yanks that thing any tighter, she'll choke. "Victoria, I'm sorry. I—we—"

Victoria's frown turns smug. "We have rules for a reason, Miss Dufour. Without them, this retreat would be chaos, anarchy." She crosses her arms.

Zoe holds a finger in the air. "Now, normally I would agree wholeheartedly with you on the virtues of rules, but really, we meant no harm."

Victoria checks the zipper of her own neck-to-toe adult onesie pajamas with "I Luv Darcy" stamped all over them and pats her hair in sponge curlers, the pink kind my mom used to put in Eden's hair as a kid before Christmas and Easter.

When Victoria shakes her head in disgust and the rollers clack together like the world's worst human wind chime, it's hard to keep a laugh from escaping my clamped mouth.

Zoe catches my eye with a twinkle of mischief in hers. I have to put a fist to my lips and feign a cough.

"Your podcast doesn't mean the rules don't apply to you," Victoria continues.

I salute Victoria, which causes one of her eyes to squint and tremor. "We get it. Rule-followers from now on. Also, it was me. I convinced Zoe to meet me here, so it's my fault. Blame me." That makes me sound like I *am* a rake from one of Zoe's stories. Things didn't usually—i.e., ever—end well for those dudes.

Victoria *hmphs*.

Zoe wrings her hands. "I was nervous about the speed dating tomorrow, and he was giving me some advice."

Victoria seems to consider this. I love that Zoe is always the peacemaker trying to reach peoples' softer side. "Maybe if you want to find your perfect gentleman like you claim to then you should spend less time skulking around in libraries alone with this rogue"—she juts a thumb in my direction—"and more time focusing on what the retreat is all about."

Yup, I'm playing the part of the scoundrel here. But the difference between me and those other fictional guys? I actually do have Zoe's best interests at heart.

We both apologize again. Victoria bobs her head, sending her rollers rattling. "Good, now get back to your *separate* wings."

She pads off to bed.

Grabbing the teacups and saucers, I return them to the kitchen. There's an awkward silence again. It slices me open. I did this. I made it weird.

We approach the part of the mansion where we'll have to split up.

Reaching out, I almost touch Zoe's arm but let my hand drop instead. "Zoe, I'm sorry. I didn't mean to—"

"I know." She smiles before studying her feet. "I'm sure my pathetic love life, or lack thereof, is truly pity inducing."

That's what she thinks? That I would pity-kiss her?

"No, that's not—"

She holds a hand out to stop me but lets a humored sound from the back of her throat break free. "It's okay, Harrison. Really. Besides, nothing happened. So no big deal."

No big deal. For me, it was like the whole world had stopped spinning. Like everything had changed in an instant. But apparently not for her.

Imitating her casual stance, I shove a hand into my pocket. "Oh, good. I'm glad. Yeah, I would never want there to be weirdness between us."

"Right. We're such good friends, and I would never want to lose that. Lose *you*." Her brows rise, an earnest, almost pleading expression on her face.

"Never. You're stuck with me." So weak. I'd love nothing more than to stick my head into the nearest expensive, antique vase and rap the side like a gong.

But her smile is warm as she adds, "Good. Ditto. Because I need you tomorrow. I'm still nervous about all of this. We both know my dating history reads like a country song."

"I've got you. I'm here." *For you. Always.* "I can act as your chaperone while I film, okay?"

She chews her lip but agrees. "You'll be by my side all day? Promise?"

"Of course. I'll help you ward off any potential disasters."

"All right. I feel better." She takes a timid step forward. "Thank you."

Then she slips her hands through my arms, threading them around my torso, and hugs me tight. I don't trust myself, so I keep my arms at my sides and then give her upper back a quick pat.

She leans her head back and steps away. "Good night."

"G'night," I mumble as I make my way to my room. The warmth of her against my chest seems to have imprinted on my skin. I place a hand where her head rested moments before.

This will be torture. How will I make it through this retreat, let alone beyond, if she does find her dream guy here? I'm starting to think my own love life sounds more like a Greek tragedy.

I've always secretly wondered what she'd do if I showed I cared about her as more than a friend and tried to kiss her again after the catastrophic first attempt in high school.

Now I have my answer.

18

Harrison

Early, watery sun is beginning to pool on the floor. But I won't sleep anymore now. No way. So this nonmorning person might as well get ready and seek caffeine in the form of black coffee. Lack of sleep and a constant looping replay of last night has me on edge.

My shower is hot and refreshing but does little to scrub the confusing thoughts from my head. After dressing and grabbing my gear, including my caricature signs I made last night when I was supposed to be sleeping, I start toward the door. There's a rustle of sheets behind me.

"Hey, wait up. I'll come with you." Jake hops out of bed. "You're up early."

"You a morning person?"

"Yeah, old habits, I guess." He chuckles before grabbing his clothes and toothbrush and heading toward the bathroom.

"Our escorts in Syria were military guys. So we were up before the sun most days."

He laughs, but there's a strained quality that says what his words don't. There's more to his baggage story than open-book Jake Rydberg divulged. I'm reminded that, despite his friendly demeanor, there's a whole lot I don't know about this guy.

My phone chirps its ringtone—the NFL football theme—from the inside pocket of my frock coat as soon as the bathroom door *snicks* shut. The juxtaposition of the nineteenth-century clothing and my smartphone isn't lost on me as I snatch it out. The screen reads, "Boss Man." I swipe it to answer.

"Hey there, Harrison. Not too early for ya, I hope." The guy expects a lot from his employees, but he's the first to arrive in the morning and the last to leave at night. With my rotating security shifts, I've seen him bent over his desk early and late.

"No, sir. Jake and I were about to head out for another day of filming, actually."

"Good, good." He already sounds distracted. I'm probably on speakerphone while he's at his desk. "I hope working with Jacob is going well so far. He was really eager to work with you."

His formal use of *Jacob* reminds me that I use *Jake* like we're old friends.

My forehead pinches together. "He was? Why?" I mean, up until this opportunity, I'd been hired to be a glorified gargoyle at this station.

"I think he's aware of some of your other work. You know, before."

Great, so everyone knows about my career-bombing experience. But if that's true . . .

I pace to the fireplace and back, gripping the back of my neck. "You know, about that—"

It's not like I didn't disclose the basics on my résumé, but does he know the details?

"Harrison, I make it my business to personally vet all employees at Minnesota Metro News and Entertainment. It wasn't a surprise, and I don't think Stan gave you a fair shake." At the mention of my previous boss, the muscles in my shoulders snap straight, rigid. "Besides, I think you showed great strength of character, doing what you did."

I guess it should be no surprise the bigwigs in newscasting know each other nor that they have the scoop on the hirings and firings in the biz.

"Sir, if I could explain—"

"No need, no need. It's all water under the bridge, as far as I'm concerned."

It *is* all water under the bridge, so why does it feel like I'm still in the bridge's shadow?

All I can muster is, "Thank you, sir."

"That's why I'm giving you a chance to prove yourself here. I've seen your work and respect it, just like Jacob. And right now, you're an incredibly overqualified security guard—not that there's anything wrong with being a security guard—but you're not using your talents there. I'd love to see you behind the scenes of one of my global news hours, orchestrating everything in Chicago."

My pulse thrums at the idea, but my stomach sinks with the weight of the responsibility and the desire to show him what I'm made of. This is my chance. I can't blow it.

A swift visual of Zoe blows through my mind. I can't let personal feelings ruin an opportunity like this. Not this time. Suddenly the thought of being just friends, which is what she wants anyway, makes all the sense in the world. I can't believe I was about to mix work with romantic relationships . . . again. You'd think I'd learn.

"Thank you, sir. I'd love that, and I'll show you I can handle it."

"Good, son. I know you will. And I know you'll do whatever

it takes to create the best show. I'm sure your last experience has opened your eyes to some of the difficult but necessary ins and outs of this industry."

What does he mean? "I understand there are difficult choices, and that editing shapes perception, but I hope honesty is first and foremost. Behind the camera and in front of it. Because that and my integrity mean a great deal to me in my work and personal life, sir."

"Mm-hmm," he replies as though his mind has already moved on. There's a *shoosh* of rustling papers. "Say, the other reason for the call is that my wife and I are planning to stop out to the retreat for the tournament. She's been asking me since we became sponsors to come out. I've already arranged everything with the hosts and the manor staff."

"Sounds good, sir. I look forward to seeing you and meeting your wife."

"I have something I'd like to go over with you at some point while I'm there, too. Something I want you to keep an open mind for. But I don't have the time right now." His voice grows more distracted.

"Sure, no problem."

"Hey, what's that cravat like? I'm told I have to wear one."

"Imagine high-class strangulation."

His laugh is one loud bark. "Great. What's a little torture if it keeps my wife happy, eh? See you soon."

We hang up.

Jake returns from the bathroom, fully ready. But I stop him before he reaches the door. "Hey, Mr. Kellsner told me you wanted to work with me . . . even after you knew about the *situation* at my other job. Why?"

"I guess because I knew enough to know that we'd get along fine. That you were a man of integrity and principles, and especially after everything with *my* last gig, sometimes not knowing who to trust in the field, that was important."

I absorb this for a minute and incline my head. Grabbing my own leather shoulder bag, we start toward the door, but Jake pauses, his hand on the door handle.

"Can I ask what really happened? Your side?" His expression is open, curious, but not greedy like so many who've asked before.

I find myself saying, "I was one of the producers and did some audio engineering at a station in Cincinnati. An investigative journalist and I started seeing each other."

My hand grips the back of my neck, heat prickling there. "Looking back, though, I'm not sure if the feelings were mutual, or if we were caught up in the excitement of our careers and similar goals."

Not to mention the fact that I'd been trying my hardest to forget about Zoe and what had happened between us at the time, but I keep that to myself.

Jake watches me without judgment in his gaze, but a wash of shame trickles down my back regardless. "This coworker and I were working on some big stories for the investigative reporting news segment—a huge drug trafficking ring, an unsolved kidnapping, and a slew of related home invasions. But as she dug deeper into each, I started to notice things that weren't right."

"Like what?"

A gust of air bursts from my lungs. No one has listened to me. I mean, Eden and Zoe probably would have if I had let them. "She lied to witnesses to get their testimonies, she bribed informants, she trespassed her way onto crime scenes, skewed quotes, or took things out of context if it supported her take on the story. I even saw her in the editing room without permission, editing her own footage to tell the story *her* way."

My jaw joint pops from clamping it. "She didn't care about the truth or the victims who she felt got in her way. I couldn't believe the person she turned out to be after I tried to do everything right to make sure her stories went well, that she had the right resources and contacts, that she knew the rules, the *right* way of doing things."

I pinch the bridge of my nose. "I had to make a choice, but it wasn't a tough one. I told her she needed to stop, but she didn't. So I went to our boss the same day we broke up. This wasn't the way I wanted things to end, but I couldn't let her continue doing what she was doing."

"Then your boss fired *you*?" His face contorts.

My laugh is without humor. "Yeah, that's the kicker. Apparently, those rules of integrity and honesty were only on paper. They looked at her willingness to bend and often break the rules as taking initiative and doing whatever it took to get the job done."

Those last words bring back something Mr. Kellsner said earlier, but I brush them away. So far he's done nothing but encourage honest work.

Jake claps a hand over my shoulder. "I'm sorry, man. That's really rough."

"Mmm," I agree. "That's why, despite what I might've said before about Zoe, I really shouldn't involve myself with anyone related to work again. I've learned my lesson."

Am I trying to convince him, or myself, or both?

His nod is doubtful. "Thank you for telling me. And for what it's worth, I'm on your side. What your ex and your boss did wasn't right."

"Thanks." And just like that, my shoulders lift, feel lighter.

We head out the door and downstairs to the drawing room.

Soon Victoria joins us with a poster full of calligraphed women's names. It really does look like a fantasy basketball bracket. "Suitor 1, Suitor 2," and so on is under each of the women's names. Zoe's has the same, with various times and activities next to each one.

The image of her rounded eyes as I slid my hand along her

jaw to her cheek last night blips through my mind. Will one of these guys do the same, maybe even finish what I started by kissing those full lips? Will they make her laugh like I can make her laugh?

Stop.

I need to stop torturing myself and find some caffeine, so Jake and I hunt some down in the kitchen. When we return to the drawing room, steaming cups of dark roast in hand courtesy of the mansion's sweet older head cook—who, as in many a historical drama, asked us to call her "Cook"—Zoe and Eden are there. Others trickle in.

Cook and her staff spread food on silver platters along a buffet table.

Sidling up behind Zoe in the buffet line, I clear my throat and say, "Hey." Smooth.

Back straight, she turns to face me. "Hey," she returns.

So she's feeling weird, too.

I rub my jaw, beard bristling beneath my fingertips. "I was wondering if we could chat before the speed dates start?"

She freezes.

"I want to go over our plan for today, for everyone," I try to assure her, including my sister and Jake in my sweeping gesture. "I had some ideas that may help you"—*never mind that those ideas were the result of staying up half the night thinking about you*—"and Eden, too, if she wants, to narrow down your choices."

Her obvious relief I didn't bring up last night writhes in my gut.

She swats back one of the curled pieces of hair at her temple. "Oh, sure. Of course."

All four of us fill plates of eggs, diced potatoes, juicy sausages, and fall-harvest Honey Crisp apples, the aromas already making my mouth water as we find a sunlit table in the corner of the window-lined breakfast room.

After I've shoveled in two mouthfuls of steaming hot eggs and gulped down the last of my coffee, I retrieve the accordion folder from my bag.

"I was thinking last night, what if we have a ranking system for these dates? Like Jake and I can be an outside perspective—"

"A guy's perspective?" Eden's brows rise.

Jake's eyes light up. "I like the sound of that." His palms rub together.

Zoe tilts her head as she seems to consider it. "What did you have in mind? I guess our listeners always hear the lady's perspective, maybe a little changeup could be fun."

I pass Jake half of the folder contents, spreading mine out in front of me. "Okay, so I drew these to represent different traits and characteristics. We can hold them up along with a number"—I pluck two whiteboard paddles and dry-erase markers from my bag—"at any time during your dates to tell you how we think the dude is holding up in that area."

They crack smiles, but I can tell Zoe is skeptical.

"What characteristics are you ranking exactly?" A cute little wrinkle forms on the bridge of Zoe's nose.

"Things like sense of humor"—I hold up a caricatured Regency-dressed guy laughing, his too-big mouth open wide, head thrown back, with the word *Humor* in huge letters above it, while Jake holds up his own copy of the same thing—"athleticism, strength, brains, compatibility/things in common." Each of the traits is accompanied by a humorous cartoonish guy in various poses or activities and the words big enough so the ladies can read them from afar.

Then I raise a caricature dressed as a knight in shining armor riding a tiny, Chihuahua-sized steed. "And one I know you'll approve of, Zoe—chivalry. Because a man *should* treat a woman with respect and show he's willing to put her first."

Zoe studies me a moment, and my neck heats under her

gaze. But she claps her hands, her face splitting into a brilliant smile. The kind that makes me feel like I'm choking on air.

I swallow past my seized throat. "Each characteristic will be ranked from one to ten. The total will be added up at the end of the date, and the score will rank the suitor in a category."

I lay out the category sheet for them to look over, and Zoe shares a smile with me. Maybe the use of her own nickname for her perfect modern-day gentleman will win her over to this idea.

> 60–48 points = Modern Lord Pembroke
> 47–36 points = Duke of Budding Potential
> 35–24 points = Marquess of Mediocrity
> 23–12 points = Baron of Meager Prospects
> 11–0 points = Mr. Collins

"Oh, my word. I should say you have way too much time on your hands, but . . . it's great. Hilarious." Zoe turns to Eden and Jake. "What do you guys think?"

Eden shakes her head and taps her knuckles against my shoulder. "Bro, you are *so* unhinged. And I love it."

Jake slaps the table. "I'm down for that."

We all agree and finish eating. Eden and Zoe put their heads together, already guessing who they may have matched with on their pre-retreat compatibility tests.

A light bell rings.

At least Jake and I will get some humor and enjoyment out of this otherwise torture session. I have to remind myself that my ratings need to be fair and for Zoe's good. Not mine. And not because I want to send each and every potential suitor packing. On a plane. With a one-way ticket. Far, far, *far* away.

I grumble on an exhale. If ever there was a conflict of interest, this would be it.

19

Zoe

It's a good thing Harrison didn't bring up last night. It's for the best. Nothing happened anyway. If I squint my brain real tight, I may have imagined the whole thing. The heated stare, his large but oh-so-gentle hand brushing against my cheek, the lean in and his eyes trained on my lips...

Yup, definitely imagined that.

I roll my shoulders back as I open the envelope Victoria hands me with a sniff and narrowed eyes. *Someone* isn't over it.

Scanning the list of eight names, I'm not surprised to find Ben Rowley there. But then my brows knit together when I stumble over Milton Birtwhistle and the older gentleman, George Fink.

"What?" I groan in a whisper.

I'm not trying to hurt anyone's feelings, but this isn't what I expected. At all.

Harrison nudges my elbow.

I show him my list. His eyes bulge as he absorbs it, and his lips clamp shut.

Eden shows me she has a date with Tom first. Another odd pairing. The guy's a total jock who has already regaled the group with tales of his best marathon times. Eden and I don't mind walking for exercise, but neither of us is running anywhere unless a bear (or Mr. Collins) is behind us or Eden's no-sugar banana chocolate cake (or Mr. Darcy) is in front of us.

Aspen, a man-bun-wearing fair trade coffee shop owner, made her list. Eden checks him out across the breakfast room with a half smile. "I bet he's a dead ringer for a regal forest elf with his hair down, and I'm not mad at it."

She doesn't catch the way Jake stops behind her, his usual easygoing smile fading.

Darren is also on her list. No surprise there, as far as their interests go.

Pointing to his name, I mutter, "Hey, maybe he'll actually show up this time."

"He better" is Jake's automatic response.

When we all turn an eye to Jake, he lifts a shoulder. "What? It was inexcusable for him to stand you up."

I raise a brow at Eden, but she's taken up watching Jake pack his equipment bag like it's now her full-time job.

Ben catches my eye from his perch by the window, the sun illuminating his hazel eyes and chestnut hair—women have been trying to bottle that color for decades. He really is handsome, and somehow, his long, lean body looks at home in his Regency attire. There's a twinkle in his eye as he points to his schedule and mouths, "See you later!" I give him a thumbs-up. At least I have one date to look forward to.

I wish Eden well on her dates and whisper to Jake, "Don't go easy on these guys, okay?"

His side grin is wicked. "Not on your life, or hers." With a wink he's gone, trailing behind her.

Sophia snags me to compare dates. "Ooh, you have Milton, too." Her eyes alight. "I can't wait to talk to him. He knows so much about the Regency period."

I point to another name on her list. "You have Matthew." I tip my lips into a knowing smile. "He's been sending brooding stares your way."

Her grin is doubtful, but she blushes at my hint about the handsome software engineer. I hug her and send her off.

Cutting through the crowd, Harrison on my heels, I hunt down Milton. My first date.

Milton eyes me, then Harrison's towering form behind me. "Hello, Zoe. I mean, Miss Dufour." His hands fidget with his schedule before he stuffs it into his inside jacket pocket.

He's sporting sideburns, or as they were called in Regency times, "side-whiskers." One flutters when he offers me a wobbly bow. I squint. Are those glued on?

I drag my attention away from the tenuous hold of his faux-whiskers and curtsy in return. "Let's go with first names, shall we?" I turn a hand toward Harrison. "This is Harrison. He'll be filming for the podcast and will act as chaperone for us."

Harrison thrusts out a hand for Milton to shake. "Yup, don't mind me. Just pretend I'm not here."

Milton is among the ninety-nine percent of the retreat goers who've signed the waivers and agreed to be filmed, so there's no surprise, only a hint of nerves and more than a little excitement on his face.

"Our activity is feeding the ducks and birds down by the pond," I read from our schedule, then stuff it into my reticule.

We start outside and descend to the small lake surrounded on one side by swaying weeping willows. Their yellow autumn leaves twirl their last dance, then blanket the grass and sprinkle onto the water's surface like confetti at a farewell party.

Milton indicates the large blanket laid out for us at the water's edge. "M'lady . . . shall we?"

He teeters, then slumps onto the blanket, but straightens his back once seated.

I follow suit, and admittedly, I'm not much more graceful. Harrison sets up the camera on a swiveling tripod behind Milton so he's within eyesight of me. Giving me a 3-2-1-action, Harrison nods and points.

Somehow I'm compatible with this guy—Lord, have mercy—and I need to give him the benefit of the doubt.

I reach for the basket of cracked corn and seeds provided for us. "So, Milton, what do you do?"

"Oh, I guess you could say a little of this and that. I run a Jane Austen fan club."

That's not exactly what I meant, but I roll with it.

"A Jane Austen fan club? I'm in a few myself. Would I know yours?"

I toss a handful of the bird feed. The geese and ducks wandering at the pond's shore push and shove like a group of toddlers at snack time, gobbling it up with boisterous honks and quacks.

Milton's chest puffs out. "You might have heard of it. We walked in the annual Jane Austen Festival parade around Lake Harriet last year. My four sisters, our pet pot-bellied pig, Bingley, and I."

Milton tries to throw the bird feed but only manages to hit the corner of the blanket. Over Milton's shoulder, Harrison holds up the Athleticism sign with a number two. I roll my eyes, but Milton doesn't catch it. He's busy shooing a determined male mallard away from our blanket, for which he receives a nip on the ankle.

My jaw aches with a held-in laugh, but I have the feeling Milton wouldn't appreciate the humor. Meanwhile, Milton's lips press together as he adjusts his cravat—high on his neck but still showing a considerable tuft of neck hair.

Harrison lifts the Humor sign with a zero. I mouth, "Come on." It's only the start of this date.

I rub the space between my brows. "Your sisters and—and your pig"—I swallow—"are in the club, too?"

"Yes, it's just them and me. I'm the president, Bingley's the unofficial vice president and official mascot. Though I think we're making progress in offering our Janeite expertise where it's so needed." He turns a doleful eye to me. "In fact, I was thinking that perhaps you'd let us be on your podcast so we can share our knowledge with your listeners." His bushy brows lift.

Glancing at Harrison, then back to Milton, I stutter, "I-I, well, maybe. We have a lot already planned out, with all of the episodes based around this retreat for the near future. But maybe after we're done with the series."

Harrison raises a thumbs-up, then crosses his eyes at me, probably because I have this tense grimace/smile I can't seem to remove. Not a great look for the camera.

"If you insist . . ." He trails off as I stand and grab the basket of bird feed.

"Come on, let's feed these birds their breakfast." I keep my voice light.

As I saunter toward the wooden dock, I pass Harrison. I cross one eye, stare him down with the other, and stick out my rolled tongue, my go-to when we were kids. This natural, God-given talent always worked wonders to elicit a chuckle from the tough guy no one else could crack.

Now is no different. He chokes on a burst of a laugh and points to the rolling camera.

Milton helps steady me on the swaying planks of the dock. I look back to Harrison, who holds up the Chivalry sign with a number five.

Milton makes a wide, sweeping gesture. "You know, this reminds me so much of that BBC miniseries version of *Pride and Prejudice*. The pond scene with Colin Firth."

This must be why we were matched because this guy might actually rival me on his love and borderline obsession with everything Regency. *And* he appreciates the "correct" version of P and P.

"Right. It's the moment I think Elizabeth starts to see Mr. Darcy in a different light. I mean, hunky and soaking wet from the pond doesn't hurt the matter, either."

He dips his small round chin. "I always felt I would've been perfect for the role."

"As Mr. Darcy?"

"Mm-hmm." Milton grabs a handful of the bird feed from the basket with gusto. The hungry ducks are already gathering beneath us when a male mallard—likely the same aggressive one from before—flies up to his hand. He pecks at Milton's fist with impatient squawking quacks.

"Let go, Milton!"

Milton emits a series of his own squawks as he bats the duck away. "Shoo, you little beast!" Both he and the duck flap. The duck manages to send himself airborne, while Milton teeters one-legged on the edge, then plummets into the water with a giant belly flop.

The cold water drenches my hem. The dock shakes, but Harrison is at my side in a second to stabilize me. His hand wraps around the curve of my lower back and waist.

Milton breaks the water's surface, gasping, his arms thrashing, grasping for anything. The lake drops off faster than I thought. It's deep here.

"Milton, over here!" But he won't open his eyes. He's panicking, not listening.

I look up at Harrison. "I don't think he can swim."

Harrison squares his jaw and starts removing his boots, waistcoat, and jacket. He dives in and swims toward Milton with powerful strokes. Milton has managed to push himself away from the dock and is nearing the middle of the lake. But Harrison reaches him, loops an arm around his middle, then swims sidestroke with Milton in tow.

When I meet them at the shore, Milton is somehow beaming. He pulls his drenched jacket off and slams it onto the ground with a *schlop*! "How's that for a Mr. Darcy impersonation?"

Mouth hanging open, I manage to stammer, "Are you all right?"

"Me? Never better." He states this as though I hadn't witnessed his near drowning.

Milton's hands prop on his waist. He's a sight to behold—his sideburns hanging off his face like droopy dog ears and white shirt now completely see-through, with the obvious outline of his *very* hairy chest and stomach. He reminds me of the way my favorite teddy bear, Bru-Bru, looked whenever my dad wrestled him away from me as a kid to wash him.

But where Bru-Bru was endearing and adorable even sopping wet . . . Milton is . . . well, just very soggy.

I whirl around, the words "Harrison, are you okay?" on my lips, but they end in a squeak.

He's catching his breath, and I have to catch my own as I take in the spectacle that is Harrison in a *wet . . . linen . . . shirt*. Whoa. A broader, dark golden-haired Darcy, every muscle in his chest and shoulders outlined to perfection. My eyes flit up to meet his. He catches me staring. There's the tiniest curve to the corner of his lips. Almost shy.

"I'm fine." He shakes out his dripping waves of gold and steps near.

I keep my gaze trained above his neck, with some effort might I add.

We all agree to cut the date short so the guys can change their clothes before the next activity.

With a bow of the head, Milton bids us goodbye but adds to Harrison, "Thank you, sir, for your assistance. I'm indebted to you."

Following Milton's *squish-squashing* steps, we crest the hill and Harrison leans close. "So any guesses where Milton landed on my rating scale?" His words are a warm whisper that tickles the sensitive skin beneath my ear as he squeezes out the sodden edges of his shirt.

I slant my head to peek up at him. "I'm thinking he didn't get the Lord Pembroke stamp of approval."

"Even without adding up the scores, I'm pretty sure he landed straight at Mr. Collins." He tips an invisible cap. "Promising start, Miss Dufour. If I had anything to compare it to, I'd call that a record."

"All I hear is there's nowhere to go but up." I wag my head a little and wink. Did I wink at Harrison? What's the matter with me?

He pulls at his drooping cravat, a tinge of red to the skin of his neck—probably the wet clothes and chilled breeze.

Seven more suitors to go. At least Ben is my last date, which is a comfort.

I best George again in a second round of a popular Regency parlor game, "I Love My Love with an A." We take turns alphabetically filling in the blanks of a little saying, first *a* words, then *b* words, and so on. We make it all the way to *u*, and then George forfeits.

He stands, giving me a round of applause. The crinkles already present at the corners of his eyes deepen. "You're too good, Zoe. And might I add, for having such an innocent look, you're a cutthroat competitor, aren't you?"

Harrison cough-laughs into his fist. "That's not the half of it."

George runs a hand through his salt and-pepper hair. "It's always the innocent-looking ones you have to watch out for."

"Don't I know it." Harrison winks at me, and it's my turn to feel heat creep up my neck.

George returns to his seat at our small round table in the drawing room, then reaches across to squeeze my hand, but in a fatherly way. "You remind me of my daughter. Headstrong. Knows what she wants. Nothing wrong with that. That's why you'll know when you find your person."

His gaze drifts across the room to the older widow, Joan, who came here with her daughter. Joan is clearly humoring a younger man as they paint portraits. Horrible, horrible portraits.

George sighs. "Finding your person may only happen once in this life. So when you find them, hold on to them. I held on to my Emmaline until her very last breath, and I have no regrets."

"But maybe you can find love again even after you've lost someone," I hint, nudging my chin in Joan's direction as she lets out a full, lilting laugh.

He makes a thoughtful "hmm," still studying Joan.

When our hour is up, with reluctance I stand and get ready to leave. "That was a lot of fun."

He takes my hand and does the gentlemanly half bow over it, then releases it. "It sure was, but I hope you don't mind me saying I can see a future with you as my feisty bridge partner, but perhaps not—"

I touch his arm. "That sounds great. I'll help you beat those guys anytime you like." He told me earlier about how he and a group of retired architects get together once a week to play bridge and pick on each other. "And, George?"

"Yes?"

"Don't be afraid to try again. Really. Who cares about what some compatibility test says or doesn't say anyway?"

His face creases with his wide grin. "I thought you were all about the rules and checklists."

I was surprised to learn the older man had actually heard of my podcast—from his daughter, of course, who also signed him up for the retreat.

Harrison's eyes are on me as I shift on my satin-slippered feet. "Yeah, I don't know. Maybe there's room for something undefined, too. Something no test or list can tell you."

Today was proof of that.

George's expression softens. "Well then. You leave room for that 'something undefined' on your other dates this weekend, too, won't you?"

The next date, after a take-and-eat lunch, flies by in a blur as we play horseshoes outside. Yup, that's just as dangerous for me as it sounds. Nate is certainly younger than George. But he might be too young for me and too ambitious. I'm ambitious, too. Maybe that's why we were matched. But it sounds like his investment banking career is cutthroat and he's either working hard or partying hard. And that's so *not* me.

The scores Harrison gives this guy with plenty of behind-the-scenes eye rolls may rival Milton for Mr. Collins status.

By the time my last date time slot arrives, I nearly launch myself into Ben's arms in a stranglehold embrace. As it is, I grasp both of his forearms, and Victoria, making her rounds, throws us a side-eye and an *ahem*.

"Am I glad to see you." I sigh and release him.

Ben grins back. "Likewise. I couldn't *speed* through those other dates fast enough."

The admission, especially after not really knowing where I stand with him, warms my heart.

"Shall we?" He offers his elbow, and I take it.

20

Harrison

Zoe stifles another yawn, and I cover one of my own. I hold in a snort at Ben's miffed expression. She misses Lord Smarmington's irritation with her not hanging on his every word—his memories of Yale, his days as a star competitive rower, which they've just discovered their shared interest for, and his travels before deciding to move back to Minnesota.

However, this conversation is better than earlier when he passed the point of polite interest in the podcast and hurtled straight to nosy—asking about the stats breakdown, how many sponsors she has and if she's pitched for more, and what kind of deals she's being offered to broaden the stage for the show. She also told him the station I work for is considering syndication and spots on the network.

They've finished their canvases, which were supposed to be of the indoor garden view in the conservatory—filled to the brim with plants and a koi pond, so basically Zoe's dream room. But with the late-afternoon sun slanting through the glassed-in room and warming it like a greenhouse, and it being the end of a long day, Zoe's eyelids begin to droop.

While Ben tries to reclaim her attention, I retrieve my own sketchbook. I try to capture those lovely lines and contours of her face. The face I see in my dreams at night and the first thing I want to see when I wake.

Yeah, so, how is that "friend thing" working out? I can almost hear Jake asking me. The answer? Not. Too. Good.

"Zoe?" Ben says, bringing me out of my concentrated sketching/ruminating.

She smiles a sleepy smile but can't hide a jaw-cracking yawn.

Rubbing her temples, she says, "Oh, yeah. Ben, sorry. I'm just tired."

I stand, leaving my sketchbook on my vacated chair. Maybe we need to cut this short.

"That's okay." Ben smiles, but there's a tightening near his chin. "This was a long day for you. We can pick up our conversation tomorrow, during the tournament."

"Sounds great." Her stomach rumbles, so I glance at my phone.

I raise a hand, stopping the camera. "Hey, it's almost suppertime anyway."

Zoe pumps a fist in the air in a very un-Regency-like way that makes me laugh. "Yes! Let me look at my blood sugar before we go." Tapping her phone app, she sighs. "It needs re-syncing. I'll have to check it the old-fashioned way. Just a sec."

But when she retrieves her backup manual glucose monitor from her bag and uses the lancing device to draw a small drop of blood from her finger, Ben jumps to his feet, making his chair skid back with a screech on the marble floor. He feigns his own yawn and stretches. "You know, it *has* been a long day actually. I think I'll head up to rest and change for dinner."

Before she has time to answer, he's already bowing his way out of the room.

Her brows scrunch in the middle. "He really does hate blood, doesn't he?"

I crouch at her side, smirking. "I'm sorry, but he loses points in the strength category because of it. That's not just about physical strength, you know."

"Yeah, and he'd need to get over this phobia if we're—I mean, if he and I—"

"First, he needs to make it past my rating system, remember?" I have to interrupt. I'm not ready to hear the end of that statement, but I smile so she knows I'm kidding. It's her choice. It'll always be her choice. Even if it kills me.

She lifts her finger to the device, but it shakes. "I'm so tired and *hungry*. Who knew dating could be such hard work?"

"Here." I gently take her hand, guiding it to the test strip. I've helped her before, especially when she was younger and she didn't have the continuous monitor. It's been a while, though.

The little device beeps—we took too long. So I reset the device, and press her finger to the strip. She doesn't even flinch. She's so strong to have endured everything she has with her own health and her mother's.

Her eyes don't leave my face as we wait the few seconds for the reading. After which she stuffs the monitor in her purse, her expression brightening. "Yup, just tired and—"

"Hangry?" I arch a brow at her but spy a dot of red on her fingertip. An extra drop of blood. I catch it with the side of my thumb before it can drip onto her dress.

She digs through her small bag, retrieving a tissue. "That's why I always come prepared."

I take the offered tissue but blot her finger first before wiping off my thumb.

"Thank you for taking care of me." Her voice is a rough

whisper, filled with something I can't place. "I'm not used to that."

"Anytime" is all I manage for fear my voice will crack like a prepubescent teen. But I want to add, *"Every time. For all time. I would take care of you for the rest of our lives if you let me."* And as the thoughts pass, I know they're true.

After inspecting her finger, now with no sign of the poke or blood, I keep her hand in one of mine and brush a soft stroke up her arm, raising a trail of prickled flesh. I don't know what I'm thinking. I'm *not* thinking. Not clearly, anyway. I have no right. But my brain is one roaring rush of bottled emotions threatening to pop open. Everything I've held in check for so long is burning through my veins.

Her lips part, and there's a little gasp that's like the flip to a switch I didn't know existed inside me.

She's pointing behind me. I turn. My sketchbook is splayed open to the portrait I drew of her. A soft smile plays upon those charcoaled lips, a sweet but vulnerable glint in drawn-Zoe's eyes.

"You drew me." Her expression is full of wonder. "Sometimes, it's like—" Her voice thickens, lips pressing together. "I don't know."

"What?"

"It's like you're the only one who really *sees* me. You see the parts of myself *I* don't even know are there."

Her gaze darts to my mouth, and she steps closer. I wrap my arms around her small frame. Fully. The way I've been dying to.

"I do see you. You're so beautiful, Zoe. Inside and out." I can't bring myself to say more. Not yet. This hug could simply mean friendship to her.

"Thank you. That's an amazing drawing," she whispers. "This was a long, exhausting day. You being with me made it so much better."

My heart thrums in my throat as she surprises me by timidly slipping her hands up my chest, then sliding them around my back. Goosebumps climb up my skin now. Her head nestles against my sternum where I'm sure she can hear the evidence of what I think of her.

Man, this feels so good to hold her. So right. I press her gently but more firmly against me with one arm and take a chance lifting the other hand to cradle the back of her head.

She makes a little contented noise. And I can't help the goofy grin that slides onto my face.

"Zoe?" Her name is pulled from me on a breath.

She moves her head so that her chin is resting against me and looks up. Her gaze roams from my eyes to my lips, then darts back to my eyes. Her fingertips still on my spine.

Okay, now's my chance. I have to ask.

There's a light cough behind us.

We pull apart with deep reluctance, at least on my part, but I keep a hand on her shoulder.

"There had better be a fire or an alien invasion," I growl at the intruder.

I tear my attention away from Zoe to find my sister and Jake in the doorway.

Jake's rounded eyes and slack jaw transform into a wolfish grin. He lets a low whistle punctuate the thick, awkward silence. Eden's hand covers her mouth.

I kind of forgot we weren't alone in the house. Who am I kidding? For those minutes, I forgot I was on planet Earth. The only thing that existed was the thrill of her in my arms.

Eden shakes her head, creases forming on her forehead. Zoe sidesteps from my light grasp. The warmth of her body removed leaves mine cold. I never meant to put that look on Eden's face.

"Eden, I—" I start at the same time Zoe says, "Eden, let me explain."

Eden stops us with a raised hand. Jake's smile melts from his face.

"Do the two of you mind telling me what you're *not* doing?" Eden's hand grips her waist.

When Zoe and I share a confused glance, Eden crosses her arms. "I must be hallucinating or this *is* an invasion of body snatchers, because you said you're definitely *not* together. That you don't feel 'that way' about each other."

Mouth clamped, I glare at Jake. The only person I told was Jake. But he waves his arms in front of him, mouthing, "It wasn't me!" Was Zoe talking about me to Eden?

Eden's eyes squeeze shut for a moment. "I can't believe you guys would hide this from me. Zoe, I told you how happy I would be to have you as a sister"—the full meaning, as in, if Zoe and I married, blasts through me—"and, Harrison, I'm *your* sister. You can tell me anything. I thought you knew that. How long have you been keeping this from me?"

Zoe's the one to finally speak while it feels like someone has superglued my tongue to the roof of my mouth. "Eden, this just happened. Like right now. We didn't plan this."

Eden uncrosses her arms and then recrosses them. "I don't like feeling lied to or like you're going behind my back or something."

Jake reaches for her shoulder, and to my surprise, she leans into his touch.

Before I can pry my mouth open, Zoe steps in again. "We didn't go behind your back because we're not in a relationship. Okay?"

I don't like where this is heading. Did the floor turn to quicksand? Because all of a sudden my stomach lurches into my throat as the wooden floorboards seem to be swallowing me whole.

Zoe gestures between herself and me. "W-we were hugging, that's all. Right, Harrison?" She looks up at me, coaxing me to back her up. "It's been a long day, and he was comforting me. That's all." Again, she lifts her brows at me like she wants me to agree.

My chest. It burns. But I manage to croak, "Right."

That's all? Like it was an everyday, ordinary hug from a friend. Like she didn't feel the tectonic plates shift the way I did. Like it was nothing to her.

Zoe throws a hand in the air and lets out a shaky laugh. "It's not like anything is going on. It was nothing."

And there we go. . . .

How is it that out of the three people in front of me, the one who's known me the shortest amount of time seems to understand the reality of the situation? It's all right there on Jake's face as he shakes his head as if to say, "Sorry, man."

Here's a list for you: I fall for my sister's best friend. Check. I finally hint that I don't think of her as only a surrogate little sister or friend. Double check. Then she immediately and with a surgeon's precision cuts my heart out of my chest and feeds it through a paper shredder by saying it was nothing. Triple check. I need to leave this room.

My fingers flex into fists. "Good thing we're not actually in Regency times, otherwise you'd be forced to marry me—you know, for being caught in a compromising position like that." I'd meant to lighten the mood with a joke, but the words rasp from my raw throat.

"I need to take a shower and get ready for dinner. Excuse me."

They're silent and watch me exit the conservatory. I know I should've probably apologized to Eden, at least for upsetting her. And maybe I will. But not for holding Zoe. Not for my feelings for Zoe. I'll never be sorry for that.

As I stride away, my hands still rolled tight and starting to ache, I realize . . . I love my sister, of course. But I also love Zoe. The big capital L love, the kind that stays, grows, holds. The forever kind. I think I have for a long, long time. I can't even pinpoint the moment my feelings turned to this deep, steadfast love for her. But they did, and there's no turning around—it's already a part of me.

And Eden's partially right. I *was* hiding something from her. I hid the fact that I feel more than friendship for Zoe. Not only from Eden. From Zoe, too. Me, the one who has hypocritically spouted the importance of honesty and integrity. But Zoe didn't hide that she doesn't feel the same about me.

A flash of her arms wrapped around me, her lips parting, gaze glued to mine. Is it possible she does feel more, or did I read everything wrong?

Maybe I need a new plan. Maybe this isn't about her finding "the one" elsewhere, it's about ruling out all of the people who are wrong for her so she can see that I'm right here. Always have been, and always will be. That I might be the right guy for her. I may not be her Modern Lord Pembroke, but I can hope my genuine care for her will cover my multitude of flaws, rough edges, and ways I may not fulfill everything on her list.

One thing's for sure, I can't sit by and stay quiet, helping her find someone else. It will kill me.

Pressuring her to accept my feelings for her or explore the possibility of a relationship with me is out of the question and something I could never do.

I still want what's best for her. But what if *I'm* what's best for her? I have to show her I'm an option. To show her how much I care. How much she means to me.

Entering my room, I stride to the desk with purpose and grab a quill and parchment.

My Dearest Miss Dufour . . .

21

Zoe

I'm supposed to be listening to Victoria's instructions about the first day of our tournament competition. We must choose a partner for each event and sign up with them ahead of time, and the individual winner with the most points at the end of the retreat will receive a prize.

That's as much as I've gathered before my mind wanders to Harrison. He's standing behind me, our backs to the breakfast room windows. His shadow merges with mine on the carpeted floor. Is it possible to *feel* a shadow on your skin?

And even though we're not touching, it's like electrical currents pass back and forth between us.

A jolt of memory—his arm pressing me to his chest, his hand cupping the back of my head—zips up my spine. I jump back with a sharp intake of breath, and my heel finds Harrison's foot. His hand reaches forward, fingers curling gently around my wrist, the rest of his arm steady and warm against mine.

"Save trampling on my toes for the ball, hmm? Of course, I *could* carry you instead, if you'd like." His soft whisper tickles against my ear.

He doesn't sound mad at me—which is what I feared after he left so abruptly last night. The exact opposite actually. And wait, I thought he said he wouldn't dance at the ball. . . .

He releases my wrist but brushes his fingertips against the side of my forearm before removing his touch. This is . . . different, and I can't decide if I should like it or not.

It's a mistake to turn my head. His eyes bore into me like the tingle along the nape of my neck had suggested. Somehow I can feel his gaze on me. A tangible thing. And where it lands, a shiver races straight to my chest.

Last night was nothing. In the real world, away from this fantasy, as Harrison puts it, he'd never go for me. And I would never choose him. Plus, look at how Eden reacted. "Harrison, about last night—"

Victoria pins us with a disgruntled glare. "Must you two always be the unruly pupils of the group? If you simply must converse and it cannot wait"—by her tone, she makes it clear that the earth opening up and swallowing Wyndmere Hall wouldn't be enough reason to interrupt her—"then take it outside." She shoos us with her gloved hands.

Harrison takes my hand lightly in his and tugs me through the room to the glass garden door. I catch Eden's intense study of us and our clasped hands and Jake's slight smirk as we exit.

A twinge pinches at the base of my throat. I apologized to Eden again once we returned to our room last night, but I still sense this invisible barrier between us.

Harrison's hand is warm through my glove as he leads us to a carved stone bench at the edge of a large fountain and high hedge rimmed with the last blooms of the season.

"Here, the stone will be cold." He shrugs off his jacket and lays it over the bench.

I sit and fidget with my kid gloves in my lap. "Thanks."

He sits close enough to share his body heat. The silence stretches, seeming to balloon out and surround us. One of us has to pop it.

"Zoe, I—" he says at the same time I say, "Harrison, about last night—"

We both let out a nervous chuckle. He jumps to his feet and strides to the other side of the circular partial enclosure and then back, palming the back of his neck.

He gestures to me. "You go ahead."

"I was going to say that we don't have to make a big deal out of last night." I hate this tension. Like with Eden, I want things to feel easy between us again.

There's a flash of something—pain?—that passes over his gaze, a tensing of his angled jaw.

That embrace wasn't for "just a friend." It awoke things in me I can't even sort through yet. It complicates things. But I need for things to be *uncomplicated*. I need to look at Harrison and *not* think about the heat that can build behind those beautiful, sometimes mischievous, and always kind deep blue eyes. Or the gentleness of his hands when he caresses my face and holds me to his chest. Or what it's like to run my fingers along the hard and soft ridges of his back, to know what it's like to be seen, really *seen* by him . . .

Oof.

Harrison clears his throat as the corners of his lips pull up a little. I'm full-on staring.

A crease forms in the middle of his forehead. "No big deal? You mean it was nothing? A hug between friends, then." He tips a brow, throwing back the words I used last night.

It *was* nothing. The more I say it, the more it will be true. I pinch the bridge of my nose and try to slow my breathing.

He seems to be enjoying my struggle, waiting with that lopsided grin.

"Right. Nothing." I swallow. Nervous energy forces me to stand. "That's why we should act like nothing ever happened, you know? Business as usual. Can you do that?"

His thumb and forefinger capture his squared-off bearded chin, like he's considering my words. Then with a decisive nod, he says, "No."

"No? What do you mean, 'no'?"

"I won't pretend nothing happened, just like I won't lie and say it was a hug between friends. It wasn't, at least not on my end." He takes another step toward me. "Maybe it was for you, but not for me." His words are a low, raw rumble.

"You're always saying how important honesty is, and I agree." His hand lands in his trouser pocket. "Now it's my turn to be honest with you."

There's something in his eyes I've never seen before. It's like he's trying to crack me open and read what's inside. I feel exposed, vulnerable, and way out of control.

How can I escape his crowbar of a gaze? "Look at what we did to Eden—"

"That's an excuse. She'll get over it. You know it. She loves us both, and we love her."

My hands spin in front of me, grasping for anything. "On paper, we make absolutely no sense, Harrison. We want completely different things, and we approach life in a totally different way."

His arms cross. "And what, you'd prefer to be with someone just like you?"

I wring my hands and walk a short distance, then return. "No, but you've got to admit we couldn't be more different." I start listing our differences on my fingers. "You're a pantser. I'm a planner. You love hunting and camping and roughing it. I've never spent a night outdoors in my life and never will if I can help it. You've never met a sport you didn't love. I would rather be doing anything else, even scrubbing the bathroom, than watch a football game. You dislike all this Regency stuff, while it's the thing I live, eat, and breathe."

I sigh, and he reaches out with a light touch to my arm. "Those are the little things, Zo. Keep them little. Isn't it our shared faith, our love of our families, and everything that makes up our personalties and who we are that add up to the big things? Those are what make us a great team."

I don't love the sports analogy. But I let it go and say the thing that's like the giant gray cloud that blotted out the sun shining through his golden hair. "Yes, but you're more than willing and always used to say you'd *prefer* to move for your career, and I'll never want to live more than thirty minutes from my parents, my mom, in case they need me."

He studies me, a sliver of something I can't place behind his eyes, and a divot forms between his brows, but all he says is, "I'm here. My job is here. Let's not worry about something that's not even an issue right now."

I want to say, *"Yeah, but what about tomorrow or the next day when you're offered that producer dream job out of state again?"*

But instead, my head tips back, eyes squeezing tight. A different kind of truth bubbles out. "Look, I've been hurt when I've strayed from what I need and want in a partner. My list. I can't afford—no, my heart can't take—"

"Let me assure you, Zoe"—he's close, but makes no move to touch me—"your heart is of the utmost importance to me. I'm making it my job to ensure it stays in one piece. It's safe, *you're* safe with me."

"But—"

His palms lift as if in surrender. "Look, I know this is a lot to process after being friends for so long." He does reach out now with a slow, gentle hand to my upper arm. "But if I'm not mistaken, the way you held me back says you might have more than friendly feelings toward me, too."

My feet shuffle under me. "I didn't—I wasn't trying to—I . . ." I trail off, unable to form a coherent response because I don't even know how I feel myself.

He gives my shoulder a little squeeze, then lets me go. "You don't have to know how you feel right now"—as if he read my mind—"but I'm here to say that I won't ignore how *I* feel about *you* anymore. Honesty and integrity are important to me, and it's time I start acting like it."

His arms cross, biceps making the fabric of his shirt strain. For an instant, I want to lay my hand there, but once again, I put that idea out of mind.

Harrison's grin turns wicked. "I'm also not standing by and making it easy on any guy who thinks he's worthy of you."

"So you're not helping me find my modern-day gentleman anymore?" Why does the thought both disappoint me and fill me with relief?

There's a tightness in his expression. Sadness? Resignation? "If you truly find someone who makes you happy and you want to spend your life with him, I won't stand in your way. But that doesn't mean I won't put my hat in the ring in the meantime."

This can't be real. Harrison, try to win *my* heart? I don't want to hurt him, and the last thing I want to do is ruin our friendship, but there's a lot to consider. Like the potential I see with Ben every time we're together, for one, despite his aversion to blood. On paper, Ben and I should be a perfect match.

"I don't know what to say." It's the most truthful answer I can give.

"You don't have to. I know I sort of sprang my feelings on you, and I apologize if it blindsided you. I want you to know where I stand. I care about you, a lot, and as more than a friend. I wasn't ready to admit it, even to myself, for a long time. And this is horrific timing, which I'm no stranger to as you know." He runs a hand through his golden waves. "But I'd like it if you'd at least give me a chance alongside these other guys. Let me court you, too."

He even used the Regency term.

Giving me one of his signature boyish grins, he adds, "I like my chances anyway. No one scored more than Baron of Meager Prospects yesterday—"

Rolling my eyes, I fold my arms over my chest. "According to you."

He keeps going, "Except for maybe George. But we both know he's better as a friend, and after your conversation, I think he might be taken."

I open my mouth, but nothing comes out. Thankfully, there's the chatter and commotion of the group heading into the yard for the first tournament.

"We should rejoin everyone." My statement is microscopic compared to his bombshell and the barrage of thoughts racing through my head.

Harrison reclaims his jacket from the bench, returns to me, and offers his arm. I place my hand in the crook of his elbow. "Would it be too much to ask if you'd partner with me for the first task in the tournament?"

There's a little flutter in my stomach. Then I remember. "Oh, that's right. I already promised Ben I'd partner with him."

We make our way out of the secluded almost-circle hedge.

"That's okay. I'll enjoy beating him."

I give his bicep a playful squeeze. The intrusive thought monster finally wins and purrs its approval. "Really?"

"Of course, it's archery. I've got this in the bag."

I snicker at his waggling brows and teasing smile. "Confidence in spades, huh, Mr. Lundquist?"

"Not so much where you're concerned, but I guess we'll see." A vulnerability I've never heard in his voice roughs up the edges.

We stop. His eyes make a study of my face. His fingers brush underneath my chin, and his head dips closer. I can't seem to move. Is he going to kiss me? In front of everyone?

"Harrison, I—"

"It's okay, Miss Dufour." The words saunter from the bottom of his deep timbre. "I will not take what doesn't belong to me. I won't kiss you until you say it's all right." He drops his hand.

"Until?" There's a tug at the corner of my mouth. The confidence in this man.

"Until." With that confirmation, we meet up with the group.

It's all I can do to plaster on a smile for Eden, Jake, and Ben. A part of me can't wait to see what Harrison will do next. But that's not really fair to him since the plan was always to end up with the person who checks off all the boxes on my list.

22

Harrison

While Zoe's reaction wasn't an immediate confession of love, it wasn't a complete denial of the possibility, either. So there's hope.

Yet how can I be both subtle and truthful while a flock of other guys are still vying for her attention? I give myself a mental slap on the back. A little "attaboy" and "you chump" combo special.

Tossing a wave, I stride past Mr. Kellsner and his wife on the sidelines, here to help judge the tournament competitions today. They're busy chatting with Victoria and a few of the household staff. Mrs. Kellsner is beaming in her Regency dress while Bill grimaces, pulling at his cravat.

"This is right up your alley, right, Lundquist?" Ben sidles up as I examine the available bow assortment.

My pocket buzzes, a pull back to the twenty-first century. It's my father texting. I shut it off without replying. He's called a couple of times this week. I'm busy, but if I'm honest, it's more than that. Thoughts of my father play audio clips in my head of our arguments, of his disappointment, and all the ways, according to him, I'm not living up to the Lundquist name.

Back to the task at hand, I peruse the bows alongside Ben. If only I had my hunting bow.

"Mmm," I agree. "And you?" I choose a quiver of arrows and a bow—not the newest, but in good condition with a sturdy string, taut but not overtightened. The newest isn't always better. Sometimes the broken in, the tried and true, not perfect but the most reliable, can be the best fit.

"Not so much, but I'm a quick study. I've done plenty of hunting with my family near the lake house." Ben's family's "house" on Gull Lake is a mansion, something of which he's always been extremely proud.

He makes a show of picking a bow of his own. Of course he would choose the newest, most expensive-looking option. The tension on that bow is too tight. I already checked.

Mr. Kellsner and his wife stroll toward us. "Harrison!" he calls, raising a hand in greeting. It's strange to see him in Regency attire, though it isn't as big a change from his regular suit and tie as mine is from my usual T-shirts, flannels, and jeans.

I search the crowd for Zoe, but my attention snaps back to my boss and his wife as Ben begins questioning him about the news and entertainment business.

Ben's saying, "You know, I majored in economics at Yale. But I've always been fascinated by television, news, reality TV, the whole process, haven't I, Harrison?" He swats my arm.

He sure squeezed Yale in there, didn't he? I lift a brow at him. "You have?"

Ben throws his head back, chuckling, and whacks me for a second time. I grind my teeth together. If he does it again, so help me . . .

His thumb jabs in my direction. "Harrison is such a kidder. We've been friends since we were kids." Friends? That's a bit of a stretch. More like forced proximity family acquaintances. "I've always admired the 'business' and his family's company. I'm sure you know about his father's work. Is he in on this show?"

Before Mr. Kellsner can answer, I do. "No, my father is not a part of this."

Ben's brows rise. "I'm positive he'd love to support what you're doing. He—"

"No." My glare hopefully communicates *Drop it*.

There's Zoe. She wanders toward us with a grin, and my shoulders relax.

After introductions and a few more questions from Ben, Mr. Kellsner's wife, Delilah, pokes her husband in the arm with her folded fan. "Now, that's all boring business." She opens the fan and flutters it like one of those gossiping mamas in a Regency drama. "Zoe, you have to give me a spoiler. How goes the hunt for your modern-day gentleman? Do you think he's here?"

Ben straightens, chin jutting out. But my breath stops, and I have the sudden urge to do an obnoxious penalty-inducing end-zone dance because Zoe's eyes flit to me. To *me*. Before she turns a bright smile to Delilah and clears her throat. "Maybe. There are certainly some good prospects."

Is it the cool autumn air that raises a flush to her cheeks? She avoids my eye while Ben grins from ear to ear like it's a slam dunk she's talking about him.

Bill tips his head toward me. "We'll be cheering you on. Come on, dear. Let's allow them to get on with their tournament."

Delilah drops the fan tethered to her wrist with a ribbon and reaches up to pinch my cheek. "May you shoot straight and your aim be true." At this, she takes her husband's arm to join the staff and anyone choosing not to participate on the sidelines.

Zoe steps forward to pick her bow from the rack. She lays a delicate finger on one. I catch her eye and give a subtle nod as Ben slides up next to her. "Oh no. You don't want that one."

He hands her one entirely too long for her. "This is the one you want." Her smile lands on me and skips away.

Ben leads her toward the end of a line of participants standing about fifty yards from the targets. Most people have partners already, and while it feels counterproductive to pair with anyone but Zoe, I have to find someone to team up with. I could ask Eden, but that's also counterproductive for her.

When I glance at Eden, she gives me a teasing grin, so maybe she's forgiven me after all.

"I already have a partner, bro. And we're going to kick your behind." Her eyes hold a wicked gleam. "You taught me well." She's what she likes to call a real Lothlorien elf when it comes to her archery skills. It was a favorite game of pretend (which started with make-believe arrows) when she was a kid.

Jake's gaze follows Eden with a look of longing I know oh so well as she takes the arm of a tall, clean-cut guy, Ryan. He's some corporate dude from Edina.

He's the sort of guy our mom would approve of. It brings back a memory of Eden's first love. She was young and chose someone more like her. A free spirit, an old soul—Colton Hayes. Mom hated him and convinced Eden to let him go and look for someone more "appropriate." Now that I think of it, Jake reminds me a little of Colton. But Colton left to "make something of himself" so he'd be worthy of Eden, at least in our mom's eyes. Said he'd come back. Instead, he met someone else, got married, and never returned.

Eden holds Jake's eye as she passes.

I scan the crowd again. There's Sophia Tuffin. I stride

toward her and bow. "Miss Tuffin, will you do me the honor of being my partner for the archery competition?"

"Oh, yes! Thank you." She beams at me as she pushes her glasses up, her braces sparkling in the late morning sunlight.

She takes my offered arm, and we select a bow and quiver of arrows for her on our way to the lineup of players. We find a spot between Zoe and Ben and Eden and Ryan.

Victoria raises a hand. "For this first tournament activity, you will be judged individually, but the way you work together as partners will factor into your total scores. We will have our guest judges and retreat sponsors, Bill and Delilah Kellsner, help score the competition today."

Sophia turns to me. "Would you like to go first?"

"Ladies first, of course. Do you need any help?"

I'm immediately chastised when she steps right up to the white toe-line. "Nope. I've been hunting with my dad and brothers since I was old enough to hold a bow and get my license."

"Maybe you'll give me some pointers." I gesture to the target. "By all means, then, Miss Tuffin. Show everyone how it's done."

She blushes, and her glasses rise as her cheeks round in a wide grin. When Victoria calls first loose, Sophia expertly sinks her arrow into the yellow bulls-eye.

I whoop and she curtsies. Her second hits just left of center. We high-five on her way to stand behind me for my turn. Milton, two places away, is staring with a dazed expression.

"Hey, great job, Sophia!" Zoe gushes as Eden on my other side chimes in, "Secret talent unlocked. Nice, Soph."

Eden's own arrows hit the second and third ring. Not bad.

Zoe's first arrow, on the other hand, sticks into the grass a good four feet from the target. The second does technically hit the target—on the white left corner.

"Nice try" is all Ben offers, with no tips for her next turn.

Removing my jacket for freedom of movement and slipping

on my three-fingered archery glove, I step up to the line, as does Ben on my right. The retreat staff remove our partners' arrows, shoo a couple of stray peacocks wandering the yard, and then clear the field.

I nock my first arrow. Man, I've missed this. The tension as I pull back feels right. I blow out a slow, steady breath, holding myself still until Victoria calls, "Loose!"

The arrow releases with a sharp *whoosh* and gust of air against my cheek. It sails forward and sinks deep into the bulls-eye. As I ready my second, I feel the heat of intense study burning on the back of my neck. I rotate my head. Zoe's staring at me.

Keeping my focus on the task at hand is more difficult the second time. But I manage to land my arrow not more than a centimeter from the first one.

Ben's arrow launches off to the right and sticks in the grass. His jaw grates together before he smooths his features for Zoe, who waits with a sympathetic smile. "It's far too breezy for archery today." She holds a finger into the nonbreezy air.

"I don't think so, but thank you for saying so." Ben returns her smile, and she touches his arm.

His second narrowly misses a peacock wandering into the field again, but it still hits the target's second ring. Maybe he is a quick study.

"Those peacocks won't take a hint." Sophia's full, dark brows dip in the middle.

"Hmm, they're pretty far back now. Someone would have to have a pretty brilliant or pretty wild shot to come close."

Zoe steps up for her second turn, and Ben is not helping her at all. Her eyes round as she tries to nock the arrow but it slips off the string.

"I'll get us something to drink while you take your shots. All right?" Ben calls to her, and he's off across the field as she quietly agrees.

"Hey, Sophie. While you shoot, would you mind if I help Zoe?"

Sophie's already waving me off. "Of course. I'm sure she'll appreciate it."

As I near Zoe, she swings around with an arrow which I duck away from. "Oops, sorry. I have no clue what I'm doing. I've never been trusted with a weapon of any kind, for good reason."

Throwing my bow over my head and across my shoulder, I gently pry her bow and arrow from her fingers. "For *everyone's* welfare, can I please show you how to shoot safely?"

There's a grudging set to her jaw, but she says, "Fine."

She takes a quick inhale as I step behind her. Can she hear my own thudding heartbeat? *Get it together.* But she's so close. If I bend just a little, I could bury my nose in the soft, dark waves piled on top of her head. Already their rose garden scent is wafting over me.

"Here, try holding the bow like this." I try for confident, but the words are a hushed rumble.

"Mm-hmm." She moves her arms where I direct.

"Pull the string back, holding the arrow between your first and middle finger." My mouth is almost against her ear.

"Bring your elbow up, parallel to your shoulder." I hold her hand steady around the recurve grip while taking her other hand to nock the arrow against the string.

We pull the string back together. "Now, empty your lungs. Slowly." Her breath is quiet, and I blow out my own on a light exhale against her ear. She shivers.

"Sorry, didn't mean to distract you." Clearing my throat, I say, "Let go." I'm not sure myself if there's a double meaning.

But we loose the arrow and it sinks into the bulls-eye with a satisfying *thunk*.

I help her nock the second arrow, but before I can coach her, she tips her face back, eyes rounding when our noses almost touch. We're close, too close for me to think clearly. There's the immediate urge to eliminate the inch of space between our lips. But I told her I wouldn't kiss her until she says it's all right.

"Harrison . . ." My name is all air on her parted lips.

Is she about to ask for that kiss now? What this woman does to me . . .

"Zoe?" It's Ben.

With that, the spell is broken and I lose hold of Zoe's hands. The arrow flies.

There's a yelp, a scream, and a disgruntled squawk. We missed the target by ten feet and nearly clipped one of the all-white peacocks. I've never seen a peacock fly that high. It takes off toward the garden labyrinth, the other peacocks trailing behind.

Zoe moves and the air cools my chest where her back was pressed moments before.

She returns to Ben and they continue the competition. But I don't miss the way her eyes keep finding mine.

After the tournament, Sophia and I are named the winners, with Zoe and Ben managing second place. I catch the boy I tasked with delivering a letter to Zoe's room. He's the son of the mansion owners and does odd jobs and chores around the estate. He confirms he delivered it.

Even though I've always said I would tell a person how I feel to their face, so far, that hasn't really worked for me. Maybe an anonymous admirer can speak Zoe's language.

23

Zoe

My Dearest Miss Dufour... Lines from the now-memorized letter delivered earlier today play through my mind as Eden and I make our way to the stables.

... I've been admiring you from afar for too long and simply had to let you know that I see you. What I mean is that I see the person you are—intelligent, kind, and funny. And although you try to hide it behind a beautiful smile that could knock even the proud Darcy on his backside, I can see that you're worried you won't ever find someone, especially someone who meets the criteria you think is necessary, to share your life with. What I'm learning after my own mistakes and heartbreaks is that finding love is not as much about holding tightly as it is about letting go. I'm finding these words much harder to say in person than I anticipated,

but I had to find a way to let you know. Besides, written words somehow have more weight, don't you think?

> Yours,
> A Gentleman in
> Training

P. S. Save me a dance at the ball? I'll be the one with fresh-cut side-whiskers and a dark blue handkerchief.

Yours. Such a simple word, and yet, it said everything. And the weight of written words? I know I've said that before. Maybe someone who listens to the podcast? I sniff the fragrant blush and peach dahlia that accompanied the letter—my favorite—once more, then tuck it into the lace embroidery of my jacket lapel.

Eden appraises me in her sturdy but elegant blue riding dress. "Thinking about your secret admirer again?"

"What gave it away?" I smooth my own riding dress, in emerald green.

"That dreamy-eyed, goofy grin." She does her best impression, batting her lashes at me. "So . . . do you think it's from Harrison?"

The light in her eyes says she's not so weirded out by the idea anymore, especially since I told her what he said in the garden this morning. She clutched her heart, "oohing" and "ahhing." But I made sure she knew I was in no way decided on anything.

My lips pucker to the side. "At first, I thought maybe Harrison wrote it, but I think that's about as likely as him willingly attending a *Pride and Prejudice* marathon. He barely texts, let alone writes to anyone—"

Eden lifts her forefinger. "Though he *is* texting full sentences now."

"That's progress." I snort. "But he told me he'd just tell a girl to her face how he felt."

"Which he did . . ." She narrows one eye as if gauging my reaction.

"He did. It wasn't a lengthy, rain-soaked love declaration or anything, but he did tell me to give him a chance to court me, too." The thought still sends a zap of anticipation racing up my spine. "Besides, he already said he wouldn't be dancing at the ball, only filming."

We discuss other mystery letter-writer possibilities—Ben? Or a shy gentleman I haven't talked to yet? Mercy, it cannot be Milton—as we saunter the remaining distance to the well-kept stables. These horses live better than most humans.

"We're collecting your waivers here. Come see me so I can check you off before heading over to the stable hands." Victoria waves us forward.

There are a few people staying back, but most of us are embarking on this ill-advised horseback hunting excursion like they did in Gladwin and Austen's day. Even if it's not historically accurate, for safety's sake our hunt will include riding helmets, and our rifles will shoot paintballs at fake foxes, pheasants, and the like across the meadow and wooded trails of the estate. A trail guide/chaperone will ensure we don't lose our way or shoot someone's eye out.

Once we have our waivers turned in to Victoria and riding helmets clasped—so much for Anne's hard work on our hair—we head to the stable yard, where there are over three dozen beautiful horses of all colors saddled and ready to go.

I haven't spotted Harrison yet, but as we move around the side of a horse barn, there he is. He's already sitting tall on a large horse with a shining black coat. Jake is atop his own chestnut horse. Both have cameras strapped to their chests.

Eden elbows me. "The line from Gladwin's *Twice the Gentleman*, when Aurelia first sees Benedict on horseback—'. . . he sits tall and proud in his seat, a gentleman to his very marrow upon his horse,' comes to mind, does it not?"

I can't seem to tear my eyes away from Harrison, but when I do, I see Eden's gaze is on Jake as she says this.

Harrison tips his head to us in greeting, as does Jake. Even the fact that Harrison has a camera strapped to his chest and is wearing a riding helmet doesn't diminish how handsome he looks.

Ben is at my side, and by the way he says my name, he must've said it several times while I was staring at Harrison like a dope. I need to remind myself all of his declarations may very well come to naught if he decides to put his career first and move away.

Ben's holding the reins of a white horse with a gray muzzle and a brown mare for me. "Hey, how are we feeling about our chances today?"

His smile is expectant.

"Oh, well . . ." We hadn't exactly made a plan to partner up again, but I guess it's a good thing if he wants to spend more time with me, right? "I suppose your skills will outweigh my lack thereof."

Harrison's boss and sweet wife follow Harrison on foot.

With a quick sweep of his leg, Harrison dismounts. Ben immediately greets Mr. Kellsner, and they chat like old friends.

Before I know what Harrison is doing, he's at my side. "Miss Dufour, may I?" He gestures to the brown horse.

"Sure—yes, please."

He bends to make a step with his interlocked fingers and helps me onto the sidesaddle. Goodness, they took the historical accuracy of this part seriously, and I'm not so sure about it. But with Harrison's steady hand, I climb onto the seat, curve my right leg into a bent position in between the padded upper and lower pommels, somehow find my balance, and slip my left foot into the saddle's only stirrup. It's not as uncomfortable as I thought it would be.

I smile down at Harrison and am aware of how his hand

still rests on my stocking-covered calf after helping me find the stirrup.

Ben eyes Harrison, then me, and claps Harrison on the shoulder. "I could've helped her, Harrison, but thank you. I've got it from here."

His tone is light, but there's an eddying undercurrent.

Delilah holds up a hand, still standing with Mr. Kellsner in her own riding gown. "You help her all you want. The audience will love this." She's eyeing me and Harrison when she says this.

The muscles in Ben's jaw bulge.

Harrison has the faintest of smiles. "Well, this isn't about the audience. Besides, of course I'm going to help my partner."

Ben and I both do a double-take.

"Partner?" I ask.

"Yup, I already signed us up." Harrison states this while he swings back onto his horse—astride, which needles me with jealousy as I cling to the top pommel and reins of my horse to keep my seat.

"But I assumed—" Ben narrows his eyes at Harrison.

Harrison faux-tips his helmet at Ben. "The early bird and all that." He winks at me. We both know he's no early bird. "That is, of course, as long as it's all right with m'lady?"

I look between them as a twinge twists in my gut. "Yes, I can partner with you, Harrison. Sorry, Ben. Maybe for the next one?"

Ben bends a half bow to me. "Of course. That's fine."

Harrison leads his horse next to mine. It shouldn't surprise me that he seems like an expert on his horse since his parents made him and Eden take riding lessons.

He leans closer, taking my gloved hand in his across the space between our horses. "I'm sorry, I should've asked you ahead of time, Zoe. Are you sure it's okay?"

I'm not sure what to think yet. He wasn't kidding about

wanting a chance to court me, I guess. But I realize I *do* want to give him a chance. So, despite my better judgment, I shove down the looming unknowns of the future, and I make my head bob up and down.

The smile that spreads across his handsome face is bright and beautiful. He lifts my hand to his mouth and presses a kiss to the back, warm through my leather glove.

Delilah calls, "Have fun, you two!" She winks and strolls with her husband to the judges' table.

"Where did you get that flower?" Harrison asks while we wait, nudging his elbow in that direction.

Fingers slipping over the delicate petals, my chest warms. "A secret admirer."

"It's beautiful, just like its wearer."

I know I'm blotchy under his scrutiny, but I can't stop it.

Ben, near us, jumps into his saddle with a little more effort than Harrison. Why am I comparing them? I need to stop that.

Eden rides over on her mottled gray horse, and Ben joins her on his white horse, pulling up on the reins until he's level with her. "Eden, would you like to partner up, or are you promised to someone else?"

If I didn't know Eden like I do I would miss it, but her eyes flicker to Jake for a quick, yearning-filled moment before she straightens and says, "I'm not promised to anyone. Sure, that sounds fun. Thank you."

And though I haven't known Jake long, there's no mistaking the pained tightness around his deep-set dark eyes.

After a few instructions from the guides, we split up into smaller groups to hunt the multiple trails set up for the competition.

Our guide—an older man with the leather-like skin of someone who's worked outdoors all his life—takes the lead. Harrison rides beside me, Eden and Ben behind us, followed by Jake, then Milton paired with Sophie in the back. Milton is entertaining Sophie with stories of the last *Pride and Prejudice* watch party he had with a game of charades and a high tea. He and I might need to compare notes on watch party ideas.

Sophie belly laughs as he describes how his cats broke into the catnip, then stole the lemon pound cake off the counter like little furry bandits and left powdered sugar paw prints in a dizzying maze across the kitchen floor.

The more she laughs, the warmer Milton's demeanor grows.

Meanwhile, there's a comfortable back-and-forth between Ben and Eden about their families as well as their mutual acquaintances.

"I'm sorry I kind of strong-armed you into this date." Harrison interrupts my accidental eavesdropping.

"It's never a punishment to spend time with you, Harrison."

His eyes flare, but then he flashes me a cheeky grin. "That's quite the compliment, Miss Dufour. It's also the opposite of torture to be with you."

"Good to know." I giggle as I grip the pommel. "But for future reference, I don't usually like my choices being made for me. I like to do the choosing."

"Duly noted. I just want you to see *all* of your options." The confident yet charming tilt of his chin makes my stomach clench into a fluttering, coiled mess.

The trouble seems to be that I can't keep my list, my reason for being here—aside from the podcast—straight in my head when Harrison is near. Especially when his eyes pierce mine, like they do now, with a dizzying combination of fierceness and tenderness.

I blow a slow stream of air to calm myself.

Because, if I'm really and truly honest with myself, Harrison is not a safe choice. Given my history, he's the "barreling headlong into the unknown, hoping there's a soft place to land but likely landing on a bear trap" kind of choice. Disaster, in other words. He loves to go where the wind blows, living a life of not knowing what's around the next corner, taking risks, full of surprises. Most of the surprises in my life have been devastating.

Disaster isn't on the list. The list isn't about surprises or unknowns. It's about steadiness, dependability, and a longstanding, well-organized plan that's best for me. No complications. No abandoning good sense or giving in to something wilder, deeper inside of myself where I lose my head . . . and my heart. And certainly finding a perfect gentleman is not about opening myself up to the loss and pain that accompanies that kind of reckless abandon.

I need a marriage of mutual respect and care like the arrangements often found in Regency times. To someone like Ben. That's what I need.

Hmm, I never realized that I'm the Charlotte Lucas of my own story, not the Elizabeth Bennet.

My parents love each other deeply. They found the unexpected, the person they never saw coming, in each other. It's what they'd love for me to have, though they've never pressured me and have told me it's okay not to marry, reminding me of that just today during a phone call. I have my friends, my family, my faith. I know that.

I've had to think long and hard about my own desire and motivation to get married when inevitably, someday the wrong diagnosis, a tragic accident, old age, or *life* hits wrong and causes devastation. There is excruciating pain in losing the person you love most or even having the life you've known together turned upside down. But to have had great love, a forever sort of love, no matter the cost, is all I've ever wanted for myself. Just like Mom and Dad. Hopefully, I can do so before all of the big surprises in life strike.

I can't chance opening my heart to Harrison like that only for him to move again. And if he stayed for me, he'd come to resent me. I can't discount our differences, either. What if we did invest ourselves in a relationship just to realize the things that make us who we are also tear us apart? He may call our differences little things, but what if they really *are* the big things? I'd surely lose him altogether then. Friendship and all.

I don't know if he could love me or where he thinks courting will lead us, but I can't take that chance.

But I *will* be his friend. I just need to figure out how to keep my heart in check and let him know without hurting him.

24

Harrison

"You look like the whole world weighs on your shoulders." I keep my voice light so I don't startle Zoe as she stares off into the woods, bobbing along on her horse.

She jumps but doesn't spook the docile creature beneath her. "Oh." The word is more of a gasp. "I-I was thinking about my parents."

"Did something happen?" The thought puts me on high alert.

There's a soft smile that doesn't quite reach her eyes. "No, they're fine. Don't worry. I spoke with Dad after lunch. Mom had a bit of a tumble when she tried to move herself to the bathroom without him, but she's okay." Her shoulders move up and down. "And I'm questioning my judgment on coming here. I usually help out for a few hours several days a week to give Dad a break. I'm sure that's why this happened. He's tired, and then Mom doesn't want to bother him with helping her."

"It's not your fault, Zo. And she's all right."

"Yeah, this time. What if she's not next time?" She turns her head away. "It would *kill* my dad if anything happened to her. He'd be lost without her, and vice versa. Me too." The words are barely more than a breath, but I catch them.

Her crumpled expression cuts through me like a jagged knife.

The pain in her big, beautiful eyes makes me want to gather her in my arms, to shield her from it. To ease it in any way I can, to protect her from the heartache this life can throw her way. It makes me want to know *everything*, more than I already know about her. All that makes her laugh, all her fears, everything that brings her pain like this does . . .

So she knows her innermost being is safe with me.

I venture further, trying to pierce that list-making perfectionism I know she uses as a shield. "Your dad. You said he's the reason you've been searching for a perfect gentleman all these years, right? Because that's what he is for your mom." I say it quietly, but everyone else is in the midst of their own conversations, not paying us any attention.

Her back straightens, rigid, which makes her wobble in her saddle. I reach a hand over to steady her.

"Yeah," she admits softly. "I'd like to have that in my life. Someone strong and steady. Predictable when life isn't, you know?"

A clawing sensation builds in my chest, and my fingers curl tighter around the reins.

She continues, "I've dated or *almost* dated my share of guys who didn't check that list and who reinforced why I made it in the first place."

My knuckles crack thinking of Chad Summers, Sawyer Perrault, and the many bozos, as her dad called them, hurting my sweet Zoe. Well, not *my* anything, but I can still hope.

"I get it." I free a pent-up breath. "I can't stand that you were treated that way. But this idea of someone who'll fulfill this list, who you categorize as a gentleman . . ."

I scrape my jawline beneath the beard. "Wouldn't you rather someone lift you up with support and encouragement than put you on a pedestal and fill you with empty platitudes or what they think you want to hear? To challenge you rather than think and do the same things as you? Someone who loves the independent, driven, sweet woman that you are without expecting anything from you? Because let's be honest, if you're expecting this perfect gentleman, who's to say he won't expect the same from you—perfection?"

I fill my voice with the passion I feel for her. "Someone with whom you can have mutual respect and honesty even if it's not built on perfect manners. Because, you know what?"

Her brows lift, but she remains quiet.

"Outward manners have little to do with the inward heart and who people are on the inside." My chuckle is mirthless. "I know this from a childhood spent around people my parents called friends. Perfectly polite with impeccable manners to your face, yet toxic behind your back."

I stop myself from mentioning that people can also seem trustworthy and pretend to be on the same page with a similar moral compass, but then emotionally sideswipe you. Thoughts of my ex swim through my mind. I sink them one by one and take in a deep breath.

She seems to contemplate my words, forehead wrinkled in thought. "You're right that people sometimes seem one way to your face and completely different behind your back. I guess that's all the more reason for me to be extra careful."

That was only part of it, but I let it rest.

"Hey." Her voice is soft, gaining my attention again. "You were talking about the woman you dated in Cincinnati, weren't you? She was the one who turned out to be someone else."

I never meant for the tables to turn, for this to be about

me and my past. But one glance at her searching expression and I want her to know the truth. After all, I know all of her dating highs and lows.

"Yes, she did." I tell her what happened, and it lifts something inside me.

Zoe doesn't judge or ask a bunch of questions. She just listens. That's one of the things I love about her. At the end, she says simply but earnestly, "I'm so sorry that happened to you, Harrison. It wasn't fair, but you did the right thing."

There it is again. Me doing the right thing, but still losing.

Even so, my next breath is easier. "I knew she wasn't right for me, in retrospect, before any of that happened. Whatever that feeling you're supposed to have, that gut-level knowing or cataclysmic, world-shattering snap of realization or even the immediate desire to see or talk to that person anytime they're not around"—I shrug—"I didn't have it."

She takes that in, mouth pressed thin, as though stopping herself from asking if I had that for her. Good thing, because I'd have no choice but to answer honestly. Yes. Absolutely, yes.

But then I turn my lips into a goofy grin to lighten the mood.

"Well, I'm sure you're excited to shoot fake animals, but try to leave some for me."

There's an adorable, silly expression that crinkles her nose and makes me want to kiss it. "As long as no real animals are hurt in the process like our almost assassination of a peacock earlier, I'm game for it."

"I think we're good. That guy's definitely spreading the word and won't come within a five-mile radius of you holding any weapon."

She scoffs. "Me? Your hands were just as much on that bow as mine, buddy."

The memory of her in my arms burns inside my chest.

After we both laugh, her expression turns sober again. "Hey, about before, do you mind if—"

"We take that part of the conversation out in editing?" I tap the camera on my chest.

She sighs. "Yes. Thank you."

I reach across and squeeze her hand, resting on the pommel. "Of course. And, Zo?"

"Yeah?"

"Never be afraid to talk to me, okay? Just because you're usually the eternal perfectionist doesn't mean you always have to be happy or never worry about anything. You're human." I study the reins in my hands. "And no matter what happens, you know, between us—I'll always be here for you."

Her eyes mist over for a moment before she turns one of her brilliant, heart-stopping wide grins at me.

"And you, good sir, as I told you before, have things to say—"

"It's getting me to be quiet once you open that door that's the problem?" I quirk one brow at her.

She tilts her head. "No. I like it. I'm here to listen, too. Anytime. Thank you for sharing what happened in Cincinnati with me. And just so you know, I don't like the reason, but I'm so glad you're back."

"Me too." I mean it, even though I'd always dreamed of living elsewhere. Anywhere but here.

It brings the question of what I'm going to do if Mr. Kellsner offers me that job in Chicago. But I brush it away for now.

With that, the mood lightens, and we stop as the guide indicates we've arrived. I reach up and lift Zoe down from her horse, hyperaware of the curve of her waist beneath my hands. We tie our horses to nearby trees and begin our trek through the woods on foot now to hunt down any unsuspecting faux-animals. We all retrieve our paintball guns and slip on the goggles we're required to wear.

"We look ridiculous." Zoe covers her mouth.

She does look adorably hilarious—the goggles enlarge her already big eyes, making her look like an insect.

Ben strides toward us after attempting to help Eden dismount, but she jumps down gracefully like the confident equestrian she is. Jake smirks.

"Speak for yourself," Ben says but flashes Zoe a smile and a wink as he slips on his own goggles like a movie star awaiting the paparazzi.

I manage not to roll my eyes. I'm proud of myself.

After several paces, I spot a stuffed-toy fox tied to a tree trunk, partially obscured by a bush. "Really?" I mutter to myself.

There's been a lot of goofy-beyond-words stuff at this retreat, but this might take the cake.

Stepping clear of the group, I take my aim. But as I squeeze the trigger, a paintball whizzes by my ear and hits the fox's side. Mine splats yellow on the tree trunk above the head. I whirl around to find Ben behind me to the right, lowering his gun. He does that cliché thing where he blows on the end of the barrel.

Eden, Zoe, and Sophia clap while Zoe says, "Great shot!" to Ben.

"Well, I had to prove I can still aim after my second-place archery scores." A self-deprecating grin slides onto his face.

Meanwhile, Milton managed to shoot himself in the foot and is wiping the blue paint off his riding boot. "Righto, jolly good shot," he calls in a Minnesotan/imitation-British inflection.

After about half an hour of walking through the woods, Ben and I are tied and Sophie is right behind us. Sophie really is an excellent shot, and judging by the moon-eyed stares from Milton, he's thoroughly impressed.

The guide, in a voice like the creaking oaks around us, says there's one more target in our designated area. By instinct, my footfalls are silent despite the dry leaves.

There it is, a plastic deer's head peeking out behind a thick maple tree. With the crunching leaves and cracking twigs behind me—Zoe's and Milton's steps—if that were a real deer, it would've disappeared into the woods before we'd even been aware of it.

I'm so caught up in winning what feels like a personal face-off with Ben that Zoe's scream behind me doesn't register until after I squeeze the trigger and hit my faux-doe.

When I whirl around, she's in Ben's arms on the ground. I have half a mind, maybe more, to take one last shot and pelt Ben with a paintball right in the chest. Right where it feels like an ax has lodged in my own.

25

Zoe

Ben's staring down at me, his arms still wrapped around my middle. His hazel eyes crease with concern, and his scent permeates the air around us. Maybe the mint is a little overpowering, but that expensive-smelling cologne knows what it's doing.

"Are you okay?" Ben's face is close as he inspects me, brushing a piece of hair out of my eye.

"Yes—yeah."

He helps me sit up.

I brush myself off. Oh, my dahlia is hanging limply from my jacket now.

Ben skims it with the back of his fingers. "I'm sorry your flower is ruined." Is that recognition in his eyes?

Harrison runs back and kneels next to us. "What happened?"

"I'm fine."

Ben takes my hands and pulls me to my feet as Harrison's arms are outstretched like he wants to touch me but doesn't. "Really. I saw a snake. It surprised me, that's all. It was hiding under a pile of leaves."

"Are you sure you're all right? Are you hurt?" Harrison's gaze rakes over me, head to toe.

"Yes, I'm sure. I'm not hurt."

He doesn't seem convinced, but that's when I hear Eden say, "Jake?" Her tone is off.

We turn to find Jake huddled into himself, knees drawn to his chest, on the ground, covering his ears.

My fear of what is most likely a nonvenomous snake—this is Minnesota, after all—slithering across my boot is suddenly silly. Jake. Sweet, easygoing, always ready with a kind word or smile Jake. Eden's at his side, rubbing slow circles into his back, a gesture that would make me smile for my friend under different circumstances. She murmurs soothing words into his ear. After several long minutes, Jake lowers his hands.

He hinted at PTSD after his work in war-torn areas for so long, but this is the first we've really seen it firsthand.

Eden picks a leaf from his disheveled curls. He catches her hand and holds it to his face as if drawing strength and comfort from that simple touch.

Milton clears his throat. "Let's get you back for teatime, shall we? My mother always says tea can heal any ache, physical or otherwise." He starts back toward the horses, Sophia trailing behind after squeezing Eden's shoulder.

I share a look with Eden that I try to infuse with all of my concern and compassion.

Even for my free-spirited friend, love, relationships, and feelings are so complicated.

I guess that's why, for me anyway, maybe I need to keep things uncomplicated.

Stick to a plan. Stick to my list. That's my safety bubble.

I can't stand it any longer. Eden, Jake, and Harrison didn't come down for dinner. Ben made a valiant attempt to cheer me with Gladwin and Austen quotes and more tales of his rowing team back at Yale. They sounded so professional that I shied away from telling him about my little hobby of solo rowing. Somehow I'd agreed to be his partner for the rowing competition tomorrow, the third part of our tournament.

But now I have to see Harrison and check on Jake and Eden. I don't mean to crowd them, but I have to know everyone's okay. Even though it's not era appropriate, I grab my favorite fluffy pink cardigan from the dresser drawer and slip it over my pale pink dress for comfort.

Within seconds, I'm striding with purpose toward the men's wing.

My chest aches with the combination of witnessing Jake's mind and body brought to his knees by memories alone, and my own toughest memories reawakened in the process.

Jake apologized, but we reassured him there was no need to be sorry. He'd said his episodes had mostly gone away since his return from the Middle East. But the sound of the guns, despite them being fake, in combination with my screams—which, of course, filled me with guilt even though Jake and Harrison both told me it wasn't my fault—triggered his PTSD.

He video-called his therapist as soon as we returned and asked if Eden would stay with him. The first blooms of love are evident in my friend and, I believe, in Jake even with his previous statements about romance.

On my way past the drawing room, I snag a few tokens of affection (or friendship, in this case) from one of the tables and scribble notes with each. A small arrangement of autumn mums and chocolates for Eden, and two satchels of what we've nicknamed the "guy snacks"—beef jerky and cashews—for Jake and Harrison.

Victoria's clipped walk echoes around the corner. I duck behind a grandfather clock and slip by without her notice. I feel like the rogue now. Harrison must be rubbing off on me.

My quick knock on Harrison and Jake's door seems to boom in the quiet hall. More footsteps behind me, heavier this time. I don't wait to see who it is, nor do I wait for an answer. Calling in a harsh whisper, "I'm coming in!" I open the door, slide inside, and click it shut behind me.

Harrison is alone in the room. He stands from his spot at the dark wooden desk.

A molasses-slow smile spreads, igniting sparks of mischief in his eyes. "Why, Miss Dufour, Look who's the rake now. I could've been in my unmentionables."

His hand hits his neckline as if reaching for invisible pearls to clutch. I roll my eyes but can't stop the tingle of heat in my cheeks.

"Oh, stop. I didn't know you were alone. I came to see how Jake's doing. And to deliver these . . ." Setting the gifts on a small table, I tread farther into the room.

The part about how I also wanted to see how *he* is—and can't seem to get his face and his concern for me and Jake out of my mind—is best left out. And how maybe if he's in front of me, I can somehow figure out what to do and how to feel about him. About Ben.

"Oh?" He stalks toward me. "So you weren't trying to find me all alone without the prying eyes of a chaperone? Scandalous, Miss Dufour, I must say." His low timbre seems to resonate not only inside the room but also within me.

He's close now, head bent to look into my eyes.

I try to swallow, but it sticks in my dry throat. So do my words. "I, no, of course not."

His intense gaze breaks into a cat-like grin, and he lets out a deep chuckle. "I'm teasing, Zo. Come in. I'm no chaperone police. You know I think—"

"They're ridiculous?" I offer.

"Yes." He indicates the other side of the room. "Eden sat with Jake for a while, then they went downstairs to the office to call his therapist and do a little editing to take his mind off things. He's okay."

"Good." My feet shuffle before Harrison points to two stuffed chairs in rich burgundy in front of a fireplace on the far wall.

"Please, sit."

I do, he takes the other chair, and the fire blazing inside the hearth reaches for me with its warmth. Even so, I secure the sweater tighter around myself like it's the armor I need to brave the confusion coursing through me.

"Is that the only reason you came here?" He's studying me.

How can he always read me like that?

But when I can't make myself spit out my mess of thoughts concerning him and Ben, I interlock my fingers and splay them in my lap. "I was thinking, seeing Jake's worst memories come back to haunt him like that. Triggered to go off at the right, I mean, *wrong* time." It's not what I thought I'd say, but suddenly it's exactly what I meant to say.

Harrison leans back in his chair, head tilting to the side, waiting.

"It made me wonder. Are the hard parts of our lives always like that? Living inside us, waiting to pop out when we least expect it?" A shiver runs through my body.

Vulnerable. Alone. Out of control. I can't afford to be out of control.

He's still, as if he didn't hear me, but then he leans over, elbows resting on his knees. His thumbs rub over the semi-hidden cleft in his beard-covered chin.

"Is there a certain memory you're worried about triggering?" His head tips the other way. "Can I ask, what *is* your worst memory?"

Oof. That's what I would call vulnerable. I'm regretting my big mouth already.

"I'll tell you mine if you tell me yours." I try for an enigmatic smile.

"It was the day you found out you had diabetes," he answers without pause.

My stomach lurches, and my ears start a high-pitched whine that only partially drowns out my thudding heartbeat. Does he know?

"But that's—"

"No, not for the reason you think." His hand raises. "Don't get me wrong, it was horrible to see you like that, and I was so worried about you when the ambulance took you away. But it was also the day my father gave up on me and my parents split up without actually getting a divorce." He punctuates this with a short mirthless laugh. "I don't know which would've been worse—a divorce or them living in cold silence under the same roof the way they did, still do."

The real, raw pain in his eyes gives me the sudden impulse to jump up, crawl into his lap, and hold his head to my shoulder.

Instead, I scoot to the edge of my chair and reach for his hand, squeezing it before letting go. "I didn't know. Eden doesn't talk much about your parents, only that you both aren't very close with them."

I can't help asking, "What happened?"

He blows out a gust of air. "That morning I'd messed up my hockey practice, royally. The coach knew my dad, so he called him to basically tell him if I didn't play better, he would kick me off the team, or, even worse for my dad's pride, he'd bench me for the season." Harrison's hand runs through his hair. "The coach called me into the office after the practice, so I heard one side of the conversation, and I knew I was in for it later with my dad."

Harrison's leg bounces and then he's on his feet, pacing away. "That's all I thought about that day. I couldn't concentrate. I failed a test I studied for, and my mile run for gym was the slowest I've ever run. It was like—" His hands juggle an invisible ball.

"You were a mere mortal. Like me?" I'm glad to coax a smile back onto his face, even though it's short-lived. "So, then what? Did you get into a lot of trouble when you got home?"

"That was the thing. I didn't *go* home." He grabs the back of his neck and strides the other way. "We were supposed to have an after-school hockey practice that day. It was intense, near playoffs. But I couldn't face the coach or risk disappointing him or my dad again. So I rode the bus home, and I walked to your house without Eden. She was at her piano lessons."

Something in me both breaks and reforms, like a shattered glass heated and molded into something new. On his worst day, he didn't seek out friends, or Eden, or anyone else . . . he came to see *me*.

"That's right. It was the first time you ever came over without her. And I told you I couldn't go to the park with you—"

He gestures to me. "You were such a little stickler for rules, even then. You had your after-school checklist you hadn't done yet. I mean, what kind of kid has an after-school checklist?"

"Hey, I had a lot of responsibilities. I made sure my homework was done, dishes were washed, my laundry was in the washer or dryer, and I always started dinner for my dad. He had so much to worry about and take care of with my mom—"

"You wanted to make sure he didn't have to worry about you, too?" One brow rises.

"Yeah, and here you were, Mr. Reckless-not-a-care-in-the-world, or so I thought." I shoot him an *I'm sorry* grimace.

"Without a list or responsibilities, wanting me to drop everything and hang out at the park."

There's a sad sort of smile tugging at his full, kissable lips. Did I just think *kissable*?

"But even back then, I used my irresistible charm to convince you to come with me. You know the rest. You said you didn't feel good, pretty soon you fell off the top of the monkey bars and passed out. I had never been more scared in my entire fourteen-year-old life or probably since when I saw you pale and not moving on the ground."

My chest tightens. "Me either, when I woke up to the paramedics wheeling me into the ambulance. I'll never forget your face. Your wide eyes as the paramedics closed the door and we drove away. You must've been in shock."

I gulp, and he nods. That scene has played in my mind at least a million times over the years. Always with the sense that I wished he could've come with me. There was always such comfort and strength in Harrison's presence, even at that age.

"After my dad found me at the park instead of my hockey practice, he went ballistic. Right in front of the crowd of neighbors." He throws his gaze skyward and runs a hand down his face. "Your parents were there at one point, asking where you were."

I pick at the edge of my cardigan, a familiar, unwanted feeling rising to the surface. One I do not, *will* not acknowledge. "Yeah, they knew I was with you at the park, so they ran to the pharmacy. There was something with her medication. They didn't know anything was wrong with me."

"Right. I ran to the house to yell for them. For anybody. But no one came."

Story of my life. There it is again, breaking through the door I shoved it behind. The hidden glass half empty inside me. The one I don't let anyone see.

Harrison clears his throat. "My father berated me all the

way to the car and on the drive home. Said I was a loser and our family didn't tolerate losers or quitters. That I needed to stop being such a wimp and do whatever it took to get ahead. Like he had." He turns away again. "That day when Dad and I returned home, Mom was in the middle of throwing his stuff from their master bedroom into a guest room downstairs. That became my fault, too."

Now I can't help it. I jump to my feet. The image of fourteen-year-old Harrison sitting mutely through a barrage of insults and harsh words, especially after he'd saved my life by calling 911, boils my blood and ignites a protective fire inside of me. How could his father be so cruel to someone so—so good? Kind? Brave?

I cross to him, his back still to me. Gently, I pull him around to face me.

Without planning it, my hands cup his face. "Harrison, you are none of the things your father called you. And whatever happened between him and your mom is the result of their own actions. Not yours. I hope you know that. But if you didn't, then know it now."

His face is stricken, as if no one until this moment had ever contradicted those hateful words. I have to blink back tears.

My thumbs move back and forth softly over his cheekbones. "You are one of the kindest people I have ever known. You're so good to Eden, and I know she adores you. So selfless and caring. Smart and funny—"

His lips hitch up. "So, you do think I'm funny."

I slide my hands down, chuckling, but I can't break contact so I leave them pressed against the solid contours of his chest. "Don't let it go to your head." I add, "And you're such a good friend to me. Always there for me. I don't deserve it."

But even as I utter the word *friend*, it seems out of place. Not strong enough. Not significant enough for what he means to me and what it would be like if he wasn't here. What it was like when he'd been in Cincinnati, the constant nagging feeling a piece was missing from my life. There would most definitely be a Harrison-sized hole right through the center of my heart if he ever left again. And at six-foot-four, that's a big, gaping wound. I'd never recover.

I can see the word *friend* hits him, too. He glances down at my hands still resting over his heart. The *thump-thump, thump-thump* beneath my fingertips accelerates as does my own, pumping in my ears.

"A good friend, huh?" His words vibrate through my hands, up my arms, and travel down my spine.

All I'm able to do is bob my head up and down.

"How good of a friend? A friend that can do this?" His hand, achingly slow, reaches up and slides the tips of his calloused fingers across my jawline, over my cheek, then brushes a curled tendril of hair behind my ear.

My throat constricts, but I manage, "Mm-hmm." I can't seem to say no or step away. I don't want to.

"What about this?" He leans closer, and my gaze flickers to his lips. Those soft-looking yet masculine lips . . .

He must notice because a smile spreads across them as he moves closer but shifts his head to the side, so we're almost cheek to cheek. His other hand holds the side of my head in a gentle grip. He turns his face in toward me.

His lips graze my cheek with a soft kiss. "I don't know about you, but I think this friendship just got a lot more interesting." Laughter lifts the edges of his voice.

"I guess so." My chuckle is cut short as he places another light kiss along my jaw, then lines it with kisses back toward my ear. Breath shallow, my heart beats faster.

I'm gripping the front of his shirt into a crumpled ball. I try to loosen my fingers but can't.

After another small kiss near my earlobe, in the hypersensitive hollow beneath it—that I'll surely dream of until my dying day—his breath and beard tickle my ear as he says, "I will be your friend, Zoe." His words are a warm, ragged whisper against my skin. "In whatever way you'll let me. Every day. Like this. Not like this. More than this. I'm yours. Always."

26

Harrison

Our noses are a finger's-width apart now, my palms resting on either side of her face, but I pin her with a look that asks for permission to kiss her lips. This is about more than just my own convictions that I need to wait for a woman to consent to intimacy before leaning in. I need to know that she feels something for me. That it's not me dangling on an edge alone. That she actually feels more than friendship for me. And I did say I'd wait for her okay to kiss her.

"Can I kiss you, Zo?"

She takes her bottom lip between her teeth, a small shy smile tugging at the corners as her chin dips once, but that's all I need. It may not be the words I hoped to hear, but it's still her lowering her guard with me. It's a step—a big one—outside of the friend zone. So I don't need any more encouragement as I close that inch of separation, fitting my mouth to hers. It's slow at first, lips meeting and discovering.

And mercy. Those lips. They're even softer than I could've ever imagined, tasting of something berry.

Her fingers have found their way to the hair at the back of my neck. She runs her fingertips through it, sending electric jolts down my vertebrae. I wish her long, dark waves were unbound, not in this tight, complicated knot. But I make the most of it, caressing the soft, smooth skin of her neck and playing with the curls left out at her temple with one hand while drawing her closer with the other, palm to her lower back. This is . . . *everything*.

She gently pulls back, but only enough to look me in the eye. "I never got to tell you about *my* worst day."

"You want to talk about that *now*?" My breath is erratic, out of control. Hers is the same. I slant my brows at her, but when I see the creases on her forehead, a determined set to her soft jaw, I ask, "What is it?"

"The same day as yours. When I found out I was diabetic."

"Of course, that makes sense." I make my words steady, careful.

"But not for the reason you think. I never—I never talk about this." She turns her head, but I catch her chin, dragging her gaze back to mine.

"Hey, you can tell me anything."

She pulls in a breath. "It was the day my family was somewhere else when I needed them. I don't resent them. How could I? When my mom needs so much from my dad and he needed, *needs*, so much from me." Her palm rests over my chest again, but this time it feels like a barrier. "He and Mom both need for me to be okay, to be self-sufficient. They need to not worry about me and if I'm taken care of."

"I know. I get it. I can take care of—" But even as I begin, I know it's the wrong thing to say.

She silences me by lightly placing her fingertips over my lips, still warm from moving over hers. "And it was also the first time I learned that losing control, losing focus on my plans for my life, and letting things slide or ignoring my 'rules' as you say, ends with everything falling apart. And it's the same hard lesson I had to learn all over again when I allowed myself to fall for the wrong guys later on."

The full meaning of her words blooms in her dilated pupils, almost blocking out the beautiful chocolate brown.

I draw a breath as if the oxygen will give me the strength I need when she says the one thing I don't want her to say. "So can we be the type of friends who support what the other person needs?"

My chest, that pain can't be normal. Surely, it's about to explode. Even so, I take her hand away from my lips, but not before pressing a kiss to the pads of her fingers, "I will always support whatever you need in your life, Zoe. Of that, you can be sure."

God, let it be me she needs.

I had a narrow shot with Zoe but somehow fumbled it at the one-yard line last night.

Rubbing a hand over my forehead, I then rake it through my hair and head out of the office, where I've been editing since breakfast.

Even though I heard her words and caught the meaning behind them yesterday, her responses to my affections were anything but a rebuff. This flicker of hope is stubborn and refuses to be snuffed out.

The warmth of her lips. I can still feel it. And her fervor that matched my own measure for measure. There's no way she didn't feel what I felt. There was nothing timid about that kiss, from either of us. It was like a dam burst open. Maybe she's lying not only to me about her desire to keep things at friendship level but also to herself.

Man, I used to be the pragmatic semi-pessimist in this relationship, convinced finding love at this retreat was ridiculous. But, well, when it's the girl you've been dreaming of for most of your life and you came so close to finally taking that next step . . .

All I can think to do for now is just be the support I know she needs, so I sent her another letter of encouragement from her "Gentleman in Training."

Early this morning was the third challenge, rowing around a buoy in the middle of the lake and then back to shore. And even though I'm usually all for competition, I can't say I was sad to see that one come to an end. Filming Zoe partnered with Ben again sent an onslaught of jabs to my gut.

But I had to be strong for Zoe and give my support to Jake. From the creased strain on his face, filming Eden with man-bun Aspen wasn't any easier on him. Jake said the guy was only a Marquess of Mediocrity at best during her speed dates because of his "way too forward" attitude with her.

At least Ben got more than he bargained for trying to row with Zoe, the petite rowing machine. I smirk at the memory.

Jake rounds the corner. "Why are you looking so smug?"

"Just having a mental replay review of Ben's oar mishap and unintentional dip into the lake earlier."

His shoulders shake in laughter. "It certainly can't hurt *your* cause, can it?"

"I don't know if Zoe will ever admit any feelings for me." I shrug. "But I still want to protect her. I'll always want to protect her. And Ben deserved that after lying about being some star rower at Yale."

And yet, she'd managed to win.

Jake claps me on the back. "Oh, man. The way his elbows flailed like a D-minus version of the chicken dance trying to keep up with Zoe before he lost his balance and toppled into the lake will live rent-free in my brain for an eternity."

I can't help the burst of laughter. "Mine too. Obviously, I'm glad no one was hurt—"

"Obviously," he agrees. With a sly smile he adds, "But . . . if you ever need a good laugh, I got a really good shot of it."

I only half admonish him with a crook of my brow.

His palms lift in defense. "I'm kidding. That'll go in the 'Do Not Use' file. You know, right next to your 'Zoe' file."

I shove his arm when he tips a knowing smile at me. I can't help it. They're shots I can't bring myself to erase of Zoe, but I won't use them in the show, either.

"You psyched about the trivia luncheon?" Jake grins.

We head toward the parlor.

I tug at the T-shirt I'm finally allowed to wear, along with my jeans, flannel, and boots. "At least I get a break from that cravat torture device. And, hey, it might be Regency trivia, but I can appreciate this kind of competition."

"Well, I can't wait to film it. And it sounds like your sister and Zoe talked about and watched Regency stuff so much while you were growing up."

"Believe me, it was like having a passive IV filled with all things Austen and Gladwin pumping the info straight into my bloodstream."

The crowd is already assembled in the parlor. It's weird but refreshing to see everyone in regular ol' twenty-first-century clothing. People sit around circular tables in their chosen teams.

You could call what Victoria is wearing modern, but it's still a full-length gown that looks like it would be more comfortable at a funeral or better left for an 1800s Victorian librarian with cats. Lots of them.

At each table, people are writing their Regency-inspired team names, ranging from "The Blushing Debutantes" (the all-girls group led by Samantha) to the "Darcy's Darlings," a mixed group where obviously the men were outvoted, except for Milton, who seems pleased with the name after his hero. A buzzer sits in the middle of each table along with platters of sandwiches and fruit for us to eat a light lunch while we play, and bowls of snacks, pitchers of lemonade, sodas, and glasses.

Zoe's across the room. There's this magnetic pull from her to me. I'm certain she could be in the middle of the US Bank Stadium and my eyes would automatically find her in the crowd.

She's laughing at something Ben says. Guess she's forgiven the rowing fiasco this morning. They're at a front table. She's forever the "good student."

Jake and I walk over and greet Zoe, Eden, and Ben.

"Are you inviting anyone over to team up?" I ask Eden.

I can tell she's being careful to avoid Jake's eye when she answers, "Not having the best experience in that department. Tonight, I want to have fun without the pressure of a date." She waves me closer. "Come on, be on our team."

"That depends. What's our team name?"

Zoe leans back and chimes in. "Lords and Ladies of Fancy-pantston." She winks.

When I sink into the chair next to Zoe, she studies me through her fan of dark lashes for a moment before murmuring a quiet "Hey." She's soft and feminine in an oversized cream sweater and jeans that make me want to gather her in my arms and bury my face in the crook of her neck.

Her hair is down—I've missed the way her silky waves hang down her back and bounce when she moves. What I wouldn't give to run my fingers through them. They waft that faint scent of roses and sweetness all her own as she turns back to Ben.

At the head of the room, Victoria, Bill, and Delilah Kellsner dive into reading the questions.

Delilah's forefinger strikes the air. "If one was wealthy, well-born, and well-dressed, as well as associated with others having the same important qualities, one was entitled to consider themselves part of what elite Regency England group?"

Before I tell it to, my hand reaches for the buzzer. "The ton."

Delilah blinks at me, then exclaims, "Correct!"

My leg brushes Zoe's beneath the table, and her piercing glance heats the side of my face.

Her astonished expression makes me laugh. I lift a shoulder. "What?"

"Nothing. Nothing at all, Lord Fancypantston." She raises her brows and bends her head in a half-seated curtsy.

Though our legs aren't touching anymore, the space between us seems filled with electricity. Warmth. Awareness. My hand rests on my chair's seat, hers a mere two inches away.

I pour a cup of lemonade and drain the coolness in one long gulp and then grab one of those tiny sandwiches, finishing it in one bite.

Victoria's face twitches with her next question. "Which of these is *not* a book published in the Regency era? A. *The Adventures of an Ostrich Feather of Quality*, B. *Memoirs of an Old Wig*, C. *"I Can't Afford It": And Other Tales*, or D. *The Many Maladies of the Chuckleheaded Chawbacon*."

Both Zoe and I jump up, raising our arms above our heads. Victoria clutches her throat like she's about to say that's not the way a lady or a gentleman is meant to behave.

But it's Milton who remembers his buzzer first. "D!" he shouts.

Victoria points at him. "Correct, Mr. Birtwhistle."

"I definitely need to check out those books based on their titles alone," I mutter out of the side of my mouth as Zoe and I take our seats again. I'd heard about them on some Regency history show Eden had watched on PBS.

Mr. Kellsner is up. "What fruit was fashionable to have on display in the Regency era? A. Apples, B. Kiwis, C. Oranges, or D. Pineapples."

I slap the buzzer, a split-second ahead of Milton. He groans, slamming his palm onto the table as Victoria gestures to me.

"D. Pineapples." I catch Jake running a hand over his smirk out of the corner of my eye. "Annnd . . . my self-loathing is complete." I slump, leaning back in my chair. "But I might as well own it at this point."

Jake gives a little doff-of-the-invisible-hat. "By all means, my good man."

Standing, Delilah reads from her card, "Women's Regency fashion of light, flowing fabrics and silhouettes was inspired by which two ancient civilizations' clothing?"

Zoe's hand shoots out and slaps the buzzer a moment ahead of another table in the back. "Greece and Rome!" Her eyes are wide and bright as she waits.

Delilah's smile warms. "Yes, my dear."

There are several questions that Milton, the "clique" ladies, and then Sophia answer.

Then Mr. Kellsner pops to his feet. And if I'm not mistaken, that glint in his eyes says he's enjoying this. "All right, what did Jane Austen's character Captain Frederick Wentworth and A. Nathaniel Gladwin's character Lord Benedict Pembroke have in common?"

Eden and Zoe squeal as they look to each other and then hit the buzzer together. Zoe gestures to Eden, who shouts, "They were both sea captains!"

They do their double-high-five thing.

We're down to the last question, and everyone's so into it that we're all on our feet now.

Victoria examines her card, a broad grin rounding her cheeks. "For the last question, there are two parts. So make sure you listen to both parts of the question before buzzing in." She holds up a hand to quiet the room. "Finish this quote by Jane Austen: 'My feelings will not be repressed. You must allow me . . .'"—Victoria waves her hand dramatically and continues—"And please, tell me from which of her novels is this quote?"

I smack the buzzer, and Zoe's hand lands on top of mine. Our eyes lock as we answer in unison, "to tell you how ardently I admire and love you."

The words remind me of the day we rowed together. It seems so long ago now.

Her eyes are wider and rounder than I've ever seen them. So big I can see the flecks of lighter brown, almost honey-colored, near the pupil. Everything seems to freeze as we hold each other's gaze. The words, though someone else's and two centuries old, somehow encapsulate every pump of my twenty-first-century heart. And, though the sentiments are simple, they're everything I feel for this woman in front of me. Maybe she can see it, written there in my eyes. The truth. An open book, just for her. Because her full lips part, forming a little "oh."

It's Victoria who calls us back to the present, plus the roomful of amused whispers. "And the second part of the question?" Her voice cracks like she's actually enjoying the spectacle.

Again, in unison and without breaking eye contact, we answer, "*Pride and Prejudice*."

Eden and Jake erupt in shouts of joy, and the room claps as Victoria announces in a very un-Victoria manner, "Team Lords and Ladies of Fancypantston, you win!"

I pull Zoe into a monster of a hug. Ben's eyes narrow behind her, but I ignore it. Lifting her off the floor, I swing her in a little arc. All eyes zero in on us again, and Zoe wiggles like she's asking to be put down. I oblige, lowering her to the floor, and reluctantly let go. Zoe ducks her head and slips a piece of hair behind her ear.

Victoria scowls at our obvious PDA, then confers with the judges and retreat staff in hushed voices. "For winning the trivia, Lords and Ladies of Fancypantston, your team members will each receive a Regency-themed gift. We also have our overall tournament winner, or should I say, *winners?*" Bill and Delilah tap a drum roll on their table. "Zoe Dufour ... and Harrison Lundquist. You've tied for first!"

There are whistles, claps, and shouts for us. Ben is the only one who has stayed quiet during the exchange. Maybe he does like her. Maybe, like me, it's tough for him to see her with someone else. There's a twinge of sympathy for the guy. Not so much that I'll stop pursuing Zoe, but with eye contact over Zoe's shoulder, an understanding seems to pass between us.

He does eventually join in with a polite clap and says, "Well done," to us both.

"Now, you two have the option to take your prize together—the romantic dinner for two, location anywhere on the grounds with the meal of your choice. Or, our retreat hosts have accommodated us with individual winnings, if you prefer. You can each pick a date to accompany you on two separate occasions for this excursion."

I motion to Zoe and bow. "Let the lady decide."

"Well ..." Her fingers fidget in front of her, and I don't miss the way her gaze wavers between me and Ben. Her lips compress and almost disappear, which is what she does when *she* wants to disappear.

It hits me. She wants to take Ben, but she's trying not to hurt me. The realization almost buckles my knees. When will I get it through my thick skull that this girl of my dreams is just not that into me? That any "feelings" I thought she had were figments of my Marianne-pining-after-Willoughby-sized-imagination. Oh, man. This is bad. Comparing myself to a Jane Austen character is bad enough. But to one of its heroines? Worse.

I clear my throat and bend my head toward Victoria and then Zoe in turn. "I wish to withdraw my win. Miss Dufour can have the prize and take whoever she wants." Then, dragging in a deep breath and squaring my shoulders, I gesture toward Ben. "Maybe Ben would like to join you."

Is that relief or shock on her face? I allow myself one last touch by giving her arm a gentle squeeze. "Congratulations. I hope it's everything you want it to be. Perfect." I try to infuse my tone with only my desire for her to be happy and fulfilled, even if it's not with me.

Then I excuse myself upstairs.

27

Zoe

Squinting against the vibrant golden-hour sun, I run a gloved finger down my to-do list for this date I planned for Ben and me. Yup. Everything is set. Perfect, like this date is supposed to be, and like Ben seems to be for me. Both lists, checked.

But why is there still a raw ache in the center of my chest? An image of Harrison's face after we won turns over and over in my mind. His gaze was so full of emotions I couldn't begin to name. But then he'd closed off, his expression becoming a wall of stone. Polite but impenetrable and not at all the open, warm Harrison I know.

Before Harrison conceded his win and told me I should take Ben, I'd actually imagined taking Harrison first. A thought that popped into my head without provocation, but sort of seemed right once it did. I blow out a warm breath into the cool almost-evening air. None of that matters now. I have to get back on track here. Harrison obviously realized what I've known all along—we'd never work out. He was just saving us the trouble of saying it out loud.

I guess that kiss—Oh, that kiss!—was nothing. Another thing to put behind me.

These past few days have given me so much to think about: Harrison and whatever's going on there, Ben and if there's something to pursue with him, and even the dawning realization that I'm actually a whole person with God in me. It's not that I didn't know that, but I've been so focused on finding my person for so long, I kind of forgot that I don't need another person to make me whole. God's love is enough.

Maybe singleness isn't a bad thing. Look at Emma. She was happy and content on her own and settled into her role as caretaker to her father and matchmaker for her friends—sort of like me with the podcast. Emma never needed Knightley to complete her. But their love did bring added joy to their already full lives.

I try not to compare Harrison to Mr. Knightley, the friend who was always there but then became so much more, *meant so much more to her.*

But where does that leave me with everything I've always believed to be true?

I've been praying that God will guide me in this, as I do still want love and companionship, the lifelong kind with marriage if that's what's meant for me.

There seem to be two opposing views at war within me.

One side brings the words of my secret admirer's latest letter reverberating back into my mind: *"The kind of love God gives has no stipulations, no checklists, and is unconditional. It's free and freeing. This is what I hope you remember about Him but also in your search for love. You're worth it."*

But the other side—the side that wants to keep hold of control, who has worked too hard to create a system to find the right person to quit now—fights to take over and give this list stuff one more try. This could still work.

Standing from my perch on a bench at the edge of the garden, where I'm waiting for Ben to meet me, I stretch and fold the list, tucking it back into my reticule.

"So, what sort of adventure do you have planned for us, Miss Dufour?" Ben is suddenly beside me. I must've been so lost in thought I didn't hear him approach.

I throw a smile on and shove away all thoughts of Harrison. "It's a surprise." I take hold of the bend of his elbow, and we start down the hill toward the lake.

His expression warms, adding softness to his sharp, angular face as he helps me step over a dip in the path. "You didn't need to do all of this, Zo. I could've helped."

For some reason, his trial of the nickname only Harrison calls me sets my teeth on edge. I admonish myself and tell my bunched neck muscles to relax. It's a silly reaction. But Harrison has called me that since we were kids, and Ben hasn't known me that long. With another puff of a sigh, I get my head back into the game. There's something Harrison would say....

"I wanted to do this." I grin up at him as we walk along the side of the lake. "It's the least I could do after my mishaps and mayhem during the tournament."

I don't have to remind him of me dropping the bowl on his foot or him falling out of the boat, though technically that was kind of on him.

"Well, whatever the reason, I appreciate it and I'm looking forward to a little time away from the crowd." He reaches over to give my hand holding his arm a gentle squeeze.

Of course, we can't come out here all alone. That would be against the retreat rules. So a retreat staff chaperone and Jake, who'll be filming—Mr. Kellsner was pretty insistent—will be with us but agreed to stay out of the way as much as possible. They came out here ahead of us to set up, along with the staff who brought out our food, and should be sufficiently hidden by now.

We hike up the small hill above the lake to the gray stone gazebo covered in climbing Virginia Creeper, now a brilliant cascade of reds, oranges, and hints of yellow with the season.

Standing at the entrance to the gazebo, we take in the lights wrapped around the arches and columns, a roaring fire blazing in the fire pit in the middle, and a table filled with candles and food, including everything we need to make s'mores. Cook and her staff did *good* and to my specifications, and I'm impressed since they only had the afternoon to put all of this together for us.

"You did all of this for me?" Ben lets his arm drop, making my hand fall to my side as he wanders into the space, then pivots to face me.

This makes me hesitate, and I'm not sure why. But *did* I do all of this with Ben in mind? He never actually said he liked the outdoors. *I* don't even love the outdoors, but I have to admit this spot is lovely. And I wanted this date to be perfect, in the perfect place.

Thankfully, he doesn't seem to notice my hesitation and treats it like a rhetorical question, perusing the table filled with covered silver platters. But he lifts one of the covers and shoots me a quizzical look. "Cheeseburgers?" He opens another. "And fries?"

Is it just me or is there a hint of disappointment in his tone?

There's a crack of a twig and someone clearing their throat on the other side of the row of evergreens behind the gazebo—probably Jake or the chaperone—as my face heats and I stumble over to the table. "Oh, I thought maybe you'd be sick of the Regency style food by now and want something thoroughly twenty-first century."

His brows lift, and I panic. I don't even know what this man likes to eat. "You hate it," I state.

Leaving the lids on the table, he strides forward and takes my shoulders in his hands. "No, no. It's great. It's perfect."

But why had I thought of burgers in the first place? Then Harrison saying he's been craving them, along with hot, crispy fries, replays in my mind.

Ben pulls out a chair for me, closest to the warmth of the fire, and takes a seat across from me. What a gentleman. That's what I need to do, mentally check off my nonnegotiables list.

He takes the liberty of serving us both until we each have a plate filled with fries, cheeseburgers, and dollops of ketchup from a fancy crystal bowl.

I have to wave a couple of hornets away. They're always out this time of year, especially if there's food.

"Let's dig in while it's still hot." His smile is bright, almost too bright. But I have to admire his precisely cut side-whiskers and the almost-regal tilt of his head, even as he takes a big bite of his tall, everything-on-it burger.

"Mmm. Good call on the cheeseburgers." He dabs his mouth with the linen napkin from his lap—such manners!—before he finishes chewing and leans closer. "So, Zoe, where do you see yourself in five years?"

My hand, holding a fry dipped in ketchup, stops midway to my mouth. "That's a big question. That's like *all* the questions in one."

His smirk is on the debonaire side and matches his wink. "Well, I'm nothing if not efficient."

I sit back a little, chewing on the fry first to give myself time to put my thoughts together. Patting my own mouth with a napkin, I say, "If things go according to plan, I'd like to be settled into marriage"—for some reason, I can't voice my thoughts on coming to a place of peace with my singleness, so marriage only if that's what's in the plan for me—"perhaps starting a family. If we move, then maybe moving even closer to my parents so I can help out with my mom more . . ."

My lips press together as I tap my chin.

"What about your podcast? Don't you want to take that to the next level? You've got such a great opportunity there." There's a spark of something in his earnest expression.

"Yes, of course." I sip my soda, nodding. "I'm hoping that in five years *Love According to Miss Gladwin* is going strong and that we're able to share it with more people, on a bigger stage. Hopefully, with Mr. Kellsner's help."

I've never met a guy who's shown this much interest in our podcast. He's already asked me tons of questions about it and seemed so excited to hear about our plans with Harrison's company and boss. It's endearing. It dawns on me that we have so many shared interests. Okay, so rowing didn't go so well, but everything else seems to line up.

His green-speckled hazel eyes study me, and I can't help throwing the question back to him. "What about you? Where do you see yourself in five years?"

Steepling his fingers over his plate, he pauses as if choosing his words carefully. There's something reserved about him. Manners held in place. Not bad, but not as open with his thoughts as Harrison. "Much the same as you. I'd love to be close to my family here in the Twin Cities. Doing something worthwhile, making my family proud, furthering our legacy. You know?"

There's a hint of something in his voice, not unlike when Harrison talks about his dad.

"I'm sure they're already proud."

"Mm-hmm" is his agreement. He adjusts the pin on his lapel, small with a black stone in the middle. Then the somber, straight line of his lips softens into a smile.

"Do you still want to be teaching in five years?"

His lips bunch to the side. "No, probably not. I'd actually like to get into something with communications. It's where I think my strengths are."

His strengths? I can't help the passing thought that as far as communication goes, between him and me anyway, it hasn't flowed as naturally as I'd hoped.

A branch creaks from behind the gazebo—probably Jake again, but he's taken a vow of silence, raised a hand and everything.

Ben takes another bite of his burger, but when he pulls away, his mouth hangs open with unchewed meat. "Ick!" He spits his mouthful back onto his plate.

"What's wrong?" I set down my own burger and half stand from my chair to see what the problem is.

On his plate is a collecting pool of juice from the medium-cooked burger. "Oh." Right. Blood phobia.

"This burger is underdone. I can't eat this." He's on the edge of the chair as though deciding whether to run from the table or not.

This time there's a grumble from the trees. I shoot a sharp look in that direction at the same time another hornet buzzes by.

"I'm sorry." I duck the hornet, stand, and move the offending plate and burger away. "I asked Cook to make them well done, but this one must've slipped through. Do you want to try a different one?"

His head shakes so violently, his teeth rattle together. Then he straightens and stands, composing himself. "No, thank you. Let's—let's sit by the fire instead. We can have dessert."

Okay, this is not going as planned. Maybe I was silly for thinking I could curate the perfect date and thereby mold Ben into the perfect guy. But I'm not giving up that easy. I send him an apologetic smile and take his offered hand to stand. We grab the s'mores fixings and the strawberries meant for me and settle onto the Adirondack chairs beside the wrought iron firepit.

Looking more relaxed now, Ben leans back in his chair,

his long legs stretched out in front of him. "Are you looking forward to returning to the twenty-first—"

I squeak as another hornet swoops inches from my nose and lands on one of the strawberries on the small side table next to me. "These hornets are determined, aren't they?"

Ben uses a handkerchief from his pocket to shoo it away.

Another buzzes dangerously close to my face so I blow at it, but in between my short gusts of air, I say, "What—were—you—saying—before?"

"Right. I was asking if you're looking forward to returning to the twenty-first century?"

The hornet finally moves on. "You know, this has been my dream for so long"—I sweep a hand over my empire waist dress, our surroundings—"to step into the pages of Austen and Gladwin." I sigh.

"But?" he prompts.

I lift a shoulder. "This whole thing has me thinking. I really put those courting tips from Gladwin and my list to the test, didn't I?"

His head tilts. "You sure did. You may have maimed yourself and others in the process, but you did it."

Guilt churns the cheeseburger in my stomach. "Sorry about that."

He waves it away. "Just kidding." Was he?

But I continue because he's staring at me intently, waiting. "I guess, after this experience, where I thought I'd find more answers than questions, where everything was going to be all laid out for me—the rules, the expectations, my own list to check off . . . I don't know, maybe no one should be listening to what I have to say about love."

Ben goes still and then swoops over to me, bending before my chair. Taking my hands in his, he presses a kiss to the back of one hand. It's warm, unnerving, his intensity. "Don't say that. You have a huge following. People out there care about what you have to say. Do you have any idea what I would—I mean, *others* would give to have that kind of influence? To make your family so proud? To matter to so many?"

His thumbs work circles into the backs of my hands while his pupils expand, wide eyes searching mine. "You have to keep going and see how big this can be. Maybe you need some extra help. I'm sure it can be overwhelming."

"I have help, I have—"

The squeeze he gives my hands is just on the threshold of painful, so I pull them from his grip as he adds in a low, fervent voice, "Don't waste this opportunity." The set of his jaw seems to be holding back more words.

He returns to his seat and lets out a breath, relaxing again. To busy my freed hands, I grab two marshmallows and thread them onto a roasting skewer.

"What are you doing? You can't eat marshmallows." He arches a brow at me.

That hits a nerve. I've always disliked it when someone told me what I couldn't eat as a diabetic, even if it's true. "You're right. They're basically pure sugar. But you can."

I move them toward the reddish-orange embers at the edge of the fire pit. "And before you say anything, I know there's a whole spectrum of 'marshmallow doneness' levels. What level are you?"

"That's easy." His tone is matter of fact. "Right in the sweet spot middle. Golden brown, with a slight crisp on the outside, warm and gooey on the inside." He kisses his fingers with a "Mwah!"

I giggle. I like this Ben. Easier, carefree, smiling.

"So, no pressure then, huh?"

"If we're going to be together, I suppose knowing how I like my marshmallows is a requirement." His tone is light, joking, but something about it still rubs me the wrong way. "What's something I should know about your food preferences?"

I turn the marshmallows, pulling back a little from the heat so they don't burn, and shake off his comment. "I hate runny yolks. With a *passion*." My nose wrinkles at the thought. "And I love strawberries."

He picks the biggest, juiciest-looking strawberry from the bowl and leans closer. "Well then. In that case, allow me to help you keep up your strength for this delicate roasting process."

He lowers the strawberry to my mouth, his eyes never leaving mine. My breath speeds up. He's close now. I take a bite. The slight tartness mixes with the sweet, running over my tongue in a gush. A stray drop of juice escapes, tickling the corner of my lips.

"Here, let me." His thumb brushes across the spot.

He leans closer, gently pulling my face toward his. Do I want this? A flash of Harrison's face this close right before he kissed me—the best kiss I've ever had in my life—doesn't help.

I'm faintly aware of a rustling noise in the evergreens. And there's a buzzing in my ears. My heart beating against my eardrums? But before Ben's lips can touch mine, the buzzing increases, becoming more insistent. I start to pull back to swat the winged intruder away when it lands on my collar. Inches away from our faces.

Ben's eyes round, nearly cross-eyed watching the hornet crawl up my collar to the sensitive skin of my neck and settle there like this is its new home.

I try to blow a stream of air down/sideways but only succeed in making a loud "*Pfft!*" that seems to agitate the hornet. It doesn't fly away.

Ben freezes, and so do I.

There's a crashing through the trees, and Harrison emerges, carrying the camera. He sets the camera on the table. I don't have time to question what he's doing here before he grabs an empty plate and rushes over to me while Ben backs away.

"Let me see if I can wave it away." Using the plate like a fan, Harrison tries to no avail to make the stubborn creature take flight.

I raise a hand, not sure if I should try to pick it up or flick it off. Before I can decide, the hornet sinks its stinger into my neck and flies off like it's sick of the drama.

The burning sting is immediate, and the pain radiates up toward my chin and face. "Ow!" My hand slaps over the spot, and the regret is immediate.

Harrison sprints to the table and grabs the bucket of ice our sodas were in while Ben remains in a silent daze.

Returning to me, Harrison steadies me by the shoulder and holds a piece of ice to my neck with the other hand. The cold takes the edge off, but *ouch*.

He's breathing hard and so am I from the pain. Face close, his eyes boring into mine, he rasps, "Are you all right?"

"Yes." I wince when even talking hurts. "Thank you." The pain floats away for a moment while his gaze holds mine. I can't help but notice being this close to Harrison is completely different than with Ben. World-tilting, body-tingling, and like an invisible magnet is pulling me closer.

But—Ben! I forgot Ben is still standing awkwardly off to the side. His arms are crossed, a brow lifted in obvious irritation.

I pull back and take a fresh piece of ice from Harrison, whose expression shutters in an instant.

Glancing between the men, I say, "What—what are you doing here, Harrison? I thought Jake was filming." I don't even want to think back over the date and what Harrison witnessed, not that I did anything wrong. But after our kiss, maybe he shouldn't be filming me on dates anymore.

He folds his arms. "Yep, he was going to, but he asked me to instead. He and Eden were invited to play games in the parlor with Milton, Sophia, George, Joan, and her daughter."

"As you can see, we're okay now," Ben starts to say.

But I hold a hand up, indicating my neck. "Ben, I can't possibly continue this date."

"Fine, fine. Of course." He rubs his hands together as if to warm them. "I'm heading in. No offense, but this was a complete disaster. Let me plan the next one, huh?" Ben's palm brushes my face, and he throws me a condescending smile on his way by.

Really? My teeth grit together and a deep snarl rumbles in the back of Harrison's throat as Ben passes him.

That's when I notice the marshmallow skewer I abandoned in the commotion. "Oh, no."

Grabbing the end, I pull out the flaming marshmallows. I shake them, trying to put them out—What do I know about roasting marshmallows? I'm not a camping gal—but they fly off the prongs like tiny meteorites and crash-land on the cement floor of the gazebo.

Harrison jumps back so they don't land on his shoes. "Whoa!" He stomps on them, and the sticky charred remains splatter his tall Regency boots until the flames extinguish. The air fills with the sharp, acrid scent of burned sugar.

After a moment, my lip starts to tremble, but not with tears. Laughter bubbles up my throat, and I can't contain it. His mouth twitches, and he lets out his deep, rich, from-the-gut laugh. The laugh I love to hear, especially if I'm the one to pull it from him. We're inconsolable for several minutes, eyes streaming even as my neck pinches with each movement.

"This was supposed to be the perfect date."

Moving closer, boots sticking to the cement with each step, he dabs my neck again with another piece of ice. His eyes brighten. "And what about this wasn't perfect, Zo?" He cocks his head to the side. It's good to hear my nickname on his lips again.

He brushes a stray curl behind my ear like he's waiting to hear something specific from me. Does he want me to say "the company"?

But instead, I send him a crooked grin. "Well, let's just say that if we were rating *me* on this date, I landed firmly at 'Mr. Collins.'"

The backs of his knuckles graze my cheek. "Oh, I don't know, I'd say you were at least a 'Baron of Meager Prospects.'"

A scoffing chuckle escapes. "You're being extremely kind. If I really was being graded, I'd be somewhere well below Mr. Collins. What exactly do you think that would be?" I tap my chin. "Potato?"

Another laugh bursts from his mouth. "Well, if you're comparing yourself to boiled potatoes, I've heard they're excellent. Besides, you're the most entertaining potato I've ever met."

"Thanks." I angle a wry smile at him.

My head spins with tonight's events. How, after all of the planning, the lists, everything I thought I knew, can I still be such a failure at finding love?

28

Zoe

My pacing the floor since dawn, the creak of the wood planks with each step toward the fireplace and back, drove Eden downstairs to update our social posts and edit with Jake about half an hour ago.

I can't stop thinking about Harrison. Most of all, about the pain I saw in his eyes as he conceded his win and told me to take Ben on the dinner date instead. Then again in the gazebo. What must he have been feeling having to film me on a date with Ben? My hand covers the ache in my throat. I wince as I brush my sting, which is better today but still sore. A groan erupts from my mouth as I march to the other side of the room again. I was so convinced Ben was right for me. And on paper, he is. But what if Ben's *not* what I want or need? Last night truly was a disaster. Ben wasn't wrong about that. Just not for the reasons he may have meant.

I'd tried to cross off the traits on my list with him, even

thought I had. But then things didn't seem to be meshing with us. We're like two puzzle pieces that look like they should fit together, but just . . . don't.

I admitted to Eden when I returned from the Murphy's Law date that I should've gone with my first instinct and asked Harrison to accompany me. She squealed and told me to stop being such a "sensible, emotion-stuffing Elinor Dashwood" and tell Harrison how I feel. But how *do* I feel?

When he said the famous Darcy quote during the trivia contest, the profession seemed to be streaming from his own heart. Or did I imagine that?

I need air.

It's surprising how natural these Regency clothes feel as I secure a bonnet over my head, slip on my short spencer jacket, and drape a thick shawl over my shoulders before stepping out the bedroom door.

Pausing only a moment, I exit the back door leading out to the gardens. Should I tell Eden I'm headed outside?

No, I can't deal with the questions. I already had an apple and peanut butter from a stash in our room, so I'll avoid having to face Harrison or Ben over breakfast. My above-the-ankle leather half boots crunch along the crushed rock path of the garden then whisper against soft grass as I leave the garden behind. The crisp air bathes my face, washing away any unease about this solo outing.

I'm surrounded by the smokey, earthy, and spicy scent of dry leaves, which I associate with Harrison, eliciting more confusion. A reel of his smiles plays for me. He has so many smiles—kind, mischievous, heated, teasing, gentle. Each more heart-stopping than the last. His laughter. Full, rich, and oh-so-contagious. And all the countless times he's been there for me. Out of obligation. Because he's Eden's brother.

No, that's not right.

Because he's my friend?

Yes, but also no. That's not quite right, either. I can no longer tell myself he did those things for any other reason than he cares about me. *Really* cares about me. The whole me. The me I can be with him, and the parts of my heart I let him see that not everyone does.

And what about him? Don't I care about *him*? About the things that make him happy, hurt him, make him laugh . . .

But he's so not part of the plan. And yet, he's right in front of me. In my life all this time, but somehow the one thing I didn't see coming.

Just like my mom and dad.

I'm already moving past the small lake to the wooded trails we used for the hunt. The gray clouds above seem to have sunk to the earth, settling among the forest in a misty fog that slithers between tree limbs. Soon the fog thickens until only the next step is visible.

The irony isn't lost on me as I stubbornly trudge forward. That's how God so often works, isn't it? Only the next step, the next shrub or tree, is visible when I want the whole forest. I need the whole picture so I can organize, mitigate disaster, plan for all possible outcomes, ready a list to ensure everything turns out the way it's supposed to. The way *I* think it's supposed to.

But *is* that what I need? Is that what God wants for me? Or would He say, "Trust Me. I've got this handled, Zoe. Let go"? Maybe He reveals one step at a time so I have to take His hand for the next one, the one I can't quite see beyond. That way He can help me when I inevitably stumble or fall.

My toe catches on a root, and I trip, but right myself before falling. I huff, sending a glance to the slate-colored sky. *Very funny.*

I've walked and walked and don't really know where I am. How much time has passed? In my haste, I left my phone behind. *Smart.*

Either side of the trail has tapered into steep hills. The

burble of a creek or small river floats from the bottom of one side. On the other, the veiled dark outlines of evergreens stand like silent sentinels in the haze.

Fine droplets of water begin to tickle my nose and cheeks. I hold my shawl over my head as a makeshift umbrella.

My next step hits an unstable rock, wobbling and precarious, which sends me toppling to the side. The slick bottom of my boots skid as I try to find purchase. I careen toward the edge of the steep hill. And . . .

I slip and don't stop until I'm tumbling down the hill. My nails scrape and claw at rocks and roots, but nothing slows me. Finally, I reach the bottom, at the edge of what I now see is a crystal-clear stream. Time to take inventory of my injuries—scratches along my fingers and palms, tender spots on my arms and legs that are already turning to bruises. My dress's hem is torn, and I'm filthy. But it's the traitorous foot that concerns me. My ankle is throbbing. What if it's broken? How will I get back?

Good thing I wasn't on camera for that. It'd be funny if it wasn't so painful. Scooting myself to my knees, I bend my good leg and push up until I'm balancing on that foot. I try putting a bit of my weight on the other foot.

"Ah!" My breath hisses through bared teeth as I slink back down and wait for the sharp pain to subside.

This is my Marianne Dashwood moment, except there's no Colonel Brandon coming to rescue me. At this point, I'd even take a Mr. Willoughby, provided he brings me wildflowers the next day. But it's me alone with these creaking, vibrant-leafed trees.

My first thought, my only thought, is of Harrison. Will he look for me? But my chest pangs bone-deep. Maybe even more painful than my ankle. Why would he? I've pushed him away too many times, and I saw the hurt in his eyes when I walked away after our kiss, and when he saw me with Ben. He made light of it, tried to hide it, even came to my aid when I needed him despite it. But I hurt him with my rejection. Harrison's probably done with me, and I don't blame him.

I was looking for the perfect modern-day gentleman. But what if the person I need isn't the perfect gentleman and instead is the perfect gentle *man?* The man who has been there for me longer than I can remember. The solid rock, the stable fixture in my life whom I've taken for granted all these years. I care about Harrison. Maybe *care* isn't even a strong enough word.

The unstable rock I thought looked secure at the top of the hill led me to where I am—hurt and alone. The irony isn't lost on me, either.

"Please, we're good on the metaphors, God. I get it." A hysterical giggle bubbles up from my chest, but it only reminds me of the times Harrison has coaxed a laugh out of me despite the circumstances, as if he knows what I need.

Images of him charge through my mind. All the times he's put me first, shown his infinite kindness and patience with me and those around him—how many times has he seen my blood sugar needs before even I have? There's his chivalry time and again as well as his respect for me as a driven, knows-her-own-mind woman. Even the way he'd been so kind to Sophia, partnering with her when she didn't have anyone just like Knightley had done with Harriet in *Emma*. And I don't think I've ever met anyone as honest as Harrison, sometimes to a fault.

"Oh," I gasp. It's a sound of pure wonder.

He *has* been checking off my list. In all the ways that matter. I cover my mouth and draw a breath from between my fingers.

All this time.

Tears spring to my eyes, prickling at the corners, then spill down my cheeks. The air instantly cools my dampened skin.

Maybe he's a *little* obsessed with sports, and he has the facial hair I always thought I didn't prefer. I laugh through my tears. But, man, that kiss. The way his beard grazed my chin and cheeks sent endless shivers through my body. Okay, perhaps *well-groomed* facial hair like Harrison's is all right.

I had never quite admitted to myself that I'd always wondered how Harrison's lips would feel on mine. *Soft*. That's how. So soft yet firm and confident, as if he'd been waiting to do that for ages and he knew exactly what he wanted.

And somehow, that is—*was*—me.

Already the cold is setting in, especially with the chill of the wet leaves seeping into my legs and backside. I rub my hands together to warm them.

A fogged breath escapes in a huff.

But then, after the kiss, every reason to say no to more had suffocated me and I'd done the most unwise thing an otherwise smart girl like me could do. I backed away—from him, from my feelings right there under the surface. I'd been too afraid to speak them out loud and grab on to them, and him, and never let go like I should have.

Oh, I've messed this up. Big time. I used my tendency toward perfectionism as a mask to hide behind. But, somehow, Harrison always seems to find the cracks in that mask and probably knows me better than anyone. Even Eden. But right now, all I want to do is talk to him. To tell him . . .

My glucose monitor beeps. A shrill, echoing slice into the quiet. Low blood sugar. I was so foolish—for so many reasons—and didn't bring anything with me other than the small monitor I'd slipped into my dress pocket. I'd chalked my hunger up to the early hour with a small breakfast, and the sheen of sweat on my forehead and upper lip to the walk and my fall. I didn't think I'd be gone long, so it didn't occur to me to bring food or juice along. Now I really did it.

"Help!" But I already know no one will hear me. My thoughts drift to Harrison again as the trees begin to spin.

29

Harrison

"Has anyone seen Zoe?" I barely poke my head around the office doorframe as the words tumble out more abruptly than I mean.

Both Eden and Jake pop their heads up. Jake leans over Eden's shoulder at the desk, the laptop open in front of them.

Eden's purple brows gather. "Not since I left the room earlier. She's been up since the crack of dawn, pacing up there."

Jake shakes his head. "I haven't either, sorry."

"What was she pacing about?"

Eden tips her head and squints like I'm a complete moron. "You."

Maybe I am a moron because I mirror her head tilt. "What? Why?"

Jake straightens, crosses an arm over his chest, and covers a side smirk with the opposite hand.

Blinking at the ceiling for a breath, Eden pins me with a

sharp look. "*Because* she's smitten with you, just as much as you are with her." Her tone says anyone with half a brain cell should know this.

"But I thought—she never—"

"She has a hard time opening up. In fact, I have a sneaking suspicion you're able to get my best friend to open up more than I can. But she's also more stubborn than two of you put together, and that's saying something. I don't think she even knows she has feelings for you, or maybe she can't admit it to you or herself." Eden stands and moves around the desk to grip my arms. "Last night I think she started to crack, to see what you mean to her. She was in a tizzy over that date with Ben."

"She was?"

"I wouldn't normally tell you or anyone something Zoe told me in private, but the girl won't get out of her own way. She needs a little nudge." Eden lets go, eyes darting as if deciding something.

"And?" I urge her.

"*And* she said that she was about to invite you on the date before you stepped in—also getting in your own way, might I add—and told her to take Ben instead. She also said she wished it had been you on the date with her."

My heart leaps into my throat. "I need to find her."

They answer in unison. "Yes, you do." Both have wide, knowing grins.

I thank them and take the stairs two at a time up to Zoe and Eden's room. There's no response to my knock. Eden gave me the key, so I quietly let myself in. The room is empty. Zoe's phone is on the side table beside her bed.

I absently pick it up, and several notifications light up the screen—all from her glucose monitor synced to her phone app. It lets out one of its screeching beeps. She's low. Wherever she is, she's dangerously low.

Sweat prickles up the back of my neck.

Keeping the phone with me, I sprint downstairs and careen into the office. I let Eden and Jake know we need to find her fast with something to raise her blood sugar. We dash down the hall.

"We'll see if she's in the drawing room." Eden pulls Jake by the hand.

I bump into Ben. As much as I loathe to, I stop him. "Have you seen Zoe? We can't find her."

His gaze flips over my shoulder to the office, then back to me. "No, I haven't."

Ben seems distracted, and for a split second, I vacillate between shaking him and racing away. Of course, with the awkward end to their date last night, maybe he doesn't want to talk about her. I'm about to excuse myself when he raises his forefinger toward the office. "Hey, is that where all the mysterious podcast goings-on happen?"

Really? That's what he wants to ask right now? But I guess I didn't say this is an emergency. "Yeah." I toss a glance behind me. "Actually, I really need to find Zoe. She has low blood sugar, and no one seems to know where she is. So . . ." *Hint, hint.*

His brows rise. "Oh, by all means. Let's split up. I'll look back down this hall and near the foyer."

My chin dips once and I'm off in the opposite direction toward the drawing room.

Eden and Jake are in the breakfast room, next to the drawing room, and there's no sign of Zoe.

"Has anyone seen her?"

Eden bounces on her heels. The worry I feel is reflected in her tightened features. "No, and I asked Victoria, too. She came from the library. Zoe wasn't there, either."

Sophia strides through the doorway.

Waving her over, I blurt, "Sophia, have you seen Zoe?"

She starts to shake her head, then holds a hand to her chin.

"Oh, wait. Now that you mention it, I did see her through my upstairs window. It was earlier, when I woke up."

This is taking too long, but I don't want to be rude. "Where was she?" I fight to keep my tone even.

"She was walking outside. Headed toward the gardens, but it was so foggy I couldn't see where she went after that."

It's started raining since then. My stomach bottoms out. Dread turns to ice in my veins.

I squeeze her shoulder. "Thank you." Then to Eden and Jake, "Hey, will you grab juice and anything sugary from the kitchen and meet me by the back garden doors?"

"On it." Jake gives me a little salute. He takes Eden's hand and I rush toward the office, where I left a backpack and a long coat earlier.

Ben steps out of the office when I arrive. "Oh, I was looking for you to let you know I didn't find her by the foyer."

After shoving my arms through the coat—though there's nothing waterproof about it, it'll have to do—I sling the backpack over my shoulders, closing the office door behind us. "I think I know where she is, or at least the direction she was headed."

He glances out the window to the rain that's now falling in earnest, the fog slowly washing away. "I could . . ." His tone is weak and ends like a question.

"No, I'll find her." There's no way he's coming with me. Besides, his offer is halfhearted at best.

He's quick to concede. "Sure, I'll stay here in case she comes back."

I'm already running toward the garden doors. There's no time to waste. "I'm coming, Zoe. Hold on."

I barely slow long enough to throw Zoe's phone, the two bottled apple juices, banana, and candy bar Jake and Eden shove into my hands into my backpack.

"I'm headed to the lake and then to the trails we used for the hunt if she's not there."

They bob their heads in unison.

Jake claps me on the shoulder. "We'll check the opposite way, back by the stables and the other end of the garden."

I clasp his arm for a split second then continue running.

Eden calls after me, "Be careful!"

If only I had my running shoes and not these boots on, but I don't let them slow me. They do, however, make me slip on the rain-slicked grass a couple of times.

In the middle of the gardens and in view of the small lake at the bottom of the hill, I call, "Zoe!"

The fog has lifted enough that I see no sign of her, but if she was this close to the mansion and able to, she would've already made her way back.

I turn in a wide circle when I hit the meadow. Where would she go? If it weren't raining, I'd use my tracking skills acquired from years of hunting. But the water will have washed away most signs she was there.

Already, Eden has texted me:

> She's nowhere on this side. Please find her and bring her back safe. She must have gone to the trails.

I fight the fear twisting in my gut against the irritation that she'd walk so far from the house alone. It's not that she's weak. No one could ever make that mistake. But everyone needs help, to be taken care of sometimes. Even my strong Zoe.

My chest burns, not just from the jog. I want to be that person for her.

Part of me warns not to get my hopes up again, but a louder part tells the pessimist to shush. This is Zoe we're talking about. My dream girl, for longer than I even understood or admitted to myself. With a jolt, I realize that she's the woman I want to spend the rest of my life with.

Racing to the first trail, the most worn in, to the right, I pray it's the one she took. She's not "The Road Not Taken" type when it comes to the outdoors. More of the full city type. Maybe I can teach her the joys of the wilderness. The thought warms me. But . . .

One thing at a time. First, I need to find her and make sure she's okay. And even after that, I have to see how she reacts to me. We have to move at her pace or I'll scare her off. But what Eden told me gives me more than a dose of hope to spur me forward.

The trail, while it's broken in, is covered with loose rocks and lifted roots I didn't notice when we were on the hunt. A snarl rips from my throat as I skid over a slippery rock and regain my balance.

The rain starts to lighten, but I still have to blink rapidly and wipe my eyes to see my way ahead. The trail's sides have steepened now. I'd best be careful or I'll find myself in trouble.

Help me find her. Please, Lord. He knows where she is, even if I don't.

"Zoe!" I don't mean for my voice to come out so raw, fringed with panic.

I freeze to listen, then call again.

That's when I hear her small, frail voice. "Harrison." It's a miracle I hear her over the rush of the stream below and above my own hammering heartbeat.

"Zoe," I call louder, nearing the edge of the stream side of the trail. "I'm here."

Peeking over the edge, I can make out the crumpled heap that is Zoe and her dress pooling around her.

It's steep here. I know it's bad when she doesn't lift her head as I slide my way down to her while the tangled undergrowth tears at my hands, face, and clothing. But when I skid to a stop and pull her against my chest, she shows surprising strength as she curls her arm around my neck and latches on.

"Harrison. You found me." Her words are a soft rasp, but the frayed edges cut me to the core.

My thumb smooths over her cool, damp cheek, and I tighten my grip around her back with the other arm. "Of course. I will always come for you, Zoe. Always."

One-handed, I wrestle my backpack off my shoulders and dig inside.

Her lids are heavy, and her small frame is shaking against me, but she licks her lips and opens her mouth. "I was so foolish. I—"

I gently shush her. "It's okay, Zo. Don't worry about that now." I slip off my coat and wrap it around her shoulders, buttoning the top couple of buttons to keep it in place, and rub her arms to warm her. "I'll tease you about being the worst diabetic later when you're feeling better. Here, I brought you a few things for your blood sugar."

Holding the apple juice to her lips, she drinks deeply. She takes several more gulps, and only then do my neck and back muscles begin to loosen.

She stops for a breath between swallows. "You know how there are animals, like dogs, that can supposedly smell low or high blood sugar?" I nod, encouraged by her stronger tone. "I don't need one. I have you. How did you know? You always seem to know when I need you."

"I went to your room to find you and saw the warnings from your glucose monitor app." Lifting the juice bottle to her lips again, I help her to finish it, then fish out the candy bar from my bag.

Shedding her gloves into the backpack, she takes the candy bar and bites into it. A little sigh passes her lips as she chews the chocolate, caramel, and peanuts.

My fingers trace along her jawline and then brush a wet

lock of hair away from her eyes. "I was so afraid..." I swallow, unable to say out loud what I had feared most. "Never leave without your support animal"—I wink and jab a thumb into my chest—"again, okay?"

Her trembling lips lift into a smile. "Deal." After she takes another bite of her candy bar, I rub a little speck of chocolate off the corner of her mouth. "Hey, before, I wasn't saying that I was foolish because of this fiasco. I mean, I am, but that wasn't—"

"What, then? Because I'm sure I won't agree."

She evades my gaze, playing with the empty wrapper in her hands. "I've been so foolish about... you. All this time." Her eyes dart to mine, then back to her lap. "Harrison, it's you."

I don't dare breathe. She can't possibly be saying what she seems to be saying.

"It's always been you." She shakes her head as if in wonder. "You were right there, but finally, I think I see you. Like really *see* you for the first time. The way you've always seen me." The words are hardly more than a whisper, but their impact is like a giant bell resounding within me, echoing on and on through every corridor of my mind, my heart, my everything.

With a hand against her soft cheek, I lean in, resting my forehead against hers, then kiss the cool tip of her nose. We both let out a shaky laugh. "And you're the girl who stole my heart, my whole heart, before I ever knew it was gone."

We stay like that for a long moment, letting our shared realization sink in.

Her dazed, awed smile turns sheepish. "Should I apologize for that?"

I kiss her forehead. "Absolutely not. You can keep it, Zo. I don't want it back. It's yours. Always."

Her hand clutches my own, still resting on her cool cheek, and pulls it to her mouth. She presses a kiss to my knuckles. "I've been so scared to let you in, anyone in. I may have made it seem like I was on a mission to find love, but I think something Eden said before the retreat might be true. If I kept my focus on perfection and checking off an impossible list, then no one could ever measure up. And if no one could measure up, no one could reject me or leave me or"—she slows, gaze moving to the stream bubbling by—"someday possibly break my heart by not sticking around through life's unpredictable challenges. Those things we can't know or plan for. But I thought if I could control everything else, somehow I could control that, too."

She's studying my hand now, clasped in her lap, running her fingers over my own. Tears mix with the drips of rain on her cheeks. I reach out to swipe them away.

"Zo, I want you to know—"

A smile peeks out, rounding her cheeks. "I know. I do. I know my heart is safe with you." Her eyes close for a moment, a look of peace softening her face.

I pull our clasped fingers to my lips now and kiss her rose petal–soft skin. "It is safe with me. *You're* safe with me. I will always protect you—mind, body, and soul—with my life."

We stay like that for a minute, but we can't stay here forever.

I draw a breath. "If we don't want to freeze out here, I better get us back to the house."

She points at her left leg. "I kind of forgot to mention, I think there's something wrong with my ankle. I twisted it when I fell. There were more important things to address first. I mean, who can think about a little thing like a possible fracture when there are rain-soaked love declarations to be had?" Her smile twinkles.

"*Love* declarations?" My heart, the one we established is firmly in her hands, stutters while I lift a brow at her.

She clamps her lips together, her already cold-flushed cheeks reddening further.

I have mercy on her and lean closer to the ankle she indicates. "Where does it hurt?"

She points to the whole ankle and down the foot. I do a visual inspection and a light physical inspection with my fingers. "Hmm. No lacerations, no obvious signs of broken bones, but I'm no substitute for an X-ray. Have you tried putting any weight on it?"

The lines around her mouth deepen, and she swallows hard. "I tried to stand on it and couldn't. It hurt too much."

"Don't worry. I've got you." My strength is bolstered by her trusting, confident smile as I shoulder on the backpack and lift her from the ground. She wraps her arms securely around my neck.

"I know you do." She studies my face. "You hurt yourself, too. Looks like you got in a fight with the bushes on the way down."

"You should see the other guys."

I hadn't noticed my injuries, either. As it is, they're only slight stings. Working in a zigzag pattern, I make my way, Zoe safely in my arms, to the top and finally emerge onto the trail.

"There, we made it." I huff and pause to catch my breath. The rest of the way will be a cakewalk compared to that.

There's a little mischievous smile playing on her lips. "I knew we would, my Colonel Brandon."

I grin despite my exhaustion. I won't let her down. Securing her closer to my chest, I plant a soft kiss on her lips before continuing back down the trail toward the mansion. "Anything for you, m'lady."

30

Zoe

Harrison's grip under my knees and around my back is still firm, his breath deep but steady. Ever the athlete. Guilt pangs in my stomach because this is entirely my fault. At least it's stopped raining as he carries me.

"My clumsiness might actually be the death of me. *And* you." I wince as I glance up at him. "I'm sorry."

"I'm not." His expression turns wry. "Obviously, I'm sorry that you're hurt, and that low glucose was too close a call for my liking, but . . . I'm not sorry you're in my arms now."

I smile in answer because I can't bring myself to be sorry that I find myself in his strong arms, either. Eden and Jake were so relieved to hear I'm okay when I called her as we started the trek back on the trail and told her what happened.

He pushes forward, one confident stride in front of the other. His eyes crinkle. "So, Colonel Brandon, huh?" One brow quirks. "Isn't that the boring old fuddy-duddy Marianne eventually settles for when her true love, Willoughby, leads her on and turns out to be a gold-digging flake?"

I can't keep laughter from bubbling out. "No! I mean, yes, Willoughby was a jerk. But Colonel Brandon wasn't a fuddy-duddy. He was dashing and a quiet sort of heroic. He might actually be my favorite of Austen's heroes." I hold Harrison's gaze, my tone turning serious.

"Oh?" His eyes sparkle.

"He was also kind."

"Mm-hmm." The sound is a rumble against my hand now resting on his chest.

"He was supportive and never tried to change Marianne. It was only that she matured and learned through experience that he meant more to her than she first realized."

"Interesting." His head tilts, as does his mouth. "Tell me more about this bloke, Colonel Brandon. Sounds like an upstanding guy if you ask me."

"Oh, he is. He's a totally underrated hero." I tap my lips. "Let's see. He's loyal, brave"—I surprise myself by running my thumb against the soft hair at the nape of Harrison's neck—"thoughtful, and always looking out for Marianne. He wants the best for her even when she doesn't see it or initially appreciate it, which is really quite silly of her. . . ."

Squinting, I add, "And Colonel Brandon may not have been the wild and untamed kind of romantic Marianne thought she wanted in the beginning, but there's something steady and calming about his presence that ultimately gives Marianne peace. Through the storms of life, he's the unmoving rock she needs." My chest heaves a deep sigh. "He was the true, devoted romantic after all."

My throat suddenly clogs.

"So what you're saying is that you think a guy like Colonel Brandon might have a shot with a girl like Marianne?" His Adam's apple moves as he studies me, waiting.

Warmth spreads across my face despite the chill. "Well, you know how the story ends...."

We hold each other's gazes until there's a little dip in the trail and Harrison's focus shifts.

My hand covers my mouth when a little gasp escapes. "I thought of something."

"What?"

"I always thought I was an Elinor—logical, doing what's right, patiently checking off a list, waiting for life to line up in the way it's supposed to, then making my move." I tug at my chin. "But I'm really a Marianne in need of my Colonel Brandon."

"Good. I always liked Marianne better. Passionate about life and way more fun." He gives me a wink.

The lake comes into view. I point to a bench beside the dock.

"No, I need to—" He sets his jaw.

"Sit. You need a break."

"But you're hurt and all wet."

"My ankle does throb, but it'll still be in the same condition if we take our time. Besides, I'm not ready for the fuss Eden will make nor the questions from everyone else." Scrunching my lips together, I point again. "Really. For a few minutes. I'll be okay."

He strides to the bench and sinks onto it with me still on his lap. I help to remove the backpack from his back and set it on the seat beside us. "I'm not sure I'm cut out to be an Austen or Gladwin hero."

I tug at the rain-dampened collar around his neck. "I don't know, you're pretty heroic in your own right. I'm not sure what I would've done if you hadn't shown up."

"Don't want to think about it, honestly. I'm just grateful I found you." He keeps hold of my back with one arm and slides me off his lap until I'm leaning against the arm of the bench and my feet rest on his legs instead. "Here, let's elevate that foot."

He digs through the backpack. "How are you feeling?"

"Much better. The sugar is kicking in." I leave out the part about the sharp ache in my ankle that has increased with all of the movement.

He hands me my phone to check my blood sugar level. "Yup, it's heading back to normal range."

In the bag is also a first aid kit that Harrison riffles through until he finds a roll of elastic bandage. He glances up at me as he gently removes my boot and begins wrapping my ankle, anchoring the bandage around the arch of my foot.

With a short laugh, he says, "After filming you at the roller-skating rink, I decided I better start carrying my own accident-prone supplies. Just in case." He winks.

I also take two of the ibuprofen from the first aid kit and swallow them with a swig from the bottled water.

He finishes and tucks in the end of the bandage. "I had more than my fair share of injuries in football, and so did the other guys. Got pretty good at these bandages."

"Thank you, it feels better like that." Reaching for the first aid kit, I find two bandages as well as an antiseptic pad.

"What are you doing?" He scans me for another injury.

I gesture to his face, and his brows furrow, making a trickle of blood ooze from a deeper gash on his forehead. He touches it and pulls away a crimson finger.

"You look quite the wounded hero, Mr. Lundquist. Very dashing. But a couple of those need to be cleaned and bandaged."

He allows me to clean them with only one wince and breath drawn between his teeth. Bending his head toward me, I blow on the wounds—not so bad once they're cleaned—then place a bandage over each.

"There."

"You're an excellent nurse." His smile warms. "Thank you."

"I had to learn a little minor medical care myself since I'm always hurting myself." His fingers rub along my arm. "And with my mom, you know."

A shiver shimmies through my body when a cool breeze hits us.

"See? We need to go back." He pulls me closer.

"No, I'm all right."

"Here." He secures me in his lap again and wraps his coat more securely around my shoulders.

There's a tug at the base of my throat. I try to swallow it. "You—you gave me your coat." With everything going on, I didn't notice. I breathe in the warm, earthy scent of him mixed with the damp wool of the coat. Our faces are close. I can see every light blue fleck in his dark indigo eyes surrounded by his gold fringe of lashes, sticking together from the earlier rain.

The significance shines in his eyes as much as I know it does mine. He hasn't forgotten my family's love stories.

"Here, let me share a little more warmth." His hand slides up my cheek, pushing the damp curls at my temples behind my ear.

He leans closer, his breath warm against my lips. It doesn't matter that we're wet or chilled or that I may have a sprained ankle. All of that melts away as his eyes pierce mine. The air seems to sweep us up into a silent, slow hurricane. Only us two caught in its eye while the world whirls a graceful, unhurried dance around us.

My hand moves from his chest, where the rapid beat of his heart thumps against my fingers, to his trimmed, bearded cheek. When I lean in, our noses touch but our lips are still a breath apart. He closes the distance. And it's bliss. Me, here in his arms, his lips on mine.

His lips are soft but firm and confident. Expressive. Like he's trying to tell me the depth of his feelings without words, and I endeavor to do the same. Our kiss deepens, lips moving in perfect rhythm—oh, we're in sync now!

There's a wellspring cracked open right in the center of me. Everything my unscaled eyes can now see, everything that's bursting from my heart—his kindness, his care, just *him*. How much he means to me. How I don't want to lose him to my stubborn hold of what I thought I needed. It's all a flood threatening to carry me away if it weren't for his strong, steady arms holding me in place.

We come up for air, and he dots my jawline with a line of light kisses, then my cheek—his breath warm against my cool skin—and one to my forehead before pulling me into an embrace. I lay my head on his shoulder, and we hold each other. No words are needed for several long minutes.

My fingers skim absently against the warmth at the base of his neck, above his unbuttoned collar. His flesh prickles. How can this feel so right? From friends to awkward whatever-we-were to friends again to *this*? But somehow it does.

A thought pops into my head. "Harrison?"

"Mmm?" His tone is languid, relaxed, his arms still around my back.

"I wanted it to be you. Before. On that special date." The truth can't wait any longer. He sits up straighter, cradling my face in the palm of his large, calloused hand with such gentleness. Like he's holding something precious. Remaining quiet as if he knows there's more, he waits.

I swallow. "And all the dates before that, even if I didn't realize it right away. I thought of you constantly, even when I tried not to." I chuckle, which makes him smile. "I measured them against all the good I see in you, against all of the things I love—appreciate about you." Oops. I didn't mean to use the "L" word again even in this context, but he doesn't flinch away from it. "Before I ever admitted it to myself, I saw you as *more*."

He strokes my cheek. "I can't tell you how many times I dreamed of this—you feeling the same way about me, of being able to hold you like this. For you to think of me as more than

Eden's brother and more than a friend." A soft chuckle, then he says, "Do you have any idea how many times *I* wished it were me on those dates with *you*?"

As he draws a breath through his nose, his jaw muscles tense and flex. "And do you know how much restraint I had to use not to crash through those trees sooner when Ben, when you were . . ."

The almost kiss.

My hand swipes over my forehead. "I don't think I've ever been so grateful to a hornet before," I say, only half joking.

He pulls the collar away from my neck to check the sting, and the skim of his fingers sends a prickle down my spine.

Guilt gnaws at me again. "I never meant to lead him on." My lower lip snags between my teeth, and his gaze follows. "I thought that if I created my own manual and checked everything off, that must mean I did it right. And, you know, I'd cut down the chance of being hurt or hurting someone else in the process."

My fingers clench in my lap. "The only thing is, I *will* have to upset someone. At least, I think it'll upset him. I have to tell him about this." I gesture between us. "But, I'm sorry, I shouldn't talk about—" I jab the air with my hand.

"Ben? Yes, we should talk about that." He sits straighter. "After so many years keeping my feelings for you at arm's length, I don't want to waste another minute with half-truths and only saying what's comfortable."

He runs a hand over the back of his head. "And that whole Ben thing? I never thought he was right for you, but I was willing to step back if you really liked him and he treated you the way you deserved."

"I didn't— I didn't know . . ." I say with wonder, turning my head to catch the soft smile at the corner of those amazing lips. "I never knew that you ever could or would feel that way about me. . . ."

He pulls my face closer again and presses a light kiss to my lips. "There you go again, selling yourself short."

We share an amused *hmm*.

"So, now what?" He angles his head to look down at me.

I sit up, tempted to half-teasingly say, *"Well, darlin', whatcha doin' for the rest of your life?"* But that might be a bit much out of the gate.

So I go with, "Well, Mr. Lundquist, I want to do what I should've done for the special date." I straighten, forming my best regal Regency air. "I'd like to cordially invite you to the ball tomorrow."

His crooked smile melts my heart. He rolls his shoulders and gives every Austen and Gladwin hero a run for his money as he pins me with the smoldering-est of all smoldering looks, never taking his eyes from mine as he takes my hand and brushes the back with a featherlight kiss.

"Why, it would be my absolute honor and privilege, Miss Dufour."

31

Harrison

"Here, let me help you sit up on your bed."

Zoe smiles up at me, looping her arms around my neck. "I would've thought you'd had enough of carrying me around today."

Placing her gently against the pillows, I bend forward to whisper into her ear, "Never."

The more I review the events of the last twenty-four hours—witnessing her date with Ben, believing Zoe would never see me the same way I see her, fearing for her life and health when we couldn't find her, relief for her safety, the revelation of her feelings for me, and the kisses—*oh, man, more kisses to keep me awake at night* . . . it seems like something my Regency-addled brain conjured up in a fever-dream.

When we returned from the medical clinic nearby, I strode past Victoria and her objections right to Eden and Zoe's room with Zoe in my arms. The doctor had looked at the cuts on my face at Zoe's insistence, but none needed stitches, as I told her. But her sprained ankle now sports a brand-new what she called her "handy-dandy and oh-so-fashionable" medical boot.

Eden's face turns pink as she ceases her pacing and perches on the end of her own bed. Sophia, who'd been waiting for us, too, excuses herself to let Milton know Zoe's okay.

This is less weird than I thought with Eden, especially since she pestered us the second I carried Zoe through the door of Wyndmere Hall after Zoe's fall—once she checked on Zoe—pressuring us into confessing that we'd finally come clean to each other about our feelings during what Zoe is calling her Marianne Dashwood moment. Eden had hugged both of our necks and squealed and then pushed us back out the door so I could take Zoe to the clinic.

As awkward as we'd all felt when Eden "caught" our almost-kiss, she's completely boarded the Zoe + Harrison ship. She's not the only one. Both Sophia and Milton said they'd been "shipping" Zoe and me from day one. The delight on their faces is only the smallest reflection of the pure joy expanding in my chest.

A knock sounds at the door.

Eden runs to answer it. Anne pokes a shy head in, holding out a tray filled to the brim with food enough for all three of us and then some. The lady's maid has a warm smile, and her gaze moves between Zoe and me.

"Cook heard you were hurt. She sent extra food for everyone."

Victoria had started a halfhearted argument about me in their room, but had backed off when I growled, "I'm *not* leaving." I quickly apologized, but it's true. There's no way I'm leaving her side right now.

Eden takes the tray.

Zoe returns a heartfelt smile. "Thank you, Anne. Please let Cook know we appreciate it."

With a quick bob of the head and curtsy, Anne's gone.

After propping Zoe's booted foot onto a pillow, I fill a tray and set it on her lap.

I hand Eden one of the extra plates and take one for myself. My mouth waters before the savory roast chicken, sliced potatoes slathered with some kind of cream sauce, and rosemary carrots hit my tongue. We didn't eat much since the snacks I brought for Zoe this morning. The nurses at the clinic had brought us each a granola bar and juice to help hold us over, but that's long gone now.

Eden and I pull chairs up to Zoe's bedside. My phone starts to ring—Father. Nope, not dealing with that right now. I don't need whatever kind of criticism he has cooked up. I hit Decline, and we scarf down several bites but are interrupted by another knock. My mouth is still full when I grunt and step to the door.

I'm expecting Victoria, here to attempt to kick me out again, but it's Jake's grinning face that appears around the doorframe.

He pulls two bouquets of flowers from behind his back.

"Oh, it's you," I grumble and swallow. Maybe I'm hangry, too. "Two bouquets? You shouldn't have." I let my tone go dry and monotone.

Jake's smirk widens as he steps into the room and closes the door. "If they make you less likely to bite my head off and possibly share some of that grub, then they're all yours."

I pull another chair over, hand him a filled plate, and return to devouring my own generous helping.

Jake bends over Zoe, squeezing her in a side hug, and sets one bouquet next to her on the side table. "I'm glad you're okay, Zoe. We were all pretty worried, especially this guy. He was *panicked*." He draws the last word out for emphasis and smacks my shoulder.

Squinting in his direction, I give him a "thanks a lot" thumbs-up.

Eden's mouth quirks to the side, the mischief in her eyes a family trait. "Only you could turn her clumsy episode of epic proportions into a swoon-worthy rescue, bro." She lands a soft slug on my arm.

Jake laughs when my response is to keep eating with a pleased grin.

Zoe tosses a dramatic hand out. "All I want to know is, was I giving elegant-even-though-I'm-soaking-wet Marianne vibes or more—"

"Soggy teddy bear?" Eden provides, all of us knowing full well we're talking about Zoe's eventful date with Milton.

Milton himself has told and retold the story so many times that it's pretty embellished at this point—and somehow I'm not the hero in it anymore, even though I saved him from drowning—and he asked if he could be in the blooper reels of the show, so there's no guilt in referring to it now.

Laughter bursts from everyone, but I reach over to squeeze Zoe's hand, then kiss it. "You were a very elegant teddy bear."

There's yet another knock at the door.

"Sprain an ankle in spectacular fashion that warrants a rescue worthy of an Austen adaptation, and suddenly you're Miss Popular." Shoveling in her last bite, Eden moves toward the door.

"Is it finally Victoria to tell us we're all irreversibly ruined with scandal?" Zoe calls to her.

Eden turns a smirk to us as she pulls the door open. "Oh, Ben. Hi."

He doesn't wait for an invitation as he marches inside. Eden steps back from the open door in his wake.

Taking in the scene of us all together, Ben's hands clench at his sides. His hard gaze settles on me, then Zoe. I don't like the look he's giving her. I set my plate down on a side table. My legs already have me standing as if they automatically know my place is between her and any potential threat.

Ben's usual polite, calm demeanor crumbles. There's a wrestling match on his face between a tight smile and a grimace. The latter wins out as his words slide between clenched teeth. "How are you doing? I was hoping to talk to you about the ball."

The bite Zoe took seems to lodge in her throat. She coughs while I hand her a glass of water. After a sip, she takes a breath. This is awkward squared, and I have to clamp my mouth shut not to tell him to get lost. Like she really needs to be interrogated about the ball right now?

I make myself take a seat again. I grab her hand and press her fingers in a gentle squeeze. Maybe it'll give her the courage to say what she wants to say. "Ben, I'm so sorry. But it's not fair to you for me to go with you when Harrison and I—"

Ben cuts her off with a hand and a glare. "No need to finish that sentence. I understand perfectly. Thanks for using me until you were able to convince Prince Charming here to go out with you instead." His finger jabs in my direction. Never been called that before. But the way he spits out the words, it's not meant as a compliment.

Now my anger flares. "Hey, watch it."

Backing toward the door, Ben shakes his head, a humorless laugh on his lips. There have been hints of this side of him over the years. But nothing like this.

Zoe's fingers dig into my palm, and her cheeks flush. "Ben, I never made you any promises. There's no need to be nasty. And I can't help my feelings for Harrison. I didn't plan it. That's actually what surprised me the most. He wasn't part of my plan but somehow makes perfect sense." She glances up at me, then back to Ben. "I want to be honest with you because honesty is important to me."

Ben rubs his jaw, a cold smirk forming. "You're fortunate that a guy like him would even go for you. With the family and connections he has? He could have any girl he wants, always could." His scoff is bitterness itself. "And he's gonna get real sick of this *La La Land* perfect gentleman stuff real quick. So have fun while it lasts." His usual meticulous Ivy League diction is now gone.

There's a hint of something across Zoe's face—fear? She can't actually believe this guy.

I let go of her hand and step toward Ben. "Don't you *ever* talk to her like that. *I'm* the one who's fortunate a beautiful and brilliant girl like her would go for *me*." My knuckles crack, sharp in the silence that follows.

Despite the tension-filled room, Ben's callous words still hanging in the air, and Eden and Jake trying to look anywhere but at us, as if it's an Olympic sport and they're going for gold, there's still expanding warmth in my chest. Zoe came right out and said we're together. To have her admit her feelings to me was one thing, but to have her open up to a roomful of people, especially Ben? That's another level.

Ben glares at Zoe but gestures to me. "Yeah, well, are you sure his reasons for being with you are so pure? Before we ever got here, he said he's only helping with the podcast until his dream job opens up."

I flinch. The job promotion, moving, yeah . . . I haven't exactly talked openly about that with her. But, honestly, I've pushed it out of my own mind. At first because I wanted to focus on the task at hand. But now, something has changed for me. Maybe having my dream job isn't worth it if it takes me away from the people I care about and the woman I *love*.

Who I really need to talk to is Mr. Kellsner, but it'll probably have to wait until after the retreat.

I narrow my eyes at Ben but then turn a softer expression to Zoe. "Not that you deserve to know this, Ben, but I did start helping with the podcast purely as a favor to Eden." When Zoe crosses her arms, I quickly turn to her and amend. "And you, of course. I wanted to have more producing experience to add to my résumé. But I actually enjoy working with you. We make a great team. Even if I still find the Regency stuff—"

"Ridiculous?" She lifts a brow and the corner of her lips.

Ben's rolling his eyes. "How touching."

I'm done, so I use one word, but it's all he needs. "Leave."

And Ben does. With one more sneer, he's gone, and Eden shuts the door and locks it.

A moment later, there's yet another knock. Every one of us lets out a collective groan.

This time it is Victoria, and from the way she eyes us guys in the room, hands planted on her hips, now we're in for the scandal talk. But I can't help a small smile. Even if it was for a terrible reason, Zoe and I just said everything—well, almost everything—we needed to, reinforcing what I already knew deep down. We have each other's backs. Always. Ben's bitter rant can't touch us.

Now it's time to show her that while I may not be perfect, I'm still the gentleman for her. Look out, Mr. Darcy and Lord Pembroke, here I come.

32

Zoe

Sophia bursts through our bedroom door, barely pausing to knock. On her heels is Anne, bearing Eden's and my dresses over one arm and the antique curling rod she uses to curl our hair in the other.

Sophia's already curled ringlets bounce as she clutches her chest. She's lovely in a deep coral hue that brings out the pinks of her skin tone.

"I'm so glad you're coming to the ball, Soph, even if it didn't work out the way you had hoped." Eden fixes a stray tie on the back of Sophia's dress. "We're going to have a blast, dates or not."

Why Milton hadn't asked, since they'd seemed to be hitting it off so well, is beyond me.

Her face glowing, Sophia gestures to me. "I was inspired by Zoe. I know you finally realized what everybody else within a ten-mile radius could see—that you and Harrison are perfect for each other." My cheeks heat as I duck my head and laugh. "But what I appreciate is your sharing with us and on your podcast updates that you came to understand that it's okay to be on your own, too. And that we can have all the lists in the world, but that doesn't guarantee our happiness in a relationship."

"It's like shopping." I laugh at their dubious faces and hold up a hand. "No, no, stay with me. My mom always said, 'Don't get something just to get something. And don't worry if it's the popular thing or the most expensive. All that matters is that you love it and it's right for you.'"

My hand absently runs over the carved wood of the desk. "I'm seeing that I was in a rush to check off boxes on my list because I had set some internal clock and turning thirty seemed to be the deadline. But it's about the right person at the right time in God's right timing, which isn't always—okay, is almost never—*my* timing. And that's okay, too."

I touch Sophia's shoulder. "I'll be praying that you'll find peace with whatever happens."

A twinge rolls around in my gut. I'll need to address these newfound discoveries more in depth on the podcast.

Her lips compress, but her eyes brighten. "Thank you, really."

I return her grin, and her expression turns thoughtful. "I've learned a lot during this retreat. About myself. About what I want but also what I need, and maybe trying to plan too much"—her grimace is apologetic toward me—"isn't such a great idea. After all, if I had stuck to everything I had planned, I never would've thought twice about someone like Milton. Now I know to get out of my own way."

Eden pats us both on the back. "I think we're all learning that we have to leave room for a little surprise in life." By the twinkle in her eye, I know she's alluding to a certain famous heartthrob cameraman.

After their hours together during the editing process but also her support after the hunting incident, Eden and Jake have become inseparable and Jake said he's changed his mind about romance . . . at least where she's concerned. He's a man who's already gone into the world to seek his fortune and come home realizing this is where he wants to be. Plus, his sweet, caring nature won her over from the start. I squealed in excitement for her like she did for me and Harrison.

"I wish Jake could attend the ball, you know, without having to film, but oh well. We've planned on going on a real date after the retreat." She sighs.

I grin at her, and Harrison's face pops into my mind. Even though he was right there, he was a complete surprise to me, too. But unbidden, tiny doubts begin poking microscopic holes into my full lungs, full heart.

What if Harrison *is* too good for me? What if *I'm* not the right girl for *him*? I've always been so busy deciding whether a guy is right for *me*. Now that I finally found the man of my dreams, how do I know I'm what's right for him?

All this time, I buried these secret fears by saying *he* wasn't the guy who checked off *my* list. That way I was the one in control. Then it wasn't about me not being enough for him. Then I didn't have to suffer losing him. That realization is like a sharp but rusted spike driven into the center of my chest.

I have to find a way to show him how wrong I was. Harrison needs to know he checks off everything I never knew I ever wanted or needed. He's not Lord Pembroke. He's not Mr. Darcy. But he's my Harrison Lundquist and exactly who he's supposed to be.

Eden excuses herself for a moment to the editing room and, promising her quick return, leaves the room.

I'm fully laced into my corset, buttoned into my gold organza and satin dress, and Anne is nearly finished with my half-up hairdo when Eden returns. Her brows are bunched in the middle, and a tense line is drawn on either side of her mouth. She leans against the door with a huff.

"What's wrong?" both Sophia and I say in unison.

I wait until Anne lowers another curl to rush to Eden's side.

She swipes at her forehead. "I'm not sure what that was. I had the weirdest conversation with Ben, and I don't know what to make of it."

I place a hand on her arm as her silent mouth opens and closes. "What happened?"

"It was so out of the blue, so absurd." Her hands flounder, upturned. "He cornered me in the hall, outside of the office. He, well, I don't know if I should say. I don't want to upset you. . . ."

"No worries. Tell me. Nothing you can say about Ben can upset me at this point. I already saw his true colors last night."

She takes in a breath and straightens. "He said he couldn't wait to work with my father and that Harrison and I would be smart to get in on it. He also said business is what he had in mind the whole time. He was never here to find love."

Even though it truly doesn't hurt me in the sense that I don't want his affections, it doesn't feel great to have been pursued under false pretenses. "What?" I exchange a look with Sophia. "Why come to the retreat at all? He could've contacted your father directly. Why the subterfuge?"

Throwing a hand in the air, she scoffs. "I don't know. He said something about needing the right environment to prove himself."

Sophia glances between us, eyes narrowing. "That's weird."

I cross my arms. "I agree. Something is off, especially considering his reaction to me breaking things off with him. And what does he mean, 'business'?"

Moving across the room, Eden leans on one of the wooden posts of her bed. "The weirdest part of all is he said he has some wheels in motion and I can either jump aboard or be run over."

We stare at each other, squinting. "That sounds ominous. What could he mean?"

She lifts a shoulder. "I have no idea."

Anne rushes Eden through her dressing process, but she looks lovely in a deep violet dress that complements her hair. Then Anne finishes the last few curls for me and pins Eden's hair into a complicated braided updo. Afterward, Anne excuses herself to give extra help wherever needed.

I pull Eden and Sophia into a huddle. "All right, ladies. That was a strange encounter, Eden." She waves this away. "But let's resolve to enjoy the ball. This once-in-a-lifetime experience is all over after breakfast tomorrow, so let's make the most of tonight."

We put our hands together in the middle, then throw them in the air.

"Let's party like it's 1814!" Eden lets out a whoop and giggles.

We slip on our opera-length gloves, mine a semi-see-through champagne color that complements my gold dress. Grabbing our fans and reticules, we join the line of ladies descending the stairs, me hobbling my way in my medical boot. As the ladies reach the bottom, a man in a white wig and vibrant blue and gold-edged jacket announces each individual or couple. The ballroom is a kaleidoscope of colors. Jewelry sparkles in the chandelier light while fans and feathers from the ladies' hair flutter as the women chatter in excitement with the men in their dapper tailed suits.

My butterflies—more like winged elephants—kick into high gear as Harrison steps into view. My breath catches. I've seen him in Regency suits all week, but this is different. This color of deep blue matches his eyes perfectly. But that's not what makes me gasp as I take his arm and our names are announced. He's shaved his beard, leaving only a pair of very swoon-worthy side-whiskers even Mr. Darcy would envy.

I lift a gloved hand to run along the smoothness of his jaw.

It's been so long—probably since college—since I've seen his face clean-shaven.

"You look so handsome." I breathe the words and lower my hand. There's a flush to his cheeks that he can no longer hide with his facial hair. "But then, you always do."

He takes my hand and kisses the back, the warmth sinking through the thin fabric. "And you, Miss Dufour, are so breathtakingly beautiful it should be a scandal. In fact, I'm not entirely sure it isn't in certain parts of the state." He winks and adds, "Don't worry, I won't tell if you won't."

Shaking my head, I touch the still-swollen sting on my neck—which Anne tried her best to cover with makeup—and kick my big clumsy booted foot from beneath my dress. He takes my hand, lowers it away from my neck, and kisses the palm.

"Beautiful," he repeats, tone firm.

That's when my eyes land on the dark blue handkerchief in his jacket pocket, then dart back to his *freshly cut side-whiskers*.

Tugging Harrison off to the side as we wait for Eden and Sophia, I whisper, "Harrison?" I tap the handkerchief. "Or should I call you 'Gentleman in Training'?"

I search the almost-shy expression stealing over his face, but then his lips twitch into a wry grin. "You caught me."

One shoulder lifts and his warm hand squeezes mine. "I know what I said about letters, but I needed to be able to tell you everything you deserved to hear, without any pressure on you. I wanted you to be happy, even if it wasn't with me." My hand rises to his smooth jawline again, and he covers it with his own palm.

The corners of my eyes prick with tears, but I blink them back. "Those letters . . . they were such a comfort, like he—*you* really saw me and knew what I needed. I can't tell you how much that meant to me." He bends and draws me into a hug.

"I'm so glad it was you." I breathe the words into the crook of his neck, his earthy, spicy scent embracing me as much as his arms. He plants a soft kiss on my forehead.

A chaperone gives us a pointed glare. We step back but keep our hands clasped as we search for Eden and Sophia enveloped in the crowd at the base of the stairs.

When Eden strides out of a throng of couples, Jake moves toward her, sans camera equipment.

Jake stands before Eden and bows, taking her hand and kissing it lightly. "Miss Lundquist, will you do me the honor of accompanying me to the ball?"

Joy lights Eden's eyes even as she tilts her head. "You have to film, don't you?"

Jake holds both of her hands. "I set up cameras and lighting. Harrison and I have worked out a schedule for checking them and taking turns with some closer shots. I wanted to spend this night dancing with you as much as possible."

Kissing her hand again, he adds with eyes full of wonder, "I don't want to waste a second of this." He gestures between them. "You know, I wasn't *looking* for romance. But who am I to argue when it just shows up—in the form of a funny, genuine, purple-haired, Tolkien-loving beauty like you?"

Sophia and I cheer as Jake leans in and gives Eden a light kiss. Harrison claps but then he and Victoria clear their throats to break it up. I swat his stomach.

Harrison shrugs. "What? That's still my sister."

Jake and Eden share a warm, lingering gaze, and there's a slight flush to both of their faces.

Milton parts through the crowd and gives Jake and Eden a belated and rather loud round of applause. "Lovely." Then he straightens his cravat, squares his narrow shoulders, and bends a wobbly bow toward Sophia.

Our shy new friend raises a hand to her throat, and my own covers my mouth.

A bead of sweat trickles down Milton's temple as he takes her hand. "Sophia, will you—"

But he's silenced by Sophia flinging herself into his arms and planting a firm kiss to his mouth. She pulls back long enough to say, "Yes! Of course."

My throat clogs. This couldn't be any sweeter.

Milton pushes his now-askew glasses back into place and beams. "It took a whole slew of excruciating dates to realize you're the one."

Hello, I was one of those dates, buddy. And come on. I will have to be intentional for the rest of my life not to picture him walking out of that lake looking like a sopping wet teddy bear. But I'm so happy for Sophia. She found her match—despite my best efforts.

I cringe at my own shortcomings, of what I tried and failed to do at this retreat, but smile at what I found instead.

And my chest swells with pride at the amazing job Harrison, Eden, and Jake have done filming and beginning the editing process so we can release a series of videos on our time here after the retreat. Good, bad, and ugly, I think people will love it. But a special episode with some of my more personal findings through this process is in order as well.

A part of me wants to grab back the reins, to seize control. But as Harrison slips his arm around my waist and we head into the ballroom, those thoughts evaporate with a twirl of my dress.

33

Harrison

Lifting Zoe to stand on my feet again, giving her ankle a break for another trip around the dance floor—she's already refused to sit down twice—I exhale as a waltz begins to play instead of a complicated quadrille or cotillion this time. Zoe's laughter lilts in my ears, a sound I would gladly listen to every day for the rest of my life. It drives away the fears that I'll somehow mess this up, do all I can to be the man she needs, do everything right, and still lose her.

Spinning us around, I continue moving us in our box steps in time with "The Sussex Waltz" spilling from the other end of the large, dome-ceilinged room, where a string quartet is playing. We weave among Sophia and Milton—Sophia the one wincing with Milton stomping on her toes—and George and Joan whirling expertly past us, Joan's head thrown back in a laugh at something George said. The older man nods in our direction with a smile I can recognize all too well.

I'll say this, the retreat center didn't skimp on this ball. Between the warm glow of candlelight, flowers and decorations dripping from every surface, and the expensive hors d'oeuvres and sparkling drinks, I don't know who they're trying to impress more—the paying attendees to elicit positive reviews or my boss and his wife. I whirl us away from their watchful eyes. The thing that I'm supposedly here for, what I said I wanted—to impress my boss and land that job I've been vying for as a producer no matter the cost or where it might take me—suddenly doesn't appeal to me as much as it once did. It would mean quitting the podcast for good, as Mr. Kellsner said. That's what I wanted originally. This part-time gig was a temporary landing, a way to help out Eden and Zoe. But somehow, over time, it has become so much more to me. And not only because of my feelings for Zoe.

She has a talent for communicating, for creating community, and for reaching people just by being herself. And she has a platform where she might do some good, albeit with a slight tweak of her message. I'm proud of what we've accomplished. All of us. Zoe, Eden, myself, and now Jake, too. He's an expert at capturing moments like no one else can, and I'd be lying if I didn't say I'd like him to continue working with us.

But the question is, after this retreat footage hits my boss's desk, will his willingness to promote and push Zoe's podcast to the next level really hinge on me taking the job he offers and quitting the podcast? Because that's how he made it seem. We'll have a lot to discuss after the retreat.

Zoe's thumb swipes lightly above my brow as if trying to smooth a crease away. "Hey, what's going on in there? That stormy scowl is too intense even for Darcy and is much too serious for lugging this fancy-dressed potato around the dance floor." She winks. "Told you I scored at potato level as a date."

When I don't return the banter, she shifts her hand to the back of my head, rubbing the pads of her fingers against my scalp. I still revel in the fact that she so freely touches me and finds any reason to be close to me. It gives me the confidence and permission I've always wanted to hold her in return.

If only I could release the tense muscles in my face. The right timing or not, I really need to talk to her about my boss's offer, even if I end up saying no to it. Moving is a deal-breaker for her, so if we're going to be together, we need to figure this out. "Hey, Zo, we need to talk about something. It's something I should've brought up before, but"—I can't seem to find the perfect words, but make myself press on—"we weren't together before and I didn't think you'd ever see me like that, but now—"

"Yes?" Her eyes are so wide, so trusting.

I dance us toward the other side of the room, keeping in motion with the other couples. We're nearing where Mr. Kellsner and his wife are drinking punch along the wall with other spectators. They seem to be in deep conversation with Ben, which makes my teeth grit together, and another man, his back toward us. The cut of the man's twenty-first-century suit is expensive. Another sponsor? Wait, the sandy hair shot through with gray, and the straight, stubborn line of his shoulders . . .

The man turns. My father.

"What is it? What's wrong?" Zoe's voice cuts through the roaring in my ears.

My feet have stopped moving, and the other dancers spin around us. "It's my father. He's here." The words hiss between my teeth.

Her gaze snaps to the sidelines, snagging on my father now chuckling at something Ben says as Mr. Kellsner joins in. "What's he doing here?"

"I don't know, but I don't like this."

My father finally notices me and tosses me a wave and sharp incline of his head as if it's completely normal and planned that he showed up here. All I can manage is a lift of my brow as if to say, "What on earth are you doing here?"

"Maybe he wants to support what you and Eden have been doing?" She watches them, too, but with a hopeful expression.

"*Hmph.*" I make a misstep, distracted, but correct us before we run into Eden dancing with Jake nearby. We set up a tripod and have moved the camera to different angles, but we're also taking turns manually filming close-ups and more intimate shots to ensure the footage, once it's cut together, isn't stagnant.

"There's no way he'd be here to support the podcast. I can tell you exactly what he thinks of it and my involvement, but it most definitely isn't complimentary." I won't, of course, because I don't want to hurt her feelings. But suffice it to say, the words *embarrassing* and *a joke* were used liberally when I first told my father about my new position the last time we talked.

"Well, it's possible he's changed his mind after seeing what a spectacular show producer you are." She beams up at me, and I can't help the warmth that swells in my chest, making me stand taller.

Eden stops with Jake near us, and her mouth hangs open as she stares at our father. "What's he doing here?"

I touch her elbow. "I don't know. I better go see what this is about." I lift Zoe back onto the floor, and Eden and I start moving closer to where they're standing.

But before we've taken three steps, Ben lowers a white screen from the ceiling on the other side of the room—the mansion is used for modern weddings and events as well. Zoe and I share a confused look.

Ben motions to the band director, who quiets the music. Then he claps his hands to draw everyone's attention much like Victoria. "Good evening, ladies and gentlemen. I apologize for interrupting. But I have an important and, I think you'll find, exciting announcement to make."

Victoria's mouth presses into a thin line at the intrusion, but she doesn't move to stop him. I return to Zoe and wrap my arm around her back to steady her.

"Arnold Lundquist, as in Lundquist and Associates, Media Investment Firm, and I, as well as Mr. Kellsner, have been collab-ing, as they say in the biz. We're talking reality show, here at Wyndmere Hall, starting with the footage our talented Harrison Lundquist and Jake Rydberg captured from this week's retreat."

Zoe's narrowed, questioning eyes find mine. I open my mouth, but nothing comes out. There's chatter, then tentative applause.

On the screen, a video begins to play a mock-up trailer for this supposed reality show. A title shot with the words "The Marriage Mart: Regency-Style Dating" floats onto the screen while a classical rendition of "Can't Stop the Feeling!" by Justin Timberlake plays in the background.

A teaser starts, and there's a sharp intake of breath, Zoe's mixed with my own as she walks into the frame alongside me. There's a shot of us laughing by the lake, her mishaps during archery—including our joint misfire almost hitting the peacock—lawn bowling, and her misadventures in speed dating. It's all very unflattering to her, making her look like a laughable clown instead of the adorable woman I love. Me saying things like "walking disaster" and "ridiculous" in jest but taken out of context.

Then there's me carrying her back to the house after her fall, us in a close, seemingly compromised position in the library, her arriving at my bedroom door and slipping inside after a covert glance down the hall, me entering her room, and her disastrous date with Ben. Most of that is our footage, shots Jake and I took but would've never cut in this way, in such an embarrassing reflection on Zoe and her personality. But some footage isn't ours, and I have no idea where it came from. It's not the quality of a professional camera but more like from a phone, probably Ben's phone. There's even a shot of Zoe in my lap on that bench by the lake, and we're kissing. We thought we were alone.

A voiceover blares over the images, promising the show will be "hilarious, and hot enough to make even the most roguish rake blush with scandal."

But the clip that clamps around my chest and stops my lungs from expanding is a close-up of Zoe's face, her wide and trusting stare—into my eyes behind the camera—as she says, "All I want is love. The kind a gentleman rides in on his white horse for, goes against conventions for, the kind he stays for, that I can set a clock to. Like the heroes in my stories. Is that so much to ask for?" She ducks her head. "I know what I want." She blushes and lets out a little laugh. "I have a list, and I'm not afraid to use it."

Then video-Zoe turns serious again. I knew when we were doing this test-filming after we first arrived that her thoughts had turned to her humiliating filmed experience with Chad Summers in high school. Her teeth dig into her bottom lip, then she holds a hand up. "Let's edit that out, okay, Harrison?" There's moisture in her eyes as she blinks and turns from the camera.

I *did* edit that out, putting it in a separate file for myself. I was the only one who was ever supposed to see it.

And the icing on the poisonous cake is a clip I thought I had deleted from the night Zoe proposed to Sawyer.

She's kneeling in her backyard, staring up at him expectantly, ring held out. "Will you marry me, Sawyer?"

His response, "I can't, Zoe. Look, this isn't how I wanted to tell you, but . . . I fell in love with someone else," still tears a hole right through me as her face crumples.

There's a voiceover saying something about using Regency-style dating to get out of a twenty-first-century romance rut—almost like Zoe and Eden's podcast idea but twisted to make

Zoe and every other woman participating seem pathetic and desperate.

My chest is burning, and my heart hammers in my ears as I look down at Zoe. "I-I didn't do this."

But it's clear the here-and-now-Zoe doesn't believe that as her hand flies to her mouth. Her breath stutters and stops as she steps back from me. Tears gather on her lower lashes and spill over, sliding down her face. She's staring at me like she doesn't know who I am. "How could you?" Her cheeks are the deepest shade of crimson, and it quickly spreads to her neck.

Her words are directed at me, and though whispered, they pack a walloping punch to my gut.

"Zoe, no, I didn't—"

"You're the only one who had that footage. You had it, and you knew how mortifying it was."

She's backing away from me but trips on the back of her dress. I reach out even as she pushes my hand away, wobbles, arms flapping, and lands hard on her backside. Eden helps her up and keeps an arm around her shoulders, then lowers her brows at me and Jake. People have started murmuring and snickering behind outstretched fans and hands.

Somehow, I did everything I knew to be right and still blew up the happily ever after—the one I didn't know I believed in. Poof. Gone. I can see it in the hollowed-out, betrayed, and angry lines of her face.

Way to go, Lundquist. Despite my best efforts, somehow I've become the villain of this story.

34

Zoe

My throat convulses trying to form sounds resembling speech. The betrayal is so raw, so deep, beyond anything I endured with Chad or even Sawyer. Maybe because I never completely trusted them the way I've always trusted Harrison. I opened my heart and entrusted it to him.

Harrison rakes a hand through his hair, leaving it standing on end. With fists clenched at his sides, he approaches Ben near the head of the room, his teeth bared. "You don't have permission to use that footage. And I have the waivers, which I will *not* be handing over to you."

Ben slides a leather bag from under a nearby chair and slips out a small stack of papers. "You mean these waivers?"

I squint. He must've gotten ahold of them somehow. It feels like someone reached through my rib cage and is squeezing my heart in a merciless grip.

Harrison is eerily still.

My fingernails dig into my palms through my thin gloves, and my feet stumble again toward the exit.

Ben turns to me. "Hey, don't say I didn't try to tell you that you'd benefit from some help. My way will make us all a lot of money and bring us the prestige I—we deserve. That's why I knew as soon as I heard about you coming here, I had to make sure we were paired up, Zo."

His use of my nickname again makes my teeth scrape together.

Ben adds with a faux-apologetic smile, "Sorry, but this was always about the next rung toward a more successful career, stepping on who we had to to get to the top." He juts his chin toward Harrison. "Right, Lundquist?"

My stomach churns, the room spins, and I hang on to Eden to ground me.

"There is no *we*." Harrison's words seethe and boil at the surface.

"I can't believe this." Mine rake over a raw throat.

Holding his hands up, Ben steps closer. "Film doesn't lie, but it *is* all in the editing. Isn't it?" He shoots a grin to Mr. Kellsner and Harrison's father. "That tends to bring out a person's true colors."

Ben's head tilts in mock sympathy.

Harrison slides back between Ben and me as Ben nears. "Yeah, and this showed yours. You've got some nerve—"

Ben flicks an invisible piece of lint from his shoulder. "Don't blame me for what you filmed, Harrison. And for what you said out in the open for everyone to hear, Zoe."

Spinning back to the screen, Ben points the small remote at the projector in the ceiling. "I almost forgot. Everybody loves a twist ending."

Harrison's face appears on the screen. It seems that Jake is filming and they're testing equipment. They're talking and laughing as they set up lighting in the dining room. No one's around. Everyone is probably dressing for dinner.

Jake's voice drifts from behind the camera. "I don't know, do you think there's anything to finding someone this way? The whole 'dating like we're in the 1800s'?"

Harrison throws an incredulous smile to the camera, rubbing at the beard that's now nonexistent. "No way. This is like trying to desperately force something that can't be forced. That isn't meant to be forced. It's foolish, plain and simple."

"Desperate?" The camera shot wobbles, perhaps while the camera is placed on the tripod.

Harrison's shoulder lifts. "I mean, yeah. If dating isn't working out in real life, basing it on an elaborate fantasy that is in no way related to the actual twenty-first-century world beyond those gates—how does that help the person? It's borderline delusional."

He said "the person," but he may as well have inserted my name. I'm not the only one with a wide stare. Grumbles start circulating the room.

"Why are you here, then?" Jake's voice is curious.

"I'm helping out my sister and Zoe. I'm trying to work my way back into being a producer again, honestly. And if I do this right, I'll be moving to Chicago for another shot at my dream job. Nothing more to it."

I always knew he was hoping to work as a producer again, but it still hurts to hear it in such a callous tone. And moving? He never said he *wouldn't* move again, but he also never said moving was a sure thing if Mr. Kellsner gave him this promotion.

The video cuts to Harrison talking on the phone. We can only hear Harrison's side of the conversation, but it becomes clear he's talking to his boss. "Mr. Kellsner, thank you, sir." There's a pause as he listens and runs a hand through his hair. "Leave the podcast? Well, I—no, of course, sir. I'd give up just about anything to produce again. Right, I'll show you I can handle it with this retreat series."

Ben turns it off and sneers. "You all should be happy. You're about to be so famous."

Mr. Kellsner steps forward and takes Harrison's hand, shaking it vigorously. "You've more than proved you can handle producing on your own. Ben can be here to oversee the Marriage Mart show, and you can be my lead in Chicago and consult on the show from there. We'll have a long chat about it when you get back."

Harrison's father claps him on the back. "That's my boy. I knew you could do it. And our investment firm would love to help sponsor this gold mine of an opportunity for you." He turns to Mr. Kellsner. "Have your assistant call my assistant. Let's set a lunch appointment sometime next week, shall we?"

Ben's feet shuffle back and forth as though to remind them of his presence. Mr. Kellsner waves him closer. "And let's not forget Ben. He was the one to fill me in on the show idea these two cooked up, which—let's be honest—is much better than the original idea."

I back away again. Harrison's gaze moves between the men surrounding him and me, then back to the screen, where his smiling face is paused. The evidence is overwhelming and condemning. He has nothing to say, nothing that can erase what I've seen with my own eyes and heard with my own ears.

Mrs. Kellsner, on the other hand, finally breaks her silence, throwing her hands to her hips, eyes narrowing at her husband. "This is *not* the reason I begged you to take a look at Zoe's podcast channel and this retreat. You took all of the heart and everything I, and so many others, love about *Love According to Miss Gladwin*, and turned it into a cheap reality show farce. How could you?"

She squeezes my shoulder, whispering a tearful "I'm so

sorry" on her way out of the room. That's my cue. I catch Eden's eye.

On the stairs, hobbling my way up with Eden's help, each step is heavier and heavier, which has nothing to do with my medical boot.

I choke back a sob. "How—why—"

Eden growls. "I don't know. I'm furious with him and with Jake, too. Let's get out of here." She pats my arm. "I'm so sorry, Zoe. I never should've asked Harrison to help us."

There's a trample of loud footsteps, then a tug on my hand. I turn, teetering on the step. Harrison is breathless, his expression taut. "Zoe, please, you can't believe I would do any of that. It's not how it looks. Ben's—"

Jake emerges from the ballroom, staring up at Eden. "That wasn't us. It's Ben—"

Raising a hand, I silence him. "Save it, both of you. Ben is, as it turns out, as disgusting as his intentions. I'll give you that. But he's right. The results don't lie. It's all too obvious what your intentions have been."

Eden points at each of the men in turn. "*You* are responsible for what you said, Harrison, and the way you cut that, Jake." She shakes her head, covering her mouth.

"Eden, that's not what happened." Jake lifts an arm like he wants to reach for Eden but then scrapes his fingers along his scalp instead. "Someone, *Ben*, must've accessed our footage somehow...."

I clutch the stair railing, turning my knuckles white, as I pin Harrison with a narrowed gaze. "I can't believe I trusted you." The words claw past my constricted throat, and I try to blink back tears, but they flow down my cheeks anyway. "You didn't care about me. You were just trying to get the right footage to win your precious producer job. Even if that meant making me look like a dupe."

Pain is etched into the lines and angles of Harrison's face, but that's probably because he's now caught and exposed. I never should've ignored the warning signs, starting with the fact that he didn't meet the criteria I laid out for myself. He's not a gentleman. He's nothing close. He's a betrayer of the worst kind. Worse than even Chad or Sawyer. At least their betrayal wasn't for personal gain.

"You got what you wanted. Your new job far away from here. I hope it's everything you want it to be. Now you won't have to deal with my desperate search for love. I thought I had found it, by the way." I start to turn, and whisper, "But I'm a delusional fool, right? What do I know?"

Eden and I ignore their pleas for us to stop. Without saying anything, we pack our things. This is what I get for veering off course. When will I learn?

My fingers grip my bag as the carriage jostles us, bringing us back to the twenty-first century, to reality. That's exactly what I need—a reality check—and it may mean some major changes ahead. How can I possibly keep recording a podcast about navigating love and relationships when my life is a shipwreck?

So what if I'd nearly completed my "Thirty by Thirty" list. My attempts to use Regency sensibilities and a nonnegotiable list didn't work. And my more trusting approach to love with Harrison left me alone and heartbroken. No one should listen to me. Maybe love *is* a fantasy, something best left to make-believe heroes and heroines. Perhaps it's not real and attainable outside of the pages of my favorite novels. No modern-day Lord Pembroke is riding in to sweep me off my feet.

I'm on my own. I have to take care of myself. Like I always have.

I wince at the memory of Harrison lifting me into his warm, strong arms after my fall in the woods, and how safe and cared for I felt in that moment. As if I'd finally found my person, list or not—kind, dependable, brave, someone I can laugh with, who sees me for me and cares about me, not in spite of who

I am but because of it. And I, him. No, not just care . . . *love*. At least on my part.

I bite my lip and let the silent tears fall as the present hurtles toward us. There's no stopping the right now or erasing the past. There's only the future, the dark chasm of the unknown, of everything out of my control ahead.

35

Harrison

I pace the floor of my clean but sterile high-rise apartment—a place for a single man, the man I've been but not the man I want to be. I scratch at the day-old stubble as I start the process of growing out my beard again. My mind wanders to Zoe and her place, warm and inviting, just like her.

She has yet to return my calls. I don't know if she ever will. She's been humiliated before by people she trusted. Maybe I should give her more time. I've already called twice and texted once since she left the retreat last night. But if I push my company on her now, she may never want to see me again.

If only I could explain . . .

But there's someone else I need to talk to, someone whose two calls I've let go to voicemail—my father.

Before I can change my mind, I hit his number in my phone's contacts. It rings once, then his commanding voice answers, "Harrison." It's a statement as if he knew I was going to call at this exact moment.

I launch right in with, "I can't believe you would go behind my back to plan this trash show with Ben and my boss. That's a new low, even for you."

The acid in my tone surprises even me.

There's a pause and an almost imperceptible exhale. "I didn't know you weren't on board with it, son. Ben told me you two had cooked up this plan, but I knew nothing about him taking your footage or filming without your permission."

There's a quality to his voice I've never heard before, something quiet and real, maybe even a hint of humility or regret. But I can't let him off easier than I did Ben—who I cornered after the disaster of a ball until he explained himself. Although the result was catastrophic, it appears Ben and I have some things in common, at least where our parents are concerned. He'd been kicked out of Yale before finishing his degree for failing grades and come back to Minnesota in disgrace—in his and his parents' view. So, with his parents' extremely high expectations in mind, he'd been trying to earn back their good opinion ever since. He thought if he could expand on the already growing success of Zoe's podcast and ride those coattails to fame and glory, he'd once again be someone his parents could be proud of. The part about teaching was made up. He's been unemployed and living in his parents' basement for the better part of a year now.

My jaw tightens as I scrape my nails against my scalp. "If you would've taken even a minute to check with me, I would've told you it was all a scam. That I had no plan or agreement with Ben."

A scoffing grunt on the other end. "And how would that have worked, Harrison? You barely ever pick up when I call, and my texts go ignored. Same with your sister."

It had become easier not to deal with him after the way he'd treated me growing up. And I'd discouraged Eden from talking to him, too, trying to protect us both. But maybe avoiding him had taken away opportunities to get things out into the open, and closing myself off from him had made those old wounds fester inside, leaking into the way I handled other relationships. The way I always thought I had to get everything exactly right.

"I never meant to hurt you, son. Really. I thought I was helping."

My father never acted like he cared. So what's the deal with this nice-guy routine now? I'm honestly not sure if I can forgive him for this, let alone the kind of dad he was to me as a kid. A kid who'd just wanted his father to be proud of him and accept him. "It still doesn't excuse you butting into my life. You ruined some things for me, Dad"—I swallow hard. It's the first time in a long time I've called him that—"and so did Ben. Professionally and with someone I care about." My chest aches again with thoughts of Zoe and the pain and anger carved into every line of her face yesterday.

There's a long sigh. "Your mother is finally leaving me, handed me the divorce papers a month ago. I'm actually surprised it took her this long." Before I can think of how to respond, he continues, "Look, I'm not telling you this for sympathy so I'm off the hook for this or anything else I've done to you or your sister. But it's made me realize how much I've messed up with you all. I know it's too late with your mother. I guess I thought if I could support you with this podcast that seems so important to you and Eden, maybe there was a chance I could begin to mend things with you two." The logic is questionable, but the sincerity in his voice isn't.

"I'm not sure where to start, but I'd like to be a better father to you and Eden. If you'll let me."

"I don't know." I rub my forehead. "There's just so much . . ." I'm not even sure how to end that sentence as a lifetime of jumbled wounds spins through my mind.

"I know, son" is his answer, as if he's heard the unspoken thoughts. "All I'm asking for is a chance."

What he's asking for is the grace I never received from him. But I guess it has to start somewhere.

"Dad, it might take time and I'd need to see you've changed." I scrub my fingers against my temple. "I can't believe I'm saying this, but . . . I'd like that, too."

The end of the conversation is sort of an out-of-body situation because hearing these things from my once cold, unfeeling dad seems impossible. Like body snatchers impossible. We plan to have coffee next week before we hang up. He'll invite Eden, too. I figure we can at least hear him out.

I'm still reeling when my door buzzer cuts through the haze. It's insistent, already buzzing again before I make it to the intercom box in the hallway.

As soon as I say "Who is it?" with a split-second hope it'll be Zoe, Eden's voice blares from the speaker.

"Not cool, bro. Let me in."

I buzz her in, unlock the door, and pace in front of it until she stomps into my apartment without so much as a knock or hello.

Her purple brows are etched in straight, slanted lines as she marches through to my open kitchen. I have no choice but to follow.

She leans an elbow onto the counter, arms crossed. "Well, I'm waiting for an explanation. What did you do?" Every word is an accusation, and I work to calm my defenses.

I lift my palms out, facing her. "Eden, you know me better than that. I didn't do any of what Ben said. I would never do that, to you or Zoe. I can only own up to what I said on camera. It was uncalled for, and I'm sorry."

Eyes appraising me for a second, she finally straightens and unclenches her teeth. "I'm listening."

I explain the confrontation with Ben and what he said after she and Zoe left.

Slumping onto one of the kitchen stools, I brace my forearms on the counter. "He must've gotten into our shared files on the laptop and even into my private files saved in the cloud to find that video of Zoe proposing." I wince at the memory. "I promise you. I didn't have that planned with Ben."

"What about Dad? What was that all about?"

My shoulders raise, then lower. "As misguided as it was, I think that was an attempt to connect with and apologize to us."

I tell her all about my phone call with him moments before she arrived. Her face is full of the shock and tiny, wary-but-hopeful spark spinning around inside me, too.

With a final huff and dip of her chin, she slides onto another stool. "Okay, I believe you. But I don't know if Zoe will, given her history, and even if she does, now she knows you've been planning to leave this whole time. Kind of hard to have a long-term relationship with someone six hours away, especially if one of those people never wants to be more than a thirty-minute drive from her parents."

I jump to my feet. I need to fix this. Right now.

"You're right."

"Can I get that in writing? Maybe notarized?" She stands, a wry grin spreading.

Pulling her into a side hug and then releasing her, I start grabbing my car keys, wallet, and phone.

"Sorry, sis. I need to go."

"Okay . . ." She draws out the word, backing toward the door. "Not to kick me out or anything, right?"

"Yeah, sorry." I shove my arms through my flannel jacket—man, it's good to be in normal clothes again. "But I've got to take care of something. It's important."

"Fine." She's on the threshold of the open door but turns with her hand on the frame. "Hey, I know Zoe isn't answering your calls right now, and I'll try to put in a good word."

"Thank you." I give her shoulder a soft tap with my knuckles. "In the meantime, maybe think about coming to the *Pride and Prejudice* watch party we're hosting next weekend at our place." She shrugs. "We figured it's the least we could do after we more or less ruined the ball."

"You mean after Ben did." My jaw still tenses thinking about it.

"Well, anyway, we thought it would be a better send-off and thank-you to everyone. Quite a few people already RSVP'd." Her hands shove into her jacket pockets. "And it'll give Zoe time to cool off and might be an opening for you to see her and talk to her. You know, if you don't before then."

"I'll be there, unless, obviously, Zoe doesn't want me there." I hold a finger up for her to wait. "Oh, and forgive Jake, will you? He literally had nothing to do with any of this."

She ducks her head, smiling. "Yeah, I figured. I was just caught up in the moment with everything. Thank you, though."

When she leaves, I head down to my truck, calling the station as I climb inside to see if Mr. Kellsner is in. Good, he is.

If I want any chance of working things out with Zoe and showing her I'm serious about us and I'm in this for the long haul, there's one major thing I need to do first.

I need to quit my job.

Because there's no job in the world that's worth not being with Zoe. Besides, I'm not that kid who wanted to escape anymore. I'm here. This is my home. This is where I want to put down roots and start a family. God willing, with the woman I've been in love with for longer than I can even remember.

36

Zoe

The earthy scent of my plant babies surrounds me as I step through the sliding glass door into my four-season porch. I use my spray bottle to mist my little succulent family lining one windowsill and sigh. "Hey, guys. Are you feeling better?"

Despite my dad stopping by to water them, they didn't fare well while I was gone. But they've definitely perked up since I've been home. Returning home to reality has been for the best for everyone. It's been almost a week and a half since . . .

I hear quick, bouncing footsteps. Eden. She bounds onto the porch. I suspect her brightness is due to having made up with Jake and their now absolutely devoted relationship status.

I'm overjoyed for my friend. If only the mess of feelings

inside me where Harrison is concerned could be smoothed out so easily.

She grins in greeting. "Be careful—talk to your plants too much and they might start talking back."

"Hey, good timing. I just put some coffee on." I finish watering my mini-jungle, then head back to the kitchen.

"Are you ready for tonight?" Eden eyes me over my steaming "Plant Mom" mug in her hands.

I tap the edge of my own "Mrs. Pembroke" cup. "Yeah, I'm ready. Bingo cards are printed, snacks and drinks are bought—"

Eden raises a finger to add, "Oh, I made my famous seven-layer Mediterranean dip, and I'll be bringing the blackberry iced tea."

"Sounds good. I have hot cocoa for later. I've already hung the white sheet and staked it for the screen. I borrowed a bunch of chairs, blankets for when it cools off after dark, and a couple of folding tables from my mom and dad."

Her expression warms. "Sophie got back to me—she and Milton are coming. And I also heard from George and Joan. They'll be here as well."

That pulls a smile from my lips. "They are all so cute together. I'm so happy for them."

But I bite my cheek and look away. A *Pride and Prejudice* bingo/watch party night should be right up my alley, but all I can think of is the fact that Harrison may be coming. Not long ago, that would've elicited excitement along with joy filling my chest. Now, my ribcage feels hollowed out. As if the rest of my body is cut off from whatever still beats beneath those bones. I haven't returned any of Harrison's calls or texts. I . . . couldn't.

It's like I'm back in high school after that humiliation with Chad but somehow it's ten times worse because I'm an adult now, and the hurt travels deeper, wider. Like when you're a kid and fall off a bike. It hurts. But you stand up, brush yourself off, and ride again. As an adult? If I were to fall off a bike now, it would be the end of me. You may as well leave me there. I'm never recovering. That hurt will be in every single bone of my body, to the marrow.

That's me right now.

"Are you thinking of Harrison?" Her tentative but honest tone cuts through the haze I've been stuck in for the last week and a half. She gestures for us to sit at the table, and I follow, slumping into the coral-painted chair.

My lips flap as I let out a long, noisy breath. "This is so hard. He's your brother, so I know you have to forgive him and, of course, you have to see him again. But I don't know if I can do either."

"The fact that he *is* my brother may make my testimony biased and null and void in your eyes. *But* it also makes me the most qualified to vouch for his character. And I think you should hear him out, Zoe." Her words are measured, careful.

This is the first time she's encouraged me to talk to him. She's told me about their conversation, and what Ben did, her father's part in it, along with the surprising but sweet news that her father wants to work on healing their relationship. But up until now, she's given me the space to think, to cry, and even to rage about the situation, never pressuring me to get over it.

Pain and longing sweep me up, wrap around me so tight my lungs can't expand, and my throat closes. I clutch my neck right over where it contracts inside and try to swallow away the invisible obstruction. "Don't you think I want to? But I can't do this. Honesty was always the most important thing to me, and he broke my trust."

The thing I had to cling to in the last week is the fact that while people, even people I love deeply, can disappoint and betray me, God never will. It gives me the strength I need to prepare to move on—with a still-broken heart that will take time to heal—and the peace to know that even if there's no future with Harrison or anyone else, I'll still be okay. That I'm still loved and there's Someone else in control. He knows everything I don't about my future, what will happen to my mom, my dad, to everyone I love . . . including Harrison. And His plans are good regardless of mine.

But I can't help the pang in my heart at the thought of Harrison. I'd just begun to hope and pray for a future with him in it. He, my perfectly imperfect match and I, his. Everything I never knew I needed or wanted. Or so I thought.

Eden reaches across the table and squeezes my hand. "I know Harrison said some careless words, and he will answer for those if you let him. Don't tell him I said this, but he's a wreck. I've never seen him like this."

My mind conjures an image of him broken and hurting at my hands, because of my silence. I clamp my lips together to keep them from trembling.

She bows her head and raises a hand. "I'm not saying this to guilt-trip you into talking to him, okay? I just want you to understand that he's not taking this lightly, and the way he cares for you wasn't, *isn't* a lie."

I chew on that for a moment and exhale. "Is he coming tonight?"

"I'm not sure. He didn't want to put you in an awkward position—"

"No, I said you should invite him. I meant it. This is for everyone from the retreat. It's the least we can do for ruining the end of the ball and making a quick exit."

"Ben ruined it," she reminds me, not for the first time. His name hisses through her gritted teeth.

Neither of us states the fact that Harrison was in Ben's crosshairs because of Ben's lifelong jealousy of him. It came to light after the whole ballroom fiasco that Ben was lying to everyone—except his parents, who were so mortified their Ivy

League son had been expelled that they were in on trying to hide it from everyone. But he'd also been scheming the whole time to schmooze his way into a television deal with Harrison's boss and Eden and Harrison's father.

Ben had contacted Mr. Kellsner and told him he was an old friend of Harrison and Eden's family and said we'd all been talking about this idea for a reality show, even promising that he could get Harrison's father on board with his media investment firm. Tempted by how much money he could make, Mr. Kellsner approved the idea and gave Ben access to the video footage via our shared files drive so he could get started on a teaser and pilot.

Somehow Ben had also gotten access to Harrison's private files, probably when the laptop was left unattended in the office at the retreat.

If I truly ask myself if Harrison could be guilty of co-conspiracy with Ben on all of this, a deep-down, bone-level knowing can't fathom it. But something still prevents me from acknowledging it, especially to Harrison.

All I can seem to muster is, "I should've known Ben was a liar of Wickham proportions. The man couldn't row to save his life. If nothing else tipped me off, that should've."

My doorbell echoes through the house.

I sprint to the door, almost expecting Harrison to be standing there, and silently scold my disappointment when he's not. It's Delilah Kellsner. Surprise makes me stutter, "D-Delilah, what are you doing here?"

"I absolutely had to see how you're doing, dear. I have something for you and bugged Jake when I saw him at the station until he gave me your address. Don't blame him, though. I can be quite persistent. Do you think my husband would've ever gotten involved in the Regency singles' retreat otherwise?"

Even bringing it up sends a renewed jolt of pain through my gut.

Something occurs to me. "Why didn't you ask Harrison where I live? I'm sure he's at the office even more now that he's working on the reality show."

She brushes my elbow with a gentle touch. "That's part of what I wanted to talk with you about. Do you have a couple of minutes?"

Delilah greets Eden when we enter the kitchen. I offer coffee, to which she replies, "No, no. I'm not like you young people. I'll be up half the night if I drink it past ten a.m. I wouldn't say no to ice water, though."

When I return with her water, I sit across from her and wait.

Delilah sips her water, then steeples her fingers. "First, I want to say I'm so sorry, to both of you, for everything that happened and for my husband's part in it. He wanted me to pass along his apologies as well. Sometimes he lets dollar signs persuade him more than he should, forgetting there are real people on the other side of that camera."

I fill my lungs and try to lift my lips into a reassuring smile. "It's all right. We don't hold you responsible."

Eden grabs the older woman's hand, squeezes. "It's okay, Mrs. K. You couldn't have known what would happen."

But is it okay? Bill Kellsner still has the waivers and will undoubtedly use the footage in whatever way he chooses. He can portray me as a fool, humiliate me like in high school or that day with Sawyer, only on a much bigger, more permanent stage.

Delilah's shoulders visibly relax. "I'm glad you say that. I've felt awful about the whole ordeal. I was the one who convinced him to get involved with your podcast and the retreat in the first place, after all." Then she straightens like there's more on her mental checklist. "But I also came to say that the footage and the story Harrison wanted to tell—"

Something bristles in me. "I saw the story he wants to tell, and it's all about how I'm the world's most pathetic, love-desperate forever-spinster."

"Zoe . . ." Eden says my name, but it's Delilah who raises a hand to stop us both.

"Hang on a minute, dear. I don't blame you for being upset. But I have to tell you that you're wrong on all counts. There will be no reality show, no show at all if you so choose. And Harrison has quit the station."

"What?" both Eden and I exclaim.

Her lips turn down in a frown. "That's right. It's his story to tell, so I won't go into detail. But I want you to know that he wasn't and isn't looking to gain anything from that footage, and when he thought it had the potential to hurt either of you, he quit. He also made it quite clear that he'd bring the family lawyer into this if the videos are used without his permission or yours." She presses a hand to her chest like she's talking about a precocious little scamp.

Eden and I exchange glances. "He's serious if he's willing to bring in our father's lawyer." Eden's voice is pitched low.

My heart drums in my ears, my throat clogging again. I try to swallow.

Delilah taps her manicured nails on the table. "We blocked Ben's access to the shared drive, so no one but Bill, Harrison, and Jake can get into it. There's always a chance Ben saved it to the cloud or somewhere else, though highly unlikely given how big those files are, but he's also been made aware of the legal repercussions if he uses any of it."

Tears sting my eyes as I squeeze them shut. Eden pats my arm. I let out a long breath. My body lets go of that girded feeling, the armor I slipped on, preparing for the world to laugh at and judge me. Oh, sweet relief.

When I open my eyes, I'm overcome but manage to whisper, "Thank you."

Her grin is kind, crinkling around the edges. "You are welcome." She scoots back from her chair. "I know you're preparing for the Regency bingo and watch party tonight, so I won't take more of your time—"

Eden jumps in. "You and Bill should come. I'm sorry we didn't—"

Delilah shakes her head. "That's okay. I understand why you didn't invite us. And, yeah, maybe we will. It would be good to set the record straight with everyone else, too."

Hands braced on the table, Delilah continues, "I think you should have this. . . ."

She digs in her purse and lays a small external hard drive onto the table, sliding it toward me.

"What is it?"

"It's some of Harrison's footage. Must've been a backup he used." Delilah points to it. "You should take a look at the file labeled 'Zoe.' You might see the story that meant the most to him." Her drawn-in brow angles at me.

"Oh, I almost forgot. Here." She digs something else out of her purse, a parchment envelope. "Harrison forgot it in a folder from the retreat. It's addressed to you."

"Miss Zoe Dufour" is written in neat calligraphy on the front. It's the handwriting he used as my mystery admirer. . . .

I'm alone in my home now. Eden returned to her place to prep the tea and get ready for the party, and Delilah excused herself to get ready as well, promising to return for the evening's activities.

I *should* be prepping the s'mores fixin's charcuterie boards—I know, I know, but I have to prove I *can* successfully roast a marshmallow without sending a fiery torpedo flying into the air—or readying myself like the other two, but here I am. Sitting on the end of my bed, staring at the still-unopened letter in one hand and the hard drive in the other.

Opening the folder on the drive seems more like a violation. Would I see myself as a fool again? Or would it perhaps show my slow—okay, painfully slow—realization I'm in love with Harrison? I don't think I'm ready for either at the moment.

My loud breath puffs my cheeks. No, I can't watch the footage. Not now. Not without Harrison's permission.

But the letter is addressed to me, so I slip a finger beneath the edge and carefully rip open the envelope.

My Sweet Zoe,

You know that I was your secret admirer at the retreat, but the truth is I've been your admirer from not-so-afar for longer than I can even remember. I don't know when my care for you went from friend of my sister to the woman I love more than I have words to express.

You're the one I want to share my best days with, commiserate with on my worst days, tell all of my secrets to, and be the man you can trust your heart to. I love you, my Zoe. But I'm not sure if you're actually mine. Not after everything that's happened. Please know I would never do anything to hurt you like that.

"You pierce my soul. I am half agony, half hope. Tell me not that I am too late, that such precious feelings are gone forever. I offer myself to you again with a heart even more your own. . . ."

Forgive me for using Jane's words, but I think in this instance Captain Wentworth's sentiments are fully in line with my own. I've only ever loved you. I'm yours, if you'll still have me. I know it's a leap of faith. For us both. But most things worth having are. I can't guarantee that unexpected hardships and challenges won't come. Life is full of the unpredictable. All I can promise you is that I will be by your side through each one.

Always yours,
Harrison

Something inside of me breaks open. It's not my broken heart scattering into more pieces. But rather, the cage I kept around my heart to separate and protect it from pain has shattered and fallen away. And those pieces of my heart that had splintered on the floor of the cage slide back into place.

I slip to the floor and close my eyes. How did I not see this before? Harrison's love is relentless. His may not be perfect, but his love is sure, it is steady, and it is unceasing. A love worth fighting for. A love that's worth the risk.

He's right—there's nothing I can do about the things that will take me by surprise in life. I can't stop aging or illness or financial struggles or any bad thing that'll ever happen to me or the ones I love. I've had to make my peace with that.

God never promised, "Take my yoke upon you, and I'll make sure your life's smooth sailing, no pain or heartache."

Instead, He said, "When you pass through the waters, I will be with you; and when you pass through the rivers, they will not sweep over you. When you walk through the fire, you will not be burned; the flames will not set you ablaze."

There's some fire insurance for you—which I should certainly invest in.

God promised to be with me. Storms may rage. The rains will inevitably come. But He's with me, just like He always has been, even when I couldn't see it or chose to ignore it, and He's blessed me with a man I love and who loves me, who will weather it all beside me.

Tears fall, and I clutch the letter to my chest. I was so scared to allow for something—even some*one*—out of my control, I almost let love slip through my fingers.

But if this letter is any indication, maybe it's not too late.

37

Harrison

Should I go to the watch party tonight? Eden said I should come, but that isn't the same as *Zoe* saying I should come.

I might have to pay back the deposit on this lifeless apartment for the track I'm surely wearing into the hardwood floors from my pacing over the last week and a half.

A text vibrates the phone in my pocket.

> **Eden**
> Way to tell your sis you quit your job. Have I been kicked out of the loop or what?

But there's a winking/tongue-sticking-out emoji so I know she's not mad.

Three little dots appear before I can respond to the first text, so I wait.

Eden
I'm proud of you, though. You know that, right?

Harrison
Yeah, sorry about that. I didn't tell anyone yet. But I guess Jake probably knows, and he's likely waiting for me to say something.

Eden
Come to the P & P bingo party tonight. It'll be fun and take your mind off your unemployed status.

Harrison
eye roll emoji Gee, thanks.

Before she can reply, I start typing again:

Harrison
I don't know if that's a good idea. I don't want to upset anybody.

By that, she'll know I mean Zoe.

Eden
We have lots to do to set up, and a little manual labor never hurts to soften someone up. Be here at 4:30. I won't take no for an answer.

I chuckle.

Harrison
Okay, I'll be there. But if she doesn't want me there, I'll leave.

Eden
You'll never know if you don't get your behind over here. Sometimes it's worth the risk.

Throwing my phone on the counter, I exhale a loud breath that echoes into the empty living room and sprint to my bedroom to change.

She's right. Zoe's worth the risk. Any and all risks.

Eden didn't give me much time. It's almost four now. The party doesn't start until six. It will be the first of a two-part bingo night, each two-and-a-half hours long since the BBC adaptation is a whopping five hours. It shouldn't surprise me that so many people from the retreat RSVP'd. These people are committed to their Regency activities.

With fresh jeans, a T-shirt, and plaid, I grab my phone and keys and head down to my truck.

Shaking my head at my own reflection in the rearview mirror, I start the drive to Zoe's place.

I have felt like a failure with Zoe, with my career, in the eyes of my father and my heavenly Father time and again. As if no matter how hard I try, I can never be good enough to please everyone.

That's the thing I've come to see. I'll never be perfect, I'll never do everything right.

But then, He never asked me to.

Instead, He said, "Come to me, all you who are weary and burdened, and I will give you rest."

I thought I needed to be and do everything right. If I was the star student and athlete for my dad growing up, if I was in my dream career, if I did things in just the right way as I pursued Zoe, then everything would line up the way it was supposed to. Like a giant soundboard I could manipulate by trying with all my strength to be right and good enough. And if I could do all of that, it would earn me the love of those I love. Earn God's love. Zoe's.

I teased Zoe about being a perfectionist. But the irony is, I was my own personal brand of perfectionist all along.

But I've hung up my perfectionist ways to show Zoe she

can, too. We can be real and only ourselves. We can trust each other completely with who we are beneath the surface. We can let each other see who we really are, every craggy piece, every deficiency.

I'm surrendering everything into more capable hands, as I urged Zoe to do with her search for love. I don't have the perfect thing to say or do, but hopefully, the depth and truth of my love for her will speak louder than any of my imperfections.

The drive sprints by in a blur, and before I know it, I'm turning onto her street.

"Here we go." I straighten my shoulders as I park and head to the side of the house where they've set up chairs and tables laden with tablecloths.

There she is. She's attempting to start a fire in the raised iron firepit. I spot a bundle of marshmallow skewers and all the ingredients for s'mores lining one end of the table.

"Trying to land yourself on the statewide fire department watch list?"

She gasps, and the lit match she's holding drops, thankfully over the wood and kindling, which ignites immediately. The sharp scent of lighter fluid wafts my way.

"Harrison." My name is an exhale on her lips, but somehow it's the sweetest sound I've ever heard. I've missed that voice.

She wrings her hands, her feet shuffling, one still in its medical boot. The silence stretches. "Zoe, if you don't want me here, I—"

"No, it's—"

Eden bursts out of the door and steps onto the shared lawn between the townhouses. "Hey, bro! Here, can you take this tray?"

Zoe shoots me a small, shy smile—which sends a jolt of hope through my chest—and I grab the plastic-covered tray of veggies. Eden walks over to the laptop connected to a projector on a table. Jake emerges with stacks of cups and plates and shoves them into my other arm, then joins Eden. He slips an arm behind her back and plants a kiss on her cheek.

"We may not be on that chaperoned retreat anymore, but you better stay in line." I dip a brow at them.

Jake angles a toothy grin at me but doesn't remove his hand from Eden's back, while my sister sticks her tongue out at me. She pulls Jake back toward the house.

She calls over her shoulder, "Hey, why don't you guys test out the video projector while we prep the pasta salad?" No doubt the Minnesota delicacy with plenty of mayo.

Her mischievous smirk and wink make me squint at her, but she shoos me away.

I unburden my arms at the food table before joining Zoe by the projector.

"Hey, Zoe, can we talk before everyone arrives?"

But she's already pressing play on a queued-up video. "Sure, let me check this first."

It takes only a moment of confusion at the missing music I know usually accompanies the adaptation, thanks to countless hours of this playing in the background of my teen years, to know something's not right.

There's her face, Zoe on the white sheet now serving as the screen. The late afternoon shade from the small grove of oaks makes every soft curve of that face I've memorized over the almost thirty years I've known her stand out.

Zoe's hand covers her mouth. "Harrison, what is this?"

"I don't know." But that's not exactly true. This is my footage. But why is it playing?

I can't move, and it seems Zoe can't, either. My breath stutters in my lungs at these shots I took. They're beautiful. She's beautiful. Her running through the garden in her long Regency gown. A close-up of her face, the golden-hour sun setting her hair aglow. Her round brown eyes through her dark fringe of lashes. Her full laugh at something I say behind the camera. A shot of her delicate hands. Her lips. Of her talking to the other guests, always trying to make everyone feel comfortable. Her serene sleeping face, when she'd fallen asleep mid-date with that snooze-fest guy. Her lips again. Her hugging Sophia, giving her a pep talk. Though the words aren't heard, Sophia's smile is proof of Zoe's kindness. Her rowing with her confident yet peaceful stroke. Playing a game of chess with George, both laughing.

It's so much of what I love about her. I tried to capture it all. Impossible, of course.

And finally, the Zoe on the screen says, "I admire my parents' love story."

My voice asking, "What do you admire about it?"

Her gaze strays past the camera, her expression softening. "They never asked for the hand they were dealt, you know? They didn't know on the day they said 'I do' that eleven years later she would be facing a life-changing diagnosis. No one can plan or predict something like that. But they never wavered in their love or commitment."

Eyes piercing the camera now, seeming to stare straight into me. Cutting through flesh and bone. Until it's me and her, left with souls bare. There's a whisper of grass and the real flesh and bone of the right-now Zoe is beside me. Her hand slips into mine, small but warm, and I curl my fingers around hers.

Screen-Zoe takes in a slow, full breath. "I've always dreamed of a love like that. Gentle but resolute. Exhilarating but steady. A love that's strong enough to weather all of life's storms." Then she looks down, cheeks tinged in pink.

In this raw moment I happened to catch on film, there's no mention of lists, Regency fairy tales, or modern-day gentlemen. There's only her simple desire to love and truly, honestly, be loved in return. *Lord, let that be me.*

When the video stops, we turn to each other. A tear slips

down her cheek. I catch it with the backs of my fingers. Her breath shudders.

"*That* is how I see you, Zo. Just you." I slide my fingertips against her cheek and tuck her free-flowing hair behind her ear, leaving my palm against the curve of her cheek.

"I love everything about you. Every part. There isn't anything I find foolish or desperate. I'm sorry if that's how it seemed from that horrible cut Ben created, and I'm sorry for what I said. I'm responsible for those words, and I wish I could take them back. They were said in ignorance and frustration."

Her eyes bore into mine as if searching for the truth of my words.

I laugh a self-deprecating scoff. "Spoken in frustration at the fact that I wanted to be one of those guys free to date you, spend time with you, but I didn't know how to tell you at the time. And if it couldn't be me, I wanted you to find someone deserving of you, not because of some list, but because he genuinely loves you."

She's still studying me, and for a moment fear grips me. Will she turn away? Tell me to get lost?

But then she places her hand over mine still resting against her cheek. A grin steals over my attempted "play it cool" expression. Her other hand slides over my heart. "Harrison, I love you. There's nothing to forgive."

The words I've longed to hear, the words I've longed to say sound like music on her perfect lips. My chest expands like it's about to burst. My breath huffs in and out. I cup her face with both hands now, trying to steady myself enough to speak.

She beats me to it. "A guy who genuinely loves me, huh? Do you think I found him?"

My mouth spreads into a smile so big it hurts. "Yes, I do. I love you, Zoe. This, right here, is for you. . . ." My voice is raw and ragged as I press her hand more firmly to my chest with each beat, willing her to understand. "It always has been.

Yours." My voice is so rough, I have to swallow to force the words out.

Her eyes mist over again, but through it, her mouth splits in the brightest, most beautiful smile. "And I'm yours. No more armor disguised as lists."

Her eyes search mine again. "But, hey, I heard what you did, that you quit your job. You didn't have to do that."

Kissing her palm, I shake my head. "Yes, I did. I needed them to know I'm a man of integrity and won't peddle unethical tripe for money. And I needed *you* to know"—I add another kiss to her hand—"that I'm not going anywhere. I'm right here, and there's *nowhere* I'd rather be."

She reaches up, arms looping around my neck. I help her out—okay, I want her closer—and pull her up until she's standing on my feet. The wonder, the love, and the joy I see in her eyes I know are mirrored in my own.

When our lips touch, it's every emotion, everything I can't put into words. Every ounce of my love and promise for our future poured into this kiss. And she returns each measure for measure, a give and take.

We pull apart enough to smile into each other's faces, keeping our arms around each other.

I trace her bottom lip with my thumb. "These lips though. If I'd had any more close-ups of them, I would've had to start a new folder...."

She giggles. "I think you may have a problem, Mr. Lundquist."

I tug her chin closer. "It's an obsession, Miss Dufour, but I'm not looking for a cure."

"I thought maybe you fell asleep behind the camera for how many times you focused in on my mouth." Her cheeks flush.

Leaning in, I whisper into her ear, "For how many times I dreamed about how soft they must feel, you're fortunate it wasn't hours and hours worth of footage. *And* that there wasn't a closed captioning of my inner dialogue."

Our lips meet again in a soft but disorienting kiss.

I plaster on my most debonair grin as we come up for air. "Because lips like these are worthy of a miniseries"—punctuating this with another kiss—"of BBC period drama proportions."

"You know, you were wrong about one thing." Her fingertips skim the back of my neck.

"Just the one? I'd call that progress." I quirk a brow at her.

Her nose wrinkles in that adorable way it does when she thinks she's being clever. "I *was* a fool. A fool not to see sooner that you are everything I never knew to ask for or imagine."

"I'll say amen to that."

The warmth of her smile is her agreement.

"Hey, hey, hey!" Eden's voice pops the bubble of our solo moment. "I thought we were trying to keep things chaperone approved?" She winks.

Jake tries, unsuccessfully, to hide his amusement, then breaks down and gives me a fist bump.

As we continue prepping for the party, I can't get over where we are.

Now it's our job to make sure we're what's best for *each other* every day for the rest of our lives. We'll need lots of practice and help, but perfection is officially off the table. For her, I'd do anything to see this thing all the way through. Even if that means growing out my side-whiskers again, attending a million more Regency-themed events, reading to her aloud from all of her favorite Gladwin and Austen stories, and watching *Pride and Prejudice* more than anyone has ever watched *Pride and Prejudice*, more than is truthfully *healthy* for anyone to watch *Pride and Prejudice*—then so be it. I'm *all* in.

Epilogue

Zoe

"You still won't tell me where we're going?" I eye Harrison's profile with suspicion.

He squeezes my hand wrapped in his on the center console of his truck as he drives us to an undisclosed destination.

"Not yet. You'll guess, I'm sure, soon enough." He looks over with a boyish grin and kisses the back of my hand. "Relax. Remember, it's okay not to be in control of everything."

His tone is teasing, but he's right. I'm learning—sometimes by pulling my own clawed grip off the reins I'm trying desperately to take back—there's a tremendous freedom and sigh of relief in relinquishing control.

Settling back into my seat, I aim the heat vent toward me. Now that the true depth of Minnesota winter has set in, with mid-February upon us, the air has a sharp bite to it. The white-frosted trees and piles of road-dirtied snow pass my window as we exit the busy freeway in the heart of the Twin Cities toward the quieter eastern suburbs.

Harrison turns on the satellite radio connected to his truck. I let out a little gasp when my own voice reverberates from the speakers.

Radio-me is saying, "It's that time again for me to read another letter, but I'm changing things up a little this time and from now on. This isn't exactly for a perfect gentleman, because, well, there's no such thing. There never was. I still believe in true love, don't get me wrong, now more than ever."

Harrison glances over, his pride evident in his smile.

"But I've come to realize that expecting perfection, listing the impossible, and refusing to open ourselves to the unexpected can undermine our desire to find love. And maybe that's it, we need to allow ourselves to work on the inside, the heart and soul stuff, to trust God loves us enough to want the best for us and that He has a greater plan. *Then* if that's what's meant for us, romantic love can find us. Like the old Irish saying, 'What's for you won't pass you by.' I know for me, my list became my armor. My defense mechanism. If no one could live up to my impossible standards, I didn't have to let them in. If I didn't let them in, I could never be hurt by them and life's challenges could never separate us or cause us pain.

"So, without further ado, here's my letter: To my dearest Lord Bibbity of Fancypantston"—Harrison chuckles, he always laughs at this part—"my gentle, not perfect but perfect-for-me man. I won't call you my Modern Lord Pembroke, because that's not who you are. M. L. P. was someone who never existed. He was someone who fit into a box you were never meant to occupy. I no longer have a list of traits or criteria that I require. Instead, I want you to be only always yourself, the person I love so dearly. Kind, steady, and a little mischievous."

Harrison is wearing my favorite smile right now as he watches the road ahead while he squeezes my hand.

"I love the light in your eyes when you're doing something you love, the kind of big brother and friend you are, the way you take care of me even when I don't know to ask, your deep belly laugh—you know the one where you can't help but admit I'm funnier than you"—he rolls his eyes at this—"but most of all, I love the depth and breadth of *your* love. How you never fail to shower me with it so I never forget, even when we don't agree. Because we don't, especially on movie choices. We're just two imperfect people leaning into and giving back the grace and acceptance we've received.

"At different points in my life, and especially during the retreat, I saw myself in just about all of the Regency heroines I love—Emma, Elinor, Aurelia, Marianne, Anne Elliot, and even Catherine Morland. But I think out of them all, I realized I'm most like Elizabeth Bennet. I overlooked someone right in front of me because of my own preconceived notions of who he was as well as who I thought I had to choose. I almost let my prejudices and certainly more than a little pride blind me to what God had planned for me—the Darcy to my Elizabeth. My opposite in many respects, but also my absolute complement in every way. I love you, my dear Lord Bibbity. My forever dance partner, my favorite archery instructor, and the one who makes me laugh from the bottom of my gut every day. Always yours, Lady McDanceton of Macarenashire, aka your potato."

Harrison turns it down, his grin still in place, once the exit message and the outro music play.

"I still can't believe that podcast episode went viral and we're still getting view after view almost four months later, along with the others."

"I can." His tone is matter of fact.

But I shake my head in wonder. After the reconciliation with Bill Kellsner kicked off with a lengthy discussion at the watch party, we—all four of us, as I made sure Harrison, Eden,

Jake, and I were all equal partners in the show—made a deal with him about the podcast/show. Now it's broadcast on satellite radio in syndication, available on all podcast platforms, and promoted on Bill's news network. Harrison took a job with Bill again, but in a producing role within the Minneapolis branch. He and Jake re-edited the footage from the retreat for YouTube episodes we were all proud to be a part of. We kept all the heart and, yes, even my hilarious, accident-prone mishaps, without all of the slimy reality-show-esque scandal-that-wasn't-really-a-scandal stuff. People love it. The Kellsners want to do more, but after the initial fiasco, they've been careful about broaching the topic.

"I'm proud of you for being so vulnerable. And, you know, I didn't mind all of that stuff you said about Lord Bibbity, either. He's one fortunate guy." He waggles a brow at me.

"No, *I'm* the fortunate gal."

We take the exit for Stillwater, and I gasp.

I know where we're headed, and with so many more good memories than bad, I couldn't be more excited to step back into the place I first realized I was in love with my best friend's brother.

Victoria greets us at the door with an uncharacteristic grin. She ushers us into the bustling foyer and closes the large double doors to shut out the frigid wind. The heavy gray skies seem to promise precipitation. It's only a question of how fast and how much accumulation there will be on the road to make our drive back treacherous.

The dining room is full, and the din is loud as we walk past. Normally it's open to the public for Regency-themed dinners and afternoon tea during the week and anytime they aren't hosting events, but I hope we helped to bring them more business. Though today is likely busy for Valentine's Day.

Victoria waves us farther in. "Welcome, welcome." She's in her Regency attire, a sweeping, deep-red velvet gown. It kind of makes me miss the Regency dresses. Not the stays, though.

She motions us down the long hallway toward the library. "We have everything ready for you, just the way you specified, Harrison."

When we enter the library, I draw a sharp breath. We clearly have the large, book-lined room to ourselves. There's a generous tea spread at the small table near the fireplace, which is dancing with an orange and amber glow. Candles are lit throughout the room, and cozy throw blankets are arranged in the reading nook with a selection of books laid out and plates of cookies and snacks within arm's reach.

I smile up at Harrison. "You did all of this for me?"

"Of course. I once heard you say that your perfect date would be in the library with books, snacks, and a roaring fire, and I know 'Read aloud together' is the last item you still have to check off your 'Thirty by Thirty' list."

Since Harrison and I have been dating, he may not admit it, but he's had a blast helping me cross off the rest of my "Thirty by Thirty" items, like "Spend time acquainting yourself with your suitor's family." As far as Harrison and his family goes, it's a work in progress. But it's so good to be there for him as he's asked me to be by his side during these early visits with his father. And I can't imagine wanting to be anything less than the rock he's always been for me.

I grab his hand, wiggling a brow at him, which makes his eyes dance with amusement. "Well, you know what Austen would say, 'The person, be it gentleman or lady, who has not pleasure in a good novel, must be intolerably stupid.'"

Victoria chimes in, "And don't forget, 'I declare after all there is no enjoyment like reading!'"

He indicates Victoria, whom I've never seen so agreeable. "Plus, I still had the special date the retreat staff insisted on giving back to me, and Victoria said with all of the extra business our show has brought Wyndmere Hall, the owners wanted to treat us."

Victoria bobs her head. "Oh yes. There has been a real boom in event reservations and diners." She clasps her hands in front of her. "Have you talked to her about the show proposition?"

I stiffen but ask, "What proposition?"

Harrison grabs my hand, giving it a reassuring press between his. "Bill and Delilah—she insisted that she help keep Bill in line this time—want to have you do a show where we participate in and maybe even help organize Regency-themed events here at the manor. We could do a variety like—"

The wheels in my brain are already spinning. "Women's events and tea socials, girlfriend retreats, ooh, and couples' retreats, of course. Regency mystery dinner theater and bingo nights!"

I've never seen Victoria look so happy.

"And maybe we could revamp the singles' week." I tap my chin. "Like let people talk and mingle without the speed dates, which made me want to peel off my own skin. Oh, and the compatibility tests, which were absolute . . ."

Victoria crosses her arms, her lips pressing together.

"Okay, okay. Too far. But we'll talk."

This seems to appease her, and she backs toward the door. "Yes, we will. Enjoy your date. We'll even ignore the whole chaperone thing. You're welcome." She bows her head as she leaves like she's doing us an enormous favor.

I hug Harrison and whisper, "Thank you."

He pulls back enough to look down at me. "For what?"

"For all of this, for being you."

We walk to the fireplace and warm our hands from the chilly carriage ride. The memory of meeting him here in the dark rushes back, including our charged moment and the feelings I wouldn't admit even to myself at the time. Then he reaches for me, filling me with gratitude for this right here, what we are now.

Threading my arms through his, curving around his back, I pull him close. The same thrill that I can do this freely runs through me, like the first time. I squish my cheek to his plaid jacket-covered chest. There's a lump against my cheek. Something hard and squarish inside his jacket. I meet his eyes, my own widening.

His gaze goes to the ceiling, then back to me with an amused grin. "I was going to wait. But I guess this is the time, since we're staying open to deviating from our own plans, right?" His shoulder lifts. "Besides, I don't think I would've been able to wait through our meal anyway."

He drops to one knee, and I do the cliché thing—my hands fly to my mouth—but I don't care. The earth seems to have shrunk. There is only this room, this moment, this man, who is looking up at me with such love, raw emotion, and adoration. He pulls the little box from his pocket and opens it, displaying a vintage white-gold filigreed ring. It's beautiful and so is his nervous smile.

"Zoe Dufour, I love that you love all of these Regency fairy tales." I giggle. That certainly wasn't where I thought he'd start. "It shows me what a hopeful romantic you are. How you believe in love that stands the test of time. But my favorite story hasn't been written yet. It's only the beginning, I hope."

There's the slightest of tremors to his voice as he continues, "The one where you allow me the chance to love you every hour of every day for the rest of our lives and stay by your side no matter what unexpected challenges come along. I love you, Zo. And I never wish to be parted from you from this day on." Each word holds every ounce of his feelings for me. He pulls the ring from the box and holds it up. "My sweet Zoe, will you marry me?"

Tears stream down my face, and for several moments all I

can do is clutch my mouth. Finally, I make my vocal chords obey. "Yes! Of course, yes."

He slips the ring onto my finger, and it's a perfect fit. I suspect I have Eden to thank for helping him with my ring size. Oh, she and Jake will be ecstatic and immediately demand their rightful spots as maid of honor and best man.

I pull Harrison to his feet and throw myself into his arms. "I can't imagine any version of the story of my life without you in it. I love you so much, Harrison."

He presses a deep and earnest kiss to my lips and swings me around until I squeal.

"It seems I have made a rebel out of you, Lady McDanceton. You've become a real rule breaker. But I have to say"—his head and mouth slant to the side—"letting go suits you."

"It really does." I laugh against his lips and pull back enough to say, "And *you*, my dearest Mr. Lundquist, are my favorite hero of all."

We are lost to laughter and joy and everything that awaits us.

Whatever my plans were, they were nothing to what God had in store for us. A future unplanned, unseen, without self-made rules, but so, so good.

This is just the beginning. And even though we're only on the first chapter and I don't know the ending, I can't wait to see the story God writes for us. Whatever it might be, I'm all in.

Thirty by Thirty List

1. Know what you want in a match and do not compromise, but let love be the governing force.
2. Inquire with trusted friends and family about eligible bachelors of their acquaintance for an introduction.
3. Attend a ball or assembly.
4. Attend chaperoned activities with your potential suitor.
5. Write and receive letters.
6. Attend a private tea or dinner party.
7. Observe whether a potential suitor is willing to make sacrifices for others.
8. Choose gowns of the latest fashion, as means allow, or of flattering shades so as to present yourself with the greatest confidence.
9. Take a promenade in the park or garden with your potential suitor.
10. Give gifts of affection or tokens of love.
11. Participate in or spectate feats of athleticism such as tennis, cricket, or archery.
12. Go for a horseback or carriage ride with your potential suitor.

13. Read aloud to each other.
14. Listen to and accept advice from a potential suitor, and vice versa, help a suitor with your wisdom.
15. Share childhood memories or recollections of the past to further acquaint yourselves with one another as well as develop a prospective bond.
16. Enjoy a friendly competitive parlor game such as conundrums or whist.
17. Bird watch or observe wildlife in their tranquil environment together.
18. Explore a library together to discern a suitor's taste in books—a high priority, indeed!
19. Engage in a creative endeavor such as painting, drawing, or composing poetry.
20. Spectate or participate in a lawn game such as lawn bowling or pall-mall.
21. Know when to speak out and when to show patience and restraint in front of your suitor. Both will surely result in the notice you desire.
22. Learn the latest dance steps to guarantee potential suitors will vie for the last spot on your dance card.
23. Host your own dinner or tea party, so you can ensure the guest list includes your suitor.
24. Plan a special outing for a potential suitor to ensure the gentleman is in no doubt of your feelings.
25. Practice proper etiquette for engaging in social discourse with gentlemen.
26. Though concealing one's true feelings may seem to protect the heart, don't be afraid of honesty when it comes to your potential suitor. Honesty is the groundwork for a successful courtship and beyond.
27. Converse with your potential suitor in a variety of

settings and situations to determine whether your wit and intelligence are a match for his.

28. Spend time acquainting yourself with your suitor's family and thereby ascertain whether the merging of the two families would suit both.
29. Compete in a game of trivia or riddles.
30. Go for a leisurely boat ride in which he rows and you engage in polite conversation or recite poetry.

Acknowledgments

I never know how to start these things! Probably because no words ever seem big enough to convey my gratitude. (And I'm terrified of forgetting someone!) Just as it may take a village to raise a child, it takes a village to send a book baby out into the world. Years ago, as I started out as a fledgling writer, I had this idea of what an author looked like—a frazzled artist locked away in some dusty nook, furiously tapping out their magnum opus with the remnants of their rejected ideas littering the floor while guzzling down coffee by the gallon. Does it sometimes look like this the closer I creep to my deadlines? Yes! But I discovered something wonderful over the years—a support system of people alongside me in the process. Some are the experts in the publishing field that this still-newbie needs, and some shower me with the love and chocolate necessary to keep going.

"Thank you" will never be enough, but here we go!

Thank you to my husband, Mark Rushmeyer. You're my biggest supporter and have helped in so many ways to see this dream become reality. A piece of you is in every hero I write because you love me and our girls so well. Your humor is in there, too (and if anyone asked, you'd say the funniest parts came from you).

Thank you, Jess Carlson and Michelle Aleckson, for the many brainstorming sessions and for your support, encouragement, and prayers. I couldn't do this without you!

Thank you to my literary agent, Cynthia Ruchti, who has worked tirelessly on my behalf. You are the best! I loved crying happy tears with you on this one.

Thank you to the team at Bethany House Publishers and Baker Publishing Group for taking a chance on me. My pie-in-the-sky dream has been to write for you. To Rochelle Gloege, who started it all and went to bat for me. To Ellen McAuley and Bethany Lenderink, as well as their team of proofreaders, who helped my story shine. To Rachael Betz, Anna Dwyer, Anna Bernin-Mallin, and Emily Vest from the marketing and publicity teams, who've been so invested in the success of this book. I know there are many more. Thank you all!

Last but never least, thank you, my heavenly Father. Look at what You've done. You are so, so good.

Mollie Rushmeyer writes whimsical romance with heart and humor. She has a deep and abiding love for all things British, bookish, and filled with history and mystery. A modern girl herself—she wouldn't want to go a day without modern plumbing and central air—she's always felt a special connection to the past. Her debut novel, *The Bookshop of Secrets*, was a finalist for a 2023 Carol Award. A born and bred Midwestern gal, Mollie makes her home in Minnesota with her husband and two spunky, beautiful daughters.

When she's not plotting, researching, and/or writing her next rom-com, she enjoys spending time in the gorgeous outdoors of her home state, trying out new recipes for her family (while listening to audiobooks, of course), watching/reading ALL the rom-coms she can get her hands on, dancing like no one's watching—because they aren't, and that's best for everyone—traveling, and hosting game nights. Though she warns in advance, things can get pretty rowdy at the Rushmeyer house!

To find more from Mollie, connect with her on Facebook at Author Mollie Rushmeyer or Instagram @AuthorMollieRushmeyer. Or visit MollieJRushmeyer.com, where you can sign up for her newsletter to receive a *free* rom-com short story!

Coming Soon from

Mollie Rushmeyer:

Another Sweet Rom-Com with a Touch of Whimsy

When ESL teacher Iris Sorensen is forced to return home to Minnesota from Japan, she doesn't anticipate that her life could be any more topsy-turvy. Then her aunt dies and the responsibility for the eccentric author's children's literature–themed estate and café falls into Iris's lap—including the guardianship of Aunt Delphie's spoiled cat, Sir Reginald Meowington III, whose care comes with some very *odd* stipulations.

Ryker Thorne is a prickly firefighter who's just been handed a life-altering diagnosis. Now he has to decide if this part-time chef gig at a neighboring estate is a fresh start for him and his retired service dog, Biff, or just a placeholder. But when his ex shows up as his new boss, Ryker wonders if his plans have already gone up in smoke.

In order to fulfill the requirements in Aunt Delphie's will, Iris and Ryker will be forced to work together for the next six months to keep the estate and struggling restaurant running all while Iris oversees the pampered cat's impossibly full calendar of activities and social engagements. With the clock ticking, navigating this unexpected new reality together could resurface the reasons that tore Iris and Ryker apart in the first place . . . or give them both the purpose—and love—they long for.

Available Fall 2026

Sign Up for Mollie's Newsletter

Keep up to date with Mollie's latest news on book releases and events by signing up for her email list at the link below.

MollieJRushmeyer.com

FOLLOW MOLLIE ON SOCIAL MEDIA

Author Mollie Rushmeyer

@AuthorMollieRushmeyer

Be the first to hear about new books from Bethany House!

Stay up to date with our authors and books by signing up for our newsletters at

BethanyHouse.com/SignUp

FOLLOW US ON SOCIAL MEDIA

   @BethanyHouseFiction